FIRE
FROM
EMBERS

BOOK 1

C. M. JOHNSTON

A life without you is no life at all.

Acknowledgments

Thank you David Haefele for working hard to edit and help make my story come to life. There are so many who helped me to get to this point. Thank you all for continuing to listen and read my on going thoughts about the story. It has truly been a blessing to have people in my life who supported and encouraged me to keep going. Thank you, Truly.

1

With every step thick mud wrapped around the bottom of my boots sucking them into the ground. I had searched for hours for any sign of movement, or inclination of life. Dark and damp woods surrounded every side, the lack of light obscured my path. Mushy ground forcing resistants with every step. At this point the very thought of moving forward was exhausting. Instead of letting those thoughts to pull me into defeat I moved deeper and deeper. My only solace, knowing the Eleith was guiding me to a potential prey.

With a heavy breath I leaned my hand against the tree next to me. The dew clinging to the wood seeped into my gloved fingers taking warmth away from the tips. A puff of air drifted from my mouth swirling up then disappeared into the darkness. I stood on shaky legs tired from the constant traction against me. Something had scared these creatures, forcing them away from where they normally graze. Something far deadly than myself.

I felt the Eleith's presence urging me forward. The little moonlight barely lit my path. Large trunks three times my size protruded from the ground; moss coated them like a blanket. Skimming over the scene, I froze when movement caught my line-of-sight, further ahead, several yards to the right. Drinking peacefully from a shallow brook, an Elk twice my size, unaware of the looming death I was going to bring.

Slow and steady, careful not to alert the creature to my

movements. I drew and nocked the arrow. Drawing the fletching back near my cheek and took aim for the kill shot. Taking a moment, I thanked The Eleith. Adjusting my stance ever so slightly, then releasing a small breath as I loosed the arrow. The slightest brush of the fletching slipped past my cheek. Soaring silently until it landed, penetrating the elks hide and piercing its heart.

Once again, my arrow never failed nor denied me of my prey. I made my way to the creature, eyes on it as I watched the life leave it. Standing over it I placed a hand over my heart then brought it to my lips. A gesture of gratitude, a sign given to those passing on.

When done I pulled the arrow from its hide and cleaned it with the wet moss on the ground. No longer waiting I pulled a knife from the sheath on my upper thigh and gutted the creature before the meat could spoil. I tied a rope to the front and back legs making it easier to pull back to my hut to finish the job. Washing my hands in the brook I wasted no more time to grab hold of the rope and began the long trek back.

After only a few steps, large droplets of rain dropped upon my face. Pausing a moment, the cold water splashed on my cheeks. I cursed out. As if there wasn't enough mud already, I thought grimly. Although tired, I forced my legs to move forward and pushed on reminding myself of the great kill made today and the families it will feed.

Although they were unaware of whom the meat came from or at least they pretended not to know. Who would want anything from someone who is considered cursed. I shook my head, bitter memories flashing across my mind's eye. The villagers made sure to remind me. I was all too familiar with their dislike of my existence.

I have trained many years to be able to stand up against those who would wish to harm me. The village I grew up in blamed me for every disease or disaster that swept through this forsaken place. It only left me with the harsh reality, one day they would finally have had enough of me and come to take my life once and for all.

The only reason I stayed this long and put up with it is because of my Grams. An old blind woman who took me in when the village would have left me to die. After my birth my parents took one look at my eyes and saw that I was cursed. A bad omen for any who crossed my path. They left me in the woods for the wolves, but instead I was found by Grams who was stopping through the village that very same day.

Grams is a Seer, there are only a handful in the world, and they were not the types of people you wanted against you. They are people treated with respect, they live where they please and mostly keep to themselves. But if a Seer gives you a warning, you take heed to their words. In history Seer's would speak and when they were not listened to entire kingdoms have been known to be decimated. Whole societies lost within days.

But Grams came through this village and decided to stay after she found me in the woods. When the village discovered she had me they begged her to return me to the woods for the wolves. They pleaded with her claiming I was cursed, and she would ruin them all. Grams only laughed at them.

"Cursed?" She'd say, "I see nothing wrong with is child." Strange words considering Grams is blind. Since the village elders had no right to force her to comply, they demanded I wear a red cloak. So they all knew where the Cursed One was at all times. I obeyed for the most part.

By the time I reached the hut I was sopping wet. The small hut had one door, one window, and one large room. I walked through the door, went straight to the hearth, and tended to the embers. I knelt beside the hearth, blowing on the embers with a shaky breath, my teeth chattering together loudly. Continuing to feed the fire with air until the flames roared back to life.

After I got the flame to a steady size, I sat with my hands out over the flickering fire. The heat radiating off, melting away the frigid cold from my fingers. It began at the tips then spread like a liquid flowing over my skin up to my arms. As I adjusted my position to warm other parts of me, I bumped the small table next to me. I nearly jumped out of my skin when a cup crashed to the ground next to me.

Snatching the cup from the ground, I went to throw it across the room when markings caught my eye. Pausing a moment, I lightly brushed my thumb over the engraving on the cup. A lump formed in my throat as I took a shaky breath and blew out the air reminding myself, I was not completely alone. Placing the cup that Grams once gifted me on a shelf next to the scrolls and maps I kept together. I leaned against it and dropped my head down. Gripping the front of my hair I squeezed my eyes shut... Standing there I let out another heavy sigh and waited for the fire to finish warming my bones.

The exhaustion weighed on me lolling me into a sleep. Before I let it take over, I went to the door and gathered the strength to finish the work I had started. Spending the next couple of hours skinning and portioning the meat for the families I planned to bring from this hunt. I set off to deliver the food, leaving my cloak required to wear outside of my hut, hoping to be done before anyone woke or be none the wiser of my activities.

No one knew who gave them the extra meat, some suspected but most never asked. Well Grams was aware and the Eleith that lingered within me as I went through each day. The Eleith guided me to the best kills I had made thus far. The Eleith was not something following me. No, the Eleith stayed with me, guided me, and helped me through the loneliest days. When I felt all was lost, it called to me, calmed me with peace and hope for something greater. Almost as if it had chosen me.

By the time I returned to the hut, the early morning glow grew over the treetops as the sun started to show its glorious face. The exhaustion finally getting the better of me, I only paused long enough to latch the lock on the door, before falling into the bed and allowing sleep to take me.

High above the ground, the wind whipped my hair back, I realized I was flying. Moving with great speed, everything a blur beneath me. I glanced to my left and noticed I was not alone. A figure of a man held my hand as we flew. His presence was comforting, I felt safe with him. Turning to get a better view of him...

I woke with a sharp pain in the back of my head. I groaned out loud and rubbed the back of my head. I found myself lying on the floor instead of my own bed. With a yawn I tried to recall my dream. Something about it was pleasant. A bang on the door broke me from those thoughts. I glowered at the door knowing all too well someone was here to complain. The door rattled again under the pressure from the person behind it.

"Shae!" a man shouted, "I know you're in there!"

Groaning in annoyance, I took my time getting up from the ground. Slowly moving about my hut, I stretched the stiff and sore limbs. Then secured each weapon where they belonged.

Feeling ready to face who was outside, already having a good idea from the voice shouting. I tapped my left boot once checking for my last hidden small knife no larger than my pinky. Satisfied, I went to the door. Taking a small breath in and then releasing it out with a sigh I yanked the door open.

The sudden action startled him and his companions on the other side. Their reaction brought me a little satisfaction. I took a step in the door frame and leaned myself comfortably against it.

"What seems to be the problem?" I said annoyed. Pulling out one of my knives I began cleaning my nails absently with the tip of it. They were all around the same age as me, some a year or two older. The difference between the village and myself was easy to find. Where they were fair and short haired, I had long black locks. Where I was fair skinned, they had a golden-brown tint. They were all tall and well-built, as opposed to me, a head shorter. Making it ridiculous that they seemed to shy away from me. Although I had made it my goal to be able to defend myself so that they would react this way.

The most frustrating difference between me and the young men standing before me were the eyes. They had soft toned eyes anyone would be comfortable looking into. My eyes..., were neither. Sharp cat-like, my right eye so bright blue you would presume it came from the sky itself. My left eye, a fiery red that danced from flames. Constantly burning and flickering like a flame.

A bad omen.

My curse, or at least the sign of my curse. The red eye brings misfortune to everyone near me and brings trouble wherever I go. I am considered the cause for any and every disaster that befalls the village, no matter how trivial.

The one at the door was an irritating existence named Brice. He had a decent face, with fine features, and a strong jaw. I would be lying if I did not imagine breaking his jaw once or twice. He thought very highly of himself and felt everyone owed him something. A spoiled and self-absorbed child if you asked me.

"You know why we're here." Brice spat at me, trying his best, I suppose, to be intimidating. Foolish really, thrusting my knife in the side of his neck before he even blinked would be so simple. The thought made one side of my lip tug upward, in a smirk.

"Is something amusing to you?" he demanded.

Shrugging, "I am not entirely sure what you're referring to?"

"Don't act like you don't know a damn thing. It's your fault. It's always your fault. You brought that curse on us!" Shaking his finger and pointing in the direction of my left eye. I lowered the knife, not foolish enough to put it away. If they had their way, the beatings would never stop if they laid their hands on me. Even though they had given me their fair share of punishments in the past. I made sure it stayed in the past. I pushed off the frame of the door.

"Alright then, let's pretend I don't know what you're referring to. Why don't you tell me what I am being blamed for this time?" My patience wearing thin with these simpletons.

"Most of the sheep have gone missing. They were there yesterday but are no longer around. Only a few are left. What have you done?" Raising his voice as he spoke.

I gestured with both my hands sweeping out to them. "As you can see, I have no sheep here." I kept my voice level even though my anger simmered to the brim.

"I see you have no sheep." He seethed. "But your curse is the cause for our misfortune, yet again!"

I took a step forward and lowered my knife down at my side. My cursed eye smoldered together with my rage. Frustrated once again for the accusations brought on by another. I never asked for my cursed eye, and it had never done me any good.

"I don't know what happened to your damned sheep. It is a loss they are missing, but it has nothing to do with me or my eye." My patience wearing thin. "Now leave before I lose my patience with you and have to drag your dead carcasses off my doorstep."

He stood there and stared, refusing to budge. With a swift motion and before he could move, I threw my knife just to the left of his face, hitting the wooden beam. The knife embedded in the post a mere inch from his face. The handle reverberating from the force. In his panic to get away Brice stumbled down the steps and fell on his back in the mud.

He tried to scramble up and run away, instead he stumbled down the road while the others far ahead of him yelled curses at me as they ran. I laughed good and loud calling out to them.

"Good thing I'm already cursed, eh! Saves you coin for paying a witch!" I shook my head as their figures disappeared in the distance. I grabbed hold of my knife and yanked it out of the wood putting it back in its sheath. Letting out a sigh. "She is not going to be pleased with me when word of this reaches her ears." Returning inside my hut I took a quick bite of bread then placed my red cloak over my shoulders. I took the basket full of meat and left to visit my Grams, as I did after every hunt.

2

Grams is a bit odd, but she was the only one who has shown me any bit of kindness. Grams taught me that no matter how much anger was pointed towards me, to always look past it. To see a person for who they are, not what they do. Even though I had a heart for the weak I still had a hard time with the rest. I still saw many as annoying existences that only caused others pain. Those were the types I did not hold back from. Even though I am treated with contempt, I wanted to be different from them, regardless of how they saw and treated me.

I would do anything for Grams, I owed her my life. So, I learned where I could be useful. I taught myself to hunt and have done so since. I decided to also share the meat with families I noticed struggling to get by. Usually, it was the families of widows or those whose husbands were gone longer than intended. The food was too much for just me and Grams anyway. I thought it better to give to someone else who was in need than waste it.

I didn't always live away from Grams, but a few years back the villagers were becoming agitated, and a sickness had come through. Even though few died it still put most people out for a week. They demanded I leave; Grams was able to persuade them to allow me to live a few miles out. Which worked to pacify them for a time, but it seems they are beginning to show their misgivings again.

The walk to Cambtem was always a pleasant time. I spent my

time in awe of the surroundings. Of the trees and the sky, I felt as though each day given to me was a gift. Cambtem was the village I was born in, as it came into view small puffs of smoke drifted into the air from the many homes and shops throughout the small village. There was one main road down the center of town with alleys spaced between each building.

A couple hundred yards before reaching the front of town another road forked off the main. Several farms lay in that direction, where the cattle were kept close to the river that flowed alongside the village. I walked through the main entrance of town toward the other end. Grams was to the left away from the main hustle and bustle of town.

I was grateful I didn't run into Brice and his companions again on my way into town. Not wanting any more trouble than I was already in with the disappearance of the sheep. The thought of having a dead farm boy on my conscience was unpleasant as well. Although it might save a few girls from heart ache in the near future. As though the mere thought of him brought his existence upon me, I glanced over at one of the small alleys, tucked between two buildings was none other than the boy himself. Brice, pressing a younger girl against the stone wall. His hands were moving freely up and down her body while she giggled under his touch.

I groaned inwardly at the scene, a memory of him daring to do the very same to me once. I had responded with a knife to his groin threatening him if he ever so much as thought of me that way again, I would be more than happy to relieve him of his manhood. A hint of a smile ghosted my lips, might be why he disliked me so intensely now.

Continuing down the main road I passed the people of Cambtem. Children played together in the street, while mothers gossiped to one another about the newest news that reached their ears. Younger woman laughed and giggled amongst themselves as they watched the farm boys work in the fields. They all briefly stopped and stared as I walked past. They watched with anger in their eyes or mocked me with crude words trying to degrade my character. I just kept my head high and my strides firm as I left them all behind. Heading toward the one person who meant something in this forsaken village.

Grams was quietly humming a beautiful melody to herself and

slowly rocking back and forth in her chair as I approached her.

"Ah, look who decided to grace this old lady with her presence." She smiled as she spoke. It never ceased to amaze me how she always knew I was coming.

"Hello Grams, you're looking rather young today." I said, walking up the steps on her porch.

"Hold your tongue." Grams cackled, "your flattery will not work on this old woman." I gave her a warm smile. Then placed the bundle I carried on the table next to her.

"Sorry Grams, I've had a hard time with the hunting this time around." Grams paused in her rocking chair.

"Hard, was it." Her tone wasn't a question, which left me confused.

"Yes, I had to move farther into the forest than normal. The creatures seem to be seeking haven elsewhere." I stood beside her not sure what else to say.

Grams looked at me, "Shae, why do you continue to wear that ridiculous cloak?" I shook my head in amazement, at this point you would think I was used to her bizarre behavior.

"Grams, you know it was part of the agreement for me to remain here." My voice came out far calmer than I felt. Yes, it was the agreement for them to continue to ostracize me and wish for me to leave. Foolish though, what will they blame all their misfortunes on once I leave? Or would they continue to blame me when I am long gone. Claiming I was here too long.

I let out a heavy sigh, frustrated with all of them, all the bad memories they gave me as I had grown. At some point I had stopped trying to win their favor and just lived to survive.

"Shae," Gram's voice broke me from the mental reverie. I looked at her and could not help but take in her beauty even at her age. Her long silver-white hair perfectly braided and swept over her left shoulder. Her face held thin arched eyebrows over eyes you could tell were once a deep stormy gray, now covered with a layer of milky clouds. Even with grams age, anyone who came across her path would see the great beauty she once held. No doubt Grams had many suitors wishing her to be at their side. The air around us shifted and swirled around our feet. Then the temperature dropped I went to stand but was stopped by Grams who reached for my arm. Slim fingers wrapped around my wrist in a powerful grip. Her nails pressed into my skin, I looked at Grams and froze in place.

Now realizing this was no longer Grams, I swallowed down the fear as bumps formed over my skin and the hair on the back of my neck stood up.

"IT IS TIME CHILD." Her voice no longer sounded her own, it was raspy, the sound of something or someone ancient. I went to pull away on instinct, but the old seer held my arm firm. Her other hand gripped my shoulder and pulled me closer.

"The time has come for you to leave. The winds have changed, and darkness is continuing to grow. Nothing is safe, beast, magical creature, human." Her Grip tightened around me as she looked into the depths of my soul. "You have a long path ahead of you, there will be few you can trust and many who will despise you. They will fear you or desire your power."

Gram's breath hitched, and she released her iron grip. As the wind and temperature returned to what they once were her gaze drifted past me. When she returned her gaze to me, Grams lifted her hand and touch my left cheek. Gently she brushed her thumb over my cursed eye.

"You are so beautiful, my child." She spoke with so much love my insides tightened.

"Grams?" Before I could move Grams burst into a fit of laughter. I jumped from the sound, almost knocking myself down the old woman's blasted steps. I let out a curse, "Grams!" I yelled, "are you losing your wits?"

"Come my child, have some tea with this old beauty, who may be losing her wits." She said patting the chair next to her. I rolled my eyes then set out to get our tea prepared. Still uneasy by the warning the Seer gave me, I decided to enjoy this time I had left with Grams.

We spoke about my latest hunt and how The Eleith led me to where I would find prey. Grams was the only other I knew of who felt The Eleith's presence.

Noticing the sun starting to get closer to the peaks of the trees, I lowered my spoon and placed it in the bowl after enjoying the last bit of my meal. I looked at Grams and before losing my nerve, "I can't leave you." My voice came out far softer than I had intended.

Grams snorted, "And why not?"

"This isn't a game, Grams." My voice grew louder.

Grams set her food down and cleared her throat. "Shae, I have been around for a long time, and I will be around for much longer. This old woman knows how to take care of herself. I do not need you to take care of me. I allowed you to do this much because it was a necessity for you to learn and to take care of yourself without having to rely on those around you. I know it has been hard. But now this time has passed, and it is time for you to move on without this old lady." Grams eyes stayed firm on my face.

My mouth had fallen open, how could she just tell me to leave? How could she say I am no longer needed? Is it so easy for her to tell me to leave and say good-bye? My face turned bright red unable to stop the frustration from bursting, I stood from my seat.

"Well, forgive me for causing you to waste nineteen years of your life to take care of an abandoned wretch!"

Grams sighed, "Shae, do not misunderstand me. I enjoyed our time together; it brought me a joy I had long forgotten. I will carry these years of memories with me. But it is time for you to go. Your time here is done." Gram's expression softened, but the feeling in my stomach was like a pile of rocks weighing me down.

"Will I ever see you again?" I waited on bated breath. Her lips lifted in a gentle smile.

"If fate would allow it." I knelt in front of her and took her hand in mine. I placed the palm over my forehead then brought it down to my lips kissing it. A sign of honor and respect. Placing her hand back on her lap, I left without another word. As I quickened my steps a silver tear trickled down my left cheek, escaping my cursed eye.

Another mystery of my curse.

3

My legs felt as though they were made from lead, each step felt like an impossible struggle. I continued down the road, my chest tight making it hard to breathe. The thought of not knowing when or if I would see Grams again choked out my insides. I stopped at the corner of a building and braced my hand against it. Closing my eyes tight, I let the last of my tears slip from beneath my eyes. Wiping them away with my free hand. I let out a shaky breath. Swallowing down the lump in my throat, this was no time to be full of sorrow.

A seer had given me a warning and told me it was time to go. I gripped the edge of the building and pushed myself upright. Now is the time for me to leave. To see what else this world has to offer. There was a shop not far ahead of me and there were only a few supplies I needed to purchase. The rest was back at the hut, I could collect the rest and be on my way at first light.

Just up head I noticed a small group of hunters, and ducked into an alley that would take another path to the shop I was looking for. I was in no mood to deal with their arrogance now. Wasting no time, I made it to the shop and quietly walked inside. Not bothering to make my presence known, I grabbed all I needed. Thankfully, the shop owner was in the back at the moment. I pulled a small handful of coin from my pouch and left them on the counter. The amount was far more generous than the actual goods. Putting the supplies in my satchel, I left the store.

On my way out of Cambtem a small irritation prickled at the back of my neck. The Eleith pressed upon me to take another route. But the easiest route to leave and be done with this place was just up ahead. Ignoring the warning The Eleith gave me, I continued forward. Failing to see past my intent on leaving the village. I didn't see the flying mud until it slammed into the side of my face.

The force caused my head to jerk to the side. Wet mud slid down my neck, with the back of my hand I wiped the mud away. The irritation grew gnawing at me when I saw Alannah. A well-liked young woman from the village, sweetly smiling at me with a wicked look in her eye. Alannah was taller than me, with long blond hair and soft green eyes. Her features were pleasant, much softer than myself, small lips with a pointed straight nose; as opposed to my sharp eyes, full lips, and thin round nose.

"My mistake, my hand slipped." She giggled as though this was an innocent game we played together. I ignored her and turned to continue forward. Another glob of muck hit the back of my head. Cursing under my breath, the irritation grew as I attempted to calm myself and turned towards Alannah.

"You're not welcome here," she spoke in that unpleasantly high-pitched tone.

"If you had just let me be, I would have already been gone." I said through clenched teeth. The smile on Alannah's face widened. Oh, I never liked her.

Her sudden scream startled me. I stared in confusion as she collapsed to the ground. I groaned and rolled my eyes ready to leave this pathetic excuse of a person to herself. When the realization that her outburst caught the attention of countless number of people, it was too late.

Unfortunately, it also caught the attention of the group of hunters I was trying to avoid earlier. The Eleith gave another warning for me to leave, it tried to push me to go to another place. I'd already had enough and there was no way this little wench was going to have the last laugh. She obviously needed a reminder of what I was capable of. The hunters already half-way to us by now. I fixed my gaze on Alannah's dramatic act as she continued to call for help. As if I was on the verge of striking her.

Well, the thought did cross my mind.

More people came to see what all the ruckus was about. I shook my head, Grams won't be happy to hear about this. But I guess it didn't matter at this point since Grams had already told me to be on my way. It was probably why she never mentioned this morning's events with those farm boys. Grams had already planned to say goodbye. The Eleith's warnings grew stronger, which only fueled my frustration more.

"What did you do to her?" The man leading the group of hunters demanded. He was the tallest with blond hair pulled back in a tail at his neck. Four more hunters followed on his heels. These men were all similar build tall and lean, definitely not like the young men from this morning. They weren't weak, probably five maybe six years older than me.

I pulled my hair back smoothly and swiftly in a few short strokes as they approached.

"Me?" I asked, blinking my eyes in disbelief. They glared at me, I glanced back and saw the smirk on Alannah's face. Oh, she knew I wouldn't be leaving without a fight. My hands twitching with anticipation.

"She fell over all on her own, a dolt like her doesn't need my help." I said with disdain.

"Don't lie." He accused me.

"Even if I was telling the truth, which I am, you are still going to believe I harmed her, which I didn't. So, can we get on to the exciting part where I humiliate all of you with a beating. And I walk away here unharmed." I rushed the hunters before they could react.

Aiming for the closest one, the shortest of the bunch. Sliding under his wide stance. I took hold of his legs as I went by and pulled them, the man went to the ground slamming his face. The blow knocked him out cold. I sprang to my feet and dashed to the one beside him. This guy also had blond hair.

This one was more prepared, he swung his fist around. I ducked under just in time to avoid it. Grabbing his arm at the wrist, I slammed my palm into his shoulder blade and twisted his arm under pulling it behind him. With no hesitation, I slammed down my elbow into his. A loud crack followed as screams of agony filled the air. The man stumbled back and fell to his knees, unsure what to do with his crippled arm. Two down and three to go.

The last three were ready now that the surprise was over. Two of them approached, swords drawn. I rolled my eyes at their same cropped cut and color of hair. They swung their swords around as though it would help them in some way. My cursed eye blazed more as my heart raced with adrenaline. Unsheathing my own blades, beautiful steel The Eleith led me to find on one of my hunts. Both blades as long as my thighs, small curves run along the metal with circular designs woven together. Each blade gleamed with anticipation of the battle, as though they too were alive.

I wasted no time and darted at them closing the distance. The hunter on my right brought his sword down toward my neck. Deflecting his blow, I turned in time to catch the other hunter from slicing me in the back. My own blades sang at the sound of their steel connecting. Shoving him back with as much force as I could muster. I shifted on my right leg and swung my left kicking him across his face, staggering back.

As he stepped back, I let my momentum carry me to a small spin and brought my right foot down on his knee cap. Another loud crack filled the air followed by him bellowing out in pain. Sensing the other hunter, I whirled around and brought my blade to meet his. He pressed in hard and shoved me back, the force knocking me on my back. I rolled to the left just as he brought his blade down, aiming to lop off my hand.

I leapt to my feet sheathing my blades and charged. As he swung his sword down, I slipped under dodging the blade. Twisting on my foot I stretched my other leg out sweeping under his legs knocking the man to his back. Leaping off the ground I brought my elbow down slamming it into the center of his chest. The force knocking the wind out of him and cracking a few ribs with it.

I got to my feet and stared at the last hunter who had spoken to me. He stood there and watched his fellow hunters get beat one by one. Coward was the only word that came to mind.

"Are you just going to stand there? Not honoring the fallen maiden, well. I see." I leaned to the side to see past him. Alannah was standing there petrified, her mouth wide open. Now that was a sight to see. "Although she seems to be just fine to me." He glanced back, then turned his glare back on me.

"you're nothing." He spat.

"Oh." I raised an eyebrow.

"You're a disgusting cursed wench, nothing follows you but bad fortune. Even your own family didn't want you. They saw you for the wretch you truly are. The only reason that blind woman took you in was because she couldn't see you. If she could, she would have known leaving you in the woods for the wolves to be devoured would have been a blessing!" A sharp pain pierced my stomach as though I had been stabbed by his words.

The Eleith pressed on the back of my mind and understanding now dawned on me. This accomplished nothing. Black smoke oozed off his skin and the irritation started to prickle at the back of my neck. I squinted my eyes trying to see if what I saw was real but then blinked and the smoke vanished. I stared back at the man showing no signs of caring for his words.

With a swift dash I appeared before him and shoved the palm of my hand against his nose. I felt the bone crunch underneath my hand. The hunter collapsed to his knees covering his nose, as he yelled out in pain.

"You little whore." I leaned down and whispered next to his ear.

"I guess it's a good thing I am leaving." I unclasped my cloak that marked me and let it fall in the mud. I walked away from the village and their frozen stares.

By the time I reached my hut the night had already set in. The moon was gone giving no light for comfort. I wasted no time gathering the rest of my supplies for the journey ahead. Putting a small bundle of clothes together. I put them in a bag, rolled a blanket up and tied it with a rope to keep it secure. The candle I had lit was my only light, I set it beside my bed. Next to my bed were some loose boards where I kept the majority of my coin, I had been saving up all these years. I reached over and grabbed my satchel, opening the flap I stuffed the bag into it.

Deciding it would be best for me to leave at first light I picked up the candle and went to set it on my table before laying down for the night. The temperature in the hut dropped significantly and a sense of death crept up from behind me. I froze in the middle of the room not daring even to breathe. In the shadow of my light, I saw two cloaked figures glide across the room.

As they slithered toward me, I let out slow even breaths while reaching for one of my blades at my lower back. A dark laugh left one of the creatures as it approached.

"Now, now." It snickered, "what are you going to do with that?" My blood ran cold at the sound of its voice, hissing like a snake with multiple voices laced together in one.

"Hello." The other spoke as though they came over for a friendly visit.

I kept my hand firm on my blade, I could see in my peripheral and the other was out of sight. Until I felt hot air slide over my ear and knew it was directly behind me. An unpleasant shiver forced its way down my neck as it spoke.

"What is this young maiden doing alone on this moonless night?" The shadow shifted just out of sight, my body was so stiff it could snap like a twig. I felt a sharp pain at the base of my neck just before everything went black.

Pain throbbed at the back of my head, I felt heavy, and it was hard to breathe. My hands were bound above my head and my feet dangled off the ground. I groaned aloud before opening my eyes. Blinking them repeatedly I tried to focus, forcing the scenery into view. Just to my right the candle was knocked over on its side still flickering in the dark. I then remembered my predicament and the creatures which ambushed me.

Taking a slow look over the room I looked to the left and found myself face to face with one of them. The sight of this creature made my entire being long to curl up and disappear if it meant never encountering them again. A black hood shrouded its face, only being face to face could you see the skin pulled tight around its skull with a sickly gray tinge. Its thin lips had two long sharp teeth pointing halfway down its chin on either side of its mouth. Where there should be a nose was only two slits in the skin and two black eyes with a deep red swirling as though blood itself churned in their depths.

It let out an awful snicker.

"Glad you are awake; we would hate to continue without your joyous screams." It smiled at me showing the full row of sharp yellowed teeth lining its mouth. Bringing up its hand, it touched the tip of its long nail to the side of my cheek. Then pressed down on my skin and slid it. Pain seared the entire right side of my face, forcing me to gasp in agony. It hurt more than just an ordinary cut.

"Such lovely skin you have." It said lifting its nail up to its mouth and licking the blood off the tip. "Hmmm... your blood. Its exquisite!" its eyes followed the blood oozing down my face. I searched the room trying to find the other one. My brain raced, desperate to find a way to escape.

"When are we going to eat?" The other hissed materializing out of a dark corner that obscured its figure. "Those sheep were nowhere near enough to slate my thirst." Irritation laced its words.

"Patients!" The other snapped.

My heart pounded in my chest, I had no idea how I might survive, the odds were not in my favor. The creature turned its attention back to me, then brushed the hair away from my face covering the left eye. It cringed back from the sight of my cursed eye, for a brief moment. Then the twisted smile returned to its lips as it leaned into me placing its face at the base of my neck. Flicking its tongue out and ran it up the side of my neck to the edge of my jaw, causing my body to stiffen and my skin to crawl. The desire to rip my own skin off where it had touched me was only stopped by my bound hands.

"What do you want?" I swallowed my fear and refused to cower no matter who they were or what they planned. "What brought you here?" I demanded. The creature pulled away to give me a clear view of its face.

"You don't know little maiden?" It's sickening smile widened. "We came. Just for you." I hung there digging my nails into my hands, confused.

"W... wh... why?" I was barely able to voice the word.

"We can smell you. And how delicious it is. Mouthwatering." As though it was confirming its claim it brought its face inches from me and breathed in. I almost gagged from its rotting smell.

"If you are going to kill me." I stared directly at the creature. "Why don't you be done with it. As exciting as it is hanging around here, looking at your face is more than I can bear." The other creature moved toward us.

"I agree with her, let us eat! I tier of waiting." It said impatiently.

The other ran its fingers up my arm, "but it's such a pretty thing and we haven't had the chance to play with one for so long. It would be a shame to not draw it out." It glanced back at its companion taking its eyes off me.

Deciding this was now or never I swung my legs up and wrapped them around its neck and twisted with all my might flipping the creature to the ground. Swinging back, I lifted my leg to kick the other, instead of making contact it grabbed my leg and yanked me forward. Pain flared in my shoulder when a loud pop came causing an involuntary scream to escape my lips.

The creature let me go and I hung limp in the middle of the hut. I bit the inside of my cheek trying to forget the pain. As the one on the ground stirred the other grabbed the back of my head and with a fist full of hair yanked my head up. I stared at those disturbing eyes that hungered for blood.

My blood.

Panic finally hit, not now, I couldn't die now. It sneered at me. A sick smile spread over its face as it read the fear in my eyes.

"I've never been one to play with my food." Its hot breath blew in my face and pulled my blade out of its sheath. Then released its tight grip from my hair took one step backward and shoved the blade into my chest plunging it deep into my heart.

I gasped out, my eyes widened from the shock and pain. My fingers gripping the ropes were losing strength fast. Blood rose and bubbled in my throat. I coughed and choked as it spilled over in my mouth. I rasped for air. Everything started to fade my every thought escaped me as images flashed before my mind's eye only to vanish without a trace. Until there was nothing but white.

4

"Shae" I heard a voice far off in the distance. "Shae." The voice was soothing and calm with an authority behind it. "Shae" Each time I heard my name it grew stronger as though it drew closer. Not knowing what transpired, I looked for where the voice was coming from and to who it belonged. Only to see an empty void of pure white.

"Shae." The voice spoke out again, as though it were standing right beside me. There was warmth in the sound, and it filled me with a sense of peace. The more the voice spoke the more I realized the words were not of my language, but I still understood it, nonetheless.

"Death will not take you." A warm breeze brushed over my skin.

"There is a sickness in these lands, a darkness with the desire to poison the very soul of every being. The road before you is long and difficult, your fiery eye is a blessing and a curse. Do not let it consume you." Then all warmth and the voice were gone.

My heart thumped... with it a pain I could never describe into words. Heat coursed through my veins as though fire boiled in my blood with every heartbeat. I gasped and breath escaped my lips. My eyes opened as I fell to the floor landing on my feet. Shocked, I saw the steam roll off my skin, I could only assume my skin became so hot it burned through the bindings.

Looking around I saw my blade on the ground next to the still flickering candle. Red glistened off the metal, my thoughts came in as a tidal wave crashing down reminding me of the situation, I was in. I grabbed both the candle and blade, turning over the hut I found the two grotesque creatures, both stunned at the sight of me alive. They were as surprised as I was. However, this was not the time for me to figure out what had transpired. No, survive now and ask questions later.

Apart from the dried blood crusted on my face and the blood all over the floor, there was no sign I had died. I was healed, there were no wounds or pain... nothing.

We circled the room, cautious of the other's movements.

"Abomination!" One hissed.

"Why are you not dead, I stabbed you myself. There was no life left in you." The other protested.

"Disappointed?" I shrugged my shoulders in a taunt. The candle flickered as it darted across the room, claws stretched toward my neck. I jumped back just outside of its reach. I brought my blade down with one easy swipe and cut clean through its arm. I felt alive! Renewed in some way. While it was distracted with its missing arm, I stabbed it in the chest, sinking it deep.

"I was never one to play with my prey." I spoke to the now lifeless figure on the floor. I wasted no time searching the room, looking in the dark places that could conceal the other creature's figure with ease. A tingle ran down my spine, sensing its presence right behind me breathing down my neck. Diving forward I tried to get out of reach. But was too slow as it racked its claws along my shoulder. Pain exploded where the claws tore through my skin. I rolled across the floor turning my body to meet it. Holding my blade firm in hand I tightened my fingers over the hilt.

"So does this mean I have an eternal meal right before me?" The creature said to me in the dark. "Will that little trick of yours work a second time?" A smile crept up its mouth showing the nasty row of sharp teeth. Fear gripped me at the horrible image of being trapped with this creature as it feasted on me day after day. Dying painfully and reviving just as painfully, if it even worked a second time. No, I shoved the thought out of my mind and pushed the fear back and focused. I had to survive. I would survive.

I darted at the creature in a straight shot. Only at the last second, I spun to the left just as it went to rake another set of claws down my torso. Turning to meet the creature as I dodged its attack, I brought the candlestick up and shoved the end of the candle in its eye extinguishing the light. The creature howled in pain and the sound cut short as I rammed my blade underneath its jaw into its head.

I pushed the body off the blade and watched it fall to the ground. Stumbling to the door, the pain in my shoulder throbbed. Only going a few steps before it began to rain. I stopped and closed my eyes, leaning my head back, I faced the dark sky, welcoming the fresh drops of rain as though it cleansed my body. The blood and smell from my encounter washing away.

As my pulse calmed, I looked out into the darkness of the forest. Checking to see if, maybe another would materialize out of thin air. Instead of waiting for another attack I went back inside the hut. Swiftly, I lit another candle and took a cloth, tore it in two and was grateful the cuts on my shoulder were not deep enough to cause concern. Using my one hand I wrapped my shoulder and tied the cloth using my teeth to tighten it down.

Satisfied it held firm, I gathered the supplies and weapons. Grabbing the oil lamp, I doused the bodies with the oil making sure there was an even amount on both. Tossing the lamp on them I took the candle and lit the bastards on fire. I wanted to make sure they were good and dead, I wasn't fond of the idea they might survive somehow and chase me down. Leaving the rising flame behind me, I was thankful for the rain. It meant the fire would not spread.

Despite the pain in my shoulder my belongings did not weigh me down. Picking up my pace I was more than ready to leave this place. Leaving at first light was no longer an option. I had looked over the map briefly before I was ambushed and had planned to go west from there.

I winced as I moved my shoulder causing a sharp pain to shoot down my arm. I adjusted the strap on my satchel and moved it away from the scratch, flexing my hand helped ease the pain.

My mind drifted to the events that unfolded as I continued walking. I mean, I wasn't insane? I had died? There was no way I could have made up the feeling of the blade in my chest. Even though I knew it was what happened I still felt my hand go to my chest and rubbed where the blade had gone through. Still disbelieving.

There was magic here and beings able to wield it. Never has there been talk, rumors, or even legends saying people can be brought back from the dead.

I tried settling my breathing before my thoughts became overwhelming. I thought of the voice I had heard, it held such a warmth, just the thought of it made me want to hear it again. So, there was a sickness, a darkness, and it had something to do with my cursed eye. Did the voices words go hand in hand with the Seer?

I couldn't help thinking it had.

One thing was for sure though, my time at the village was done. I clenched and un-clenched my fist and focused on the movement to rid myself of the uneasiness spreading inside my stomach.

Cambtem finally came into view at the end of the small trail where the trees broke open to the sleeping village. Picking up my pace I shifted my stride making my feet lighter and silent when it touched the ground. I moved along the wall behind any object I could sneak around. It was late, and I was in no mood to deal with anyone tonight. In the past years I have learned ways to sneak around. To be unseen and unheard to hide from the people of this village.

Sometimes, I did not fair too well when they were able to find me. So, I had to get better at hiding, better at being invisible. Those were not my fondest memories, but I did learn from them. Most of my knowledge came from what Grams taught me or the scrolls she kept for me to read. She is why I can even read and write and how I have learned to live off the land.

How to survive.

I passed the buildings in no time at all, only a few people staggered around. No doubt drunk from the night of drinking at the pub. I reached the end of the street and turned towards Grams. As I approached something felt wrong. There was silence over her place.

"No," the word came out barely a whisper and I moved before thinking. A sharp pain in the pit of my stomach.

Dread.

I pushed past the door and looked everywhere. There were no smoldering embers from the fire, no fire at all. The place was cold, every room was empty, there was no Grams to be found. The problem was not only that she was gone, but any sign of her once living here vanished. There was nothing. My world started to spin. Grams what is happening? Maybe she'd known the creatures were coming? But if that were so, wouldn't she have warned me? Well, technically she did...

The wooden door creaked from pressure, and I whirled around to see the intruders, knife already in hand. My eyes narrowed at the two figures standing in the doorway gaping at me. I dropped my hand and glowered at Alannah and Brice. I could see they had been drinking from the way he stumbled, and she clung to his arm, trying with an effort to keep them from toppling over.

"Can I help you?" I said not hiding my irritation.

They both jumped from the sound of my voice. Not realizing, I stood there.

"What are you doing in here?" Alannah's voice held all the disdain she felt. Then she lifted a candle in my direction. I tapped my foot on the floor, impatient with the two for entering here at such a late hour.

"Are you going to leave my Grams home, or will I need to make the two of you leave?" They stared at me as though I lost my mind.

"Whose home?" Brice said confused,

"My Grams. You know, the blind woman that lives here. She raised me." I couldn't believe I was explaining this.

"Has your curse finally caused you to lose your mind?" He laughed, "there is no blind woman here, there never has been. No one raised you, of course they wouldn't, you're an abomination your very existence is repu..." His sentence was cut short as my hunting knife embedded itself in the wood next to his head. Alannah let out a short ear-piercing screech.

I walked over irritated at him for running his mouth. I was getting tired of listening to the same dull sentence repeatedly. That's fine, if Grams was gone there's no more need for me to linger here. I reached up, pulled the knife out of the wood and looked over at them. With a smile I told them.

"Good luck with all your misfortunes." Then left them swaying back and forth in their drunken state. One, seers have far more power than I realized. Two, something was after me. And three, whatever this curse is, it's only going to bring me trouble.

5

Two days have passed since I left Cambtem. Maedoc was the closest town to the small village, it was much larger than Cambtem. I traveled with caution and made sure there were traps set when I stopped for camp for the night. After those creatures ambushed me, I didn't know what else could be hunting me, and I didn't want to find out.. I leaned down next to the stream I stayed next to while traveling. Cupping a handful of water, I brought it to my lips. The cold liquid made me shiver. Although I was grateful to have it while traveling, what I would kill to have a warm bath at this moment.

After another day of travel in seclusion seeing signs of other people in the same area, helped me to relax knowing my destination was near. I decided it was best to move towards the road and swept my hair over my cursed eye to not draw attention to myself. I kept only a light curtain over it, just enough to keep it hidden. Not keen about the idea of being caught off guard.

Up head the trees staggered further apart until there were less and less. In the clearing, a cluster of homes gathered on the right. A large field with crops next to it. Livestock grazed absently while groups of people tended to them. The stream continued on the other side of the homes. Further down the road the town Maedoc came into view. It was a considerable size town with many shops and taverns and a few inns. It also had weapon, and armor shops. Two places I planned to stop before leaving town. But first, I needed a hot meal and a place to stay. Walking to the closest inn that caught my eye, the Elieth pressed upon me to move further into town.

Sighing, I decided it was better to listen and changed my direction walking past the inn. I took in my surroundings, people were everywhere going about their business, but something... felt off. It was as though there was something thick in the air, like it was choking out any real joy people might have. I kept my pace and moved past the shops and trading goods. There were several guards patrolling the streets making their rounds. I filed away how many there were and which streets I saw them on. I walked until the Elieth let up, in front of another Inn.

Inside, the inn had round tables spread out with a huge fireplace. The fire blazed bright, making the large room warm. Stone ran along the walls no higher than my waist, timber finished the building to the ceiling. People filled the tables with loud groups, while others kept to themselves. I walked up to the counter on the left of the room, a long wooden counter ran down the length of the building leaving a break at the end for stairs. Keeping my eye covered, I cleared my throat.

"Sir." The innkeeper turned.

"Why hello." His voice was gentle. "How can I help you?" I reached my hand into the satchel.

"I'd like a room for the night and also a hot meal." I put coin on the counter and pushed it towards him.

"Thank you miss, there is a room for you and food will be brought right to you." I thanked him. Then turned and sat on a small table on the side, away from the large groups of people. It was 20 paces away from the entrance. After finding my seat, the barmaid brought out the food and drink.

Grateful it came so quickly, I ate my food while monitoring the people in the room. Even though the people were boisterous, there was still a tension in the air that could suck any genuine enjoyment from every single person.

As I took my last bite of bread the door I entered burst wide open. Instinctively, I gripped one of the knives in my right hand, ready for a fight. But instead of a fight a woman ran through the door screaming and crying for help. Long Sandy Brown hair, a small figure, her height only a few inches taller than my own. Creamy brown eyes with worry wrinkling her slim eyebrows.

Her hands trembled.

"Please! someone help, the... they... they have my son! They will kill him!" Panting, she grabbed a man standing next to her "Please!" She begged. The man shrugged her off like she was an annoying mouse that kept pestering him. "Please!" She went to the next person not bothered by his gesture or too frantic to care, "help him, he's an innocent boy!" She kept pleading to the unmoving group of people crowded together in the inn.

I looked over the room and noticed several people were looking down or trying to avert their gaze from this woman's pleas. I felt the irritation rise like water boiling to the surface. Shoving the chair back, I stood and felt the tingle from the Eleith once again. Now knowing this was the reason for me to be here I called out to her.

"I will help you." If it was quiet before, it was dead silent now. Not waiting for her reply, I headed for the door, the woman pushed past me, beckoning for me to follow. We ran towards the side of Maedoc I had entered. There was a crowd not far ahead of us. I could hear the voices and laughter in the center of the people grouped up watching the festivities. My frustration grew at the entertainment these people were getting out of another's suffering. Moving closer to the crowd I began to make out their words.

"That all you got boy?!" One guard said with amusement thick in his voice. "Not much of a man, are you?" He laughed, I pushed my way through the crowd to get in the middle. Shoving past a young man it revealed seven guards standing in group. All sneering at a boy no older than eight years.

He had short sandy brown hair longer on the left side of his face, freckles across his nose, his eyes a deep forest green. The urge to rip the mouths off all their faces was like an electric shock. I calmed the twitch in my fingers. The boy stood with his fists clenched out in front of him, doing his best to be brave against them.

He had cuts and bruises on his arms and legs and one under his right eye. He looked up at the guards with rage.

"Alright boy, enough play time give back what you stole." The commanding guard said, pushing past the rest.

"I stole nothing!" The boy yelled back, "I took back what you stole from us." He said breathing heavy.

"That coin belongs to the King, it's payment for protection in this poor excuse of a town." The guard took a step closer.

"It belongs to us! We already paid our fee to the Kin..." The guard stuck him across the face, sending the boy tumbled to the ground. He struggled to get up before being overtaken.

"I think we're done here boy, it's time for your punishment, for stealing from the King." The Commander sneered at him, pulling his sword out, the mother shrieked when he swung his sword down. Instead of the sick sound a head being lopped off, the sound of metal colliding rang through the air. I knelt before the Commander blocking his blow. Shoving him back I caught a glimpse of surprise flash over his expression.

I glanced back at the boy hiding his head under his arms waiting for his fate. He peeked out, eyes wide as he realized death wasn't coming for him. I gave him a small nod.

"You did well. Now, run." Without waiting to see if he listened, I turned my attention to the seven guards standing feet from me. I sheathed the blades. I may handle against some gruff hunters, but these were trained guards. I didn't like my odds. Movement caught my peripheral, sight of the boy running to his mother's arms, the next instant they disappeared into the crowd. Hopefully to get what they need and leave.

"You've just interfered with the King's guard. Do you have any idea what you are doing?" The Commander looked down on me, his eyes danced with amusement. He was a tall man with short cropped black hair and deep brown eyes almost as dark as his hair. His build not small, this man spent his life training and fighting battles.

"The King's guard? Looked to me like a bunch of cowards pushing around a defenseless child." I folded my arms over my chest.

"You will be punished for your crime." A smug smile formed on his face.

"What crimes have I committed here? All I saw was a boy fighting for his life and helped him." I fumed.

"You have aided a thief to escape. It's only fitting you get punished for his crimes." He took a step toward me.

"Then what is the price I must pay for saving the boy from pathetic cowards." I spoke despite the predicament I put myself in. He took the last few steps to me then grabbed a fistful of hair and yanked my head back. Forcing me to look at his face when he spoke.

"Twenty lashes a day for every coin the boy stole." He paused and glared at my face. "What are you?"

"Human, same as you." I said through gritted teeth. He pulled tighter on my hair, then shoved me to the ground before the other guards.

"Twenty lashes for ten days." A smile crept back onto his face and excitement danced in his eyes, as though he had found a new toy he could take apart. "Starting now, take her weapons and put her on the post." He barked orders. Two guards grabbed my arms on either side pulling me up to my feet. Another guard removed my weapons. He took one weapon after another then made it to the knife on my thigh, his hand lingered groping the inside of my leg.

I promptly smashed my knee into his nose. The bone crunched under the pressure. He toppled back, cursing, holding his nose while blood spilled from under his hands. My small victory was short lived when another guard slammed his fist into my gut. The force made me double over, a wave of pain rushed up making me cough. They all laughed, except for the one franticly trying to stop the bleeding. One side of my lip curled up, he shouldn't be bothering me again.

They pulled me through, and the crowd backed away splitting in half as they walked by, taking me to their so-called whipping post. It was more like a large stump in the ground with shackles bolted on one side. Shoving me to my knees, they pulled my arms around the stump and clamped them down. A guard paused behind me to rip my shirt, exposing my back.

The cool air brushed past my skin, causing an involuntary chill to run over my body. The Commander leaned beside me and whispered in my ear.

"I am grateful for the interference. This will prove to be far more entertaining than killing that little bastard." He chuckled under his breath. Choosing to remain silent, I could feel my cursed eye pulsing alongside my anger over the guards abusing their powers. I wondered how many people had stood in this very spot waiting for their punishment. Just for mere entertainment for these bastards.

"Make sure you scream and beg loud enough for everyone to hear." He pushed off my shoulder then stepped back. The sound of the whip cracking as he warmed up, and the crowd before me flinched back reminding me to breathe. I clenched my fist down and took a breath out of my mouth. I could do this, I had endured much, this was just another one of those moments in life... pain sliced through as he slashed the first lash, cutting into my train of thought.

I bit my lip not allowing a sound to escape my mouth, I wouldn't give him the satisfaction. His whip went down again, I gripped the post harder and reminded myself to breathe. The last things I wanted was to pass out when they were just getting started. Another crack filled the air, it sent my flesh screaming. The whip continued never letting up or giving me a reprieve. I had lost count long ago, I remained conscious and allowed no sound to escape me as he carved my back. There was no cheering except for the guards in the back, they laughed and mocked me as I endured one lash after another.

Finally, the whipping stopped, my entire body cursing me for allowing it to endure such pain. Two guards came over and unshackled my hands. Then hauled me to my feet. I tried my best to keep myself upright but staggered as they pulled me forward.

"Take her to a cell, she will stay there until she serves her punishment. If she survives that long." A smile crept over the Commander's face, showing a row of straight white teeth. I couldn't stop the rage from pulsing in my blood as I stared him down while they dragged me away. These bastards were not going to let me leave alive and I wasn't entirely confident I would come back from the dead a second time.

6

The guards took me to a building close by, fifty or so paces from where I had received my lashings. I had to make an effort not to pass-out. I needed to know which direction they took me. I needed to know what was where if I was planning to escape before they ripped every bit of my flesh from my back.

Inside the building the first room was empty save for a table and a couple of chairs. There was a door directly across from the entrance and a hallway to the right. They took me past the table, down the hall where there were two more doors on the left wall. At the end of the hall was a metal door. Stopping in front of the door I heard keys rattle then the door opened. Revealing a lengthy set of stairs leading into the darkness.

The stairs were made of stone as well as the walls. We descended for half a minute when the walls split free to an area with several smaller rooms. All created with stone and metal. Tall metal bars only four inches apart from another. Each corner had a pillar of stone and bars forming the walls and doors. A wave of nausea hit me when I noticed the smell of rotting bodies lingering in the air.

They passed several cells a few had bodies in them, not sure if they lived, from the smell I expected not. After they crossed the row of cells, the guards stopped at the end and opened the last cell straight to the back. Throwing me to the ground, I groaned from the impact of my back scraping along the floor. There was a small window with bars above a bench running along the back wall.

"Enjoy your stay, wench." The guard said. I made no attempt to respond, I only stared at him. The other guard didn't seem to appreciate that, he strode up and kicked the side of my face. Knocking me back to the ground. I spit blood to the ground, another blow went to my gut. Doubled over in pain... there was so much pain at this point, I almost felt numb. Coughing, I wiped my hand over my mouth traces of blood smeared.

"You bastards, don't know when to quit." I rasped. They laughed together.

"Quit? We are just getting started, by the time we're done with the lashes tomorrow you'll be begging us to kill you." He reached down and grabbed a fistful of hair then slammed my head into the ground.

Darkness took over.

I woke with a start, it took me a few minutes to recall where I was and the events that had brought me here. The ache in my body helped to remind me of my predicament.

A groan escaped from me when I tried to shift my body around and feel the damage done. There was barely any moonlight shining in from the small window above me. I heard movement and whispering from the other cells, so there were some still alive. Pushing myself off the ground I stood up. Almost toppling over from the room spinning, I caught hold of the wall. My body barked in pain from the sudden movements.

I let out a shaky breath, gritting my teeth, I moved to the bench and sat down carefully. Leaning over I laid my head on the bench, the cool stone touched my head giving me comfort. Shifting slowly, I laid on my stomach. My shirt was torn in the back and the bindings I used for my breasts now shredded, leaving my back exposed. I had just closed my eyes when the sound of a heavy door opened in the distance. Footsteps followed and grew louder by the second.

A young woman came into view, she carried a bowl with rags on her shoulder. Steam drifted up from the water showing how hot it was. She was followed by the pair of guards who dragged me in here and gave me their warm welcome.

The cell door creaked open, and the woman went straight to me and knelt by my side. She began tending to my back. Surprised they would even bother I remained still and allowed the woman to do her work. She was a simple woman with plain brown hair, blue eyes, and soft features. She took a cloth, dipped it in the bowl of water and wiped the dirt away from my back.

The sting from the boiling water seeped into my skin. I couldn't help but wince as the woman pressed on the wounds. I eyed the guards as the woman worked, my body tensed when one of them moved towards me. Before making a move thinking I would be struck again, the man dropped a bowl of food next to the woman. It splashed on her from the impact. Irritated, there was little I could do at this point. I would bide my time and figure out a way to escape.

"Eat up, you got a big day tomorrow." He laughed telling the woman she was done with her job. He grabbed hold of her shoulder and pulled her along with them leaving the bowl and wraps behind. I stared at their backs, watching them ascend the stairs until their figures disappeared.

My back still stung from the hot rags on my back, I closed my eyes and let out a breath. A warm breeze brushed over my face followed with the fresh scent of woods after the rain. The pain seemed to ease, and my body felt lighter. A calmness swept over me, and I finally relaxed enough, sleep took me once again. This time without pain.

Bright clouds zoomed past me as I flew fast into the deep blue sky. Freedom enveloped me as I sailed over the vast amounts of land beneath me. I moved faster, soaring higher. A hand grabbed me, and I stopped. Looking ahead of me, I almost entered a land swept with darkness. Where there was once a beautiful blue sky now an empty blackness roared with rage. Frozen, I turned to the person holding my hand...

I woke to the reddish orange glow seeping through the window above where I lay. Blinking several times, I rubbed my eyes to clear the blurry vision. Bracing my fingers around the stone bench I took a deep breath before getting up. I winced from the movement then sat for a moment. The gruel left on the ground caught my eye, deciding it was better to eat something rather than starve. I slowly picked up the bowl then forced down the badly cooked meal.

Moving from the bench my body remained stiff from the lashings I received yesterday. I placed a hand on the cool wall steading myself as

I moved to ease my body. Getting it used to moving with the damage done. Despite the protest my body gave I forced my legs to move. First slow and steady, before long I could walk at an easy pace. Pacing back and forth in my cell I contemplated finding a way out.

If I could get out before the next set of lashings, all the better. Pausing, I tapped my boot checking for the knife I hid there. Satisfied, it remained in place. I felt for the one kept in the sleeve of my shirt or what was left of it. The hard steel was easy to find, using the tip I tore a small hole and pulled it out. Cutting a slit in the sole of my other boot I slid it right under my foot. Only a thin piece of leather between my skin and the cold steel.

I scanned over the other cells noting the prisoner's glancing in one cell after another. My eyes stopped on the cell next to mine, locking on an unmoving figure. He sat on the ground leaning against the wall, knees up with his arms resting on each. Both eyes closed, his dark brown hair fell past his jawline with a thin line of facial hair along it. His jaw sharp and defined, lips full and smooth.

I caught my breath when his eyes snapped open, his gaze piercing, their depths a smoldering gold, drawing me in as though they were bottomless. His gaze lingered, keeping me frozen in place. I couldn't help but feel a familiarity toward him, which was strange considering I have never encountered him before. My heart thumped as his gaze still lingered. I felt trapped like a caged animal by his stare. A smile tugged on one side of his lips revealing a slightly elongated canine, as though he could hear my heart respond under his gaze.

The thought I may be at his mercy from a simple look annoyed me immensely. Never had I reacted in such a way. The contact broke when the heavy door swung open in the distance and a group of footsteps rapidly approached. They stopped in front of my cell, the three guards standing there leered inside the cell. Anticipation of my next flogging written all over their faces.

"It's time wench." The guard in the middle said, opening the door. I turned in their direction, frustrated with myself for wasting my time not devising a plan to escape. I waited for them to enter, not taking a step back or fight when they took hold of both my arms. Now was not the time to fight back. Besides it was pain, pain I could handle, I would endure and not be afraid.

There was no way I was going to give them the satisfaction in believing they could break me.

"Just wait until we get you latched on that post; you won't be so calm then." The guard muttered yanking my arm forward. Cracking any scabs that may have formed over the night. It didn't matter at this point it was all going to be fresh in a few minutes, anyway. I glanced back at the male in the cell next to mine, his golden eyes never left me. As though they could burrow deep into my soul. A shiver ran down my spine at the thought.

It didn't take long for the guards to return me to the post, blood still lingered in the dirt from the lashings I took yesterday. I glanced around noticing the crowd grew today, oh wonderful, I thought more bystanders to watch the guards abuse their power. A breath of relief blew out, when I wasn't able to find the woman and her child anywhere.

They pushed me on my knees again and pulled my arms around then shackled each wrist, making them tight enough to cut into my skin. The sun was high, making it midday, the heat from it made my back sting even more.

"Second day." The Commander's voice boomed over the crowd, I recognized it from yesterday. "Twenty lashes." He spoke to the crowd watching the punishment about to be delivered. The example being made telling them anyone stepping out of line would not be tolerated. His shadow blocked the sunlight covering me. He stood close enough I could feel his breath down my neck. The man had a real issue with personal space.

"If you beg and plead, I may be lenient on you," he spoke pleased with himself for a reason I could never fathom. Pulling the whip out of its belt he brought it up and brushed the handle against my cheek. "Are you going to scream for me today... hmm... wench?" I spat in his face.

"Get on with it coward," his lip curled into a snarl wiping the saliva off his face and stepped back.

I braced myself as the whip came down on my back with a loud crack. I knew it would hurt but the feeling of the whip on my fresh wounds made the world spin. Pain surged through me, my fingers dug into the post. He brought the whip back than unleashed another, my eyes stung. I forced back any tears threatening to escape. Refusing to give in, another pain searing crack, my lip bled already biting into it. Have mercy I spoke to the Eleith it was only the second.

The whip went down again, my body betrayed me when it began to tremble from the abuse it received. The crowd remained silent once again, the only noise came from the guard's laughter and the Commander's grunts from the amount of force he used and the crack of the whip with each motion. Another blow, I gripped the post harder, I felt the wood cut into my fingers. I tried in vain not to count my lashes one after another as he continued at a constant pace.

Thirteen.

Fourteen.

Fifteen.

Sixteen.

I squeezed my eyes shut, jaw tight and focused, almost done a few more to go. Remaining conscious and keeping silent throughout it was nearly impossible, but I refused to give the Commander the satisfaction.

Then the lashing stopped.

Two guards unchained my wrists and pulled me off the post. There were stains of blood where my fingers pressed into the wood. I trembled, my body refusing to listen to me, willing it to stop. Unable to support my legs they dragged me to the Commander.

"No scream? No begging? Such a shame." He looked at my eyes an expectant smile twisted. How I longed to rip that look off his face. He ran a finger over my cheek, I moved away from his touch with as much strength as I could muster. He chuckled darkly and continued to chuckle after ordering his guards to take me back to the cell.

They dropped me in the cell like a sack of potatoes than brought in the same woman who tended to me last night. Laying on the bench I waited for them to leave doing my best to keep myself sane from the pain coursing up and down my back. Glancing at the male in the next cell, I could have sworn his eyes glowed as he watched me lay on my stomach.

The woman finished tending to me than stood next to the guards, one of them looked at me before he spoke. "Not very tough now are you." I just closed my eyes and ignored their laughter as they left the prison. A warm breeze brushed past me again calming any doubts I may have had. My pain lessened, it became easier to breathe until I could no longer stay awake and fell asleep shortly after.

7

I jolted awake from the sound of my cell door creaking open, everything was dark I could barely make out a figure walking into my cell. I went to push upright, but a hand flashed past my vision and clamped down over my mouth. Stopping me from yelling out, as though it would help. The person slammed me back against the stone wall, lights danced around my vision from the pain shooting through my nerves.

I tried to focus on whose arm it belonged to, as my vision came to focus. Short sandy blond hair, dark brown eyes with thin lips and a round face became clear. Realizing with disbelief the guard had a bandage covering his nose. He was the one I had broken his nose over my knee.

"Shh... shh, quiet now... we wouldn't want to disrupt the other's sleep now would we." He whispered in my face. The reek of ale from his mouth hit my nose, I grunted a reply of disgust. "Hmm... if I had known how happy you would be to see me, I would have come sooner." Running his free hand up the side of my arm.

The man wasn't just drunk, he was delusional. I shoved his hand away from my arm and gripped the one over my mouth then yanked two fingers back. He yelped in pain.

"Bastard!" I growled, he ripped his hand away and seized a fist full of hair with his other hand then slammed the side of my head into the bench. Dazed by the blow I was unable to stop him from climbing on top of me.

"I'm juss going to show you a good time. After all you'll die down here, I am doing you a favor. Letting you experience a real man." His voice slurred as he spoke. I threw my arm at him in a panic, he snatched it and shoved it against the bench. Pressing his knee over it pushing my arm into the stone. Yanking my head back he forced my face near his then shoved his mouth over mine.

My insides recoiled from the touch, shoving down the repulsion I felt for what I planned to do next. I unclenched my jaw and parted my lips, believing I was no longer fighting him. The man slid his tongue in. As soon as a good portion made it past my teeth, I chomped down with all my might. The taste of iron flooded my mouth as his blood poured from his tongue.

He ripped himself from me and thrashed around the cell screaming. "You ore..." at least that was the sound that came from his mouth. It was hard to tell with his tongue half gone. I spit the piece out of my mouth along with the blood. Wiping it with the back of my hand I held back the urge to gag. Then went to him while he rolled on the ground squealing in agony and kicked him repeatedly. This bastard would remember to stay away this time, let him be an example to any other who might try.

The pain from my lashings in the back of my mind, all the adrenaline coursing through my veins made me feel invincible. In the distance I vaguely heard a door slamming, numerous footsteps grew louder toward my cell. I looked over in time to see the Commander leading a group of guards. He walked into my cell and waved a torch in my face. The bright light forced my eyes to squint and the heat from the flame warmed my skin.

"Why is there blood on your face?" He demanded. That was his question? Raising an eyebrow at him I lifted my chin to the now unconscious guard on the ground.

"He came where he wasn't welcome." He struck me across the face with the back of his hand. The blow sent me against the bars to the cell next to mine. Golden eyes appeared in the dark. The Commander pressed me against the bars and dug his fingers in my back then racked them across my wounds. Unable to suppress the scream from escaping my lips, it echoed over the dank rock walls. I panted from the pain.

He leaned into me, bringing his mouth next to my ear.

"Since you gave me such a lovely sound. I will overlook this tonight." He paused a moment and clicked his tongue seeming annoyed. Then, shoved off my back, barking orders at the other guards to pick up the mess on the floor. He stopped at the cell door and turned to me. "I look forward to hearing more of your lovely sounds." Then slammed the cell door shut.

I waited for the echo of their footsteps to disappear before I allowed myself to collapse to the floor. I covered my face with my hands, my body trembled from all that transpired. Struggling to keep my tears from streaming down to no avail they flowed freely. The silver mixing with the clear in the palm of my hands.

"Concentrate." I told myself, "You have endured much, this will not break you."

A hand brushed the top of my head, I jerked away from the touch and looked up. I found myself seized in the stare of those mysterious golden eyes.

"I don't need your pity." I snapped pulling further away, his eyes still watched me as he let his hand fall back into his cell.

"You have a name?" The sound of his rough voice caressed over my skin. Leaving me wanting to hear more and again the familiarity pressed in the back of my mind. I felt my brows knit together in confusion. I ignored the draw I felt toward him.

"You assume I'll just freely give you my name? What concern of it is yours?" What were his motives? Everyone had a motive no matter the realm, whichever he belonged to.

"I have no ulterior motive, just wondered what they call you." He ran his fingers through his hair. For a moment I thought he could read my mind. Biting my bottom lip, I mulled over my options.

"Before I give you mine. What is yours?" I turned the question at him wondering if he would comply. A chuckle escaped from behind his lips.

"Faelan."

"And where are you from Faelan?" I continued to pry.

"I believe it's only fair you answer my question first before getting ahead of yourself." His eyes burrowed as though he could, will the words from my mouth.

"But you know where I am from." I challenged.

"Do I?" He answered.

"We are in the Human Realm after all." I watched him carefully.

"True, but how can I know for sure this is the realm you belong?" He got me there. I sat quietly for a moment.

"Shae," I relented figuring this was as much information I would get now, he released me from his piercing gaze.

I took the chance to grab the bowl of water left and cupped a handful then rubbed it over my neck, ears, shoulders, and face. It did little to help the smell, but it was better than nothing. Ignoring the throbbing pain radiating off my back I cupped another handful and put it in my mouth. Swishing the liquid around then spit it to the ground, I tried several times to get the taste of iron from my mouth. All the while eying Faelan who remained by the bars.

Feeling as though I had rinsed enough, I sat next to him. Unable to ignore the unusual draw I felt toward him.

"So, why are you in this wonderful place?" I cocked my head to one side.

He shrugged "Right place right time." Raising my eyebrows at him, I nodded my head with my lips in the shape of a silent O. He seemed to not be right in the head.

Before I could back away his eyes blazed to life and a warm breeze brushed across my face again. My eyes closed and I welcomed the feeling and scent of the forest after rain.

"Does it help?"

My eyes shot open and saw him staring at me. "Excuse me?" I said confused.

"Does it help?" He asked again patience laced through his voice.

"Does what help?" Raising an eyebrow, a rush of warm air hit my face, and his eyes blazed again.

My breath caught, it now dawned on me what he was. "You... you're an elemental!" I choked out in disbelief. The corner of his mouth twitched then pulled up to a half smile revealing his canine. That is a dangerous look to have, I thought. Because what it did to my pulse was unexpected.

"I can help with the pain." He said in a calm voice, "I cannot heal you completely, but it will help."

"Why would you go to the trouble of helping a nobody?" I asked unaccustomed to people offering to help. "It will only bring you misfortune, you shouldn't involve yourself with me." I made to touch my eye but dropped my hand and looked at him. "I am cursed." I felt my eye blaze as if responding to my claim.

His golden eyes flashed then a wave of heat rushed through me leaving no room for any chill to linger. My eyes rolled up and my lips parted, a sigh of relief left me as the pain from my lashes lightened immensely. I groaned involuntarily at the sensation of heat coursing through my veins unable to deny the pleasant feeling it brought.

Remembering myself, I closed my mouth and opened my eyes, I could feel the heat rise to my cheeks embarrassed by my unintentional response. I stared at him, unable to read his expression.

"How?" I whispered.

"You are not cursed Shae, if anything you are blessed beyond all reason." Faelan said nothing more and went back over to the stone wall where I had first found him. He sat down and leaned his head back against the wall then closed his golden eyes vanishing them from my sight.

I didn't remember falling asleep, but it was the best sleep I'd had in a long while despite the situation I was in. I stretched my body wincing when the movement cracked open a few spots on my partially healed back. My eyes unconsciously drifted to Faelan's cell. The pit of my stomach dropped when I saw he was no longer there.

Frantically I looked from cell to cell, thinking maybe they moved him to another. But there was no sign of the striking golden eyes. I sank down on the bench and dread began to fill me. I could only hope they had released him.

The sunlight streamed into my cell; I realized my next set of lashings was not far off. My blood boiled from the thought of what these bastard guards were allowed to get away with. What kind of King allowed the men who were supposed to protect his people treat them so horribly? The sound of footsteps approaching interrupted my train of thought.

I looked up to see whose steps they belonged to, when the Commander stormed down the hall followed by two other guards. He had a scowl on his face, jaw clenched. He reached the cell door, then opened it with so much force it nearly came free of its hinges. My eyebrows shot up.

"Lovely morning. Commander?" I made my voice pleasant.

"You are free to go." He let out in between clenched teeth. I cocked my head to the side, the corner of my mouth twitched.

"Then I will be on my way, can't say it was a pleasure." I said and made my way out of the cell. As I passed, the Commander's arm snapped up and grabbed the back of my neck. I stopped in my tracks, I could feel the tips of his fingernails dig into my skin. Every muscle in my body screamed to react and pull his sausage sweaty fingers off and break each one of them. But I was almost out of this hell hole, and I would not give him any reason to throw me back in.

"Do not think I will just let it end here, wench. We'll see one another again and I will be looking forward to it." His voice was low, venom seeped out of every word. His grip tightened.

"That will make one of us Commander. Now, release me." I said tightly.

"Drask," he said, "my name is Commander Drask, remember it." I turned my head to look at him, my eyes blazed with rage.

"Release me." I said again, this time my voice was lethal. Commander Drask let go and I left with no concern of him watching my figure disappear up the stairs. I didn't get far down the hall before I caught sight of my satchel. Not waiting I went into the room and picked it up. Pulling an extra shirt out then pulled it over the rags still on my body. Satisfied, I removed the torn-up shirt and tossed it to the ground.

My weapons lay along the wall across the room, nice of them to keep my belongings in one place. Taking what was mine, I left with bitter memories and one good one.

The sun was bright as I left the building, my eyes squinted before adjusting to it. I needed a place to stay for the night and didn't know how bad my back truly was. Thankfully it didn't seem to hurt as much as it should. And I needed a place to lie low and figure out my next move. I stayed to the shadows, moving in and out of secluded areas away from the crowds and the streets the guards patrolled on.

I looked behind me as I entered another abandoned alley making sure I wasn't being followed. As I turned, I slammed into a hard, unmoving surface that knocked me to the ground. Pain flared up my back. Looking up to yell at the person but was stopped short when I saw Faelan looking down at me. His hand was out waiting to help me up. A wave of emotion rolled through me.

"Faelan?" I breathed; a half smile crept on his face. "You mind telling me how you crept up on me?" Was all that had come to mind.

"Crept?" His facial expression was playful. "I was right in front of you, you just didn't see where you were going." I got up despite how much my back hurt, ignoring his hand in front of me and dusted myself off while looking him over.

"Well, you seem to have got out just fine." I noted.

"Were you worried." His smile widened.

"No." I said too quickly, his eyebrows went up.

"I see they let you out. Released early on good behavior?" He said in a light tone, then glanced over his shoulder. "We should get you some place to rest."

I cocked my head to the side, "We?" I gave him a questioning look. "Although I am grateful to you for your help last night. There is no we." Faelan returned his attention to me, is face showing no sign of being bothered by my statement. Pushing past him I left before he could reply.

As I went to leave the alley, I realized he was following me. Turning on my heels I stepped in front of him forcing him to stop.

"What do you think you're doing?" He looked me up and down. It wasn't the way most men did. The way it would make my skin crawl like I wished I could just vanish. No, he was mulling over some idea. Like he was assessing his options.

"I'm walking," he said.

"Walking?" I gave him a look of disbelief.

"Yes walking, I can't walk?" His tone turning mocking.

"The same direction as me?" I lifted an eyebrow at him.

"Is that wrong? Can I not go this way?" A little miffed by his question I stepped to the side and put out my hand as though giving him the go ahead to pass.

"No, Please, do continue." I gave him a sarcastic sweet smile as he walked right past me. Glancing behind me out of habit when I looked back Faelan was no longer in sight. Stunned.
I looked around to see if maybe he was still around.

"What in the..." was this normal? Is this how elemental's acted appearing and disappearing at any moment. It's not like I've had interactions with any elementals. I shook my head and left to get past a crowd of people heading in my direction. At the end of the street, I found an inn near the outskirts of town and entered.

I asked the inn keeper if they had a room and food. After paying for a room, I asked them to have a bath prepared while I ate my food. It was more coin for the bath, but I needed one and rest, so I paid it willingly.

After eating the well-prepared meal, I headed to my room. It was small with two areas, one with the bed and the other had an open-door frame with a tub of hot water. Steam rose in the air above it. I groaned at the sight of it, looking forward to the clean water, I checked my room quickly. Satisfied no one was there I latched the door behind me. Paranoid someone might have been there to cause me trouble.

Placing my belongings next to the bed, I took one of my hunting knives along with me and entered the room with the bath. I tossed aside the dirty clothes that were useless now and put one foot in at a time. Sinking into the water, I savored the heat wrap around my body. It stung my back when it reached the partially ripped skin. After a minute the stinging subsided, and I was finally able to relax a little. Washing the dirt and grim off my body, dried blood flaked off my skin before the water hit it.

Deciding it was better to clean, I didn't linger in the bath long after washing. I dried myself off and went to the satchel looking for a roll of bandages I kept. The roll lay at the bottom of my bag, I got them and began to wrap around my stomach just above my belly button. I worked my way up; I was unable to cover the whole of my back but was satisfied with what I did cover. I could tell they were far more healed than I originally thought. The Elemental had done far more healing than I believed he was able.

If I was honest with myself, I didn't believe their kind could even heal to begin with. Faelan... I mulled over his name, his half-smiled face appeared in my mind. I swallowed down the excitement but couldn't deny the pull I felt toward him. Elementals were not the type you'd find in a small town like this, let alone hidden in a prison. They kept to their own territory northwest of the Human Realm.

Their race is superior in strength and speed, even the Fae and Elves know to deal with them with caution. Beings with long life such a long life you'd think them immortal. Warriors who possess the ability to control elements. There are only four known elements, none have to do with healing. So, it was a wonder how he could heal. I filed the new knowledge away.

I doubted I'd see him again, I felt a small twinge in my chest at the thought. Biting my lip, pulling out my map, I ran a finger along the wrinkled paper, I stopped and tapped it on the town Lira. It was only a half a day's walk north of here and I thought it would be a good place to go next. Staying here any longer would be dangerous and my back is better than expected.

Tossing my stuff back in my satchel, I slipped the knife under my pillow and laid my head down and drifted to sleep.

8

I woke before light and changed into a green top. My black pants fit comfortably along my legs, and brown boots that reach above my ankles. I finished strapping the leather buckle around my waist to secure the blades on my lower back. Taking the rest of my belongings, I left.

The place was quiet downstairs not a soul in sight, a small bowl of fruit and bread was on the counter. I helped myself, leaving a few coins and left the inn without a sound. The air was light, a chill showing signs of fall not far off. Sensing someone's eyes on me, I halted and scanned the buildings and alleys. Finding no evidence of life, I continued on.

The woods were calm and silent, nothing like the rowdiness of Maedoc. Breathing in the fresh air I quickened my pace forcing the air push past me, enjoying the cool rush it gave. Darting back and forth from tree to tree, ducking under branches and jumping over bushes. A smile touched my lips, I relished the solitude of the forest. My solitude in the forest

My exhilaration was short-lived when I heard a twig snap in the distance, slowing my pace. I searched the trees in the direction of the sound. My breath came out heavy as my chest rose and fell. A small stream of smoke rose a little in the distance. Movement caught my eye before the clearing where the smoke rose from. Five figures moved in a semicircle converging to that spot. I watched as they closed in, all of them oblivious to my observing. They pounced through the brushes and screams erupted.

In the next instant I was on the move, trying with everything I had to make it there before it was too late. Shouts and laughter came from the attackers, a woman cried out screaming at them. Drawing closer, I pulled my blades from behind my back. I rushed past the trees and into the opening. A small camp appeared, a woman with five children from the looks of it ranged from five to thirteen.

The woman was struggling against one man kicking and screaming, another attacker had two children in his grip holding them up. Two other attackers were ransacking the family's supplies, and the last one held his sword up taking the rest of the children hostage. I ran targeting the attacker with his sword out first before they saw me. I brought my blade down, severing his hand from his arm.

The weapon clattered to the ground and taking my other blade, I slashed it across his throat, cutting off his screams. This wasn't like the hunters, this was kill or be killed. I couldn't afford to hesitate. The two rummaging through supplies froze in their place seeing their comrade fall. The man holding the children dropped them and charged. Jumping back out of his reach I rolled away.

Springing back to my feet only to meet a fist smashing the side of my cheek. Knocking me to the ground, I used the moment to tuck and roll into a crouch. The woman still struggled in the background yelling for her children to run into the woods.

The stunned men finally unfroze and joined in. I stood up slowly. They stood around me in the form of a triangle, I slipped one blade back in its sheathe. Pulling the knife from my thigh I flicked it forward to the one who had landed a hit, embedding it into his jugular. He dropped to his knees then to the ground.

Enraged, one of the other two charged me, I quickly pulled the knife from my boot and sent it flying at him, missing the mark and burying the blade in his shoulder. The impact did little to stop him. As he continued to charge me his friend began to move around to flank me. Slashing my blade across the chest of the one charging, as he dodged my attack, I jumped and spun at him while unsheathing my blade from the back and planted into his spine as he charged by. I pulled the blade out and let him fall to the ground.

The second man flung his now drawn sword at my arm. I

deflected it and brought both blades across his stomach and chest. His eyes wide in disbelief as the blood flowed from his body. I watched as his knees buckled from beneath him, no longer able to support himself.

Before I could even pity the man or think my next move, I was slammed into and hammered against a tree. The blow forced the wind out of my lungs. Before regaining any breath, a large hand clamped onto my throat and thrust me up against the tree. The force knocked the blades from my hands and clattered to the ground next to my dangling feet.

He squeezed tighter, the pressure cutting off the air flow. I tried kicking his sides, but he held firm, fingers digging in as I struggled to breathe. It didn't stop me from ripping at his hands, I fought him in vain as he made no signs of swaying. I on the other hand became sluggish my movements slow and clumsy.

The ferocious look on his face dropped suddenly when a sword protruded from his chest. His body went slack, and he released his grip on my neck. I collapsed to the ground, gasping for air, coughing, and retching trying to remember how to breathe. I held my hand close to my neck and looked to see who the sword belonged to. Only to find those mysterious golden eyes blazing down at me.

"F... Fa... Faelan?" I choked out, he stood holding out a hand to help me. I took it this time gratefully. I was about to find out whether I could come back to life a second time and I wasn't looking forward to it.

"Can you stand?" Worry was woven in his expression. I gave him a slight nod still not able to speak well. He pulled me to my feet placing his hands over my shoulders to steady me. The touch was foreign to me, and I staggered away from him. My gaze drifted over the scene, the children grouped together kneeling by their mother. My heart sank, I left Faelan and ran over to them, stumbling as I went. The Elieth drew on my senses telling me to get to the woman. An image flashed in my mind as I pushed past the children and knelt beside her.

The woman's body laid lifeless, her eyes were wide, stricken in fear. The children wailed in agony at their dead mother. I lightly touched her face, my hand trembled as I placed them over her eyes closing them. My heartbeat loud, drowning out the sounds around me. The Elieth pressed on me a weight that grew heavy with each passing second. I licked my lips feeling unnaturally parched, staring at the woman.

I hesitated. Unsure of what the Elieth was asking me to do or why. But the weight grew, and my shoulders felt as though they may collapse under the pressure.

Deciding it was better to follow through then ignore the Elieth, I pulled her upper body on to my lap. Her body still warm, I brushed my fingers against my left eye and pressed them to the woman's chest. I leaned down and pressed my forehead against the mother and closed my eyes.

A fire ignited beneath my left eyelid, with it, pain surged through my veins like liquid fire. I kept my arms firm around her and sat still. As I silently felt the battle rage within me over this woman's life. After what felt like eternity a silver tear trickled off my cursed eye and splashed onto the woman's face. The mother gasped, her eyes fluttering open, I pulled away from her panting as the pain subsided. The mother stared into my eyes, tears overflowed and spilled over the brims.

I released my firm grip from her and saw her mouth form words of gratitude. Giving a slight nod I backed away from her, allowing her children to embrace their mother. All crying tears of joy. I turned to walk away, and stopped. I saw Faelan standing, watching, his golden eyes never leaving me. Those eyes looked bright; excitement filled them. I forced my feet to move past him.

"Yes?" I said brushing past him to gather my weapons. He turned and followed.

"How?" He was in awe.

"What do you mean?" I acted ignorant.

"That woman was dead, there was no life in her." He spoke in disbelief.

I knew.

I knew how impossible it was, but I saw the image. The Elieth saved that woman and used me to do it. Or maybe the Elieth showed me, I could, do it? Either way I was just as surprised as everyone else. I turned to Faelan.

"Obviously you are mistaken, she is clearly alive." Why did I lie? It was obvious to everyone here what happened, but I lied to him like a fool? I still didn't trust him, though he had saved me. I looked to the ground, breaking our eye contact.

"I am in your debt," I changed the subject, "you saved me again." Continuing not to meet his gaze.

"You should be more careful." There was concern in his tone. My brows drew together, and I looked up at him.

"Why do you care? We only met a few days ago." I reached to pull a knife from the man's jugular and cleaned the blade off with the moss on the ground.

"We may have just met but that doesn't mean I am heartless enough to not be concerned. This is the second time I've found you in a compromising situation."

Well, I couldn't deny that. I sheathed both the knives after having them cleaned, then turned to Faelan.

"Something you should know Faelan, in case, we ever cross paths again. I'm not very good at being careful." I went to retrieve my blades that had fallen to the ground and cleaned them off as well.

"We could always travel together." He offered, I scoffed.

"Come again? I mean don't get me wrong I am grateful for your help and all but why would I travel with you?"

"Seeing how you have a knack for trouble, and I am handy in a bind. We could be of use to one another." He paused.

"And how would traveling with me be useful?" I lifted an eyebrow at him in challenge. Although the idea piqued my interest.

"I've been alone for far longer than I would like and am in need of a companion. I will make it worth your while."

My mouth almost dropped open. Was he serious?

"Apologies, even for how eye catching you are I don't plan on being your *companion*." I emphasized the word.

He cleared his throat, "As flattered as I am at the statement. I meant more as a comrade in arms than for warming my bed." A half smile touched his lips.

My cheeks burned at my misunderstanding,

"And... there is something about you Shae..." His eyes lingered.

"Ex... excuse me." A young voice interrupted. Glad for the distraction I turned to him still flustered from my blunder. The boy in front of me was none other than the boy who was fending against the guards in Maedoc.

"Yes," the boy looked down in embarrassment.

"I don't mean to bother but are the both of you perhaps... heading west toward Sinbury? We are traveling there now to meet with our father but need protection." He pulled out a pouch, and it was the very same he worked so hard to defend against the guards.

"W... we have little coin with us, but we can pay you more when we've reached Sinbury." Trying his best to persuade us.

"You have a name boy?" I asked.

"Drustan."

"Well, Drustan," putting my hand over his, "it would be an honor to escort you and your family to Sinbury, free of charge. You fought bravely for this, and I will not take it from you." I smiled at him.

"I believe it's decided then." Faelan spoke beside me. "We will be traveling together to help get his family home safe." He said with his sly heart stopping half smile, I rolled my eyes at him.

"How lucky," I said not concealing my sarcasm, hiding the excitement that made my pulse quicken. He chuckled in response. "We travel together only until they are home safe." I stated firmly, giving him no room to argue.

9

We gathered supplies that were scattered everywhere, the attackers laid still on the ground. Never to draw breath again. Did I regret taking their life? If I was truly honest no, there was no regret when defending their family. Most of the children stayed away from me however, keeping their distance from the stranger who killed and then mysteriously saved their mother. Well, all except for Drustan, he seemed to have grown attached to me.

The mother's name was Aliyah, she was taking her children to meet her husband. He had to go before them to secure his trade in Sinbury before they could settle there for a fresh start. He meant to return and travel with them, but with the circumstances of the guards in Maedoc Aliyah felt waiting for him any longer would result in losing her children. So, they packed the important belongings and left shortly before me.

The attackers had been lingering in the woods to pick off easy prey, so much for paying the King for protection. 'Worthless guards' the thought only made my anger grow. memories of Commander Drask entered my mind. Thankful I was no longer in that wretched prison, I wondered what made him release me so soon before I finished my sentence. His obvious disdain for me made it evident he didn't do it willingly. Shaking my head, I sighed and forced the thought out of my mind for now, before my mood worsened.

I remained silent during the journey doing my best to ignore the constant stares from Faelan. I was unsure of his interest in me, other than the obvious... my cursed eye, which was usually what everyone made the fuss about. Never good though, he didn't seem to be after my life. No, in fact he has saved me twice now. He had a look of amusement cross his face and I realized I had been staring at him intently. Embarrassed at being caught, I showed him a rude gesture and walked away. His laughter trailed after me as I stalked off.

As we traveled the family remained a few yards ahead of us. Drustan fell behind to walk alongside Faelan and me. He asked me many questions, mostly to do with my fighting and how I was taught. I did my best to answer but told him I was self-taught, never officially trained so most of my moves were made up. His eyes seemed to sparkle at that. When I thought about it, I realized I had learned rather quickly. He was a cheerful boy, and it was refreshing to walk with him.

"We aren't far now," Drustan said after a half of day of walking. "Will you stay for dinner to show our gratitude for all the help you've done for us? It's far more than we can ever repay." His voice filled with excitement. Before I could protest, Aliyah stepped in front of me.

"He is right, you are welcome to a meal and any meal after. You have done more for us than can ever be repaid." Her face welcoming.

"That is unnecessary, I didn't help you for you to be in debt to me I was just doing what I believed to be right." Aliyah was a kind woman, she even did something only my Grams would ever do. She looked directly in my eyes, both eyes, with a warm smile.

"Please stay for a meal and stay for a few days, I know your wounds need healing. Allow us to give you a warm place to stay until they have been mended." Her voice was filled with so much tenderness I couldn't help but take a step back. I was unaccustomed to people's kindness. Before the words of refusal spilled from my mouth Faelan stepped in front of me.

"We would be grateful to have a warm bed and meal to stay in before we continue our journey." I glared at his back, displeased with his sudden intrusion. But also relieved because he excepted what I could not. Faelan glanced back noticing my glare and smirked at me unconcered by my unhappy expression.

"Splendid!" Aliyah clasped her hands together and smiled pleased to have us agree.

She wasted no time in getting us to move along, the road to Sinbury was just ahead and she was in a hurry to make a fine meal. There was still plenty of daylight and she planned to make a very fine meal indeed.

The trees ended abruptly and revealed fields in a bowl surrounded by tall trees. The fields were a beautiful bright green, the lands were large filled with crops, many people working together tending to them. Most of the homes had lots of space between them, the buildings grew closer the further you got to the town of Sinbury. In Sinbury stood more buildings where inns and shops did their business.

I pulled my hair down to cover my left eye, there was no need to draw more attention to us. Aside from the elemental with eye catching features. I caught myself following is every move and averted my gaze before he found me looking. We followed Aliyah and her children to a small house outside of Sinbury. The land next to it vast, she steered them directly inside her home. Before entering there was a loud crash from the inside. My hand instinctively went for a knife, only to be stopped by a firm grip on my arm. I looked to see Faelan shaking his head at me.

"Your weapons aren't needed here." He gave a nod toward the inside of the door where I saw a couple embracing. The children jumped in to show their father love, I felt a tightness in my throat at the sight of the their father. His eyes glossy as he held Aliyah brushing her hair back and caressing her face, a tender smile on his lips from the sight of her. He would be what Drustan would look like when he ages. Sandy brown hair, deep green eyes, with a cluster of freckles over his nose.

"What are you doing here?" He asked confused but his voice still held a gentleness.

"We had to leave." Aliyah was crying, burring her face into his neck. "The guards were looking for trouble." She pulled her face away but never let go of him. "They were going to kill Drustan." She continued. "But he was saved. We were attacked in the woods on our way here. They were going to do awful things, but we were saved again." She stepped back, letting go. Her husband looked even more confused.

He looked in the direction his wife Aliyah turned to.

"But she saved us both times. Her name is Shae." She walked toward me, "we are alive because of her." Aliyah gave her husband an affectionate smile. The lump in my throat grew to the point I feared I might choke. I let out a small breath overwhelmed by this woman's gratitude. This was never my intention, I never planned to follow this family home. My emotions were beginning to threaten to overcome me. Before they could consume me and tear down my composure, I bit the inside of my cheek. It helped to distract my mind and gave me a chance to swallow the sobs that threaten to rend its way to the surface.

"Shae, this is my husband Turi." Turi walked up and stood beside his wife. He bowed deeply and brought his hand to his forehead. The tip of his fingers touched in between his brows, a gesture of gratitude. I tipped my head down and made the same gesture with my hand in return, showing I accepted. Aliyah put a hand on her husband's shoulder.

"Now it is time to make us a meal, something to celebrate this wonderful reunion and meeting new friends of a lifetime." She beamed at me then called her two daughters in to help her prepare the meal and called the two boys to go prepare baths for their guests. Not long after Aliyah and her daughters left to prepare dinner. I stood awkwardly in their home taken aback by what had transpired.

"Shall I show you two where you will stay," I stood frozen until Faelan nudged me out of my stupor. Instead of replying to Turi I turned and scowled at Faelan to which he returned with his half smile.

"Why don't we follow this good man," he suggested turning his attention to Turi. "Lead the way."

Turi nodded and led us out of the house, we walked around the outside. On the other side there were a few smaller huts spaced out between one another. The huts stood not far from the tall woods surrounding the entire of Sinbury. We stopped at the one furthest away, Turi gave Faelan a short nod telling him this was for him.

Faelan gave him a nod with gratitude and disappeared into his hut, pushing past the flap the was made for the door.

Turi continued to the one beside it and gave me nod to go in.

"It's not much," he said.

"It'll do just fine." I replied, I noticed his shoulders relax some.

"Someone will fetch the both of you when supper is ready." I gave him a look of gratitude and went inside.

It was a small open space with a spot for sleeping and a tub, hot water already steaming inside of it. Excited to have a nice hot bath, I wasted no time shrugging off my clothes and setting them next to the bed. Stepping into the water, the hot water stung at the open scrapes on my back. After my body grew accustom. I relaxed inside, dipping my head back into the water, closing my eyes and savoring the fresh feel water always brought me.

After making sure all the dirt and blood was washed off, I dried myself and wrapped a large cloth around my body. There was a fresh pair of clothes lying on the bed, sadly the clothes left were dresses and that is something I didn't wear.

Putting it aside, I pulled a fresh pair of dark brown pants and a form fitting black shirt and put them on. Satisfied I decided to pull my hair up for once, pulling a leather cord around until it secured the damp hair in place. My face usually covered. now clear. I discarded the dresses and put them on a small table with a look of distaste. Unable to resist, I collapsed onto the bed rolling over onto my back. I held a hand outstretched in front of me then let it fall over my eyes.

I let out a long sigh, as I recounted all the events that led to this moment. It had only been seven days since I left Cambtem and already it felt like a year.

"Why the long sigh?" Jolting upright, I found Faelan leaning on the door frame.

"How long have you been there?" I demanded. He raised his hands up in a truce.

"Long enough to notice you discard a nice dress left for you." He glanced over at the clothes lying on the table. My face flushed, why was he so infuriating? I stalked toward him, placed both hands on his chest and shoved him back hard.

"Haven't you anything better to do than stand here and annoy me?" I glared at him.

"At the moment..." he said playfully shrugging his shoulders. Then he took a moment to look me over. I would be lying if I said the look didn't excite me. "You look good, although I'd pay to see a dress someday." His half smile played on his lips.

"Unless you are willing to pay me a very handsome amount, you can just forget that day ever coming." I said, annoyed and flustered at the same time. Was that even possible?

"Hmmm... I hope you remember those words, Shae." He looked at me again and held my gaze. "I do enjoy being able to see your face." I ignored his comment and pushed past him to see Drustan heading our way beaming.

"Shae!" He called out waving his hands over his head, I couldn't help but smile and wave in return.

"Drustan."

"Ma says supper is about ready. She asked me to fetch the both of you." He gave Faelan a nod.

The table was full of meats and breads, there were platters of fruits and steaming vegetables. This was quite the feast set before them.

"Welcome," Aliyah said with a warm smile. "Please sit, eat your fill." Everyone was already seated at the table waiting to eat. Faelan sat at the only other seat available, next to me. I didn't know what to do with him. At one point he was infuriating, at another intriguing, and let's not forget there was a draw I felt toward him that was unexplainable. Plus, I was still annoyed with the encounter earlier.

The Eleith seemed to hum within me, enjoying the warmth their family radiated. There was laughter, exchanging of stories. Turi spoke of how well his trading was, the children spoke cheerfully and shared good food with one another.

"I will be in town most of the day tomorrow." Turi was saying.

"Are there any blacksmiths or weapon shops?" I blurted out. He gave me a gentle smile.

"Yes, there are a few I would be more than happy to show them to the both of you on the way." Turi replied. Looking between Faelan and myself.

"May I come too?" Drustan asked excitedly, Turi's smile widened.

"That would be fine Drustan."

10

The night was cool and crisp, winter wasn't long off. I lay in bed welcoming the soft sound of critters singing outside my window leaving a peaceful atmosphere. Sleep quickly took me, my dreams filled with flying in the bright blue sky with my unknown companion once more. I was free.

Morning came too soon.

I woke early, before sunrise. Wondering over to the bowl of water, I splashed some on my face and wiped my neck. Taking my bow and quiver of arrows, I went into the woods in search of a deer to thank the family for all their kindness. I didn't go far before one crossed my path. Finishing the hunt quickly, I returned to my hut and set it on a bench outside of the room.

My hands moved steadily as I skinned the animal humming to myself as I kept my hands moving. I stiffened when I sensed the onlooker behind me.

"Don't you have better things to do?" I huffed out in annoyance and glanced over my shoulder to see Faelan leaning on the side of the hut staring at me.

"What could be better than watching you skillfully cut your prey." He admired my handy work.

"I suppose after so much practice it's become natural now." I continued. Pleased with my finished work I separated the meat and wrapped it in sections placing them in two baskets I found in the room. I set them aside for Aliyah to take care of later. Faelan brought a clean bowl of water so I could clean my hands and knife.

"I am staying with you whether you like it or not." He surprised me by breaking the silence. "If anything, traveling with you will lead to many interesting encounters." He held a half smile on his lips.

"Nothing interesting happens, only tragedies follow me." I had no humor in my voice.

"All the more reason for us to travel together. I can help keep you safe and you can help keep me company and watch my back." His lips now stretched to a smile, showing his canines.

"You don't even know me! We have only met one another a few days ago, and you believe I will watch your back!" My frustration rising.

"Yes... yes, I believe you would." He didn't hesitate with his answer, which caught me off guard. "Regardless of what you may think of yourself Shae, you are a kind human to your very core. You will help when no one else will lift a finger, that is the type of human I want by my side. And despite what you may say, there is a part of you wishing for me to stay. Besides, I see your eyes following me everywhere I go." His eyes danced with amusement.

I scoffed, "I believe you may be delusional, Faelan." I shook my head in denial, but in the back of my mind I knew he was right. How my eyes seemed to search for his figure and the attraction I felt. "Never a dull moment when you are with me."

"Then it's settled!" He put his arm in front of me and held it in the air, anticipation floated between us. In the heat of the moment before I could cower away. I clapped my palm to his forearm gripping it in my hand with a firm shake.

"I hope I don't regret this." I sighed, a little unsure of my choice but was not going to back down now. The excitement of traveling with him outweighed all else.

Not long after, Drustan came bouncing over to inform us food was ready and should eat before setting out for town.

"What do you have there?" Drustan asked me, eying the baskets we were carrying.

"Meat, for your Ma and Pa." I replied.

"Did you hunt it yourself?" His eyes lit with excitement at the thought.

"Yes," I gave him a small smile.

"Wow!" Amazement sparked over his facial expression.

"I wouldn't be too excited Drustan, it's taking a life. You need to be skilled, so the creature does not suffer unnecessarily. If hunting is what you want to learn, you should know it is not something you should do lightly." I reached up and ruffled his hair trying to lighten the mood. I always took hunting as a necessity not a sport, some hunters were known for. They would compete to measure who was the best and waste the meat. I never knew what it accomplished for them other than bragging rights. Unconsciously I looked over in Faelan's direction and noticed his silence on the topic. His eyes seemed dark as he stared ahead of us. All I could wonder is why his expression seemed so haunted.

The food tasted pleasant, and the atmosphere around the family was just as bright as before. Turi finished his meal and asked Drustan if he was ready. They gave the family their farewells and he kissed Aliyah before walking out. Faelan and I followed him to town.

I wore the same attire as the day before and kept my hair pulled back, partly from Faelan's comment, though I would never admit it. Faelan wore simple black trousers and a gray shirt close enough I noticed how fit his chest was. A black vest lay over with knives aligned his right rib cage and a sword lay across his back.

The sun was rising above the trees, no clouds were in sight. I enjoyed the warmth it left on my skin taking away the cool feeling in the air. By the time we reached the town people were out chatting and trading among themselves, also enjoying the bright sky. Turi took us to the street with weapons and armor vendors and left us on our own, saying to stop by when we were finished.

The sound of metal clanging on metal worked its way to my ears. The hot smell from the fires they used to create their trade always left me excited. I walked past the smiths and noted the line of daggers beautifully crafted. One caught my eye and I stopped to look it over.

"Anything catch your eye, my dear?" I glanced up to see the smith watching me.

"Yes, this dagger is well made." I stepped closer to him and looked in his eyes. The blacksmith paused and did a double take. His eyes narrowed and he took a step away from me.

"Leave," he demanded, "I will not serve the likes of you." He bit out with a shaky finger pointing it outside his shop. I froze, remembering why he suddenly became panicked by my presence. I knew I shouldn't be surprised by his response, the kind of treatment I received from Drustan and his family for a moment I felt normal. I took a step back then turned and walked away, frustrated the rumor of my curse had spread even to this small town.

What was I hoping for anyway, this was normal, this is what I was accustomed to. As I walked away from the shop, I caught sight of Faelan eying me from the armor shop across the street. I turned and headed away from him. I made no attempt to speak with him or search for his comfort. He was part of the reason I let my guard down when I should have never done so.

Irritated with myself and the whole scenario I walked into an alley up ahead, not waiting for him to follow. Then disappeared from his sight. The alley took me to the next street over where more people bustled about the street minding their own business. I only took a few steps into the street when I heard shouting up ahead. I caught sight of a group of boys gathered in a semicircle.

Then, noticed Drustan was standing among them, yelling at the boys partially surrounding him. They appeared to be a few years older than him. They laughed at him after he finished what he was saying and one kid who was the same size as Drustan, shoved him over and over. He gave one last good shove and knocked him to the ground. The boys laughed in unison.

I made my way to the boys sensing Faelan trailing behind me at a distance. I pushed past them and took hold of Drustan's arm hauling him to his feet.

"We got a problem, boys?" I turned to face them.

"No problem." The boy that shoved Drustan spoke, "we were just helping this kid know the rules around here." He smiled as though he was doing Drustan a favor.

"As important as your 'rules' maybe we have a prior engagement to get to." I forced Drustan to move past the group of boys. The boy who spoke latched his hand onto my arm as I brushed past him. He pressed his fingers in my arm and stared at me as though he was remembering something.

"Wait... that eye..."

I yanked my arm out of his grip, his eyes turned black, and a shadow hovered over his small build, and everything froze around me.

"yesss.... those eyes." There was a voice, but it didn't come from the boy. He just stared frozen in place with empty black eyes. The air shifted, a cold feeling began to creep in around me. Darkness ran along my skin as though it would engulf me.

"You..." The voice was nothing like the one speaking to me when I died. There was no warmth here. Ice seemed to form over my very being with every word. Darkness seeped from its words, like a thick cloud dulling the senses.

"You are nothing, there is no hope for you. Your life will only know pain and suffering. No one will love you and everyone will abandon you." It paused and I felt a breath beside my ear. "Then I will come and claim you." A dark chuckle resonated beside me, and my stomach twisted in pain as my heartbeat picked up in speed.

"No." I could barely form the word, everything around me was going black. The once sunny day turned dark, and the shadow now almost completely enveloped me.

"Help," I tried to choke out, as the darkness was crushing over me.

A pair of golden eyes came into view. They blazed to life. The face belonging to them appeared and I noticed his lips were moving. But no sound was coming from them. Concern wove throughout his face.

"Shae," his voice reached my ears. Heat surged over my body, melting away the coldness from the fog.

"Faelan," I breathed. "Wha... what happened?" I looked at him confused. I trembled and tried to soak in the warmth he was giving.

"You weren't moving, those boys ran away long ago, and you weren't responding. It was as though you were not even here." His gaze dropped scanning over me, checking to see if there was any damage. A wave of vertigo hit me, and the world toppled over. I lost my bearings, Faelan caught me before I collided with the ground.

"I'm fine." I reassured him which he did not believe in the slightest. So, he picked me up in one easy swoop and held me across his arms. "What are you doing?" I protested weakly, "I can walk just fine."

"Really?" Faelan arched a brow, "you collapsing to the ground tells me otherwise. I will carry you until we find food and a place for you to rest." He allowed no room for argument.

I huffed a pathetic excuse for a protest and allowed him to have his way. In all honesty, I was too shaken to fight back. I took the cord from my hair so it would serve as a curtain and pushed some over my cursed eye more so than normal. If Faelan wondered about my actions, he made no mention of it, just continued walking as Drustan followed behind.

"Tell me tonight." was all he said. Those simple words helped shake off more of the still cold feeling lingering within me. I laid my head on his arm taking in the warmth his body radiated. Trying to forget whatever nightmares awaited me.

11

Turi was at the end of the street we were currently on. He was busy when we made our way to his small shop. Drustan ran over to his father to explain what had happened, at least what he knew, anyway. I wasn't even sure myself what had transpired.

"Is there a place we can rest and have a small meal?" Faelan spoke with Turi.

"Yes, of course follow me, there is a place in the back. Aliyah has made food for us to eat as well." Turi led the way. He was a good man; I could tell he did his best for his family. Faelan followed him back to a small room with a bench, two chairs, and a small wooden table. He placed me on the bench, then handed me a piece of bread that was in a basket on the table.

"Here," he said worry in his voice.

"I am fine Faelan, truly." I was, my body had stopped shaking, the cold feeling that crept over me had dissipated. Turi gave us both a nod and said he would return after the people around the shop dwindled down. I let out a long sigh holding the bread in both hands.

"I can't stay here any longer." I took a bite out of the bread. "First thing tomorrow before sunrise. Too much for an elemental?" My tone playful, feeling more myself again. Faelan's lazy half smile was his only reply. My heartbeat sped up in response.

Turi came back after a short while, his expression troubled. "I am deeply ashamed for what happened earlier. Those boys used to never act that way." He let out a long sigh.

"What do you mean?" I became curious.

"They used to help around town and with their families, hardworking boys. But a few weeks back they started terrorizing other people, causing problems. Telling the other children, they better listen, or they will regret it." I sat back listening to his explanation, my thoughts went to the smoke that appeared from thin air. Could that have something to do with the voice I heard? Or their behavior changing so drastically.

"So, they weren't always this way." I said.

"No," Turi sat at the table, "in fact there are a few others in town who started acting out of character as well." I glanced in Faelan's direction, if he had any idea as to why people were acting out of character, he showed no signs.

By the time we returned from town the sun had made its way down and nightfall settled in. I lay in my room alone on the bed. Trying to keep my memory of the encounter at bay for fear the voice would return and claim me like it promised. I stared at the ceiling wide awake when a knock at the door startled me. Sitting up I looked to see Faelan standing in the doorway.

"You know it is not time to leave." I laid back down and continued staring at the ceiling.

"I came to check on you." He whispered.

"It's unnecessary, I am fine." My voice came out far harsher than I had intended.

"What happened today?" He asked as though I had never spoken rudely. I knew I should tell him, I owed him that much. But would he believe me? I barely understood what had happened. But the thought of that voice haunted me. Closing my eyes, I released a breath and looked over to him.

I nearly jumped out of the bed when I saw him kneeling next to me. He was so silent I was unable to detect his movements. Settling on my side I stared into those golden eyes and hoped they would melt the memory away. Then the words just poured out of my mouth and I explained when the boy latched onto my arm. I told him how the words didn't come from him and the black smoke that hovered over his head.

I even told him how the freezing darkness kept me in place, as it tried to consume me with that horrid voice still speaking to me. After I finished, we sat in silence for a while until Faelan finally spoke.

"I will stay here for the night." He got up from his spot beside my bed and leaned against the wall by the door, just like how I first met him.

"You don't have to go to such measures," I found myself relaxing into bed realizing the dread I once had now gone.

"I figured if I stay here, your presences will keep the critters away." I laughed at his words.

"I didn't peg you as the type to be afraid of bugs." I countered.

"Only few know of my secret." He gave me a wink and settled back against the wall.

"I will do my best but no promises." I said facing him.

"Sleep Shae, we have an early start and a difficult journey ahead of us." I liked the sound of him saying us. My eyelids grew heavy than closed over my eyes.

I woke to Faelan calling my name, which surprised me considering I usually woke myself. After gathering our supplies, we set out before anyone was aware. I left a letter for Drustan, giving him and his family my gratitude for their help and the delicious meals they shared. I also left him one of my knives for him to use and practice throwing since he found interest in them. And I wanted to leave him something to remember me by.

The air felt crisp and fresh as we walked side by side in silence. Faelan was tall and lean, the top of my head reached just above his shoulders. His arms smooth, muscles well-formed, every part of his body seemed like a masterpiece of strength. There weren't many words spoken between the two of us, we spent the better part of traveling in silence.

Honestly, I didn't know what to say, I was unfamiliar with company, and he seemed content, so I made no attempt to converse. As the sun neared the trees Faelan caught a bird for us and made a small fire where we stopped for the night in the woods. I watched as he rotated the bird over the fire on a stick.

"So," I broke the never ending silence to try and get a feel for him. He lifted his eyes to me, giving me his attention. "Is this what traveling together is like?" I felt awkward just saying it. He gave me that awful yet wonderful half smile.

"It varies,"

"Do you travel often?" I asked.

"Yes. I've traveled and done many things," his gaze became distant, absently splitting the share of the bird with me, and we both ate in silence. Great going I thought, if it wasn't awkward before, it is now. I had only taken a few bites when Faelan's head snapped up and scanned over the woods. He killed the fire with his element, pulled me into him, wrapping a cloak over the two of us. Holding me tight in one arm, before I could complain he launched us straight up into the air, landing on a branch off a large tree next to where we made camp.

I was about to yell at him for his absurd behavior, but he clamped his hand over my mouth and drew me into him. Pulling his cloak further over us almost covering me entirely. His breath blew over my cheek as he whispered low next to my ear.

"Remain silent and still. Trust me... please." His low voice sent a shiver up my neck making my heartbeat quicken. Glancing at his face his eyes glowed, showing he was using his element. The slight breeze that pushed past us confirmed it.

His gaze was looking over our camp and I turned to see what made him so tense. Even though the camp lay far below I could never mistake those figures gliding below moving around the spot we had just occupied. My body went ridged at the memory; Faelan tightened his grip in response. There were five of them moving around unaware we sat right above them.

"I sssmelled her," one of them hissed loud enough I didn't even need to strain to hear them. I pushed myself further into Faelan after hearing its voice, for fear it may find me. My heart picked up and my breath became shallow.

"Shhhe'ss here!" said another, its tone impatient,

"Then where iss sshe?" a third screeched.

"Ssshe could not have ssenssed uss coming." The first one spoke outraged.

"I want her blood!" Another screeched louder. My skin crawled knowing there were more of them out there hunting me. Faelan leaned down next to me, whispering again so softly I could barely hear.

"Relax Shae, they will soon leave... I am here, I will not leave you." Pulling me closer to him he increased his breathing to match mine. Then slowly worked it back down bringing our breathing to a single rhythm.

The warmth he always carried melted away my fears. We stayed this way for what felt like hours but was only a few minutes. The creatures began to depart one by one, fading into the darkness. Faelan continued to stay in place loosening his grip only slightly and leaning back against the tree. Pulling me with him to keep me close. I could feel his body relaxing and his breathing evening out. Looking up to him I searched his face.

"What are those?" I asked barely a whisper, Faelan look down at me after hearing me speak.

"Sliske, nasty dark creatures that suck on the blood and soul of anything that crosses their path." He kept his voice low.

"I didn't realize there would be more." I huffed out.

"You've encountered them? And are still alive?" He said surprised.

"Yes, of course, I am here now aren't I. Why do you sound so surprised?"

"Because they travel in groups as you saw and dealing with one is nearly impossible for a human." I knew he was not intending to be insulting, he was only stating a fact. But I was frustrated with him anyway, blaming it on my competitive nature.

"This mere human faced two together and killed them both," I boasted. He cocked his head to one side. A slight smile of amusement touched his lips which stopped me from continuing any further. Sadly, the amusement faded, and he asked.

"When did you run into the Sliske?" My fingers pressed into his chest.

"The night I planned to leave the village I grew up in, they ambushed me."

"Ambushed? And you still made it out in one piece?" He looked at me with appreciation.

Thinking back on the event I didn't believe telling Faelan the little detail about me coming back to life after they killed me was a good idea. Let alone him thinking I was mad for even believing it. Someone coming back to life after they died the way I did was not heard of.

So, I told him about my fight with the two Sliske and left out the parts that would leave him asking more questions. He shook his head in disbelief.

"My, my, Shae."

"Yes, yes, I am full of surprises. So, when are we getting down?" I asked changing the subject.

"We aren't, we will stay up here. I don't want to risk them catching your scent again since they will be wondering around the area until daylight."

Sighing, I supposed this was better than fighting for my life again. Although the thought of fighting alongside Faelan gave me comfort. I felt we could out match the Sliske if it came down to it.

Relaxing against him I allowed myself to immerse in his warmth. It sent my pulse racing, I recalled our position hoping he wouldn't notice the change in pace. I lay there listening to the steady rhythm of his heartbeat. Oddly comforted in the arms of this elemental where I have never once felt the comfort of being embraced. My eyelids slowly closed, and I quickly drifted off to sleep.

12

I woke to the morning light shining on my face, I breathed in the musky scent of pine that always followed Faelan. The smell was more prominent since I was still buried into his chest from the night before. My gaze followed along his body until it landed on his face, his eyes open, how long he was awake, I didn't' know. His face held a calmness, any tension from the night before long gone.

"Why are they after me?" I found myself asking him, as if he held all the answers, pulling him away from whatever distant thought had him gazing deep into the woods. Faelan's eye met mine, gently he brushed my hair away from my cursed eye. The simple gesture sent chills done that side.

"I suppose it might have something to do with who you are." His face looked grim.

"But I am nothing special, I'm an outcast. A being that was never meant to exist." He tucked my hair behind my ear and gave me a soft smile.

"This is something we disagree on."

"I don't believe you have been paying attention. There is trouble wherever I go." My eyebrows pulled together.

"Isn't it more fun that way? Keeps me on my toes." His smile turned playful.

"I'm glad you are happy with it." I spoke with sarcasm and pulled further away from him. Assuming he still didn't understand. We have only known one another for a short time. He will learn though, I have learned misfortune truly does follow my every step.

Sighing, I shook the thought away from me and gave Faelan a sly smile.

"Well, see you on the ground." Then leaned back and slipped off the branch. I held my arms out, bracing for the one just below us. Grabbing hold of it I swung myself down moving from one branch to another. Then landed on the ground with an over-the-top back flip I held a smug look on my face looking up toward Faelan. Only to find him already on the ground waiting for me.

I rolled my eyes at him leaning on the tree applauding my performance. Then walked over to collect my supplies.

"We will travel with caution from now on with the Sliske hunting you more adamantly, now that your scent is so close to them." Faelan put his own supplies away. I had put the last of mine away and hefted the bag over my shoulder when a twig snapped closer than I would have liked. Jerking my head in the direction of the sound, I noticed Faelan already looking that way.

His arms were crossed over his chest, a scowl marring his handsome face. Commander Drask walked past the bushes concealing him and several guards trailing him. I stood frozen in place at the sight of him. Memories of the time in that hell hole flooded back.

Although his looks were not in the same league as Faelan, Drask was still easy on the eyes. Black cropped short hair, sharp curved features. A strong build, his biceps nearly as large as my thighs. His dark brown eyes took away any appeal he might have held. Whatever cruelty this man had, his eyes did not hide one bit.

His eyes searched the area until they landed on me. A sinister smile spread across his lips, and I felt a chill run down my spine. This was not good.

"Shae," he spoke coolly, "I told you we would meet again." His dark eyes looked over my body in one easy swoop.

"What do you want?" I said with caution, "I was released. You were the one who released me. Why are you here now?"

"Oh well, yes. It's simple I came because there is an order out for your capture." He moved toward me but was halted by Faelan stepping in his path.

"On whose orders." Faelan spoke with a calm commanding voice,

"She has done nothing wrong." He stood firm in his path.

"Pardon me General... orders come from the King himself, if you have a problem you must take it up with him."

"General?" I blurted out confused. Commander Drask looked over me again, an amused look clear on his face.

"Yes, General. You didn't know who you were traveling with?" He scoffed.

"You work for the King?" I took a step away from him.

"No, I am a General. But not for this King." Faelan lifted his hand toward me in an attempt to console whatever fragile relationship we had.

"And when were you going to tell me?" I asked, stepping back out of his reach. My brain was trying to keep up with everything. Commander Drask stepped in the middle before Faelan could respond.

"Yes, he's the General of an allied realm so naturally when I found him in my prison, I had to release him." His tone held more amusement, obviously pleased watching me squirm.

"Shae..." Faelan began but was cut off by Commander Drask once again.

"Well, I imagine a four-hundred-year-old elemental gets bored once in a while and likes to pick up pets here and there to amuse himself." He looked over at Faelan. "Don't you have somewhere to be General? I am sure you have other... obligations to attend to rather than skirt chase this cursed wench." Commander Drask Signaled for his guards to put me in chains. "But You're welcome to tag along. If you have nothing better to do." He added with a smug look.

I stood with my feet planted as the guards circled me. My mind raced, there were too many to fight, and running was nearly impossible. I couldn't rely on Faelan, I wasn't entirely sure which side he stood on. Even after the few days we had grown closer, he could have been bringing me to the King without my realizing the entire time.

Commander Drask pulled me out of my thoughts from the sound of shackles clanging together.

"We can do this the easy way, but honestly. I would very much prefer the hard way. I have missed watching you fight with all your might in vain." My blood boiled, but instead of fighting. I hurled my supplies to the ground and brought both hands up. Instead of putting the shackles on Drask threw his fist and connected with my face forcing me to stagger back from the blow. My expression did not betray the rage seething inside, blood trickled down my busted lip.

"Now that's more like it." Two guards seized both my arms and held me in place as Commander Drask struck my ribs. He got one good hit in before Faelan's voice cut through.

"Enough!" He demanded. Commander Drusk whipped around drawing his sword and placed the blade along Faelan's neck. I caught a glimmer reflect beside Faelan as he drew a knife just as quickly as Commander Drask. Pressing the Dagger near his gut. If he noticed, he made no show of it.

"Are we going to have a problem... General? I would hate to see our treaty end after so many years. Because you could not respect our King's wishes, while remaining in our territory." Faelan's eye's hardened staring at the Commander. He blew out a sigh and withdrew his dagger just as swiftly as he drew it. He took a step back the sword sliding away from his neck.

"I don't believe it's necessary to treat her with force when she is willing to go." Faelan returned to his calm posture as though he had all the time in the world. I licked my lips, my heartbeat pumped in my chest. The frustration of not knowing whether Faelan could be trusted or not ate away like a starved animal. Allied to a King who is cruel to his subjects, people he should take care of and protect. Instead, he stole from them and abused them with his power.

Commander Drask pulled hard on my hair forcing my mind to return to another more important predicament. The reality I was once again imprisoned to the demented Commander.

"She is a prisoner, and she is my prisoner at that. I will treat her as I see fit. She needs to be taught a lesson in manners and understand who is in charge here." Commander Drask sneered in my face. He gripped my hair tighter. I could feel the strands ripping from my head. I glared back at him, my eyes held the promise of death.

"If you're going to kill me, be done with it. But I am sure your King wants me back alive. So, I suggest you take your grubby hands off me." A smile crossed his face that never touched his eyes.

"Yes, he did mention bringing you back alive, but there was nothing said about the condition you had to be in when we arrive." He slammed his fist holding the shekels into my gut. The blow made me double over, releasing my hair I fell to my knees. I gritted my teeth determined not to falter any further.

Commander Drask didn't wait to drag me back on my feet and shackle my hands. I felt a pit in my stomach at the thought of what was to become of me now. I caught a glimpse of Faelan watching it all unfold. I turned from him knowing I would find no help from him here. A sharp pain filled my chest from the pain and sorrow with each and every thought of him.

I shoved the pain down like so many times before and forced myself to remain firm. To prepare for what could be next for the trouble that was sure to come with Commander Demented. And I refused to let him get the better of me. I felt hard cold close around my neck and jerked back from Commander Drask. My hands flew to my neck touching the cold metal shackle he had placed there. I gripped it and pulled trying to remove the solid piece, now more unsure of my future.

The Commander laughed at my reaction to his metal necklace then jerked me forward with the rope tied to it. He yelled for his men to get back to their horses. His gaze drifted to me with pure delight in his eyes from whatever he had instore.

"Oh, don't worry cursed wench, you won't be needing a horse." He said amused then turned to Faelan. "General, as I said before you are welcome to travel with us or leave to your lands and cry to your ruler. The choice is up to you." I looked over in time to see Faelan's eyes blaze.

"I will accompany you, Commander. I am sure you will not be competent enough to follow your King's wish to bring the prisoner back to the capital alive." Any amusement the Commander Drask once had vanished. He pulled the rope attached to my neck to get me moving towards where he had come. The guards gathered waiting for their Commander. He mounted his horse in one easy motion and grabbed hold of the reins. Sitting straight on his horse he wrenched the rope attached to me.

"You'll do well to keep up or I will drag you along." Another one of his perverse tortures, no doubt. I held my chin high not showing emotion giving him what he wanted. Faelan came into view on his own horse, how he come by it I had no recollection. A black beauty holding itself with a commanding air that suited Faelan too perfectly. He seemed so far away from me, it appeared the last few days we shared had been just a dream. The sharp feeling hit me again as I watched him bring his horse alongside Commander Drask.

"Time to leave Commander." He said as a command not a request. If Drask was bothered, he didn't' show it. Signaling his men to move forward, I swallowed hard and took a few deep breaths prepare for however long the trek ahead may be.

As they rode, I allowed my mind to wonder helping me keep my mind off the burning in my legs. I thought of Faelan and realized I didn't know anything about him. The fact he was a General or that he was four hundred years old! The thought was beyond me, four hundred years was a long time to live. There was so much he must have done, who he was with.

The thoughts only spiraled as I trailed behind Commander Drask's horse in a steady pace. My only grace in this whole scenario was their easy pace rather than me sprinting the whole way. I was sure if he hadn't, I would have collapsed and been drug long ago.

13

After what felt like eternity Commander Drask brought his horse to a stop after Faelan's protest, saying their horses were tired and needed water. This is where I wondered whose side, he was truly on. His face was stone cold for a long while and he never looked in my direction. But it was obvious the horses were fine and could go for a while longer.

My legs burned and screamed at me, I could barely muster enough strength to keep standing. But I would be damned before collapsing in front of Commander Drask. I supposed I was damned anyway. Trying to catch my breath with each lungful. Short, shallow dry breathes scorched my throat. Commander Drask yelled out orders to his men to set up camp. The horses were left by the stream so they could graze and rest.

He hauled me over to a tree outside of where the men made their camp and tied the rope to a branch, like I was one of the horses. Tugging the rope twice to make sure it was secure he turned and walked away, continuing to bark orders at his men as they scrambled about.

My body gave up supporting me and collapsed to the ground, I was sticky from sweat and dizzy. The cool air brushing against my face helped to clear the spinning. I leaned back against the tree trunk and closed my eyes enjoying not moving for now. Trying to adjust the iron shackle hanging around my neck as best I could. It had rubbed my skin raw and no matter which way it laid left my neck itching.

Every muscle and nerve suddenly tensed when a bucket of cold water was dosed over me, followed by a roar of laughter.

"The Commander ordered us to give you water." One of the bastard guards spoke laughter still on his voice. Glaring at them was my only response, I was at the edge of camp. The few fires they had going were far from me and small fires at that. I looked over the camp and caught sight of Faelan standing in front of Commander Drask. His arms crossed over his chest while the Commander had his clasped together behind his back.

Faelan gave a curt nod, appearing to have reached an agreement between the two of them. I watched as he walked back to his horse. He glanced in my direction our eyes met for a moment before he turned away, paying attention to me no longer. A sharp pain hit my stomach as though I had been stabbed. I rubbed the spot in an attempt to alleviate the pain. Frustration nagged at me from the lack of knowledge I had of him. Why would I allow myself to trust him so fully in such a short time. The thoughts spiraled in my head like a storm. Everything he did either drew me in or left me confused. I swallowed, trying to shove down the feeling threatening to consumer me.

Shifting my attention back to the guards still standing before me. I moved my wet hair away from my face, no longer bothered about hiding my eye. There was no point now. My clothes were sopping wet, even if they had meant to humiliate me. It only accomplished cooling my skin down from its heat and rinsing the sticky sweat away.

"What happened?" Commander Drask's voice barked behind the guards. His bulky build stomped in our direction.

"Your men felt I needed a bath." A slight smile touched my lips amused at their sad attempt to humiliate me. Drask breezed past his men and went straight for me. The strike from the back of his hand snapped my head to one side.

"You will do well to know your place, cursed wench." I wiped away the blood that trickled down the side of my lip and returned my glaring gaze up at him.

"Maybe if your men were better at following orders... or maybe it's just a lack of authority on your part?" My tone dripped with mockery. He roared with laughter, causing me to nearly jump out of my skin.

"Authority?" He repeated while laughing. Turning to his men the laughter stopped. "Who brought her the water?" He demanded. All the men there stood in attention wherever they stood. "Step out!" He spoke with more force.

"Me. Commander." The guard who dumped water over me spoke with a shaky voice. Commander Drask took a step toward him, pulled his dagger from his side and slashed it across the young man's face. Leaving a long bloody gash. The guard clamped his hands to his face and screamed in pain, trying in vain to stop the bleeding.

"Now I am assuming it was an attempt to humiliate the cursed wench. But while doing so you defied my orders which will not be tolerated." Commander Drask looked down at him on the ground clinging at his face. "Someone take him to the healer and get him patched up." Then, kicked him once before returning his attention to me. "Satisfied?" His voice filled with his own mockery.

"Yes Commander, I see what amazing fear you hold over these foolish young men." Commander Drask no longer held any amusement. He reached down and grabbed hold of my face and pulled me up until the shackle tightened enough to cut off the air flow.

"You will do well to remember I can continue our sessions of lashing anytime I please." Then shoved me away. I rubbed my jaw, sure a bruise would develop.

"I am sure your *King* wants me more intact than you're letting on. Otherwise, those lashings would have been the first thing you did when you found me." His jaw tightened at my words.

"Well... Shae," hearing my name from his mouth made my skin crawl, "I guess you are more intelligent than you let on. Make no mistake, I will make this journey as unpleasant for you as it will be pleasant for me." A slight smile touched the corner of his mouth then walked away yelling orders to get the meal prepared.

I closed my eyes and leaned my head back, rubbing my jaw trying to ease the lingering ache. I found myself trying to remember the warmth I felt from Faelan the night before. Breathing in, I remembered how my pulse rose from his tight grip over my skin and his steady breathing that calmed me down. A bowl was dropped at my feet, interrupting my peace that was short lived.

I ate as best I could with bound hands and no complaints. My stomach grumbled at the very smell of the food. As I ate, I scanned for Faelan's figure, but he was nowhere to be found among the men sitting in groups around their small shelters in case of rain. The clouds were heavy, and chances were good for it to come down.

The men laughed and talked with one another like normal young men. It was hard to imagine they were the same guards mistreating the very people they were charged with to protect. But here I was, sitting tied to a tree in the chilly weather while the clouds made night come that much quicker. While they sat around small fires warming their hands. I supposed I was a prisoner, so what did I expect from their treatment.

The sun had set within an hours' time, no light to see. Which put me more on edge, only a few men were up in shifts to stand guard, and they kept their distance from me. I sat silently in the dark staring out in the abyss the fires now faint glows radiating by their camps. I fumbled with my shackles in vain trying to find a weakness something to break loose from the damn steel. Failing miserably and giving up my attempts, I found my eyes grow heavy from exhaustion.

Just before I fell into a sleep the temperature dropped around me and my eyes snapped open, on high alert. I studied the camp, no guard appeared to sense the sudden change in the air. The hair on the back of my neck stood up and a cold chill ran down my spine. Then, I felt the presence behind me, directly on the other side of the tree I was tied to.

"I smell you..." the Sliske hissed, my heart stopped knowing they had found me.

"Hmmm... you smell mouthwatering." Another voice spoke on the other side. My blood pumped knowing there was no way I could escape. I went to scream, yell, anything to alert the guards of danger. But my voice caught in my throat failing me, I searched for Faelan in the dark and couldn't see anything outside the glow of the small fires. The guards making their round oblivious to the creatures just outside their camp.

"Let's take her now," the one on my right said.

"No," the first Sliske spoke, "we can't now. Patience." Their voices low enough only for my ears.

"But we've waited so long," the other urged. "A taste, just to make sure it's really her."

The one on my left was silent for a moment.

"Yes." It finally agreed with delight. My stomach clenched, I opened my mouth only to choke on the words I tried to force out. They moved slowly on both sides of the tree. I caught sight of their figures creeping along the tree. Their hands moved one after another along the trunk.

My eyes locked with the Sliske's eyes, black orbs with red swirled inside their depths. The Sliske on the left placed one hand lightly on my shoulder. Everything inside me screamed to get away, but I was frozen in place unable to escape from this nightmare. Another hand came into view, long sharp nails pushed into my skin and brought its face close to my arm.

Opening its thin mouth revealing the rest of the long thin fangs hanging from its mouth. Pain exploded from both arms in unison as they punctured the skin. I could feel the blood draining slow at first than it flowed faster. Its eyes stayed locked on mine; the red swirls seemed to grow with every drink. I remained paralyzed staring into the eyes of these creatures. Until they finally pulled away.

"So sweet," The Sliske on my right hissed.

"She's the one," The one I kept eye contact with spoke, a smile crept on its face that would haunt my dreams. My body still suffered from whatever substance lined their fangs that caused the excruciating pain. "Hmm... I look forward to our next meeting, Blood Bearer." It spoke as if promising a lover, the voice horrid. I stayed motionless watching its figure and blood swirling eyes vanish into the darkness where they came from.

The blood rolled down my arms from my shoulders where they had left their marks. I sat there petrified; my eyes stung as tears ran down. One normal, the other silver once again reminding me how cursed I truly am.

A familiar warmth began to grow within me, I searched until they landed on a pair of two glowing eyes staring at me. The heat rose inside sending a pleasant feeling throughout my body replacing the pain in my arms as the skin began to mend. I felt relief from the thought Faelan had returned, accompanied by frustration of the many questions rolling in my mind.

Why did he loom in the dark? Where did he vanish to? Can I still trust him? Will he help me from the sidelines without being noticed? I leaned back when his eyes vanished, leaving me in the dark once again.

14

I woke to a sharp pain in my side, I opened my eyes and pushed off the ground just in time. To see Commander Drask pulling his leg back to kick me again. I tossed my hands up blocking him from landing a strike to the face. The shackles bit into my wrists from the blow.

"Oh, good your awake." He announced overjoyed, "Ready to travel." He stepped past me, untying the rope. I took that moment to stretch my limbs, hoping the travel was not as long as yesterdays. The stiffness in my legs and arms made me weary and less hopeful.

I didn't linger when he tugged on the rope, the men were scurrying around putting the last bit of supplies away and getting their own horses ready. With each step I took my body moved easier...

"Get on," Commander Drask commanded, breaking my focus. I gave him a look of confusion. "Mount the horse," he said impatiently.

"With you?" I raised an eyebrow at him.

"Get on," he repeated from the top of his horse.

"I'd rather walk," I said without a second thought, Commander Drask grunted.

"I was hoping you'd say that." His facial expression brightened with a cruel delight. I realized my mistake too late, He kicked his horse hard and took off with no warning. I was unable to get a footing before the horse yanked me forward. I bit the inside of my cheek as I hit the ground and grabbed hold of the rope and held on so my neck wouldn't snap.

The pain had no time to register before my body was drug along the ground trailing behind the racing horse. I could barely hear the roar of laughter coming from the Commander over the pounding in my head. My body screamed out as he wrenched me across the tree roots jutting out of the ground. My muscles were on fire while I desperately kept hold of the rope. I kept my eyes closed and mouth shut, holding tight to the rope. Struggling to keep my mind intact while the body endured the beating.

The pulling stopped and my hands still clutched onto the rope. There was a fog over my senses making it hard to make out the voice off in the distance.

"...DO YOU... KILL..." The voice was loud and furious, followed by a cruel laugh.

"Kill... hardly." I looked at the two figures on their horses. A figure blocked the other, I tried to get a clear view, but my vision blurred, and my body barked in pain from the movement.

"How incompetent are you?" Faelan's voice echoed over the woods and my heart thumped from the sound of it. "How are you going to follow through with the King's orders if you kill her before you even get there?"

A chill ran down my spine at the sight of Faelan, the rage that radiated off him would make any man or creature cower. Faelan got down from his horse and Commander Drask followed suit.

"I see you're displeased General, but she is the one who decided not to ride. I will not force her into the saddle." Amusement filled his words as he spoke. "And honestly what are you going to do about it. If you try to step out of line in our realm, the treaty will end and we would start picking your people off one by one."

My chest tightened, realizing the predicament Faelan had been in getting mixed with my troubles. But he surprised me, instead of backing down he moved closer to Commander Drask and spoke so low I could barely make out his words.

"Let me make this crystal clear for you, Commander. If you continue to put Shae's life at risk. I am going to set your veins on fire and run them through your body melting you from the inside out. It's a very gruesome way to die. You know I am more than capable of doing so. My people are not so easily to pick off as you might think. The treaty is more for the safety of your people, not mine." Faelan stared down at him for a short moment. Then pushed passed him nearly knocking Commander Drask to the ground and walked straight to me.

I had been sitting on my hands and knees frozen in place, watching the scene unfold. His expression softened when our eyes met, but there was still an edge that lingered in his. Faelan bent down after reaching me and pulled a knife from his belt. He cut the rope attached to my collar, sliding the knife back he scooped me up in one fluid motion.

He walked in easy steps barely jostling me as he made his way to a small stream we had been following since Commander Drask captured me. I looked up and saw his jaw tight, anger still visible. He let me down and set me up against a tree.

Clear water calmly flowed over the smooth stone, the sun reflected its surface shining brightly. I watched as he tore a piece of cloth into strips and dipped them into the stream. The silence stretched while he used a strip and dabbed it over my face gently wiping away the dirt, grim, and blood.

The air was tense, and I didn't dare move, even knowing his rage was directed elsewhere. I wanted him to know how grateful I was for what he had done, what he was doing. How do I go about saying such words. Nothing seemed to be enough. My Grams was the only other person I felt this grateful to and I never expressed the words. Clearing my throat, I casted my eyes away from him.

"Um... I... ah, am grateful." I managed after fumbling over the words. A slight smile touched his lips when I glanced up at him. The expression left just as quickly.

"What were you thinking?" His voice hard. The anger rose inside, and my facial features hardened.

"I was thinking I would rather tear my own limbs off than mount a horse with that twisted bastard!" Faelan continued to clean off my arms and wrap a few strips and tie them in place while I continued. "I may cause more suffering for myself, but I would rather endure any manner of pain than to grovel in the dirt begging them to stop." My voice rose. "They will not break me!"

My arms trembled as I kept going. "I will never bow to anyone who abuses their power or treats others as insignificant wretches. Just because they are more fortunate or better off. I have dealt with enough fools like that and will not back down from it!" Breathing hard, the furry gnawed at me. Faelan stopped mending and held both hands together in a tight fist.

"You could have died." Frustration and worry laced in his tone.

"I would rather die than give into those bastards." My brows pulled together. "I apologize, I am truly grateful for all you have done for me, but I will not change in this. Knowing this are you still willing to continue with me?" I looked at him worried, a part of me thought he may be done with the trouble I brought.

Faelan unclenched his hands and placed them on either side of my face. So that his fingertips slipped into the back of my hair. To my surprise I didn't flinch away from his touch. I was finding more and more there was something else to his touch. Something right about it.

"I will be honest, you... are more than I expected and each day we are together your presence grows in me. I am not sure what the future holds, but I am with you, and I will not leave you. That, I am sure." He spoke softly, his deep voice caressed over my ears giving me hope for more.

"Well, isn't that sweet." Commander Drask stood leaning onto a tree a few yards away. The sound of his voice startled me as I turned in his direction. Faelan released his hands from my face. "A well renowned General falling for a cursed wench. What will your Queen think General?" Commander Drask enjoyed every word he spoke.

"It is none of your concern." Faelan reached out a hand to help me up. I grabbed hold without hesitation.

"It is, if you are consorting with my prisoner." Commander Drask pushed off the tree. He walked toward him in a smug way. Then stopped in front of me. He brought his hand out from his pocket the sound of keys echoed as he reached for my neck. I stood frozen eying the Commander not trusting him.

Faelan stood next to me, his posture tense. He clearly felt the same way. Commander Drask placed the key he carried in the hole and turned it once with a click. I couldn't stop the relief that flooded through as the fresh air kissed my neck. Stinging the raw area left from the constant rubbing. Still eying the Commander, he reached down and unlocked my wrists.

"Now I am assuming you will not give me anymore trouble while we move forward. Because if you try to escape, I won't even chase you. I will turn my men around and we will travel straight to that little town Sinbury you were at a few days ago. I will find that little bastard and his family and make sure they all suffer in the most gruesome way I can make up in this brilliant mind of mine. By the time you reach us, their entire home will be set fire and simmering in embers. I will be waiting for you over their bloody carcass, to muzzle you and bring you back to the King. Now I would prefer to do it that way. But we have a time limit, and I must get you back so if you would do me the pleasure of being a good, cursed wench and get on my horse. We can be on our way."

The relief I had once felt left me completely as the images flashed across my mind. He would do it.

"You would bring in innocent people?" My anger getting the better of me at the thought of Drustan and his joyful family together eating a meal.

"Yes." He spoke lazily, as though it would just be another day to him.

"Someday Commander, you will stop breathing and I hope to be the one who slits your throat." I said through clenched teeth.

"Yes, well, you have made my life far less boring." He glanced over at Faelan with a smug look as though he won this round. For a man who was recently threatened to be melted Commander Drask seemed awfully calm.

As disgusted at the thought of riding with him, Drustan and his family were far more important than my pride. I could take all the beating but to bring innocents in, I was not willing to bet on someone else's life.

"Right then!" Commander Drask clapped his hands together as though they made a good bargain. "Time to set out." He shot Faelan another smirk then left in the direction he came. I touched the back of Faelan's arm causing him to flinch.

"I will be fine." I reassured him and gave him a small nod before following Commander Drask.

15

His men were all gathered in attention waiting for their Commander's orders. He stood by his horse, one foot tapping impatiently as I approached. I fought the childish urge to walk slower.

"Get on." He Demanded, slipping a foot into the holster I hoisted myself onto the horse despite the treatment my body suffered recently. Commander Drask promptly pulled himself up, adjusting in his position behind me sitting far too close. My nerves on edge in high alert, I felt far more in danger than being dragged along.

Commander Drask chuckled darkly noticing my body tense after he settled in. Reaching over me he made his movements exaggerated while grabbing the rains.

"Let's have a good ride." He whispered in my ear so close I felt his lip graze over my skin. Kicking his mount, he urged the unfortunate beast forward. My rage flared from his overbearing attitude. He was becoming a serious problem. I could do it, I thought, it would only take a second.

Imagining connecting his nose with the back of my head, wrapping my arm around his neck rolling off his horse. Pulling one of the daggers that were hidden away, while I rolled swipe it across his throat and watch him choke. I could see the blood spilling over his fingers as he gasped for air, clutching his neck trying to keep it from spilling out. But the Elieth tugged at me, an unpleasant warning the fight would not go in my favor. So, I kept to myself, while every movement he made had me stiff as a board.

Frustrated I was at his mercy. I contemplated the reasons the king requested me brought alive. Did Commander Drask plea to his king about me slipping through his fingers before completing the lashes? I caught sight of Faelan's majestic black beast in the corner of my eye. My stomach tightened remembering Commander Drask's words about his Queen. Was he close to her? He has been around for hundreds of years they could have known one another for most of those years. What could I even compare to hundreds of years together?

A sharp pain lit in my chest, I shifted on the horse rubbing at it, as though to remove an unwanted stain. So many questions swirled in my mind as my thoughts continued to wonder. Commander Drask kept an arm on either side of me while holding the reins, Faelan stayed close by as they moved.

"Something bothering you, cursed wench?" His rough voice pulled me from my thoughts.

"Only considering whether I should slit your throat or snap your neck like a twig, and wondering when the best time would be to relieve you of life." I replied keeping my eyes forward.

Commander Drask leaned his head in brushing his lips over the nape of my neck, my stomach tightening from the feeling of his breath over my skin as he spoke.

"You should be more worried I don't run this blade through your spine, filth. My fingers have been itching since we left." His voice was low, only I could hear, or so I thought until I noticed Faelan, who shifted on his horse.

"As pleased, as I am sure you would be, Commander. Your king will not be." Commander Drask leaned back letting one arm fall to his side he guided the horse with the other. The gesture was like a wave of relief to not be so crowded. We continued, no longer speaking a word, until we reached a small town at the edge of the forest.

I knew the Sliske were somewhere out there, still following me, so the fact we would be staying indoors gave me some comfort. The town was quiet as we made our way to the inn. There were no shops open, very few people walked along the streets eying our group moving further into Morcan, a small town southwest of Sinbury. Commander

Drask stopped his horse by the one inn in the middle of Morcan. He got down from his horse then told me to follow him inside after telling his men they had the night to themselves.

I made no protests, just quietly followed him. I looked around in hopes to catch sight of Faelan, but he was nowhere to be seen. I headed inside trying to not allow his once again sudden disappearance to bother me. The inn was like walking into a completely different place, it looked as though half the town was inside on the side that looked to be a pub. The chatter and laughter left me wondering if the quiet from outside was real.

"Upstairs," Commander Drask grunted, motioning for me to follow. We walked down a long hall with five rooms on either side. He stopped at the last door on the left and unlocked it. The room was simple, a bed, table, a couple of chairs and a wooden tub in the corner. Looking around the room I turned to see Commander Drask glaring at me.

"Problem Commander?" I said without emotion.

"No problem, just... pondering," his voice held amusement.

"Don't let me stop you." As I turned, he launched himself at me from where he stood. I barely slipped past him then spun around with my knee and connected with his side causing him to stumble. Losing reason to my rage I went on the attack. Bringing my right fist across his jaw, then my left followed suit. My knuckles jamming into his cheek. Commander Drask staggered back, I took the opportunity to hook my right arm behind his neck. Dragged his head down and connected his nose with my knee.

I only got one good hit before stumbling back onto the floor after he grabbed hold of my leg and yanked back. Rolling away I pushed off the ground in time to catch a shoulder charge. The blow slammed me against the door, knocking the air out of my lungs. My vision blurred, trying to focus, I saw his figure slowly make his way to me wiping the blood from his face. I shook my head and forced myself to my feet and swung a fist blindly.

He caught the punch and shoved it back against the wall above my head, pinning it down. My free arm went for his throat, but he intercepted before it connected. Then shoved it together with the first, latching one hand around both wrists with ease.

"Now that was a surprise. Didn't think you would be foolish

enough to fight back." He said as blood ran down his face from the gash I left on his cheek.

"You thought I would miss an opportunity to smash your face in?" My voice came out shaky from the heavy breathing.

"What to do with you now?" He tapped one finger against the wall above my head ignoring my response. "What bothers me is why the sudden interest in you? You're nothing more than a cursed little wench. But everyone wants something from you." As he spoke, I could feel the anger rising. "What gets me is why the General is so fascinated with you. I've never seen anything bother him, nothing ever gets under his skin. That is... until you." His eyes scanned over me, the hair on the back of my neck stood from the look in his eyes.

This man was far more demented then I could have ever imagined. He placed his free hand over my cheek and caressed along my jawline down my neck.

"You have such lovely skin. It's a shame to leave as is." Every alarm in my body went off, I shoved my arms hard only to move them an inch before he pinned them again. My knee went up, but he blocked it with his leg. Then slammed his fist into my gut, pain exploded all over my senses. "Now, now you didn't actually believe you could overpower me, did you?" He said entertained.

Yanking me forward he shoved me on the bed face first, the sound of cloths being ripped filled the air. I tried to pull myself together to run, but my body refused to move. Commander Drask gripped my arms behind my back and tied them down along my lower back. His weight pressed down on me, then he ripped the back of my shirt wide open.

"Don't worry now, I am only leaving a small message for the General." His voice sounded off like something sinister was being released. The sound of a blade leaving its sheath caused my muscles to tense up. The blade felt cool before it was replaced with a sharp pain slicing into my back as he wrote his message. I gasped and grunted, digging my nails into my hands. I bit down on the bedding to hold back any screams trying to escape. He whistled to himself while he wrote, a happy tune not matching the agony he caused.

At some point the blade stopped moving along my back and his weight lifted. Too tired to even look, I laid there focused on breathing and imagined the many ways I would cut or break his neck.

"I am so glad you're here, Shae. General Faelan has always been a thorn in my side. But now that you're around I feel as though it has been plucked out." He said while patting my shoulder.

"I. Will. Kill you." I promised with as much strength as I could muster. He laughed at my pathetic excuse for a threat.

"Don't worry, we will have many fun times to come. Your General should be along shortly I am only sad I won't' get to see the look on his face when he sees my message for him." Then he left the room.

I made no move to get up, I had lost all feeling in my arms long ago. Blood dripped down my sides from his damned message carved into my back.

16

I wasn't sure how much time passed before hearing those all too familiar footsteps draw near. The sound stopped just outside of the room. My heartbeat rose, a lump formed in my throat at the thought he would once again witness my pitiful state. The door creaked open, another couple of steps. My breathing picked up making it hard to control. 'No' my thoughts screamed as I lay there helplessly, the pit in my stomach so overwhelming it hurt.

All emotions spiraling inside of me broke through when his weight pushed down next to me, and a warm hand lightly began stroking the back of my hair. Tears broke free from me, and a noise erupted from my throat as I lay there and wept. Heat flooded through my veins, soothing the sting from my back. I felt the skin itch as it stitched itself together, Faelan continued silently stoking my hair and released my bound wrists. While he used an element to heal the wounds Commander Drask left.

"The message?" I mumbled, "... what did the message say?" I turned my eyes up to him. His gaze was gentle but mixed with sorrow and anger.

"It's... not important right now." He took his hand and wiped a tear from my left eye, I watched as he examined the silver tear.

"Yes," I broke the silence. "It is. He dug a blade into my back just to make sure you saw it. What did it say?" Faelan sat for a moment the muscles in his jaw tight. "I know you believe I am weak, all you have seen is me being beaten or dragged, even strangled..."

"I have never once thought of you as weak," he interrupted me. "As for the message, it was a challenge, and he chose the best way to get my attention." A dark shadow crossed his face.

"What was the message, Faelan?" I repeated not letting the issue go. He let out a long sigh,

"Try and stop me." I saw his jaw tighten, my brows pulled together confused and frustrated how much I endured for a simple taunt.

"Why does he despise you?" I asked in a quiet voice still processing his words. His eyes shifted to me.

"It has less to do with me and more to do with him. The more he watches a person suffer the more pleased he is. And when he finds someone who fights with all their might. He is beyond thrilled." He held my gaze; I caught a bitter tone in his next words. "Commander Drask did not earn his ranking; it was given to him. I have not bothered with him sense our first encounter and with my reputation I am sure it gets under his skin."

I went to stand and was stopped by him placing a hand over my shoulder.

"You need rest. Drask will be more difficult now. I have already taken care of the Sliske from last night so you can rest easy now." My eyebrows went up.

"You killed them?" I said in surprise, even though I should know better by now. "Is that where you have been since we arrived?" He gave me a small nod.

"Yes, I went hunting." A smile touched his lips.

"Do me a favor. Next time you go hunting." He waited for me to continue. "Take me with you." Venom filled my words, remembering the encounters I've had with them, and I was done being at their mercy. His half smile appeared, making the idea even more thrilling.

"Should be interesting." He replied, Faelan then lightly pushed me back down on the bed. His gaze drifted to my neck, and he paused. Running his finger over my collarbone, I shivered under his touch. "Let me heal your neck. It looks worse." I gave him a small nod and watched as his eyes glowed in the darkness between us. The warmth put my body at ease as the discomfort from my neck faded.

"Now rest. I will bring food and clothes and remain by your side tonight." He then placed his hand over my eyes. The familiar breeze drifted over, and I found myself drifting off to sleep.

It was still dark when I came to, blinking my eyes a few times adjusting them to the dark. The hair on the back of my neck stood up as the Eleith urged me to rise. I looked over to the window and noticed it was open. Moving from the bed I made no sound as I made my way to the window. The cold air grazed over my still bare back and a chill ran down my spine as I pressed it against the wall next to the window.

Peeking outside the window I saw what caused my senses to jump on high alert. The voice below drifted up toward the window. They spoke low, but their words were clear. Three figures stood in a triangle. My blood ran cold I would never mistake two of those figures and their horrid, voices only confirmed what I saw.

"We want her now!" The Sliske demanded.

"You can do what you want with her after my master is done with her." Anger rose as I realized the third figure was Commander Drask.

"We want her blood we know it's her, and she belongs to usss." The Sliske hissed.

"You already know the bargain, not until we are done with her. My master needs her to resolve his problem." Commander Drask's voice sounded impatient. "I have another day's ride, and I am tired. Be grateful I even allowed some of your kin to have a taste of your precious Blood Bearer last night." Commander Drask turned to leave but was stopped when a hand darted out, grabbing hold of his cloak.

"What of my kin?" It demanded.

"If they haven't returned yet I am sure he has already killed them." There was amusement in his words.

"Who killed my kin?" The Sliske yanked on his cloak. I could almost see a spark in Commander Drask's eyes as he responded.

"Faelan of the Elemental Realm." The Sliske pulled its arm away as though it was suddenly burned and hissed.

"Faelan... Faelan the slaughterer,"

"The destroyer?" The other hissed. "Murderer, abomination!" It shrieked.

"He will die a very painful death for all of my kin he has killed." The first one said in rage.

"I am glad to hear that." Commander Drask said pleased. "He is traveling with your Blood Bearer. When you get one you will have the other." The Commander turned away and all three figures disappeared into the darkness where they belonged.

I didn't realize I was holding my breath until a wave of dizziness hit me and I collapsed. A strong arm caught me before I could crash to the floor.

"Easy." Faelan whispered next to my ear. A shiver went up my neck in response. Sending a fresh sensation at the base of my scalp.

"How long have you been there?" I couldn't hide the shock.

"The whole time." His eyes held mine, and I could not break away from his intense stare.

"What is going on, Faelan? Why is everyone after me and who are you? Really? Why did the Sliske call me the Blood Bearer?" Wrapping his arm over my shoulder, he guided me to the bed. We sat and he kept his grip tight his expression was unreadable. I still held his gaze the glow from the moonlight coming from the window reflected half of his face. We sat in silence as I waited for his reply.

"There are dark creatures moving, even more horrid than the Sliske. They hunger for the Blood Bearer. It is said the Blood Bearer will bring anyone great power with just a drop of their blood." He was so close to me but also felt an eternity away.

"I still don't understand what that has to do with me. How am I this supposed Blood Bearer?" I shifted in my spot.

"The Blood Bearer is marked by the Eternal Flame." He tapped above my brow over my left eye. "They will be called cursed, and misfortune will follow them wherever they go." His voice dropped lower.

"Faelan, I may be cursed, but I am not this Blood Bearer you speak of. For one those Sliske you killed, they didn't have any great power. And they drank a lot more than a drop of blood." He sat still for a long time and didn't speak. Thinking he would no longer speak I went to get up. Faelan latched a hand onto my arm holding it firm.

"Whether you believe it or not there is more happening than you know, and you are in the center of it all." His grip dug in with each word.

"Faelan." I tried to pull from him. His grip lessened but he didn't let go. Frustrated I asked.

"And you? If I am this Blood Bearer, what business do you have with me?" His gaze dropped from me.

"That is not for me to tell." Yanking my arm out of his hand I took a step back.

"What do you mean it is not for you to tell. You follow me around all this time and now run your mouth about some damned Blood Bearer and Eternal Flame it's not for you to tell? Was meeting in that prison even a coincidence... Faelan?" I was fuming and him keeping his eyes away from me made me even more angry.

"I swore an oath, Shae." He tried reaching for me, but I took a step back out of his reach.

"An oath! Oh, how convenient for you. So, there is more to us meeting. You came to me because you and your oath takers want something from me?" I could feel my voice rising and used all my energy to keep it level. "This will not go your way for you or the people you took your oath with. Do not think I will do as you say. Whatever you have planned I will have no part in it." My voice trembled.

"Shae, it is not what you think." I was so angry I couldn't even think straight, there were only thoughts of pain and betrayal.

"I can't believe I fell for it. I almost fell for you and this whole time you have been with me just to fulfill some kind of duty. Was any of it real? Did you really mean the words you said to me yesterday? Or was that just you trying to sweeten me up, for me to follow you around?" The words flew out of my mouth after realizing he truly did have an ulterior motive. It struck me like a fiery arrow. "There anything else you can't tell me, General?" I took another step away from him and he just watched like he allowed me to make the distance. "Why don't you return to your Queen or oath takers if they are even one in the same. Whatever my fate with the King, it has nothing to do with you."

Fury boiled inside me, and I went to the other side of the bed, not sure if I would have another chance to sleep in one after this. I curled into a ball with my back to him and closed my eyes trying desperately to sleep the rest of the night away.

I found myself running, my breaths came out short and labored as though I had been running for ages. I dodged branches and jumped over bushes. Roots tripped my feet in the dark. Around me figures dashed back and forth behind hunting me. That voice came to me whispering my name and getting louder. A black form dropped in front of me forcing me to halt. It latched onto my leg and pulled me to the ground. I screamed as it crawled up, my leg disappeared under its form. Clawing at the ground I grabbed roots, rocks, anything I could get a hold of franticly trying to pull myself loose.

My fingers and arms left trails of blood as I thrashed around trying to escape. My heart pounded so loud I thought it would explode. Tearing the ground desperate to get away the dark voice spoke next to my ear.

"Shae." I swung my arm in the direction of the voice, only to swipe through thin air.

"You cannot escape me." It spoke sweetly in my other ear.

"No!" I screamed, no longer able to move my arms, the black form had reached all the way to my neck. "No!" Screaming again. It made its way to my face, covering my ears, mouth, then nose, until all that was left were my eyes. I saw golden eyes dark, red blood woven into them. I choked trying to breathe as the black blob crept down my throat, tears spilled over.

"Shae!" Jolting back to reality, my fist came up. Slamming into a large mass. My breath came out in short, ragged bursts. Sweat dripped down my entire body and every part of me trembled.

"Shae?" I scanned the room until the figure of the familiar voice came into view. Faelan stood at the end of the bed worry written on his face.

"Are you alright?" He took a step closer. I shook my head unable to find my voice. It felt so real I had to look over my body just to make sure the black form was truly gone. I looked over the room, trying to see if the figure to that voice was anywhere to be seen.

Faelan stood unmoving, watching me with caution, clearing my throat I felt for my voice.

"Cloth..." I managed a whisper; still frozen I sat bracing myself up with my arms and watched as he moved across the room and rummaged through his bag then tossed the cloth. Its white color illuminated through the air, landing in my lap. My hand trembled as I wiped the sweat from my face and neck. Breathing a little easier I willed my nerves to calm.

"Are you going to tell me what just happened? You were thrashing all over then started choking violently. I practically shook you like a rag doll to wake you." Faelan said still standing across the room.

"Are you going to tell me about your oath?" I said bitterly.

"Shae, I swear I am on your side I will not harm you. Haven't I proven that time and time again. If that was my plan I would have done so long ago. I wouldn't waste my time following you around." He said in a low soothing voice.

I sighed, "I know... you have saved my life far more than I can repay. I am just... tired of being left in the dark. I would like to know the truth and know more about you. But I would prefer from your own mouth rather than from the lips of another." I said now wiping my arms.

Faelan sat next to me, but he did not sit on the bed, however. He knelt next to me on the floor.

"I do have a mission. No, we did not meet by accident. I caught word of the village you lived and saw you in the streets with the guards as I was passing through. I waited in the crowd and when I learned they were taking you to the prison, I slipped into a cell unnoticed and made sure we stayed together. My oath and mission may have brought me to you but know when I tell you I am with you no matter what must be done. I will be with you Shae."

Sitting there in the dark, my terrors seemed so far away now. I felt as though that dark voice had no power over me any longer. With Faelan near me, I could once again fight any pain and any hardships awaiting me.

"I will try not to explode on you again." He chuckled deeply.

"I highly doubt it, but I look forward to seeing you try." I tried to remember what it was like before Faelan, but I couldn't imagine it anymore. Which scared me. What if I lost him? The very thought sent a stab of pain into my chest and tears began to fall unwillingly. I closed my eyes and shoved it back out of my mind.

We laid next to each other as I drifted off to sleep. I slept dreaming of the sky. Soaring high with the same figure beside me but this time when I looked over. Faelan was the one flying with me his hand in mine holding it firm. Warmth surrounded us.

17

Morning came far too quickly, waking me out of blissful dream and pulling me back to reality of a door slamming open. The dreaded voice of Commander Drask barking my name along with insults filled my ears. I barely had time to get out of bed before he yanked me up and shoved me to my feet.

"Get up, wench!" He spat throwing a pile of cloths at me. "Wash and get dressed quickly you stink of filth." Movement caught my eye, and I noticed Faelan already lugging his supplies over his shoulder.

"Get a move on." He snapped.

"I plan to after you leave." I retorted. He erupted in laughter.

"After I leave? You don't get that kind of modesty." His hand shot forward grabbing the shoulder of my sleeve and tore it. I pulled back yelling.

"Bastard." Faelan was at my side in the blink of an eye. Commander Drask pulled his sword out and placed it on the General's neck. He pressed it against his skin hard enough blood trickled down his neck.

"I don't think that is a wise decision General." Commander Drask smirked.

"Let her be Drask there is no need for this." His smirk turned into a sneer and his eye shifted to me.

"She is my prisoner, and I will do what I please. You had your night with her, I hope you enjoyed her to the fullest. Because I will not give you another opportunity. Considering she will be the King's little whore when we reach the Capital, and I have been just itching to see the rest of her." Command Drask yelled for his guards to enter. "Escort General Faelan to his horse before I send a message of him interfering with the king's order's."

"This has nothing to do with your King's order." Faelan spoke with his jaw tight. His eyes began to glow.

"Ah. Ah," Commander Drask pressed the sword even harder. "Don't think I won't slice your throat before you get your magic out, General. Now be an obedient ally and go wait by your horse while I clean the prisoner up for his Majesty." Faelan's eyes went to me, the look of anger filled his eyes. I stared at him knowing there was little he could do.

Faelan shut his eyes tight for a moment when he opened them there was a darkness that hovered over his eyes. He shifted his gaze to Commander Drask.

"Remember who I am, Commander." Faelan's voice low and filled with venom.

"Oh, I know General, I know very well." Faelan moved his neck away from the blade and pushed passed the guards, disappearing out the door. I turned my gaze to see Commander Drask eying me.

"What?" I spat at him. Sheathing his sword, I waited for his next move and debated on fighting back. Or fighting with everything I had to make it out.

"So, did you have a good night? Did the General ravage that cursed body of yours?" I gave him no response for his crude question. "No, I can imagine he didn't. It's a pity, he's such a bore. When I practically gift wrapped you for him. I would have thought my bloody message would have been enough to get the mood right." He brought his arm up to my face and I slapped it away.

"Don't touch me with your filthy hands." I said taking a step back looking in vain for an escape.

"I'm filthy? Look at you, you're covered in mud, dried blood all over no part of you isn't covered. It's disgusting to look at you. Now get undressed." He lifted his hand towards me again and I took another step back.

"Stay away from me or I will break every finger you touch me with." Commander Drask smiled at the challenge.

"Is that a promise?" He went for me, throwing a fist at my face. I turned my head just in time before connecting and dashed for the door. I made it to the doorway when a blade came into view through the doorway. Ducking my head I dodged the blade than a large hand clamped down on my arm and twisted it behind my back, putting pressure on my shoulder.

"Do you feel that cursed wench? That is five fingers you promised to break. It's my right hand if you'd like to be sure you get the correct fingers." He shoved my body into the door and jammed my chest against the wall. He took his free hand and tore the rest of my shirt off. Heat flooded my face knowing my body's exposer to all the onlookers around the room.

"Now isn't that a sight," Commander Drask said next to my ear. "Never would have imagined this would be under those filthy clothes." His grip tightened on my arm, putting more pressure. I felt a slick warmth rub across the back of my neck under a hot air. I shuddered, sickened knowing he licked the back of my neck.

"The one spot not filthy, I just had to taste. Now, let's see about this arm." Commander Drask clutched tighter, pushing until the pressure became unbearable. A loud pop echoed in the room along with the screams that erupted from my lips as he dislocated my shoulder. Shutting my eyes tight, I forced myself to breathe through the pain.

"There now maybe you will give me less trouble. Let's clean all that filth off." He grabbed a handful of hair and pulled me off the door jamb, dragging me across the room and tossing me in the tub. The side of my head hit the wooden rim. A flash of pain shot past my vision. All my senses jolted when they doused me with cold water dumping it over my head. My breathing came out in quick sharp bursts and entire body shivered under the cold water, the guards roared with laughter at my humiliation.

I held my arm against my stomach careful not to move too much when Commander Drask took out a knife and cut away the pants. He paid no mind to the blade that grazed over my skin leaving shallow cuts.

"What do you think now? Should have undressed when I told you? It could have been just me watching your delicate body shiver. Shall I just leave you this way for the rest of our journey? Think your

General will be pleased? I suppose he wouldn't be able to concentrate on riding, he might want to try giving you a ride instead." His guards laughed at his crude remark. I refused to turn my eyes from him I wouldn't let his humiliation get to me.

Grabbing a cloth along the side of the tub I started scrubbing my legs, the small drops of blood on my calf dripped in the water. Commander Drask watched me a few moments, then barked at his men.

"Get out, get ready to leave."

"Commander." A guard began to protest but never got to finish his words, a knife stuck from his neck after the Commander threw it.

"Did I stutter? Leave and take that body with you." He pointed at his men who now obeyed immediately. He turned to me and pulled the cloth from my hands and started scrubbing my good shoulder.

"I see the General mended you. Too bad he can't heal you completely." He paused lingering over the scars he left on my skin. "You have such lovely skin once it's nice and clean, it's just asking me to leave more of my marks on it." I leaned away from his touch and got out of the tub taking the closest cloth to me, covering myself with it.

"You're sick." I said through clenched teeth.

"Oh? That is a matter of opinion. The lady's swoon over me everywhere I go." He said following me and stopped just behind me. I could feel his gaze burrow into my back.

"You are demented." I could feel the anger pulse in my cursed eye.

"You really have no idea." He said as I turned around to face him. His brown eyes lit with a cruelty in them I only saw in murders and thieves. Without warning he smacked me across the face hard enough it sent me tumbling to the ground. My vision blurred, then felt his knee press against my chest the weight drove the air from my lungs. My eyes came into focus as he grabbed hold of my shoulder and popped it back into place. I yelled out in agony as tears leaked from my eye involuntarily.

"There now you can dress yourself..." He paused looking at my face, keeping his knee pressed against my chest he leaned forward. "Now that's interesting." He said as his hand wiped under my left eye. "I have never seen this before." He examined the silver tear that escaped me. He licked the tear off his finger like it was liquid sugar.

"Are you done?" I grunted under his weight. He returned his attention to me and stroked his hand over my left cheek. Just then a guard came to the door.

"Commander." Drask turned and looked at the young man.

"Yes." He made no attempt to move.

"We have a small complication we need you for." Looking back at me he remained silent for a moment longer before speaking.

"As much as I would enjoy causing more tears to come out of that pretty face. It seems there is something that requires my attention." He got off me and went toward the door. "You have one minute to clothe yourself after that this fine young man will drag you out in whatever you have on. And you will travel that way." Then he left the room.

Furious, I got up from the ground and forced my clothes on, wincing every time I moved my shoulder. By the time the guard entered I was panting for air. He led me out of the room and outside where the rest of his men waited for our departure. Drask came around with two horses in tow. He paused and gave me a look that was exaggeratedly disappointed.

"That's too bad I was looking forward to the General's face when he saw you." The sun was a bright hot day for the time of season we were in. Commander Drask pulled me to one of the horses he led behind him. Noticing my stare, he said.

"We picked up another horse, the inn keeper was kind enough to... lend us another one." His face twisted into a cruel smile. His expression left me wondering what they made the inn keeper suffer through.

Shoving my hands together, a sharp pain shot down my arm. Commander Drask grabbed a rope from a nearby guard and bound my hands firmly together.

"I thought we were done with the bindings." I said watching my hands be tied together.

"I changed my mind. Now get on the horse."

I did as he demanded without another word. This morning's activities left me already tired. The peaceful dream now felt like an eternity away. Struggling to get up with only one good shoulder I managed to swing my leg over and settling in the saddle. Commander Drask made no attempt to hide his delight from my struggle. I ignored his gaze and looked for Faelan who I found sitting on his own horse a dark expression covering his face.

He stared at me, his eyes wandered to my shoulder, and I thought he could tell of my discomfort even from there.

"Move out!" Commander Drask yelled after tying the other end of my rope to his own saddle. All his guards followed in two single file lines as we made our way out of Mochan. It remained just as eerily quiet as when we came.

18

Our travel along the road was nothing like the time I had with Faelan. He remained a distance from me at the front of the group. We traveled in the sun, no clouds in sight. Its rays glaring down from directly above making it far hotter than it should be. Sweat trickled down my face and neck. The men remained silent as we moved forward. Trees stood tall on either side of the road; a bright blue sky always beautiful regardless of my circumstances. The thought brought me hope for another day, a better day.

They stopped after a long while for a short break, his men stretched their limbs and ate from their provisions. I caught sight of Faelan making his way to me while the men chatted among themselves. Again, I sat further away from the rest tied to a tree branch.

"You're hurt." He said as he approached

"It's nothing," I leaned on my good shoulder.

"It is not nothing. Why would you say that?" Frustration filled his voice.

"What would you like me to say?" My tone came out far more bitter than I intended.

"Tell me the truth, tell me it hurts when you hurt. Tell me when you are angry. You are not alone."

"I'm not alone, am I? Where were you then? When he tore the rest of my shirt off. Shall I tell you how he disgustingly licked the back of my neck, right before he dislocated my shoulder. Do you want to know of the hair he ripped out of my head as he drug me across the room and threw me in the tub? Or how they dumped cold water over me and watched me sit there naked, humiliated from their stares. Would you like to know how he slammed his hand across my face. Pinned me down while he re-located my shoulder? Should I weep for you, I am at his mercy until I can become strong enough to repay him tenfold?" My voice came out in an angry whisper, not wanting to draw attention to us.

Faelan never once took his eyes off me, and I could see the silent rage boiling behind those golden eyes.

"Forgive me." I dropped my head into my hands. "I know your hands are tied in this and I do not blame you." I felt his hand brush over mine and heard him rummage through his sack of provisions.

"You should eat." He said holding a piece of dried meat near me. I bit my lip at the guilt for lashing out at him while he only showed concern for me. And let out a heavy sigh before raising my gaze to meet his.

"You are kind, but I cannot lift my arm properly." His eyes shifted to my bound hands.

"Are you asking me to feed you?" His playful tone shifted the mood.

"Are you offering?" I gave him a sly smile. Faelan tore a small piece and brought it to my lips.

"Will this satisfy as my atonement?" The half-smile touched his lips.

"Hmm." I took the meat from his fingers grazing my lips against them, his eyes brightened from the touch. "Depends, how often do you plan to feed me?"

"As many times as, it takes." His gaze drifted to my lips. I looked away unable to contain the heat flooding my face. He laughed lightly at my response then stroked a stand of hair and the light-hearted feeling left us.

"He will pay, that I promise you. He will not be protected by his master forever. Once that protection no longer applies to him. There will be nothing left but ash." There was a darkness to his voice.

"If it is not you, it will be me. Although I don't think I could do something like melt him from the inside out." Faelan caught me eying him and his smile returned.

"You heard that, did you? I thought I kept my voice low enough, I guess you are full of surprises." He gave me another piece of meat. I accepted it graciously.

"Never a dull moment with me." I showed him a winning smile and he chuckled, feeding me another piece. We sat together for a few more moments before he got up from his spot next to me. Helping me from the ground he put a hand on my hurt shoulder. I winced under his touch, then a familiar heat rushed through my arm. I closed my eyes, and a pleasant sound slipped from my mouth. Unable to deny the relief from the pain no longer weighing me down.

"I don't think I will ever get use to that." I opened my eyes to him staring at me.

"I don't think I will ever get use to your responses." His gaze made me squirm as I felt the heat rise in my cheeks again forcing me to look away in embarrassment. The men gathered back to their horses, and I could hear Commander Drask barking orders again. Turning back to Faelan.

"You should go..." I met his gaze. "I am glad you are with me Faelan." Bowing his head, he ran his fingers along my skin while removing his hand from my shoulder. Sending a shiver down my arm. I watched as he walked toward his horse watching his stride, a pleasure, I enjoyed for myself.

Commander Drask's solid frame blocked my view as he made his way toward me, two guards following behind him.

"Time to go." He signaled one of them to untie me from the tree. "I hope you're ready to meet the King?" Amusement in his voice.

I remained silent while the guard tugged me back to the horse, able to move easier after Faelan mended my shoulder. Pulling myself up I settled in the saddle. I noticed Commander Drask eying me, sure he noticed the difference in my movements. He was the type to pay attention to detail, especially if it's someone he is looking to make suffer. But I didn't care. I wanted him to know, I made sure he would notice the difference to see whatever he does will not stop me.

He moved on to his own horse, yelling at his men to move out. We rode in two single file lines. Some men riding beside one another chatted quietly among themselves as we continued our journey. The woods still on either side of the dirt road we traveled, not a clearing in sight. Now with it being later in the day the sun's rays no longer beat down on us. I overheard the two guards assigned to me mentioning us going southwest to Thornden where the Kings' castle resided with several towns living just below it.

As it began growing darker, I was led by a guard that had untied me, instead of trailing behind Commander Drask. He was at the head with Faelan next to him, both riding without speaking. Far ahead of us, I noticed a break in the trees along the road. We were about to leave the tall trees surrounding us I was starting to feel them closing in wondering if there would ever be an opening. By the time we made it to the opening, it was dark. Strange we had not made camp, but Commander Drask kept pressing forward, no orders given to stop.

Making our way past the trees it was quiet, even the men no longer talked among themselves. As we made our way forward you could only hear the hooves of the horses pressing into the dirt. A chill ran down my spine and the temperature dropped, my muscles tensing something... was coming. Glancing around, no one around me seemed to notice the difference. They all kept their gazes ahead.

It happened all at once, Faelan's warnings shouted out, up ahead figures darted out of the darkness pulling men from their horses.

Screams echoed all around me.

Fighting broke out in every direction, men dropping one after another and the Sliske moving to their next prey. A guard behind me went down with his horse, the Sliske jumped on top of him cutting off his screams. I kicked my horse getting him moving only to be wrenched off, I hit the ground hard knocking the air right out of me.

Dazed, I Got back up pulling hard on the rope still secured by the guard. He looked down at me, fear in his eyes from all the confusion roaring around us.

"Untie me, I can help." I yelled, he only shook his head and gripped tighter. A hand snaked out of nowhere and latched onto my arm. I yelped surprised and yanked away kicking the Sliske hard enough to break from its grasp.

"Shess here!" It hissed. "Found you," it said hurling itself at me, diving back I landed just out of its reach. Backing away, my rope tightened as I reached the end of my slack. It snickered at me and looked up to the guard still holding it. His eyes grew large, fear consuming him. Knowing he would be no help, I yanked as hard as I could on the rope pulling it from his grasp and took off toward Faelan.

I only made it a few feet before I was jerked back again, throwing me off my feet, hitting the ground hard I coughed on the dust in my mouth. The rope tightened, continuing to shorten as it pulled me closer. Scrambling to get a foot hold my heart raced as memories of my dream flashed through my mind. That voice seemed so close once again shaking me to my very core.

"NOOO!" I screamed so loud it rang past the clashing of monsters and men. A blue flame erupted from the ground encircling me in a cage of fire, I heard Sliske screaming and hissing on the other side of the flames. My rope went slack, sending a wave of relief over me. A familiar arm reached in grabbing my shoulder firm, Faelan walked past the flames and pulled me in a crushing embrace. He took a deep breath and brought his hands up to my face.

"Are you hurt?" His eyes searched mine. I only shook my head watching his glowing golden eyes scan me over, not believing my words.

"Truly, I am fine." Feeling completely safe surrounded in his blue flames standing taller than even him. Before the thought of him using another element stopped me, I moved my face closer.

He leaned down, as if he also had the same desire. Those blazing eyes searched mine for a moment until, he pressed his lips to mine. His lips soft and unyielding as they moved, pushing mine apart with his, sending chills down my spine. The flames surrounding us reacted with the heat rising in me. His mouth moving on mine, I felt a pleasant shiver as his long fingers slid through my hair.

Breaking away too soon he leaned his forehead on mine, eyes closed, both of us breathing heavy, I could feel my heart pounding in my chest.

"Apologies." He breathed.

"There are things for you to be forgiven for Faelan, but that is not one of them." I said breathily.

"What's going on, General?" Commander Drask yelled over the roaring of the flames, reminding me we were not the only ones in this world. Faelan lifted his head from mine and gently pushed me back. I watched as the glow in his eyes died out with the flames. The action was almost heart wrenching to watch. The wreckage from the ambush left us with only a handful of men the rest lay bleeding on the ground. Heads torn off some faces so distorted you would have thought they died from pure terror. Small piles of ash laid in every different direction, no Sliske in sight, I looked over to Faelan eyes wide.

"You did this?" I said astonished.

"Well, you're not the only one full of surprises." He said with his half smile, which was short lived when Commander Drask came stomping in our direction.

"You couldn't have done that in the beginning?" Commander Drask demanded of Faelan.

"I am only here for her Commander, as long as she lives the rest is no concern of mine." I waited, standing beside Faelan, Commander Drask stood there nodding his head.

"Ah yes, that's right, the cursed wench you are protecting for some unknown reason." He said as he looked me over. Taking hold of what was left of my rope, he pulled me forward. "Looks like you'll need to take up her life with the King, she will be his property soon." He said looking towards Faelan.

"I am no one's property Commander, least of all the King's." Annoyed by his statement, he turned, putting his face directly in front of mine.

"Guess we will see, Thornden is just beyond that hill and my master is expecting to meet you tonight. Let's try and get along for the last bit." His voice was low. "Anyone still breathing get back on your horses take any others that are still alive and can walk leave the rest." Walking back to his horse, I kept my eyes from looking at all the bodies lying on the ground, my stomach tight from the massacre. The ones left alive pulled themselves together grabbing any horse, still mobile but lost its rider.

"Get up." Commander Drask barked. Looks like I was riding with him again. I got on his horse with no protest and waited as he did the same. Faelan was already ready and waiting next to us, his demeanor unshaken, I realized this scene was one he was familiar with. Holding on Commander Drask spurred his horse, and we continued onward, leaving the wreckage behind us.

The ambush probably only lasted a few minutes, but it felt much longer, the men that survived traveled in silence, some with torches now to light our way.

Traveling with Commander Drask always made me tense, I never knew what this man was thinking. What I knew was he thrived off torment and suffering, I could count on that from him every time. So, I waited and kept myself on guard, but he remained silent as we pressed forward. He seemed to have one goal in mind, and that was to make sure I made it to his master tonight.

19

By the time we arrived in the city, the streets were empty, all doors and windows closed shut for the night. It was late, and the night did not seem to be over anytime soon. Faelan remained next to us the entire way and kept to himself, only glancing my way a few times, I kept composed the entire way there. Commander Drask remained silent as well, it was hard not to feel my impending doom was all that awaited me in this city.

With every step closer to the castle the walls towered over us. Being in Thornden made me more nervous about what kind of King I would meet shortly. We rode through streets one lined after another, small houses pushed together and stacked on top of one another to make room for people to live. Further in I could see a few souls wondering around, dashing in and out of the shadows, stalking whatever prey they may be hunting. Commander Drask turned onto a street and stopped in front of an inn.

"Time for you to leave men, there will be food and woman for you here." His men slowly got off their horses, filing inside. Their spirits long gone from the ambush. Drask turned to Faelan, "This is as far as you will go tonight. Someone will come tomorrow. You may have an audience with the King then, but for now I am taking her with me. You have any complaints you can take it up with the king." He spoke impatiently and started to walk away.

"Call for me if you need me." He said then turned and disappeared into a dark alley, I knew he spoke to me alone. Commander Drask continued us down the street in the castle's direction not far ahead of us. We walked in silence; I made no attempt to escape. I felt the Elieth's warning me, growing the closer we got to the castle. The feeling was both good and bad I knew what was to come would not be pleasant but there was something here I needed to do. What that would entail, I had no idea.

The buildings had ended, the street opened into a large circle with stones built in the middle of it, a fountain with a statue of a woman standing. She looked composed, one hand to her side the other out in front of her, as if she were offering a gift. Water came from that hand pouring down into the pool of water flowing at her feet. Staring at her figure as we went by, I noticed her face looked strangely similar to Grams, a younger version but very similar.

"Something catch your eye, cursed wench?" Commander Drask spoke, breaking the silence.

"No." I replied.

"Don't get too comfortable, since that dog is gone, we can spend some time to get to know one another much better." He spoke with a smile in his voice, my throat felt tight by his words reminding me Faelan was not here.

"The only thing you will be getting to know, Commander, is my fists connecting with that ugly face of yours." I said, but I couldn't deny his features were one of the nicer ones to look at. But it only made him that much more dangerous, if I was not able to read his eyes. I would have been far more surprised by his constant torments.

He breathed out a laugh, "You are in far deeper than you realize cursed wench." Spurring his horse on, we turned down a dark alley. We walked in that direction for a short while until Commander Drask stopped his horse and hopped down. "Time to get off." He said, yanking at my rope, tossing one leg over, I slid off his horse and followed him in the dark. A wall made of stone stood high above us, it ran a long way down past the streets and buildings.

"Is there a reason we are sneaking in the dark when the front doors to the castle are in the other direction?" I said, observing my surroundings. "I'm sure your King is that way, probably a warm welcome for your loyal service." I said, mocking the Commander.

"We are not going to the King." He said quickening his pace.

"So, when you talk of your master, he is not the same as the King." I said, tucking that little information away.

He ignored me entirely and pulled me along with him. We walked further past the buildings and into a small break into trees where everything was wet and mushy. My feet stuck in the ground as we walked, causing me to fumble a few times. He yanked on my rope, making me keep pace with him.

"Keep up, we don't have all night, and I want a warm bed to sleep in before the sun comes up." He spoke without looking in my direction. Commander Drask halted. A ditch lay just in front of us. "This is it." He whispered then hopped down, dragging me along. I looked to the wall noticing a large dome shaped hole in the wall bars lined the entrance further inside with a lock on the latch.

A set of keys jingled at Commander Drask's side, he picked through them until finding the one he was looking for. He put the key in a dark hole, turned it until it clicked then pushed the door of bars open, creaking as it moved. "Time to meet my master." He said to me without a smile. The tugging of the Eleith pulled at me leaving me with dread of whoever this 'master' he spoke of may be. For one thing, this will not be a good encounter.

We walked in a damp tunnel, the smell made it hard to breathe. There were other openings with more tunnels, this place was like a maze. I paid attention to the surroundings in case an escape may be necessary. Commander Drask must have taken this way many times to know where he went with little light to guide him. He took only one turn as we walked for about ten minutes and came to a stop at a brick wall.

"Now where Commander?" He looked down at me, put his hand in a small hole to his left. I heard a small click then the wall slid open, and we stepped through. The hall was large and empty, a few banners ran along them but otherwise not much else. He stopped to check both directions then took a right pulling me along, his pace quickening.

"In a hurry to get rid of me, Commander? And here I thought we were on our way to become fast friends." My sarcasm was hard to control when I became nervous, thankfully a trait he was unaware of.

"Shhh." Was the only response he gave me. The hall came to a T, we took the left. Doors started to appear on both sides of the walls and a few torches were lit evenly spaced between them. Another turn to the right and up some stairs that spiraled at the end. After the stairs there was a large wooden door with metal for the latch and bars holding it together. He stopped before the door, the Eleith gave me one final warning to tread carefully.

He knocked once then stepped back the door creaked open shortly after a young boy appeared. Blond hair pulled to one shoulder tied neatly, it reached to his chest, blue eyes a beautiful boy with features any woman would envy, he couldn't be more than fifteen.

"Yes?" The boy said calmly.

"I am here to see him." Commander Drask spoke formally, a side of him I didn't believe he was capable of. The boy nodded his head and opened the door wider, stepping to the side allowing us entry.

Commander Drask made his way past the boy and walked into the room. There was a table with three chairs around it over to my right, a large white rug on the floor from some beast. A fireplace burned just behind it directly in front of us, a few other doorways leading to other rooms. A man stood on the rug with his back to us. His hair was long and straight, golden strands reaching the middle of his back half pulled back in a neat braid. His demeanor strong, proper a man raised in higher status.

Commander Drask stopped just short of the rug and knelled on one knee, his fist to the ground head bowed. I hid my astonishment there was no way I would have ever imagined him kneeling at someone's feet.

"Commander, you're late." The man spoke, his voice smooth, but there was an edge not something you would catch if you were not listening for it.

"Yes, master." Was all he said keeping his head down I watched remaining still not daring to move an inch.

"Can you give me a reason as to why you kept me waiting?" He still spoke in his smooth voice while turning around.

"There were... complications, master," he continued to speak formally.

"But you were to have arrived last night, so I would have a whole day with our precious guest." He had turned around fully, looking straight at me, not bothering to even glance at the Commander. He kept his hands clasped together as he moved in a graceful feminine manner. His skin was pale ivory and eyes a deep blue so dark you could scarcely tell the color of them. Although he was older Mid-thirties it seemed, his beauty rivaled even grams. "But now I only have a few hours with this lovely creature." Every word he spoke was smooth and sly, like a snake.

Everything in me told me not to make any false moves, he was not someone to be taken lightly. His eyes slowly scanned me over from head to toe. The slight smile made my skin crawl from the possible thoughts he had.

"I apologize master, there were many problems, the prisoner was not corporative, General Fealan from the Elemental Realm was following along with her. The Sliske...." The commander was stopped dead sentence with a loud smack to his face, blood tricked down the side of his cheek.

"I don't need your excuses, what use are you to me if you cannot accomplish a simple task. Would you prefer to go back to that hellhole you were rotting in before I found you?" His voice no longer held its smooth tone, it once had, venom filled his words.

"No master," Commander Drask said shaking his head, I noticed his fists clenched and his jaw tight.

A part of me found enjoyment watching him at the mercy of this man, considering all the torment he made me suffer through. Although I would rather, he be on his knees at the mercy of me, I suppose this will do for now.

"Now leave, I will send for you when you're needed." He ordered, Commander Drask got up immediately and left the room leaving me to the man staring me over never once taking his eyes off me. "Calum," he said, motioning to the boy closing the door, "leave." He bowed deep.

"Yes, master." Opened the door once again, walked out and closed it behind him softly. Now it was just me and him standing in front of one another. I kept my pulse normal, my breathing remained even, I stayed unmoving as I waited.

"Now," he said clasping his hands together, his voice returned to his usual alluring sound. "Aren't you a dirty creature?" He brought his hand to my ropes, snapped his fingers. The ropes fell to the ground I watched with a neutral expression rubbing my wrists trying to get the feeling back in them. They were raw and sore.

I kept silent while he continued to examine me. He brought his hand up in one fluid motion, his finger grazed my wrist, the long-pointed nail trailed up my arm reminding me of the times with the Sliske. I watched as he moved it closer to my shoulder, pushing the tip of his nail into my skin. He slid it along the shoulder over my clothes, the fabric slicing underneath it. He continued to move his finger over my collarbone and did the same to the other side. He left no mark on my skin, just sliced right through the fabric on top of the skin.

I watched as his eyes danced with anticipation as he moved his finger down along my side all the way to my hip.

"What do you want?" I said, breaking the silence, tired of being toyed with. His hand stopped, his eyes locked with mine a smile touched his lips, one that made me want to run.

"Well, to wash you of course, you are to meet the King tomorrow, and we can't have you looking." he paused and looked me up and down again, his nose wrinkled in disgust. "Like this."

"If all you want is for me to bathe, I can do that on my own." I said, not hiding my annoyance.

"And where would be the fun in that?" He said stripping my shirt from me. "I would prefer to be called master, but you won't call me that, will you?" His smooth voice made my insides cringe.

"I have a few names for you, but master is not one of them." I said lifting my chin slightly not breaking eye contact.

"Well, you are quite the creature aren't you." He looked me over, I realized he had more than one meaning to his statement. "Morfran," he said. "My name is Morfran, remember it well." He then turned away, beckoning me to follow him into one doorway. Keeping my arms crossed over my chest, I followed, cold from the lack of clothing.

The room was round with a good-sized tub in the middle, deep red and white flower peddles lay on top of steaming water. The room smelled of oils and perfume, Morfran glided past the tub, picked up a small bottle from a table with more elegance than I could ever muster, pulled the top off and poured it into the bath. An aroma filled the air sending chills down my back.

"Come," he said excitedly, clasping his hands together. "Oh, but you won't be needing those," and snapped his fingers removing any clothing I had left, furious I plunged in, the heat burning my skin till my body grew accustomed to it. Unable to hide the enjoyment of the hot water soaking in, washing away any cold I had just felt. My thoughts went to Faelan when he wrapped his arms around surrounding me in his warmth and scent. The thought alone pushed away any effect the aroma may have had on me. Wondering where he was if he remained close somehow 'if I call for him now, would he come?' I thought and wished he would come and replace this perverted bastard standing behind me watching my every move.

"Comfortable?" He said, interrupting my thoughts.

"I would be more comfortable if you weren't here." I said, irritated at his very existence.

"Don't say that. Shae, we could be allies. I can help you more than you realize." His cunning voice spoke too close for my liking.

"I'm sure anything you offer Morfran, all of it comes with a price," I said running a handful of water up my arm.

"Mmm... not for you my lovely, you are a precious existence." His silver-tongue continued as he ran one of his fingers along my neck. "I can offer you safety and a warm bed, this bath is only the beginning, you can be treated like a queen waited on hand and foot." With every word, he spoke I could tell how easy it was to fall into his trap. He made everything sound so pleasing, so easy to come by. The Eleith's warning pressed in reminding me of the truth.

"I am no fool, whatever you have to offer, I do not want any part of it." His cold bony hands wrapped on either side of my shoulders.

"Be wise Shae, I will not offer my help to you again, things can go well for you, or it can go poorly. I can make your life a living misery if you decide not to take my side." The venom he once held towards Commander Drask he now held towards me. The pressure of his hands increased on my shoulders, causing them to ache. Knowing my words would only cause me more suffering, I didn't hold back.

"I knew before I even came to this place Morfran. You... are no ally of mine."

In an instant he shoved me down, pushing me under the water holding me in place. Gripping his hands, digging my nails in deep pulling and yanking on his arms trying to get him to release me. He held firm, a smile wide across his face showed his teeth shining from above. Air bubbles escaping from my mouth as I thrashed hard against his arms, I racked my nails over his skin streams of blood flowed through the water. Just when I thought I wouldn't be able to hold my breath any longer Morfran released me, I emerged out of the water gasping for air. His laugh filled the room, a wicked sound putting my nerves on edge.

"Don't you feel clean now," he said as if he helped. Still coughing, my body fought to remember how it once breathed, I sat both hands braced on either side of the tub. "Now that you are clean, let's get you ready to sleep, you'll need a good night's rest. Tomorrow, we'll dress you properly for meeting the King." He clapped his hands once and Calum came into the room with a robe far quicker than I would have imagined possible. He walked over holding it out for me, I stood still conscious of Morfran's eyes. Stepping out of the tub, I quickly wrapped myself in the soft fabric grateful to be covered finally.

Morfran lead us out of the room and into another, a large bed lay in the middle of the room with a window on either side of it along the wall.

"You will stay here for the night." He said not as a request. I made no reply and walked to a bed that was larger than any I had ever seen. Suddenly he latched hold of my arm and pulled me close. "One more thing before I leave," raising a hand to my face his finger ran over my forehead pushing back the wet hair revealing my cursed eye to him. I could feel the flame dance from within, smoldering a deep furry. "Yes... That is lovely. A very fine creature indeed." He crooned.

"Are you still gawking, or may I sleep now?" I said impatiently. His serpent-like smile never left his face.

"Until tomorrow," and left the room, the boy Calum following him and closed the door behind him. Standing in place waiting a few moments longer, making sure he didn't feel the need to return. I wasn't looking forward to the morning and all he had planned to get me ready for seeing the King, something told me I would not be very comfortable.

Scanning the room there was a fire lit on the right side of the bed a few chairs on either side they looked more comfortable than any bed I slept in. Realizing I had no other clothes than the robe I had, I wrapped it tighter and jumped on the bed snuggling in the center, my entire body sunk in softly. I laid there staring at the ceiling knowing to well sleep would not come soon, this place was a place to sleep with one eye open. I had no weapons at my disposal and any comfort I may have once had was long gone.

20

The soft rise and fall of my breathing was the only sound filling the room. I wasn't sure how much time had passed when they finally let me be. But I was no closer to sleep then when they had left. A small sound came from the window. I was upright in the blink of an eye looking in the sound's direction. I cautiously crawled from the bed and made my way to the window. The only light was from the moon, a blue glow shining through. Leaning in I tried to get a view of what made the sound. A large hand suddenly smacked onto the glass. I yelped leaping away, my heart nearly jumping from my chest, then a chuckle and Faelan's smiling face appeared from the other side.

Relief flooded through me seeing him. Opening the window, I glared at him.

"If I wasn't so glad to see you, I would close this window in your face for scaring me half to death." He chuckled again, his half smile always making my pulse rise. The playful moment was short-lived as his eyes searched mine.

"I can't stay long, but I wanted to make sure you were unharmed." His tone serious.

"As unharmed as I can be I suppose." I paused "You knew of Commander Drask's master Morfran?"

He nodded silently, eyes grave; I sat on the windowsill next to where he stood, leaning my head onto his chest, I closed my eyes and breathed in his scent. His hand slowly stroked my hair, his heartbeat and breathing were even.

"I guess asking you to steal me away from here is out of the question." I looked up at his face as he shook his head.

"No. I would be the first they would suspect. You have to walk this out, see why you are here. You are clever, I am sure you already know to be weary of Morfran. He is more dangerous than most." He spoke in a calm voice.

"Yes, I caught that in our first meeting. He offered being my ally." I said with a small laugh.

"He made that same offer to me once, the fool. He may be cunning, but he's too arrogant believing no one would refuse him." He said amused.

"Did it anger him?" I said curious Faelan snorted.

"I am sure he was furious. He only turned on his heels and left…" he paused "What did he do?" He always seemed to catch the little details.

"After I refused him?" I said.

"Yes," he urged.

"Well… he just, you know… acted as if he would have drowned me." I said, his hand stopped, and eyes began to glow. Anger radiating off him.

"Faelan, there was nothing you could do, I am more resilient than you know." Trying to ease his anger.

"That does not make it any easier to except. I know I will not always be there to intervene. But when I hear of or see how any of these bastards treat you my vision goes red. It takes everything in me not to rip the throats out of them all." He spoke through gritted teeth; I placed a hand on his cheek.

"As long as you are with me, it all seems like dust in the wind." I whispered with a light kiss on his lips. Letting go I hopped off the windowsill. "I appreciate the late-night visit, I will be able to rest now." I said, closing the window, "Until tomorrow." Not wanting to say farewell, I glanced over, quickly checking my room. When I looked back Faelan was gone.

Locking it shut I walked past the bed to the fireplace snuggling into the chair closest. Pulling my feet up I curled into a ball, laying the side of my head to my knees. I stared into the flames, mesmerized with the flickers and colors dancing around. My eyes grew heavy, and I finally fell asleep.

I woke to the sound of footsteps in the distance. Remaining in place, I waited for whoever came to enter. I watched the embers in the fire radiate its heat. I enjoyed this part of fire. Even though the fire is not ablaze the heat still simmers underneath, it would only take a little to bring it back to a full flame once again. The door opened, leaning back I stretched my limbs looking to see who entered. To my surprise the boy Calum was the only one walking in, he closed the door behind him. The boy was far too beautiful first thing in the morning. His Blond hair shined, he wore it in the same fashion as last night. The light blue shirt fit him tightly till his waist then loosened and stopped at his knees. His eyes didn't take away from the rest of his features in the least. Fair skin, small nose that rounded perfectly and full pink lips, a soft jaw with fine edges. His pants a clean white, the collar of his shirt stood halfway up his neck. He walked with a grace that made him even more eye-catching. Carrying a tray of food and drink, he set it on the table next to me and walked back out without saying a word.

Knowing better than to eat the food, I got up from my chair and stretched, loosening the rest of my body. The door creaked open again and Calum walked through with a bundle of supplies in his hand. He walked over to another set of chairs by a dresser and a bowl.

"Please." His voice was soft and kind he did not resemble one ounce of his master. Nodding his head, encouraging me to sit down in the chair beside him. I stood assessing the young boy. I wasn't sure if I could trust him, he was loyal to his master for all I knew. I didn't take Morfran as the type to allow people who were not under his complete control to stay near him.

"Please." He spoke again just as softly as the first time. Slowly I made my way over to the chair and sat down, my back to him.

"You do not have to be afraid I am not here to harm you." He said,

"It's more caution than fear. You are with Morfran, and he is not a man to be trusted." I didn't hide my disdain.

Calum placed the bundle on the dresser and rummaged through it. He pulled out a comb and moved my hair back, laying it on the other side of the chair I sat in and began running it through just as gently as his voice.

"Morfran likes pretty things," Calum said, I thought it was the only thing he had to say. "He makes sure to only surround himself with such objects." Calum caught my sight in the mirror for a moment. His facial expression was strange.

"One day I was in the market with my brothers there was a formal procession that day. I was pushed into the street while we played in front of Morfran, his eyes locked on me as he continued to pass by..." He paused a moment, still running the comb through my hair. "I thought nothing of it until the very next morning there were guards at our doorstep demanding my parents hand me over. They were not willing at first, but after a few days we learned he was not a man you defy. They came to our home again, killing my oldest brother and told them. if I did not go with them that day, they would kill the other two of my brothers and take me anyway, leaving them with none." He became silent.

Calum stopped running the comb through my hair. I caught sight of his features in the mirror on the dresser. The boy's tormented face was heart wrenching I swallowed down the lump beginning to rise.

"Yes, I am a servant of Morfran he has trained me well there is much I will never forget or forgive. But I know better than to defy that man. I have also learned many suitable abilities from his as well. There is one thing for sure though." He locked his eyes with mine and his expression change from pain to rage. "I am no alley of his, I am only here for the safety of my family and nothing more." Calum finished talking and continued to comb my hair.

"Why are you telling me this?" I said before stopping myself.

"I didn't want you to believe I was associated with that man willingly," his face grim. "I am the one that has to dress you, and I wanted you to know it is not my choosing." I snorted.

"Of course it's not your choosing, I am sure that bastard has picked out quite the attire." I rolled my eyes.

"Or lack thereof." He said and I turned to him.

"Pardon?" I said, unhappy.

Calum turned to the dresser pulling a piece of cloth out of the bundle there was not enough to fully cover me. Running my fingers along the deep red material as soft as silk, it glistened in the light.

"I believe you're missing some material." I held it in my hands annoyed.

"No, that's all of it." He said a small smile appeared on his lips, the first time I had seen it on him.

"Glad you find this amusing, but I will not wear this." I went to hand it back, the little smile he had left, he returned to his usual self.

"Apologies, but Morfran said if I could not dress you, he would do it himself."

"That piece of scum." I said, snatching the silk from him. He turned around for me as I changed, even though there was no point in him turning the gesture was appreciated. The cloth grazed my skin gently as I stepped my feet in and pulled it up. Tying it in place on the back of my neck, the back remained open revealing any kind of scars mister demented Commander had left me. The cloth was only wide enough to run over on either side of my breast. A split in the middle, leaving the rest of my skin bear that stopped just beneath my belly button. It hung loosely on my hips reaching to my ankles, a slit on either side that exposed from my thigh all the way down. I heard a jingle and realized Calum was rummaging through more supplies.

"I few more things." He said apologetically. He brought over a long golden chain wrapping his arms around he clasped the chain on my waist pulling together any loose silk left. The chain ran down the side of my leg, stopping just before my ankle.

"Any other awful attire for me?" I asked, tired already.

"He requested your hair be pulled back. If you could sit, please, and try to eat I prepared it myself, there is no poison or strange drug added, you will need your strength." He said bringing the tray over and placed it on the dresser beside us. Knowing how hungry I felt, I was grateful for his kindness.

I ate silently while he pulled my hair up high on my head, looking like the tail of a pony. Which left my eyes clear for view. Obviously, he wanted to make the cursed part of me seen. I was definitely being presented as a whore or some form of entertainment for that snake Morfran. Calum left me barefoot after he was done and asked me to follow him.

"I know I can do nothing for you, but I pray good fortunes on you." He said as I followed behind him.

"I am grateful" I told him, then kept silent preparing myself for what may await me with the King.

I was chilled from the lack of clothing and uncomfortable, but I kept my head up no matter how I would be presented I would keep my dignity. Calum brought me back to the room where I had first met Morfran who was standing in the middle of the room. Commander Drask joined him. Morfran turned to me as we entered the room, a sly smile spread across his face at the sight of me. I groaned inwardly, wanting very much to choke the life out of him.

"Yes, yes, very lovely. Red is a good choice." He said while scanning me over from head to toe. "Now, I must leave the King requests my presence before you are to meet him. For your sake, I hope it is a good meeting." He kept smiling like there was something amusing only he knew of, some foolish joke that only he was in on.

"Commander," he nodded once and glided his way out the door. Calum followed without looking in my direction once, a sharp boy I am sure he has picked up a lot working under Morfran. A hand drifted along my back, reminding me I was not alone in this room. I turned my head slightly, knowing Commander Drask was admiring the scars he once left me. The feeling made my insides twist, disgust rising and clawing at me.

"There is nothing more exciting than seeing fresh scars mar perfectly smooth skin." He said continuing to run his fingers along my back tracing along one. "Too bad we don't have enough time to give you some fresh ones." Moving away from him I turned to look at him directly.

"Would your master be pleased? If you get punished again, I would be more than happy to continue." I watched as his smile disappeared from his face and he looked at me, his eyes had a hint of fear. "You afraid of him?" I asked, part curious, the other part enjoying his suffering mildly.

"Don't speak to me of fear whore, I have had you squirming under me enough to know I have the upper hand." I laughed at him as his eyebrows pulled together.

"Yes, you've made me suffer, you've tormented me with physical pain numerous times. But fear?" I shook my head. "No, I have never once truly been afraid of you, Commander. Your twisted yes, a sick bastard who gets off on hurting others but that is all you are. You cower from that snake you call master and only come at me when I am weak, you are a pathetic existence." I kept my eyes on him and watched as his face grew angrier with every word I spoke. "And because you fear your master you will do nothing to me, you can't do anything to me." He raised his hand up to strike, when a knock on the door stopped him in his place and he dropped his hand back down.

Calum opened the door, "it is time Commander." He said holding the door open for us. Commander Drask grabbed hold of my arm squeezed tight sending pain up and down my arm. He leaned down as he whispered.

"You know nothing, when I am free from this wretched place. I will hunt you and I will show you what true terror I am capable of." Then pulled me forward out of the door, letting go as we left the room. The blood flow returning to my arm sent thousands of needles prickling through until it returned properly. I am sure he would be disappointed if he knew how unafraid I truly was. But after my run-ins with the unknown figure in my dreams, it was hard to be afraid of Commander Drask.

I kept to myself and followed, still barefoot walking behind Commander Drask. Calum walked just behind me. The walk was quiet except for the echo of Commander Drask's sword and armor clashing as we went. My steps remained silent on the cold stone floor, the halls empty and unwelcoming, the sun streamed through the open windows. It looked to be a beautiful cloudless day, I wished very much to be out in the sunlight rather than this dreary castle. We took several turns, and I mentally noted each one and what was where, in case I needed to make an escape.

21

The cold air pricked at my skin, the dress, if that's what you could even call it brushed along my legs as we walked at a steady pace. Commander Drask took another turn, which brought us to an open square area. Filled with small trees and flowers arranged neatly. Stone benches placed on every side. In the center a statue of a woman kneeling with her head bowed, a man cloaked looking down at her hand on her head. The image left me with the feeling of pain, a cold sense of loyalty, a betrayal she would later regret with her life.

The feeling left me and we continued past the area, stopping in front of two large doors. So large it needed at least two men on either door to open. A low rumble followed by the large doors cracking open slowly, the space getting wider by the second. As the doors continued its slow and dramatic opening the space between was dark and hard to see after walking in from the brightly lit hallway. I kept my features neutral and everything inside calm. Commander Drask led the way with his brisk pace through the doors. A large, enclosed room with statues of men standing tall in a line on each wall, four statues on either side. The marble floor clopped beneath Commander Drask's boots and remained silent beneath mine. I could even hear a slight tapping from the slippers of Calum behind.

Groups of people stood on either side of the room, leaving the center open for us to walk through. Everyone silent, all eyes followed me as I passed, their looks made my skin crawl, some accusing others of lusting. 'Bastard.' I thought, for making me parade in such ridiculous attire. Keeping eyes forward I scanned the rest of the room, it was cold like a tomb, this place reeked of death. I saw the King sitting on his throne, far too large for his size, an iron chair with intricate designs woven along the outsides The back reaching higher than the two guards standing on either side behind him. He was young, no older than fourteen, rich curly brown hair with beautiful green eyes. The life emitting off him did not match the feel of death in the room. Two men stood on either side of him, one among them the snake Morfran. He had a smirk on his lips that made my fingers twitch, the urge to rip it off his face strong.

I got the feeling of being watched, it wasn't from the many eyes already upon me. No, this made my heart thump as a sense of dread weighed on me. I kept my head high, my face forward where the King and his advisors stood beside him. In the corner of my eyesight stood Faelan. He stood to the far right out of sight, his eyes followed me a hint of glow filled them. You couldn't tell of his position as a General by his posture. Casually leaning on the side of a pillar, hands crossed over the dark brown leather vest on his chest. A blade across his back, two curved shorter blades on either side of his belt. I knew as he watched the rage building inside him by how Morfran disgustingly paraded me around as some exotic creature waiting to be bid on for a new master.

He remained in place and kept with his casual demeanor but there were small tells, the tight jaw muscle and his eyes, always his eyes, it was as if he could see right into the deepest parts of my soul. The thought sent pleasant chills down my spine. Commander Drask's steps finally stopped echoing as he stood in front of the King, four large steps of stone separated us from him. Kneeling on one knee, he bowed his head before speaking in a loud voice.

"I have completed my mission My King, I have retrieved the Cursed One with two different colored eyes and she is standing here before you now." He said, standing grabbing hold of my arm and pulling me forward. The King stood his eyes on me, no smile, no amusement at my arrival. This King did not look pleased to see me.

"You have my gratitude, Commander. I will see that you and your men are rewarded for daring to embark on this quest and returned successful." He nodded to him once and returned his gaze to me. "So, you are the Cursed One." He stated as a fact, I remained silent, noticing the smirks on the advisors behind him. So, all of them were snakes and Morfran probably pulls all the strings, most likely won them over without the King knowing.

"There has been misfortune and disaster throughout my lands. Towns burning, people starving, crops rotting, and livestock missing. There have been rumors of a small village having similar issues but have been caused because of a cursed woman staying just outside of their village. Now my father did not seem to burden himself with a hunt for you as it was only a small village. But this misfortune has spread considerably in my lands, and I will no longer turn a blind eye to your... existence." He paused, taking a brief glance in Morfran's direction, who nodded encouragingly. Ah yes, he is certainly the one pulling the strings, the King swallowing before he continued, I noticed his uncertainty. The boy had never done this before.

"You will be sentenced to death for your crimes that have been committed against the kingdom." He said firmly, Faelan who has remained unmoving so far pushed himself off the wall before he was noticed I spoke.

"Pardon me Majesty, but have you proof my curse causing your misfortunes and disasters of the kingdom?" I asked, knowing it was a long shot, but I did not want to involve Faelan more than necessary. The King paused, confused.

"Proof?"

"Yes, Majesty proof, I do not recall doing anything that would cause such disasters. I have an odd-colored eye, yes. The people in my village did not take well to it, they began blaming me for every little problem that went wrong for them. I do not see why I would need to be punished for a crime I have never committed." I said with my hands to my side Commander Drask grip on my arm becoming tighter, as I spoke, I kept my voice calm and even.

The King's expression softened, almost relieved. But Morfran noticed his waiver and did not seem pleased by it. Morfran stepped forward, speaking in a cunning voice.

"My King if I may." He said, hands clasped together,

"Yes Morfran," The King said turning to him.

"I do not believe that is how curses work. I believe this woman has no ill intentions to the kingdom and its people. Just her mere existence would cause the curse to be in effect, so keeping her alive would only fuel the curse to continue the disasters. She needs to be put to death, My King only then would your kingdom be safe from her curse." He said bowing his head and slithering back to his place, a triumphant look set in place. The King's face turned grave again as he looked over to me.

I did not turn away or falter as he searched my eyes, his gaze staring into my blazing eye.

"What do you say to this Cursed One, it seems I must put you to death to save my kingdom and its people?" He said frowning.

"Majesty, have you been outside of your castle?" I asked, remaining calm.

"I do not see what this has to do with your sentence?" He said confused again.

"It's simple, if you have left from your closed doors, you would see there is more going on in your kingdom and its people's suffering than this curse everyone keeps going on about." I replied

"What do you mean?" He asked. His brows knit together in confusion.

"Your people are being mistreated, abused by the very people that are charged to protect them." I glanced over at Commander Drask whose grip dug deeper into my skin if he had long enough nails, I am sure there would be blood dripping down my arm.

"Are you accusing my Commander of taking advantage of the people? That is impossible." He said upset. "Who are you to make accusations? You are the one being punished, you have no right." My face hardened as I looked at this misguided young King.

"Who are you to come hunting for me, blaming me for all the misfortunes? When you have not once stepped out of your castle to see the way your people are being treated. I will not stand here and die just because you are not willing to see the truth of these greedy men taking advantage of you." I said, nodding my head toward Morfran. The King looked behind him to see Morfran's exaggerated outrage of my claim.

The King looked back at me and before he spoke Faelan advanced. He calmly waved a hand up trying to gain the attention of the King, again not formal for a General.

"My Lord," he said. The King broke his contact from me and

looked over to Faelan. His entire expression lit up at the sight of him. He was someone the King admired 'hmm' I thought to myself a little detail he failed to mention again.

"General Faelan." The King said excitedly, "I had no idea you were here." The boy truly did not know Faelan stood over to the side near to him. I caught a very slight facial change in Morfran, the other advisors did not hide their dislike so well. It seemed Morfran did not allow the king to know much of what was happening around him if he could help it. I could imagine he was capable of hiding many things from this young King.

Walking towards the king, Faelan kept a gentle smile on his face.

"King Anwyl, it is good to see you, although I reget it is in the middle of an unpleasant circumstance. If the good King would allow a suggestion, I may have a solution to your problem." He said, turning an eye to me briefly and back to King Anwyl again. The young King's face seemed relieved at the suggestion and nodded, giving Faelan his approval to continue.

"In my homelands if someone is accused of said crime, they allow the person to choose a trial by fire." He said keeping his calm demeanor,

"Forgive me General, I am unfamiliar with that term." King Anwyl said, confusion lighting his face.

"Oh, I've no doubt you are King Anwyl. The Trial by Fire is a series of difficult obstacles surrounded by flames. A battle being the last of them where the accused must last until the fire turns to embers against another opponent or they will face their punishment without objections." Faelan finished his explanation, Morfran approached once again, obviously displeased with this idea.

"My King." He said right next to King Anwyl, "If I may, we are not in his lands we do not have a right to use his customs." Bowing his head to the king.

"Yes, that is true," King Anwyl said slumping his shoulders slightly.

"If the King is worried of offending there is no need to concern. I have the authority to allow such a trial to take place outside of our realm. If you are willing to accept this as a solution and if the Cursed One is willing to take the challenge of Trial by Fire." Faelan said looking over to me instead of returning his attention to King Anwyl.

My pulse rose and I swallowed, this was not the time I told myself. However, a deep fire simmered from within, I forgot everyone in the room Faelan was all I could see. His eyes on me, that deep golden color watching waiting patiently for my response. Jerking my arm out of Commander Drask's grasp. My arm felt relier from his fingers digging in the entire time and took a step forward.

"I choose Trial by Fire. If the good King will allow it?" I said firmly, without faltering. Faelan then looked to King Anwyl and waited again.

"Then we shall see if you can earn your freedom. We will proceed with the Trial by Fire three days from now. Until then you will remain in the dungeons awaiting your fate." King Anwyl waved a hand to Commander Drask, telling him to take me away.

Before he could pull me, I blurted out.

"If his Majesty is feeling generous, some clothes less drafty would be grateful." The King looked down as if it was the first time, he noticed my attire and blushed, revealing his age and innocence.

"Yes, I believe I can allow that much." He said still beat red. Taking one last look at Faelan I walked out of the large cold room, Commander Drask gripping my arm in the same spot he had already left bruised.

22

I was thankful I would be out of these damned curtains, the sooner the better. I walked with Commander Drask in silence, his anger boiling over, furious with me for revealing how him and his men abuse their power. 'Three days' I thought I would have to find a way to pass this trial so I could walk out of here alive. I will have to give Faelan my gratitude for once again saving my neck.
It grew darker and darker with every turn we made. One less torch light with every new hall. He turned again, at the end of the last one stood a wooden door. Bars lined at the top showing only darkness behind its ominous hinges.

Stopping just before it he knocked twice, two short pounds. After a few minutes the door creaked open a large man stood on the other side. He was almost the size of the door itself shirtless with a mask over half his face, the mouth was open, but three metal bars came over his lips.

"Cursed wench meet Graa. Graa, this is the cursed wench." He grunted his response scanning over the new prisoner. His eyes were black as if there was no soul attached to them. He turned and walked down a long dark hall of stone steps, there were fewer torches down here, the smell getting worse as we descended. Graa grunting to himself as he led the way, Commander Drask remained silent while we walked, and I waited for the torture I knew would come shortly. Preparing mentally, holding firm to the Eleith, I knew was somewhere nearby.

We reached the bottom. Dirt covered the ground with no solid stone to walk on. Brick walls lined along each side and split them into different rooms. Passing an open door, I saw chains dangling from the ceiling. I wondered if it was like that in every cell. A scream at the far end another wooden door closed, put my nerves on high alert. More screams erupted from behind that door, Graa walked up to the door. With one pound the screams halted. Commander Drask stopped in front of a cell and opened the bar door, pulling me inside with him. The cell was damp and the ground cold, he shoved me against the stone wall, my back became slick from the moist rock. Glaring at Commander Drask he moved his face close to mine, his eyes searching over my face. I kept my hands to the side, one of his hands pressed against the wall next to my head.

"Wha…" before I could finish, he pushed his mouth to mine both my hands went up. He snatched one then shoved it into my chest hard as the other grabbed at his face. I tried viciously to remove him from me, but he kept his mouth firm on mine. Pain shot through my lip as he bit down hard, I could taste the blood that sprouted from it. Grabbing hold of my hair he yanked my head back, leaving my neck wide open. I connected my open hand to the side of his face, only stalling him for a moment until he brought his mouth to my neck. I could feel his tongue trace its way down, following his mouth. My stomach dropped from the feeling, a sickness rising inside, chasing away the once simmering fire left with just a look from Faelan.

He let go of my hair and brought his hand down to my outside thigh, sliding it up along my skin. He gripped it then pulled my body up, scraping my back along the wall. I felt no pleasure as he pressed his body up against mine. Or from the filling of his hand gripping far too high up my thigh, marking where no one has touched before. Sickened, I screamed. "Let go!"
Brining my arm down hard on his shoulder the blow caused his hand to release, I dropped to my feet. More pain shot through the base of my neck, warm blood trickled down matching the red color of the silk.

Grabbing hold of my other hand he shoved both back into my chest. He looked up to me, his face inches from mine, I could see my blood slide down the side of his mouth.

"YOU… humiliated me in front of the King and Morfran!" He

raged. "So, I will return the favor. What do you think your precious General will do when he notices these marks I have left on you?" He emphasized by running a free hand up my thigh. "You think he will understand how much of a whore you truly are when he sees how I have ravaged you. Your delicate body trembling under my touch. Or how you will spread your legs for me when I touch in just the right spots." Taking his thumb rubbing it over my lips smearing what blood dripped off. The throbbing pain now became just pain.

His cold eyes watched, waiting for me to show some fear or panic from what he planned to do. I never gave him the satisfaction, I knew Faelan. I knew he would not leave. In the short time we had together there was an unbreakable bond formed between the two of us. It was something Commander Drask could never understand.

"It won't work. You will only be disappointed." He grew furious, eyes murderous. He pulled my entire body off the wall and shoved me back hard, knocking the air from me, yelling in my face. He continued to yank me off the wall and slam back while still screaming in my face over and over again. My body finally went limp from the many blows. I could only hang there while he took his rage out on me. A tap on the cell door stopped Commander Drask entirely.

"Are you going to let her go Commander or will I need to rip your hands off your arms to remove you?" Faelan's familiar voice spoke through the haze I was in, his tone deadly. I could still feel Commander Drask gripping my hands to my chest, I didn't have the strength to lift my head. He let go and my body crumpled to the ground. Unable to catch myself, the side of my head smashed against it. I laid there pain throbbed in my skull. Taking a few breaths I waiting for enough strength to return so I could manage some support. Listening to the footsteps shuffle around the cell. There was a loud bang and the sound of a man panting Faelan's voice was low and lethal.

"Let's make one thing clear, Commander." I mustered enough strength to look over in the direction of his voice. Commander Drask's feet were dangling off the ground as he was struggling to get a hold. His hands were clinging at his throat where Faelan held him with one hand against the wall. His eyes raged as he fought against him, unable to get away. "This will not happen again. If I so much as sense you are planning to harm her, I will suck the air out of your lungs and watch you struggle to breathe. Get it in that dim brain of yours. And do not think your master can save you." Faelan released Commander Drask who dropped to the ground clutching at his throat coughing and gagging trying to breathe.

I watched him scramble off the ground rushing out the cell door tumbling over himself, never looking back once. Graa stood at the door watching, for how long I was not sure, but he stood there, eyes lifeless as if this was nothing to the horrors he had seen.

"Leave." Was all Faelan said and Graa turned, heading to the wooden door that had the continuous screaming behind it. Faelan turned to me rage radiating off him. Pushing my body up I leaned myself back against the slimy wall, the cold stinging my scrapes. I managed a small smile, his eyes burned, jaw tight, fists clenched from my once again ruined appearance.

"Hey," I forced out. "Nice meeting you here." He didn't seem amused by my humor. He pulled a cloth out from his back pocket and began wiping the blood off the side of my head. Somehow the dry rag was damp with warm water.

"You came prepared, it's like you have found me in this predicament before." He ignored my attempt again and continued to wipe the blood moving down to my lip, cleaning it next. His gentle touch chased away any bad feelings Commander Drask forced on me.

"I saw the look on his face when he was leaving the throne room, I knew whatever he planned was not good." His voice still had an edge to it. "Forgive me for not getting to you sooner. I had to make sure Morfran did not change King Anwyl's mind about the Trial by Fire." His eyes were hard, unforgiving of himself, I reached a hand up and placed it on his face.

"I owe you my gratitude on numerous occasions, late or not, you have helped me again." I said, he looked me over and he noticed for the first time where all the bruises lay along my body. Where he had placed his hands, putting my hand on his arm bringing his eyes back to mine. "I am fine. Truly." I said softly, "Just having you next to me is more than enough." I waited for him to calm down and felt the pleasant warmth run through my veins as he used his element to heal the wounds just given to me.

Faelan wiped off the rest of the blood as best he could with the little cloth he had with him. He then stood, walked out of the cell and picked up a bundle I had not noticed before lying next to the door.

"Here I brought you more comfortable clothes less.... breezy." He said as his eyes wandered down to the little, I have been wearing for far too long. I snatched the pile from him, waited for him to turn then quickly changed savoring the feel of the cloth and leather it came with.

It was an improvement, but I still felt empty without weapons. My fingers itched to have them back where they belonged. "I don't know if I can ever be more grateful," I said as he turned back around. "So, what's next?" I asked. "You kept me from dying for another three days. But how am I supposed to beat this Trial by Fire?" We sat on the cold ground again, leaning against the stone wall separating us from the cell next to me.

"Calum will be down with some food soon. I cannot stay much longer it will not be wise to leave King Anwyl in the company for Morfran and his conniving advisors for too long. Plus, he has requested me to join him for dinner, I will try to get his permission to keep you under my supervision considering what just happened with the Commander. But it will be hard with that snake next to him whispering poison in his ear." He said annoyed.

"How long have you known King Anwyl?" I asked curious, Faelan froze, suddenly realizing his mistake.

"I did not intend to keep it from you." He said honestly, panic in his eyes. I couldn't help but laugh at the worry on his face.

"You should see your face though," I laughed again but his panic was replaced with irritation. "Where was my warning? You had some idea of what that bastard would have you in. Do you know how hard it was to not erupt a ring of fire around you so no one could see?"

"A ring of fire." I said eyebrows raised "Don't you think that would be a little extreme." I said amused,

"No, I believe it would have been perfectly reasonable." A tap on the cell door pulled us from our own little world. Calum came in with a plate of food and it looked delicious.

"I have your dinner for you," he said, stopping before me kneeling to hand it over. "You have my graititude, Calum." I said with a smile.

"I am glad you are well." Was all he said to me then turned to Faelan "King Anwyl is expecting you." He said bowing before he left the cell, Faelan looked over to me once brought his hand up and brushed my cheek with his finger.

"I will see you soon, then we will talk of your Trial by Fire." He left me in the dim cell to eat my food in silence, the once peaceful atmosphere now gone just like a swift breeze.

23

The food was delicious, I was grateful to Calum. After finishing the food, I pushed the tray over, picking up the blanket in the pile Faelan brought with him. I leaned my back against the stone wall, not wanting anything to sneak up on me. Wrapping myself in it, I watched as Graa's figure walked back and forth past my cell door making his rounds. My plan was to remain awake, but my eyelids grew heavy, and I could not keep them open. Before I knew it, I was already asleep.

It was dark, there were no lights in sight, I could not even see my hand in front of my face. The only thing I could hear was the sound of my heartbeat growing louder and my breathing becoming faster. I felt a strange pressure behind me, throwing my hand back my arm passed through thin air. The hair on the back of my neck prickled I could feel a presence behind me, and it wasn't the Eleith.

"Shaaeee." The voice whispered, flinging my arm around again, trying to connect with whatever belonged to that voice. Nothing, as my hand swept through thin air.

"Shae." It whispered again, its voice was more alluring this time. Everything in me said to run away and my legs started doing just that as I ran blind. "Shae." It snickered.

"Where are you going Shae." Its voice purred still so close, as I ran, my legs strained, lungs burning, I couldn't slow my heartbeat down. An awful feeling crept up my spine, the terror returning knowing it was about to get me. A bright flame erupted just before me, stopping me in my tracks shooting higher than the *tallest treetops. Dark creatures scurried away from all sides, crawling, slithering, dragging their limbs behind them. Some larger than what I would have liked. Their numbers were endless.*

A cold fingernail slid down the back of my neck and I could feel breathing in my ear as the voice spoke.

"Time for me to go, my lovely Shae, but I will see you again." And just like that the voice was gone, the flame still roared before me. Beautiful colors dancing inside blues, reds, yellow, orange, and many more. The flame felt alive melting away any fear I had.

"Shae." This voice was wonderful it was warm and kind more loving than any Grams had ever spoke "My Shae. Be strong, the young King is lost. He will need you to guide him." The flame grew smaller, but my heart longed for it to continue raging. But the light became smaller until it was only embers left radiating the heat. "It is time to wake Shae."

My eyes snapped open. Graa stood at my cell with the door open, one foot in his lifeless eyes watching, waiting. It sent an icy feeling in the pit of my stomach, he turned around and left my cell, shutting the door behind him. Something told me he would have crushed my skull in my sleep if I had slept any longer. So, I kept myself wide awake for many hours. After having nothing to do, I worked my muscles with the training I knew best and continued for hours more. By the time Faelan had returned I was sweating from head-to-toe breathing heavily. He stopped dead in his tracks at the sight of me and whistled.

"You couldn't have waited so I could watch." His half smile fatal.

"Next time," I said breathily. He handed me a jug mercifully, he brought water.

"You are in a particularly good mood did negotiations go well with King Anwyl?" I asked, analyzing his face.

"Why yes, yes they did." He said happily, "Shae you are to accompany me. You are now under my watch." I sighed with relief.

"It's good to know something is going our way." I said before taking another long drink.

"You will remain in shackles outside of the room we are staying, however." He said with a sheepish grin I rolled my eyes at him.

"Do I have a necklace to match?" I said sarcastically.

"We could find one if it will make you feel more comfortable." He said with a devious grin.

"Get on with it." I said, holding my hands out. Faelan put the shackles on my wrists, stepping aside his eyes watching Graa who stood staring through the bar door watching our every move.

"You should go first," he said eyes beginning to blaze I nodded once and moved with a fast pace, Faelan walked right behind me. We reached the door shortly, my eyes stung at the light as little as it was, it was brighter than below.

"He seems to have his eyes on you." He said walking next to me, I glanced back a sharp sense of fear hit my stomach. when I saw those lifeless eyes peering from behind the bars, looking straight for me. I turned back quickly, looking at Faelan.

"I didn't think you meant literally?" Faelan paused momentarily, jaw tight and put his hand on the center of my back pushing me forward.

"Can he leave from there?" I asked, fear coating my voice. We rounded the corner, pulling ourselves from his sight. Faelan stopped, grabbing my shoulder and pushing me, my back hit the wall as he leaned down, his hands raised on one side of me. I felt my pulse rise and my heart beat a little faster from his sudden proximity.

"No, he remains in that hole, but that is the first time I have seen him follow anyone up. He listens to the darkness, Shae. Morfran believes he controls him, but there is only one master to him. I will be with you, but I don't know what he is or what he can do." His eyes searched mine, worry lining his face there is so much he was not telling me. Another time I thought let's get out of this alive or at least out of this without knowing if I really come back from the dead.

Faelan glanced at both sides of me, then pulled away from me and encouraged us to move out of the dank area before we really find out if Graa will leave the prison or not.

"How long have I been in there?" I asked as we walked.

"It's been a day and a half, I imagine you are hungry, and your feet must be cold." He said examining my bare feet along the stone floor. I looked down the halls filled with the sound of my shackles clinking together.

Surprised, very little sound came from Faelan who was armed and wearing boots. I noted I needed to work on my stealth better when I retrieve my belongs once again. We took the numerous turns back to the square Commander Drask lead me from, when we first left the throne room. The Sky was a beautiful blue, a crisp cold lining the air. If there were rain I am sure snow would fall instead. I watched the hot puff leave my mouth with every breath, my feet starting to sting more and more with each step from the cold stone touching my bare skin.

Faelan walked next to me, our paces matched perfectly, must have been hard considering I was much smaller than him. He walked with authority, a confidence that came naturally or from the many years he had to refine his demeanor. I frowned at the thought, realizing I had yet to learn more of him. I longed to hear his stories, hear of his life before me, the many ventures he has made. I held on to the one thing I knew for certain, there was a purpose for our meeting.

I remembered my dream, how he flew next to me, the feeling of his hand on mine, how it felt right where it belonged. I searched the area as we walked, remaining silent. Servants eyed us while they tended to the square garden, where the flowers still bloomed wonderfully in the cold air. Groups of upper class stood together, giggling and glancing in our direction as we stepped by. Some just plain stared, not pretending to hide it, whispers followed us as we passed through the garden and into another hall.

Faelan kept close to the wall, large round pillars reached the ceiling. We walked in between them and the wall, beautiful swirls etched into the pillars showing a wonder of silver lining the edges. The walls, a dusty stone with white curtains running down them, a few feet between them. Rows of benches filled the inner part of the hall with a long empty row down the middle. I realized when I saw a man dressed in white and blue robes this was meant to be a holy place. He wore a funny hat far too large for his head that hung down the middle of his back, an old man with wrinkles visible even from where I stood.

Faelan stopped at a small opening, a passage it seemed for the servants and workers to walk through easily. We turned in and left the old man to his prayers, the passage was narrow we could walk next to one another, but our arms brushed past each other.

The passage came to a wall with a split either to the right or the left, the dark stone made it hard to see it was not a dead end. Only a few torches lined the walls. Faelan took the left, and we continued in silence, not wanting anyone alert to our existence. There was a turn to the right this time, no left turn was available. Little torches lined higher on the stone lighting the way to the next split. Taking a left here, we walked for a few more minutes when light showed at the end, smells of spice and meat filled the air the closer we got. My stomach rumbled, eager to fill it full of what made that delicious aroma. Faelan stifled a laugh after hearing my stomach complain aloud, I elbowed him in response.

"You'd be hungry too if you were locked up a whole day without food." I grumbled at him. We made our way past the opening lights filling the kitchen, people working paying us no mind. As they scrambled around trying to make food for the meal that needed preparing. There was a huge fireplace in the middle with four openings on all sides, large pots hanging over the fire, steam pouring out of them. Five large wooden tables in a line, one in front of the other.

One table had desserts scattered along it, another had bread and pastries, biscuits steaming in baskets several had meats and pies overflowing.

"King Anwyl expecting a celebration?" I asked, glancing around the room watching the cooks scattered around putting finishing touches on dishes.

"No, this is just another normal meal." Faelan said, frowning. "A lot of food goes to waste while his people are starving in the streets just below. King Anwyl doesn't even know his people are suffering because of his own advisor's." Faelan said, leaning down to whisper in my ear sending a chill down my neck. I Rubbed my ear with my shoulder to chase away the feeling. Faelan looked at me quizzically.

He brought me to a small table in the corner just outside the kitchen, grabbed a plate and started filling it with whatever he saw. By the time he came back to me, the plate was overflowing with food and set in front of me. He un-cuffed my shackles, then handed me a fork so I could eat. I ate as he scanned the room, taking in the people moving in and out of the kitchen. A cup of ale was brought over for both of us by a wondering servant looking in Faelan's direction. Realizing who he was the boy didn't waste any time. Faelan thanked him and watched the little fella scurry away putting the trays on large platters and carrying them out a large door leading to the banquet hall.

I heard laughter, the loud roar of many people talking all at once, and a very lite sound of music filling the background.

"Must be dinnertime." I noted.

"It is just beginning, upper class is still filing into their places, making lots of racket while waiting to be served." I noticed his face darkened at the mention of them.

"I have a day left then?" I said, before I continued, he cut me a look that said to keep quiet, his eyes searching the room. A shadow caught my eyesight, and a figure seemed to materialize out of the dark, Morfran came slithering his way in our direction Calum right behind him.

"Not joining the festivities tonight, General?" Morfran spoke in his sly voice that always seemed to have an insult lined in his words. Just his presence annoyed me.

"It is strange to see you missing out on them yourself, Morfran." He noted.

"Oh, do not worry about me General I will join shortly, I was checking in on the prisoner making sure she was not too difficult... for you to handle. We would not want her to escape just before her trial." He said with that nasty smile always plastered on his face, a warning it seemed.

"Your concern is noted counselor I believe I have the prisoner under control as you can see." He said glancing at me while I had a mouth full of food, not bothering to stop during their conversation, if you could call it that.

Morfran's eyes were wandering over in my direction, acting as if he had just noticed my presence.

"I see you still lack manners." He said clasping his hands together and sizing me up like I was some filthy dog not trained properly. I made a rude gesture at him to show him how well they were. Which he then dramatically looked appalled by my behavior, backing away like I had just slapped him. "I can see this is not a good time General, if you please, keep your pet leashed before she gets put back in the dungeons at my request." He spoke to Faelan like it was some kind of favor. I rolled my eyes and continued eating, the chicken leg greasing my fingers. Wondering for what purpose his attitude had changed drastically towards me.

I watched as Morfran left in the same manner he came, with Calum trailing behind him.

"That went well." Faelan mused while watching me lick the grease off my fingers savoring the flavor. I shrugged.

"We know he has something up his sleeve if I win the Trial by Fire the question is what." I said, remembering the warm voice speaking to me about the King. "There somewhere I can wash?" I said, catching Faelan stare at my lips making my heartbeat jump a moment, he nodded at me.

"Good," I said with a sly smile.

24

After leaving the kitchen, my body felt renewed from the feeling of a full stomach. Faelan and I disappeared into another tight passage out of sight from most the onlookers. We headed past several doors on either side of the wider halls lined with torches and windows. He stopped in front of a double door with two red banners and larger torches on either side of it. Faelan opened the door, stepping aside.

"After you." He said with a light tone.

The room opened into a large area. Across from us lay a black rug along the floor from some massive beast. Just beyond it was a fireplace with chairs lining the rug. The room was large enough we could have fit a tavern from our earlier stops inside. A bed stood next to the wall, larger than the one I slept in the first night I'd arrived here. An open room stood to the very right with a screen just inside the door separating it from view.

On the other side, steam rolled up from the water I heard flowing in.

"I had a servant prepare it when I came and got you. I knew you would die for one." Faelan gave me a side smile, then unshackled my wrists. I shook my head with a smile in disbelief. Rubbing my wrists, I stalked over to the bath, the smell drew me in, it had a much more pleasant aroma than the bath Morfran had waiting for me. The petals were a bright pink floating over the water. Dropping the dirty clothes off I stepped into the warm water enjoying the way it felt running over my skin. I washed myself thoroughly scrubbing all the parts Commander Drask touched, the memory of it made me repulsive. I closed my eyes and let my head sink under the water relaxing, for a moment, engulfing myself in the heat, pushing everything away.

A tap on my head made me realize I was in for far too long poking my head up, I saw Faelan's back to me.

"I was just checking, you got quiet." He said while walking out. Getting out of the water I wrapped myself in one of the fluffy soft robes, the rest of me dripping. Faelan sat at a chair near the fire, his gaze fixed on the flames flickering. I noticed as they grew smaller and larger, the glow from his eyes controlling the flow of the flame.

"Is it hard?" I asked walking over to him, looking over as I approached his gaze lingered.

"No." he said, no pleasure in his words. I stopped before him while he sat unmoving, the glow in his eyes faint.

"Can you teach it?" I asked curiously.

"Only to those who can wield it." I sat in the chair next to him and observed as he watched me the air felt tense, it seemed to be a hard subject to approach. Curiosity getting the better of me, I asked, anyway.

"You have the fire element?" His eyes searched mine. He was debating, debating on what he should tell me. A hint of frustration sprouted within me. I got up to walk away and he reached for my hand, those long fingers wrapped around my wrist stopping me in my tracks.

"Yes." He said looking up at me pulling my arm back, "I have the fire element." The way he said it felt as though he was only telling me part of a truth, so I asked before I lost my nerve.

"And air? Do you have air as well?" I asked, starting to put the pieces together. Faelan kept his hand firm, and I noticed his mouth twitch in the corner. Pulling my wrist from his grasp, he let go easily. I made my way to the chair and watched his head fall into his hands, his hair tumbling to the sides of his face.

"In my realm," he began, "It is a well-known fact what I am capable of. But it has come at a price." He said, his voice low. I waited for him to continue, it took him a few minutes. But I waited and watched as he battled within himself something dark and unforgiving seemed to hover over his shoulders, a past I knew nothing of. The words fell out of my mouth before I could stop them.

"How many elements do you have?" I asked, already knowing the answer. He lifted his head up, his eyes looked haunted, a sorrow I could never fathom.

"All of them." He breathed, it was rare for an elemental to have two but for there to be someone who had all four.

My Grams spoke to me about it once speaking of a legend, but right here in front of me was that legend. My entire body felt electrified by the excitement. I felt overwhelming questions rise and suddenly drop away as he took his eyes off me. His gaze in another world, another time. Suddenly scared he would vanish right before me, I grabbed hold of his arm.

"Faelan." I said panicked, his eyes snapped back, the life returning to them. "Are you with me?" I said to him, making sure he didn't drift off on me again.

"We have more pressing matters." He said, "You only have a day left before the Trial by Fire. King Anwyl said he would be the one coming up with the challenges, but we both know Morfran will worm his ideas in his head. I will be the one setting the flame ablaze given I am the only one capable in the Human Realm. You will have three challenges, the last, you will battle an opponent without killing them." He said, my heart sunk at that, he smiled at my response knowing what I was thinking. How much easier it would be to take a life instead of holding back.

"You will have to dodge and maneuver your way out. You are just as good at that as you are at killing." He said with a bit of a twinkle in his eye. "Since we know Morfran will be the one setting up the trials. Be sure to think fast and move quick, time will not be on your side." He said.

"How can Morfran handle the trials?" I asked, confused.

"Have you not noticed?" Faelan said a little surprised.

"Noticed what?" I replied annoyed.

"Morfran is a sorcerer. Why do you think he is so dangerous?" Faelan held my gaze as everything started to come together. There was a tap on the door as he finished, we both froze. Faelan pulled a dagger from a sheath on his side before walking over to the door. I stayed just beside him. He opened the door, Calum stood at the other side, a bundle of leather and cloth in his arms.

"Good evening." He said before walking into the room. "I came to give you clothes at the Kings request. He wishes you the best." Calum said, while putting the pile on the bed. I looked out the door for anyone else behind him and figured he was alone considering he was good at moving around undetected. I assumed he lost whoever may have been following him.

"You have my gratitude once again." I gave him an honest smile.

"It was good to see you earlier." He said with a sharp smile, remembering my rude gesture, I am sure. "If you'll excuse me, I am expected elsewhere and cannot keep them waiting." He said with a bow and left just as easily as he came. Faelan closed the door behind him, setting the latch with a click before he turned to me.

"It is late, you will need rest. We train at first light." Watching him as he passed me there was a hint of weight still following him, a shadow I hadn't noticed before. Deciding it would be better to leave for now, I made my way to bed and laid down snuggling in the warm blankets. I fell asleep shortly after, not realizing how exhausted my body truly was, glad no dreams followed.

I woke suddenly and the room was dimly lit. I scanned the quarters and noticed steam rolling off the water at the far end of the room. Water splashed and the sound of feet padding over the stone. Faelan appeared from behind the screen, water dripping from his hair, a towel only covered his lower half leaving a full view of the strong body fine-tuned for battle. His muscles flexed as he used another cloth to dry his hair. His chest and stomach were formed perfectly smooth and defined, not leaving me with any kind of disappointment from our close encounters. There was a long scar across his chest and another scar on his shoulder, as though something had pierced it once long ago.

Faelan stopped, his gaze went to me and a slow half smile crept on his face.

"Awake I see." He said then continued to where he had meant to go before noticing me staring. 'Oh, I was staring.' I thought to myself. I was sure I could feel the heat rising on my face when I turned my back where his clothes lay. Getting out of bed I snatched up my own I hid away and dressed myself. After fitting in a smooth black shirt, a dark brown leather vest fitting perfectly, my black pants closely fit my legs. I put on a pair of dark brown leather boots that made it halfway up my calf, sticking close to my legs. The clothes fit comfortably, making it easy to move around without restrictions.

Faelan stood by the fire lacing his dark brown boots up over his black pants and a white shirt lay under a close fit light brown leather vest. My ears warmed thinking of the beautifully sculpted body under those clothes, shaking my head trying to get the images away.

"Are you ready?" He said breaking me out of my thoughts, a half-smile still dancing on his face.

"Yes." I said far too loudly. He chuckled at my discomfort, annoyed I stomped over to the door. "We don't have all day." It came out a bit too harshly, he only smiled and walked out the door.

"You're right." He said far more amused than necessary.

We had a light meal in the same place we ate the night before, it was just as noisy now as it was last night. We remained silent while we ate, I glanced in his direction every now and again watching him observe our surroundings. I finished my last bite a few moments before Faelan stood and we left out of the kitchen towards an open entryway. The entry took us down two halls after a few minutes of walking. We turned into another hall opening to the fresh sky. There were archways on either side of the pillars.

We walked down a balcony into a large courtyard, with weapons lined against one side of the stone wall. Further in the distance you could see targets placed next to one another for archery. This was a training area for the guards I realized. I glanced around and noticed not a single guard was in sight, no one was training, the entire place was empty. The balcony stretched past the courtyard. Faelan turned continuing down stone steps leading us to the training area.

The air was chilled but the sun's rays just heading over the mountains far off touched my skin, warming with its light. I took a calm breath savoring the fresh smell in the air, a puff of hot air tumbling out of my mouth. Faelan was standing in the middle of the courtyard observing me take in everything. I turned to him, noticed his calm demeanor and wondered if he was actually here to train.

"Alright, attack me." he said, slightly amused. I raised one eyebrow at him.

"If you say so." I said and dashed straight for him. He stood there unflinching by my fast approach. I leapt from the top of three large steps leading down to the spot where he stood. I brought one foot around and kicked it through the air aiming for his head. Somehow my foot passed through thin air where his head was supposed to be. He had ducked under my kick stepping to the left of me, I landed light on my feet springing back up launching a fist at him this time he only evaded me with movements I could barely detect turning just outside of my strike.

As he alluded my punch, he slapped down on my forearm leaving a red mark, stinging my skin already cold from the crisp air. I yelped, pulling my arm back glaring at him. His half smile lined his mouth.

"Apologies," he said, not apologetic in any way. Turning on my left foot, I flung my knee up to ram it into his side. He only stepped closer brushing against me. He spun and swept my foot out, knocking me to the ground. I caught myself just before hitting the ground, twisting to a roll instead of landing flat on the ground. I sat crouched eying him while he waited and observed my next move. The bastard was playing with me. 'Fair' I thought he has been alive far longer, battled far more and, his race superior. Still an annoyance struck, I was not one to be taken so lightly.

Rushing toward him, I let out a series of punches and kicks and with every strike I threw he avoided it with ease. Stepping outside of reach, spinning around, dodging in a fluid motion and, slapping my limbs that lingered for too long. Sweeping one leg under him he jumped over, my breath getting ragged, face bright red from the constant movement. Throwing a punch towards his chin he reached out a hand wrapped it over my arm stopping its pursuit. Twisting down forcing the rest of me forward and pulling my arm tight, a pressure pushed on my shoulder. He stood just behind me. I threw my free hand up and he caught it just before landing a hit on his cheek. Twisting it down as well, now both arms locked in place behind my back.

My breaths came in quick bursts while Faelan's remained even, he didn't even break a sweat. His body warmth on mine I felt his breathing near my neck, the feeling sent chills causing my body to tremble involuntarily.

"You're going to have to do better if you want to land a hit on me." His voice deep, amusement lining his words.

"I was just going easy." I fibbed, my pride a little hurt by how much faster and stronger he was. He chuckled in response, reading me easily. The sun was now fully over the mountains shining bright. Sweat coated my skin, his hands were slick on my arms but still held firm, the several spots he smacked stung, red welts formed in place.

Releasing my arms, the pressure on my shoulders eased and I pushed off him rolling my shoulders and neck from the strain.

"We'll switch, you will be needing to avoid getting pinned in any form if you are to last until the fire goes out." He said seriously.

"Yes, I am sure I won't be going against an elite elemental who toys with his pupil." I said hotly, his face neutral, then rushed at me.

I didn't have a chance to blink next I knew he was in my face so close to mine our noses nearly touched. His eyes fierce, a hint of glow behind them radiating that beautiful gold. His hand came up and flicked my nose then winked at me before dashing away. The shock on my face still lingered as I rubbed my poor nose. Standing just a few paces away I waited for his next move, looking for any kind of sign from his movement. He came at me, his speed slower this time, he tried latching onto my arm and yanking me in. I was able to twist my wrist from his grip, stepping out of reach only to run into his hard body. He had moved right behind me before I realized wrapping his arms around my entire body holding me in a bear hug.

"Got you." He said putting me back down I rolled my eyes getting back to my spot readying again.

We continued for hours, I was getting better, dodging and rolling out of his reach I even slapped his arms a couple times in retaliation from earlier. I bobbed and weaved away from punches, slipped away from his kicks. My movements started slowing as my limbs burned, it was getting hard just standing, a wave of nausea hit me, and I doubled over falling to my knees. Fealan was there in an instant, he reached over me looking for the source of my discomfort.

"I'm fine," I said after a moment, the feeling gone. "Just a little hungry." I said, my stomach rumbling in agreement. He sat up leaning back on his arms.

"It is well past time to eat." Almost as if Calum had heard Faelan speak, he came around the corner with food and drink on a large plate. I smiled at his approach.

"You will have to tell me how you do that one of these days." I said, taking a drink gratefully. Calum returned my smile, setting the tray next to us.

"Hmmm… do what?" A sly smile slid on his face, I rolled my eyes dramatically and turned to the food to enjoy the meats and bread given to us. Calum straightened his attire as he stood, which was a white shirt lined in gold thread. The front and back reached to his knees leaving a gap on the sides showing his black silk pants.

"King Anwyl requests your presence for the banquet tonight." Calum said looking at Faelan.

"We will have to wash than." Faelan said, starting to stand.

"Not the both of you. Just you." Calum said not hiding his displeasure from the message.

"I am charged with watching her, I cannot just leave her." He said, his jaw tight.

"I am only relaying the message, General." He said apologetically.

"I understand Calum, I will see to it." He said, looking in my direction.

"Morfran suggested she be brought back to the dungeon for the night." Calum added, my heart stopped for a moment and all I could see were those lifeless eyes watching me.

"No!" I said, far too loudly. Faelan's eyebrows frowned together.

"You are not going back down there." He said looking over to Calum. "Inform King Anwyl I will make sure she is secured for the evening and will join him at his table briefly as I have duties to attend to." Calum nodded and bowed.

"Of course." And left us alone in the training yard. Faelan growled deep, a low rumble sending shudders down my spine.

"That bastard is planning something tonight." Faelan's eyes glowed with anger. I waited a few moments before walking over in an attempt to take his mind off. I placed a hand on his forearm. My fingers lingered on his muscles, the feeling made my fingers tingle a little.

"How about a competition before we leave?" I said, nodding my head toward the targets. A sly smile crept up to his face.

"And what makes you think you can beat me." He replied.

"I never miss." I said winking at him before heading over to the bows searching for one suitable for me and grabbed a quiver. I could feel his gaze on me, 'the small enjoyments we gave ourselves makes me feel the rest is nothing' I thought.

25

Stepping on the mark, Faelan stood nearby, leaning against a wall. The target about seventy meters. We each had three arrows to shoot, the one with the closest to the middle wins. A slight breeze ruffled my hair, the feeling was pleasant bringing back fond memories of the Eleith. Drawing an arrow from the quiver I nocked it to the bow standing with my feet apart. I took a breath. Pulling my elbow back making the bow taut the bowstring steady next to my face. The feather from the arrow brushed my cheek. Excitement rolled through me as I focused on the target, keeping my eyes steady, with a small breath I let loose the first arrow. There was a thud, it sunk deep into the bullseye of the target. I smiled at myself, pleased my body remembered the feeling.

Glancing over, Faelan still stood leaning against the stone wall, his eyes intent, words formed on his lips but I couldn't not decipher them.

I tilted my head confused. Pushing off the wall he stood at his mark drawing his bow the muscles in his arms rippled from the strain. He let go, the arrow sorrowing with a silent whistle through the sky, landing with a thud in the center of his target. He looked over his shoulder at me, his eyes bright with anticipation.

"Your turn," he said.

I huffed and walked back to my spot, looking at the target. I readied my bow sending another arrow it went straight for the target piercing through my first arrow hitting the target. Faelan whistled at my shot then took his next shot I watched the same scene unfold before me. The arrow whistling through the air, landing through his first arrow the replica of my shot. He looked at me again now his eyes danced with amusement.

"Not bad if I say so myself." He said, leaning himself back on the wall. I shot him a death glare, which he responded with his hands up.

"Your idea." I took to my spot again taking my last arrow from the quiver, enjoying every moment, every movement I made for the shot. The feel of the bow and arrow savoring it. Releasing the arrow, it sorrowed past hitting through the second arrow leaving it in splinters. I looked at Faelan and gave him an innocent smile. Then sat myself on the ground and propped my hand up, leaning it against my face dramatically, waiting in anticipation. He shook his head while pushing off the wall again, seeming to be amused by my behavior.

Setting his feet in place, he pulled the last arrow from his quiver, nocking it to his bow. His jaw was firm, arms steady. He stretched his arm, dragging the bowstring with it. There was a small cracking sound, and the wood of the bow snapped in half, falling to pieces. The look on his face disbelieving. I roared with laughter at the sight of him standing there.

"Looks like I win by default." I said, still laughing. He looked over to me, his eyes seemed to say just you wait.

"They don't make them like they do in the Elemental Realm." He said shaking his head.

"When we reach your lands, we will have to have a rematch." I said, still shaking with laughter, wiping the tears from my eyes. He stared at me, face unreadable.

"When?" He asked.

I stopped laughing. And stood up, then brushed the dust off my legs.

"Why are you surprised? Didn't we agree to stick together?" I said, returning the bow from where it came.

"Yes. I mean, I know... I... just didn't... think about it." He said stammering over his words.

"Is it a problem?" I asked, staring at him.

"No." He said finally, but something hung in the air, something he wasn't telling me, and I could not help but believe it had something to do with his past.

Faelan was already walking up the stairs when I finished my thought, he paused a moment looking back at me, his expression unreadable.

"Coming?" He said stiffly and just like that the good feelings were gone. I followed him back to the room where we spent the night before. I washed all the dirt and sweat off from the day's training while Faelan stood by the fire manipulating its element deep in thought.

Before leaving, Faelan took a moment to clean. Considering all the training we did he barely broke a sweat. Washing his face and arms, he dressed for the evening with King Anwyl. I was cleaned and dressed in a simple white silk shirt, the neck cut in a V and sleeves reaching down slightly past my elbows. Black silk pants that grabbed around my ankles hanging loose off my legs. Passing back and forth in front of the fire, I chewed on my lower lip, thinking of what might come for me tonight. Faelan came out dressed in his usual leathers and blades strapped in their designated places.

My eyes drifted to him while he tied one of his wrists up, a cuff made of thick leather it covered the lower half of his forearm. He placed thin round metal objects into an unseen spot of the cuff, each metal glinted in the light, the tip sharp at the point. I stopped my pacing, shifting my gaze to the fire staring into them. Bottomless flames mesmerized me, making it hard to break contact. I spoke while trapped in those flames.

"What is the plan?" After a moment, Faelan's voice sounded far off in the distance when he spoke.

"You will remain here while I make an appearance with King Anwyl. Since I am sure Morfran is scheming, we will cover our bases." He said, a rattle sound of a chain came from his direction, I finally broke my hypnoses from the flames focusing on the metal shackle Faelan held in his hand. The Shackle had a long chain attached to it.

"What is that?" I said, not pleased with whatever he was thinking.

"Don't worry, you will only appear to being locked up. If he plans to make me appear incompetent and unable to secure you, he will probably force the King's hand. If he plans an attack while I am gone the shackle will be easy to remove." He showed me by removing a metal bolt from two holes, keeping it together. I glared at him, unhappy with his plan. His features softened from my expression. "I know it's not a great plan, but I must stay in the Kings favor. If I don't go or bring you with me, he will lose faith in me and as fond of me as he is, there are lines even I cannot cross. Defying the King is one of them, even if he is not my King."

I understood where he was coming from, but I was tired of being locked in chains, dropping my shoulders with a long sigh.

"Fine, let's get this over with." I slumped in the chair next to me, watching him cross the room, the chain dragging along the floor behind him. Kneeling next to me he took the shackle wrapped it over the silk pants I wore, inwardly grateful it was not touching my skin. Clamping it together and slipping the metal bolt through the two holes, securing it in place. His hand holding the back of my calf lingered while he brought his gaze up to me, desire filled those golden eyes. I felt his hand slide gently up my leg, never breaking contact. A shiver surged up my leg and my heartbeat picked up in response. I searched his face, taking in his features the raw attractiveness would take any woman's breath away.

He dared continuing to move his hand along my leg reaching up to the middle of my thigh. Then bracing it against the back of the chair. His knee pressed against the cushion between my legs. Moving his other hand up brushing his thumb along my jaw, his fingers reaching across my neck entangling them in my hair. I could feel the tips of his fingers caress the back of my neck, my body trembled from his touch.

Keeping his eyes locked on mine his face moved closer daring me to stay, my eyes closed as his lips touched mine. My mouth remembered those soft lips instantly, breaking contact for a moment he pulled away just enough to search my eyes. The look in his were full of craving, a need as though I could quench it for him. Letting out a small breath he closed them from sight and moved in continuing where we left off.

His fingers on my neck pressed in while his mouth gently yet decisively moved, taking my lips with his. His tongue lightly brushed against my lower lip sending a shiver surging throughout my body, gently grabbing my hair where his fingers entwined, he gently withdrew, leaving my neck exposed. Heart hammering against my chest, I felt a brush against my neck as his lips roamed further down, caressing it with his canines. Without realizing my mouth parted open, a breath escaped me, leaving an unfamiliar sound rushing out. A low rumble reverberated from Faelan's throat in response. My toes curled at the sound, making it hard to think.

A small knock on the door had Faelan releasing me instantly and out of reach, his expression torn as if weighing his options. He ran a hand through his hair closing his eyes momentarily when they opened, he seemed to have come to a decision. I leaned back in the chair, catching a breath from what had just transpired, my heart still beating loudly. Faelan walked to the door he opened it slightly Calum was the one on the other side he spoke briefly bowed and then gone again. Closing the door, Faelan stared at me a moment before speaking.

"It's time." He said running another hand through his hair "I won't be gone long..." he paused for a moment. "Stay in the light." He warned before leaving me alone, disheveled and flustered.

Running my hands down my thighs, I rubbed them trying to shake away the sensation but everywhere he touched felt as if it left a mark. The room was quiet with Faelan gone, it seemed more empty than usual. I remained in the chair watching the room, checking for things that may lurk in the shadows every so often.

After a while I calmed my nerves, snuggling in the chair next to the fire, the chain following my movements. Returning my gaze to the fire, mesmerized by the way its flames flickered.

26

I didn't realize I had fallen asleep when I woke to the fire gone, no heat remained in the hearth. It looked stone cold, as if there was never any fire to begin with.

I froze...

A feeling crept up my spine, that cold uncomfortable darkness lurking nearby. Looking around the room without moving a muscle, I searched for its place. My heart stopped when my gaze froze on those lifeless eyes standing in the open doorway it locked on noticing my search. In a heartbeat he moved, the way he walked was off, uneven, and disfigured almost, I grabbed at my shackle with shaking hands. Trying to get my fingers to hold tight to the bolt and pull it free from its notches, but it refused to let lose its grip.

He made his way to me, mumbling incoherently as he went. I tugged hard and a sharp pain shot through my knuckles blood sprouted from my hand after it slipped scraping over the shackle. Graa suddenly froze, staring in my direction lifting his chin up sniffing the air dropping his head back down even in the dark I could see his eyes go wild.

"BLOOD!" He yelled a deep haunting roar that made my entire body quake. He bolted for me far faster than a man his size should have been capable. I leapt from the chair diving from his pursuit just before he crashed into the chair smashing it against the wall.

I swallowed looking at his figure on all fours turning his head to me, those eyes hungry. I could almost make out saliva spilling from behind the bars of his mask.

"BLOOD!" He roared again. Crawling backwards, I tried to get my footing to stand up, he dashed for me on all fours in an inhuman speed. Gripping the blankets on the bed I yanked myself upward, rolling backwards onto the bed. He slammed into the side, making a loud rumble that should have woken anyone sleeping in the castle.

Leaping over him I ran for the door, only to be stopped when a sharp pain cracked in my ankle, screaming out, I fell to the floor. I cursed aloud remembering the shackle still latched to me. Reaching down to search for the bolt again fear gripped me when I was pulled suddenly by the chain. I looked back, Graa stood one hand on the chain, the other reaching for more to pull me closer. I grabbed at the floor frantically trying hard to latch on to anything, trying to keep away from him.

He pulled me one arm length at a time, all the while speaking to himself.

"Blood.... Blood.... Blood." My heart hammered so loudly I couldn't manage my own thoughts. Sausage fingers draped around my lower calf, as my hand ran past something hard grabbing it, I twisted and swung as hard as I could at his head screaming in defiance. The object shattered against Graa, unfazed as he latched his meaty hand onto my skull and lifted me off the ground, my feet dangling I could hear the chain rattling beneath.

Gripping at his hand, I tried tearing and clawing, anything to get him to let go. The pressure of my head was becoming intense, it felt crushing. I thought any second now my head will crumble, and we would see just how well I can come back to life. A large rough hot wet feeling run along my hand, I shuddered realizing he was licking the blood off my hand.

"Blood... Blood." He said over and over licking the flowing blood from my knuckles. Disgust rose I would have hurled had my head not been smothered by his overly large hand.

Suddenly I felt a swift motion next to me, the pressure on my head released and I hit the ground hard. Screams exploded in front of me as Graa roared clutching his arm, half of his forearm missing. No, not missing it laid on the ground just before me, its fingers twitching blood pooled the floor. Faelan stood just to the right, blade in hand pointing to the ground, Graa's blood dripping from it. Furry emanated off him, a glow resounded to life as the surrounding air went still.

I watched frozen by his ability to shift the air, Graa fell to his knees, one hand gripping his throat fighting to breathe. All the while keeping his cold eyes on me staring down at the blood dripping off my knuckles. If he could speak, I believe, it would still be the same words he'd already been repeating. I waited for him to fall over, those lifeless eyes, to no longer have any movement in them. But they remained staring, haunting me even now as life drifted from him. A blue flame erupted, engulfing his figure entirely. The heat emanating from it so intense my body felt as if I had a fever. When the flames finally died out there was nothing left of the soulless Graa.

Not a moment later guards flooded into the room surrounding us, Commander Drask coming in behind them, I remained where I sat unmoving. Faelan wiped his blade clean then sheathing it behind his back he knelt in front of me examining my head, then my hands, then he removed the shackle. His fingers moved swiftly and quietly, making one easy tug on the bolt. The clattering to the ground was heavy and loud.

"What is the meaning of this?" Commander Drask demanded, "you mind explaining yourself." He pointed a finger in Faelan's direction. Although he made himself appear surprised by the scene, everything in me said he knew very well what had happened here.

"I disposed of an intruder Commander" Faelan said standing to his feet. The guards held their weapons out like they were prepared to defend themselves.

"An intruder?" Commander Drask sounded appalled, looking at the fresh arm laying on the floor next to me.

"He came into MY quarters, Commander. He came to take the life of the prisoner I am charged with. To murder her while I was away, summoned by the King. I dealt with it in the manner I saw fit." Faelan said not bothered by all the guards surrounding us, the once large room felt extremely small.

"She will be in my..."

"No!" Faelan said cutting Commander Drask off, his voice commanding, "She will remain under my custody. If you have a problem with this, then take it up with your *master*." Faelan said, emphasizing the word master in a mocking tone. Reaching his arm out to me, I took it without hesitation and allowed him to pull me to my feet. Commander Drask was fuming but Faelan showed no sign of caring. "Send someone to clean in here before we return." Faelan commanded. "Excuse us, Commander." With a push on my lower back he led us out of the lion's den.

We walked at a fast pace, I did my best to keep up but with my ankle injured it was difficult, I limped next to him, if he noticed he didn't show it. I decided not to make a point to bring it up. I didn't want him to believe it was his job to heal every little scratch or bruise left on me.

"What happened?" He said his anger seething after we had taken a few turns, leaving the guards behind us.

"I... think... I think he tried to eat me." I said, remembering the feel of his tongue on my knuckles. Faelan halted in the middle of a small quart yard the moon lit up the area making everything glow with a blue tint. A small square fountain sat in the middle with white roses on each corner. There was a bench for every side of the fountain and two pedestals on either side of the benches.

"I cut my hand fighting to get the shackle off than he went crazy yelling about blood repeatedly." I said, the image still fresh in my mind. I looked over my shoulder sure it would still be standing in the shadow, its eyes hunting me. Faelan brought a hand to my face, gently bringing my gaze back to him.

"We must see the King and explain what happened, do not mention the darkness that consumed him. King Anwyl does not know of the darkness lurking in every corner. I'd be surprised if he even knew it is this close. We do not want him to believe you insane before even getting the chance to prove yourself." Faelan pressed his lips to my forehead, "I thought I would not make it." He said through my hair, backing away from him slightly I gave him a kind smile.

"Shall we meet with King Anwyl?" He nodded in agreement, and we continued our way to see him.

27

The night was cold the brisk air kissed at my skin leaving me feeling exposed more than usual. My fingers gently brushed against his, the touch electrifying. I glanced in his direction as we went, his jaw was tight eyes forward the look of a warrior, not just any warrior however, one of renown. He has been many places most would not dare to even speak of. How I longed to hear those stories, even be a part of them.

Limping next to him, I thought to myself about how I had died once and still hadn't mentioned this small detail to him. Honestly, I wasn't even sure if it would work a second time, so I decided to keep it a secret a while longer. Maybe it wasn't right to long to hear of him if I wasn't willing to share myself. I pushed the thoughts away for another time.

The King was not in his chambers, which surprised me, the room we walked in was not bed chambers. We stood outside double doors, two guards stood on either side. One held a sword to his side, it had a tassel signifying he held a high command like Drask.

"We wish to have an audience with the King." Faelan spoke to him.

"It is late for an audience General." He replied. The man was older maybe by ten years to me.

"If it wasn't urgent I wouldn't be here. Cynwrig." He kept his shoulders square and waited for the guard to reply. Cynwrig sagged his shoulders than leaned in to open the door.

"You're the only one I would let pass at this hour." He said than glanced at me.

"It concerns her. She will be coming with." Faelan didn't ask. Cynwrig looked at him skeptically then, glanced at me again worry lining his features. "She is no threat to him." Faelan reassured him. Cynwrig's shoulders sagged again then opened the doors.

"If it was anyone else Faelan, you would be on the ground and in shackles."

"I wouldn't expect it any other way." Faelan clapped him on the shoulder and pulled me along with him. Large, tall shelves lined in several rows all beautifully crafted with intricate designs. Inside the shelves lay hundreds of parchments, scrolls neatly rolled up and put away. This room was the library where they kept their knowledge. I froze for a moment taking in the sight, windows cut out of the wall high between each shelf allowing the moonlight to stream in. Benches and chairs littered the room, some together surrounding stone tables, others separate. The two guards that were standing with the King before were the ones standing next to him now as he leaned over a table candlelight next to him. Torches hung at the end of each row of shelves, lighting the room.

Faelan grabbed my hand pulling me out of my amazement he looked at my face a smile touched his lips realizing why I stopped.

"Later," he said, tugging me forward. The guards just now noticing us enter the room stood in a defensive position ready to fight. Faelan released my hand, raising his in the air. "I am here to ask for an audience with the King," he said calmly, King Anwyl recognized his voice immediately lifted his head, eyes bright from the sight of Faelan. The light died however when his sights caught me.

"What is it you need at this hour, General?" He said displeased, I was not sure why he disliked me so. I mean, other than the obvious curse.

"There was an intruder in my chambers, I came to inform you." Faelan continued, "it was while I was joining you for dinner the intruder attacked the prisoner you gave me charge over." The King pursed his lips together.

"And why would you need to inform me?" He asked.

"Because I disposed of the intruder myself. He was aslo one of your men from the dungeons." The King's face finally showed concern.

"I see." He said, Faelan looked to me to continue. I kept my tone respectful and even as I recounted what happened, I never took my gaze from his. I explained how he had kept a close eye on me when I was in the dungeons and did not think he would come above in search of me. The Kings face looked horrified from my story and concern woven into his face. He was a kind king it seemed. His distaste of me was most likely Morfran's doing. He probably filled the little King's head with horrid stories of how I am the only reason his people suffer so.

"That is truly shocking." He said rubbing a hand on his neck.

"Forgive me King Anwyl for not keeping better watch, I will keep a closer eye on her." Faelan said as if the fault lay with him. He nodded his head.

"Yes, yes. Well, her trial is in the morning you will not have to keep watch for long." He said bringing his gaze back to me. "I do not know if you truly are the reason for the disasters happening in my lands. But if you pass the trial by fire tomorrow, I will forgive any charges against you." The Eleith pressed on me.

I responded to the King with a bow, lowering my head to him.

"I am grateful for you giving me the chance instead of an immediate execution that some of your advisor's wished for. You are a wise and gentle King who cares for his people I can see that now." I finished, raising my head up, watching him stand in astonishment from my behavior. Recovering from his shock, giving me a slight bow to the head.

"I wish you luck tomorrow and may the fire judge you fairly." He said, then motioned for his guards to escort him out of the room.

After he left, my body remembered the pain in my ankle and I slumped down on the bench closest to me, letting out a long sigh I closed my eyes. Faelan scooped me up, carrying me in between his arms.

"What are you doing?" I protested.

"Just be quiet you can barely walk, anyway." He continued walking ignoring my protests.

"Whose fault is it I can barely walk." I said a little miffed.

"Yes, the shackle was a bad plan." He said, his face returning to a haunted look. "I will fix you up when we get to another room. Returning to that one would not be wise. I had Calum prepare another one just in case something like this happened." He walked in a steady pace, never jostling me as he moved. I relaxed my head on his shoulder, the heat coming from his body was soothing chasing away the shadows that lurked around us.

The room was much smaller than the last one we stayed, still it was better than the dungeons. Faelan lit the torches with his element, lighting up the room as we walked in. There was only one window on the opposite wall from the door, a small fireplace to the left with chairs near it and a small bed to the right. The walls were made of stone, just like the rest of the castle. He set me in a chair next to the fire Faelan's eyes glowed bright as the pleasant warmth flooded around my ankle.

"How do you do that?" I asked, mesmerized by his radiant golden eyes.

"Secret." He said with a half-smile, moving his gaze to mine. I crossed my arms, leaning back in the chair.

"Hmm." I returned my own half-smile. The pain I once had disappeared along with the many wounds Faelan had healed in the few weeks we spent together.

I laid in the bed watching Faelan remain next to the fire, his gaze seemed far away as he stared in the distance. My eyelids grew heavy, soon I was fast asleep dreaming of the pleasant dream souring through the sky, Faelan in hand free of any darkness or looming death.

I woke to the gentle feeling of Faelan brushing his fingers over the side of my face pushing back my hair tucking it behind my ear. My heart thumped at the touch, unable to conceal it, a slight smile hinted at my lips, a soft sigh left me as I opened my eyes.

The colors were rich streaming in from the window, the light just before the sun came over the horizon. A deep red with creamy oranges and yellows mixed, swelling the room with its radiance. Faelan's outline shadowed by the beautiful colors, even with my impending Trial by Fire I could not help but be amazed by the brilliance of first light.

Taking a moment to soak it all in, I quietly thanked the Eleith then stretched my limbs while preparing every aspect for what may await me in a moment. I dressed in simple black leathers a small light green shirt that fit my form comfortably, the sleeves stopped just passed my shoulders. My dark brown boots came just above my ankles, the extra leather folded over the sides. There would be no weapons for me until I completed my task, and even then, it would be debatable.

Faelan armed to the teeth in his usual leathers and vest, he approached me with a commanding presence, I was taken aback from the sight. I've often forgotten how truly fearsome he is. There was a knock on the door, Faelan put his hand on the handle before he opened the door. He looked down at me, ran his knuckles gently across my cheek. Leaning in he brushed his soft lips over mine, my mouth twitched burning for more.

He pulled back, "Are you ready?" He said eyes searching mine. Giving him a nod, his fingers fell from my face and the door opened with Calum and several Guards behind him waiting to escort me to the Trial by Fire.

28

The walk was long, and quiet, only the sounds of our steps echoed through the halls of the castle. We passed many areas some familiar, some new, very few servants scurried around as we passed. The buzz of royals nowhere to be seen. We came to a long hall of stone, the ceiling arched over our heads eight or nine feet above us. Well, mine at least since I stood at least a foot shorter than the tallest guard who stood just above Faelan's height.

You could see bright light shine at the other end of the stone walls as we walked, the light came in brighter. Calum stopped just before the entry and looked over to Faelan giving him a nod telling him to proceed ahead. I am sure if it was anyone else, Faelan would not have left so easily. I watched his back as his figure disappeared into the light.

Calum turned to me, his eyes steady, "After we enter you will have until the fire goes out to complete your trial. You will have three tasks. I wish you luck." He said and turned away from me walking into the light.

I continued forward with the guards, my eyes squinted at the bright light shining on us from the sun. It was brighter than usual today, the sky a clear blue, the ray of sun chased away any chill in the air. We stood outside before a large stadium reaching further than the throne room. People filled the seats; I could see there was no empty spot throughout the ring of seats circling the arena. The people speaking among themselves was a low rumble as they waited for my trial, as though it was a sport for their amusement.

We stood on a platform above the ground beyond the platform ditches dug out in the ground parallel to one another, leaving a six-foot walkway. It led to a larger circular area which led to two more opened areas stretched out each arena surrounded by the ditches. The ditches were filled with large amounts of wood piled just above where they began there was no space unfilled. My hands twitched at my sides; my legs restless. I scanned the arena, searching until my eyes stopped on the young King sitting in a seat above the platform high enough to see the entire arena. Faelan stood next to him the snake like advisor's sat in seats on the other side of the King.

Morfran then stepped up and clapped his hands. The sound loud enough the people throughout the stadium became quiet. All eyes on him.

"People of Thornden, you have all come here to bear witness to the Trial by Fire! We are here to watch the Cursed One go through the trials and face them to prove her innocence! She is to complete three tasks before the flames around the arena die out! Now I hope you are ready Cursed One!" Morfran finished speaking looking down at me, a sly smile plastered on his face.

King Anwyl looked to Faelan gave him a short nod giving him the go ahead. I watched as he stepped forward, eyes blazing to life. A roar filled the air and blue flames erupted from the piles of wood starting just before me. It moved like a wave flowing down the line, racing past the people awing at the sight of fire illuminating the whole area. I kept my eyes on Faelan as the beautiful glow died out of his eyes.

"Begin!" was all the young King said to me before I ran forward straight past the flames into my first set of trial.

The heat from the flames radiated instantly, I stood in the first open area waiting for the first trial to reveal itself. The blue flames danced around me, heat flickering off its tips into the air. The ground below me began to rumble, it suddenly cracked open. I dove forward, leaping over a gaping hole so far down you could not see where it ends. The ground continued to quake, opening other various spots leading down to the depths of darkness. I leapt from one spot to another, trying to stay ahead of the gouges formed deep into the earth.

I could hear the mass of people making cheers and boos at my every move. Distracted, my foot slipped just as I leapt over the next gap I fell into the whole.

Panic hit me, staring down into the dark abyss.

Flinging my arms out reaching for the other side of the rock frantic. My heart pounded as I grabbed for the side of the wall, fingers digging into the rock. Pain pierced through my nerves as one of my nails tore off from the impact. Wincing, I kept a death hold on the side of rock taking deep breaths calming myself and willed my hands and feet to stay steady. I racked my brain, searching for any kind of hole or rock sticking from the ground to reach onto. It looked as though I was four feet from the surface.

I caught sight of a thick root jutting from the ground just above my head. Taking hold, I tested it to see if it would hold. Slowly I pulled, putting more weight on the root. When I felt it would stay firm, I pulled myself up. Looking for another source of anchor I held tight to the root. The ground rumbled around me as I continued my search. Using my free hand, I felt for a hole that was big enough for me to grip. To my relief there was one at the edge of my reach. Taking hold of it I felt the strain on my whole arm as I used all my strength to pull up. Bracing on the root I pushed up with one arm while pulling with the other. 'don't look down.' I told myself while my feet fought to lose grip on the side of the wall. A rock just above the hole caught my eye and I pushed off the root to take hold of it. Replacing my hand with my foot on the root.

I hung there with one foot up and the other dangling below with no footing and a death grip with both hands. I took a heaving breath and let my forehead rest against the rock. It was only a matter of time before my fingers would lose purchase and I would fall. I shook the uncertainty and went for the next spot. Pulling my body up I found another hole with ease. Thankful the closer I got to the surface the more places there were to grab hold of. My fingers trembled fiercely and my arms shook.

"Keep going." I whispered, another spot, another pull, "almost there." I grunted out the last word. So close to the top I raised my hand over the edge and slammed it on to solid ground I could feel the heat from the flames course over my skin.

I reached the top.

Using every bit of will I pulled my head up above the crack, the ground rumble with the roar of the crowd cheering. Holding firm, I heaved the rest of my body over lying flat on my back, I tried to take control of my heavy breathing. I closed my eyes. I felt the tremble of my arms from the over exertion. Staring at the bright blue sky, it looked distorted from the heat of the fire surrounding me. Pushing myself off the ground, I looked back, where the ground once stood level was left with craters and holes tore into it.

Taking another deep breath, I shook my arms and moved past the flames to the next open area for my second task. The sweat dripped down the side of my face, running along my neck and disappearing into my shirt. I walked into the open area scanning round looking for what could be against me this round. I took one step and felt a crushing weight suddenly hit me, knocking me to my hands and knees. I felt the rocks press into my skin, dig in deep as the weight continued to press down. I looked for the source of this pressure and found nothing. Realization dawned on me remembering what Faelan told me of Morfran the night before.

"Sorcerer," I said under my breath. As if he heard me speak the biggest smile spread across Morfran's face. I tore my gaze from him and focused on the task at hand. My heart hammered in my chest as the flames that had danced so freely had dwindled to a smaller flame. Pushing up with all my strength I slowly pushed back up to my feet, the weight on me felt suffocating. Taking another step my foot barely left the ground, the exit of the area suddenly felt miles away. Licking my dry lips, my throat parched as I tried to swallow it felt like dirt. I took another step. Each step felt heavier I was starting to just drag my feet along the dirt.

Another step.

Then another.

Shifting my feet along the dirt, my muscles strained to keep going. I felt the burn from the overuse of each limb. It felt like hours had passed when in reality it was only a few minutes. The end was so close, only a couple more paces away.

The pressure suddenly became unbearable, and I crumpled to the ground. The mass of people gasped at the sight of me hitting the ground.

I coughed on the dust that slid into my mouth.

Pushing up again, my arms shook from the strain. I forced myself to focus on the end of this trial and took a shaky hand forward. My fingers screaming with each grip in the dirt as I pulled my body along the ground. Keeping steady I took another crawling step, inching forward one hand after another. The dirt, sweat, and blood mixed over my skin as I moved along the ground with force, not stopping for anything.

My hand reached into the next narrow path and the weight suddenly lifted. I moved and sat still on my hands and knees breathing, heavy drops of sweat sliding off my nose dripping into the dirt before me. I looked up to where the King sat, Morfran stood beside him, his eyes looked triumphant. I noticed the flames were much lower and got up. I had one more task to complete and this I would face a champion. Rushing, I felt much lighter after the heavyweight suppressed me.

Morfran's voice rang out above the noise of the crowd. All went silent, "YOU HAVE FARED WELL CURSED ONE! YOU WILL FACE YOUR LAST TRIAL. YOU MUST FACE THE CHAMPION OF OUR CHOOSING AND RENDER HIM IMMOBILE BEFORE THE FLAMES DIE OUT! AND FROM THE LOOK OF THE FIRE, I WOULD SAY YOU HAVE TEN MINUTES!" He said with that never ending smile on his lips.

By the time he was done talking, I reached the last opened area. I stopped just before entering my anger seething at the sight of Commander Drask standing in the center waiting for me. He had a sinister smile on his face. This was the first time I saw him without armor over his chest or weapons at his side. He was in regular clothes black with a deep red line running down the center of his sleeves.

My cursed eye roared.

My fingers twitching at my sides, itching to grip his throat until the last breath left his mouth.

"You ready to be humiliated, wench." He said standing ready. I was barely aware of the roaring crowd cheering for the Commander, telling him to finish me quickly. I stepped into the threshold, moved towards him in a slight crouch, watching his moves for any attack.

"Times ticking cursed whore I only have to stand here, and you lose." He said relaxing his stance mocking me. But he was right, time was not on my side and instead of evading him they changed the rules making it impossible for me to win.

Or so they thought.

I dashed.

Full speed, I went straight for him. I didn't slow, his eyes assessed my movements still standing not fazed from my speedy approach.

He brought his fist up to meet me as I ran in. Instead of connecting with it, I ducked under the swing. Took the chance and slammed my fist into his gut once. Twisted around I slid past him, turning to come face to face with his sinister smile. He threw another punch in my direction I leaned to the left as it swiped past my face. I moved with ease, keeping just out of his reach. He threw punches in every direction. my pulse rose from every attack. I stayed steady, looking for another opening while dodging the rest.

He landed a blow at the back of my shoulder in the middle of an attempt to evade. I hit the ground rocks embedded in my skin and scrambled to get up before he was upon me. Sliding out of reach just as he bulldozed by.

"Tick-tick, wench." He said between clenched teeth. I could see the rage radiate off him. I glanced, noticing the fire barely a flicker off the wood. I didn't have longer than five minutes.

I stopped and looked straight at him.

"What's the matter Commander, am I too fast for you?" I cocked my head to one side, knowing he couldn't help but take the bait. "Oh, that's right you're only good at beating on others when they're tied down. The pathetic kind of man who can only handle someone when their weak. No wonder Faelan sees you as nothing more than a filthy dog." His face turned bright red.

It wasn't but a few seconds until he let out a hoarse laugh.

"It's over." He said coming at me in rage. I latched my hands round his right hand just as he went to strike. I twisted with all my strength, pulling it over my shoulder as I pushed my body against him. I moved with speed I didn't believe I was capable of and launched his entire body over my head, he landed with a heavy thump. Pulling his arm around I twisted it around, bending his hand backward. Then placed my foot on his shoulder and pressed down hard.

I waited as he struggled for a moment beneath me. Knowing I beat him, he remained still, trying I suppose not to appear humiliated. I interlaced my fingers with his, squeezed tight and bent them back until the snap echoed around us. His body convulsed from the pain, a short yell escaped his mouth. I leaned down watching the angry rage in his eyes, the look of what he would do if he ever got his hands on me.

Putting my hand on his thumb I spoke, "Your right hand, correct? Remember. I warned you." Then snapped his thumb, I heard no sound from the crowd of people watching us in the arena. Honestly, I didn't care being the bad guy was something I was good at. Morfran clapped again the sound resonated throughout the arena.

"The Trial by Fire is finished. The Cursed One has passed all tasks." King Anwyl said stepping in front of Morfran who appeared to be displeased being pushed to the back. I dropped Commander Drask's hand and stepped away.

29

My body shook.

I sat in a dark corner, out of sight of all the people raging in their seats, from the results of my trial far behind me. As soon as the King announced I passed my trial, I left the arena not waiting for an escort.

Leaving Commander Drask furious on the ground after I snapped his fingers. I found Faelan waiting for me on the other side of the long tunnel, eyes ever watching as I approached. We left the area and headed to a small place tucked away while I tried to regain my bearings, he stood with his back to me keeping an eye out.

"What now?" I asked my arms on my legs, skin still hot from the massive flames that had surrounded me.

"You rest. And we wait." He said glancing back in my direction. I slumped back, the cool stone felt wonderful on my feverish skin. "Why did you break his fingers?" He asked curiously. I looked at him with an emotionless expression.

"I wanted to make sure he knew I'd keep my promises." My tone level.

"The people are angry, most of them look at him as a hero here." He said eyes careful.

"The ones who know otherwise will not hate me. And I am not here for the wealthy. The sooner I leave here the better." I said looking at my hands, the feeling starting to come back to them, my fingertips screaming at me for my little climbing stunt earlier.

"Let's get you cleaned up." Faelan reached under my elbow and gently pulled me towards him. The touch alone made me shiver.

I let him lead me out and we walked back in silence to our room keeping to the shadows and out of sight. The room was clean, a bowl of water sat on the table with the surrounding chairs. Strips of white cloth laying just beside it.

"I assumed you would have needed mending after." He said to me with a side look. I sighed.

"I suppose I do." Looking down at my bleeding fingers, the one with the missing nail still throbbing. We both sat together at the table, he then took hold of my hand and examined the fingers whistling.

"You do nothing halfway, do you." I tugged my hand away.

"Well, it was that or tumble into the abyss below." I said annoyed.

"Relax Shae." He said, tearing the strips of white cloth into smaller pieces. I watched as his eyes brightened, the rich gold radiating a halo around his deep pupil. Steam rose from the water as he heated the bowl of water. He laid his hand out before me and nodded at me encouragingly. The annoyance melted away as I placed my hand into his palm and observed as he took a cloth. He dipped some extra cloth into the steaming water and gently started brushing the blood and dirt off my fingers one by one.

It stung when the heat touched the open scrapes and cuts. "No healing magic?" I asked.

"No, it is custom to allow your body to heal... naturally. It is also part of the trial. Although the people here are unaware, I will still follow the traditions of my realm. In their eyes it is finished." He said brushing my fingers his skin was smooth over my dirty and rough hands. Considering he was a warrior, his hands were quite soft. Or maybe mine were just that callused.

After he wiped the blood and dirt away Faelan took the thinner pieces of cloth and wrapped each finger covering the tips. When he was done my fingers looked as if small white caps sat at the end of my fingertips. He knelt before me and unlaced the leather cords of my boots gripping the back of my calf, he lifted my leg and dragged my boot off. Then reached behind my other leg and did the same. Rolling each pant leg up above my knees, his fingers grazing over my skin leaving a lingering feeling of heat in every spot.

My pulse rose from his touch.

Blood crusted along my legs from the little gashes in my knees when rocks had embedded into my skin. He took another clean cloth and cleaned each knee just as gently as he was with my hands, wiping away all the blood and dirt.

"I will prepare the bath for you to clean the rest of yourself. I can call a servant to come in and help you wash." He said getting up and disappearing into the washroom.

He reappeared and vanished once again leaving me alone in the room without another word. Fumbling over my clothes, I attempted to remove my garments without help. Mostly because I wasn't fond of someone helping me remove my clothes. It was hard without the full use of my fingertips. I gripped the clothes in between my palm and inner fingers. I cursed every time I bumped the tip sending a shooting pain through my nerves and up my arm.

After what seemed like an eternity, I finished removing all my clothes, tossing them to the side. I went directly into the steaming water, careful not to place my newly bandaged fingers in it. Sinking deep in the hot water, it stung my knees for a moment, then the pain subsided. I leaned my head to the back of the tub, my arms laying along the sides, hands dangling on the outsides. Closing my eyes, I breathed deep and slow, soaking in the comfort the water always brought me.

It was only a few minutes of peace and quiet until I heard the door open and close. The steps walking in my direction gradually getting louder as they approached. I waited, knowing who those familiar steps belonged.

Keeping my eyes closed.

"Were there no servants available?" I asked Faelan as his footsteps stopped just behind me. "None that I could trust." He said, his voice low, gruff. I glanced up at him, his eyes were cast to the side. "Will you help me?" I asked, glancing over to the oils and cleansers. He looked down at me, his eyes held a look of craving.

"I don't think that is a good idea." He said looking me over. Sitting in the water. My heart thundered just from him, observing.

I swallowed.

Looking away I leaned forward, gripping the sides of the tub. "I think your rig…" He touched my shoulder, stopping me mid-sentence.

Brushing his fingers over my skin he pulled my hair along with his hand dragging it across my shoulder blades draping it over my other shoulder. His finger gently ran up to the back of my neck, my entire body quivered from his touch. The smell of lavender filled the room, a cold liquid poured down the center of my back causing my body to shudder. He gripped the back of my neck moving his fingers in a circular motion pressing them into my skin.

My head rolled back into his working fingers.

I suppressed the groan of pleasure rising in my throat, threatening to escape my lips. His other hand pressed in on my shoulder and he began massaging the oil over my skin. Although his touch was warm, it left a chill over my skin leaving small bumps along my arms. His hands moved gently, kneading along my back.

My pulse sped and my breathing picked up.

My mind could only focus on the pleasant feeling rising within me as he continued to rub his hands along my back. My lips parted and my eyes closed, enjoying every moment of his strong fingers running over me. He brought his hands to my head and started running his fingers through my hair, tugging it back to the center of my back again. More lavender aromas filled the air as he rubbed through my hair, cupping water in his hands to soak my head.

Running his fingers along my arms, his grip tightened, I felt him lean in next to my ear.

"I think this is enough." His voice rough and low, a tremor ran down my neck from the sound and feel of breath on my ear.

He let go.

I heard his steps leaving the door open then closed and silence.

My Fingers were numb from clutching the tub the entire time. My heart raced as heat filled throughout my entire being from his touch.

I craved for more.

30

I had spent the rest of the day alone in the room left with my thoughts to myself and the feeling of Faelan lingered with me the entire day. I cursed myself for being so foolish to ask him to help me. I could have managed just fine myself, I mulled over and over what had possessed me to do something so daft.

It was dark by the time Faelan returned to the room. Calum came in behind him. He carried a tray full of food. My stomach rumbled at the sight of it, knowing it hadn't been fed the entire day. I smiled at Calum who returned one to me.

"I'm shocked Morfran even allowed you near me." I said looking over the splendid food sitting on the table before me.

"Yes, well, he still wants to keep an eye on you. And I am the best way to do so." He said with no smile.

"I am grateful for the food. Yours is always delicious." I said taking a bite of bread savoring the buttery flavor. He sat down at the table with me, giving me an affectionate smile. You wouldn't think he was only fourteen from how he acted. The boy was more mature than most men, ten years older than him. Faelan stood by the fire, keeping to himself. I glanced in his direction briefly, then went back to the food. "Is there anything I should know while I'm waiting?" I asked aloud.

Calum put down his plate of food and looked serious once again. "Morfran has something planned. I don't yet know what it is, he never reveals his most important plans to me. But he is not as angry as he should be considering you have beat him and turned down his offer." Chewed on a piece of meat, the taste was mouthwatering leaving me wanting more. "

"I can imagine he has something up his sleeve. That smooth talking snake is the type to scheme several plots at once." I said not bothered by Calum's warning.

"In the meantime, will I get my weapons back since I am no longer a prisoner? I'm getting lonely without them." Faelan cleared his throat from where he stood. I blushed from remembering our earlier incident.

"Is something the matter?" Calum asked, reaching over he touched my forehead with his hand. I looked up at him.

"No, I am fine. Just. A little hot." Fanning my face like it would help.

Faelan approached the table, he reached over me brushing his skin over my shoulder grabbing bread for himself. His half smile in full view. I leaned away from his touch, annoyed just the very contact had my nerves reeling.

The bastard was playing with me.

"When we are summoned by the King you can speak with him about your weapons." Faelan said, walking round to the other side of the table. "We can train each day for the time being, Commander Drask almost got the best of you. With the display you made of him in the arena, he is sure to be aiming for you." He said, his eyes careful. I snorted.

"That bastard has been on my neck since the day I met him." The taste of my food suddenly felt bad, and I pushed my plate away from me leaning back in my chair, crossing my arms over my chest.

"We are not trying to make you angry, Shae." Calum said gently. "You have a lot of enemies, and you have to watch your back constantly. We are just trying to help." I glanced over at Faelan his golden eyes were dark, darker than their normal radiant gold.

"We can leave as soon as we meet the King, and you get your possessions back." Faelan stated.

"No." I said without hesitation. "We have to stay longer, there's... something I must do here." I said, my thoughts returning to my dream a few nights ago. "The King is in danger. You both know it just as well as I do." I stood from the chair and walked over to the fireplace. I sensed their eyes on me, assessing my every move both with a different meaning.

"Then we will remain here." Faelan said, glancing over to Calum. "Looks like we will be in your care a while longer Calum." Faelan said, bowing his head slightly. Calum smiled gently, a slight pain shown in his eyes.

"I will keep my eyes and ears even more sharp. I will help you in any way I can. I have a few spies of my own Morfran is unaware of. It's amazing what loyalty comes with kindness." He said smiling to himself.

"Be careful Calum. Morfran will watch you just as carefully as he is us. You need not put your neck on the line for me." I said, gazing in his direction. He nodded in response.

"It is getting late I will excuse myself for the night. I will bring word when the King summons you." And with that, he left us alone.

I sat by the fire in my fine silk clothes, a beautiful jade shirt and black pants it fit my form nicely. Faelan lingered by the table a few more moments before he came to my side.

"We should change your bandages." He said setting a bowl of water next to me. He held his hand out waiting for me to give him mine, I gave it to him without complaint. Gently he touched my hand, his thumb pressing into my palm, his fingers easily reached over my hand. I looked up watching as he concentrated on taking off the bandages one after another, my fingers felt lighter after it was removed.

His strong jaw relaxed as he focused, his lips parted, air flowing in and out between the smooth surface. Shadows flickered across his face from the flame beside us. His eyes sparked to life as he leaned over the bowl of water, steam beginning to rise from it. Taking my hand, he dipped my fingertips in, they stung from the hot water.

Stealing another glance from under my lashes, Faelan was staring down at me. I retreated quickly, my heart pounding from being caught. He put my hand on my knee and reached for the other one.

"I have been meaning to ask you." He began. I looked back to him, watching as he pulled the cloth off each finger once again. "Where did you get that line in the middle of your chest?" He asked, stopping his hands to look at me.

"Line?" I returned his gaze confused. "What line?" He brought a finger to the middle of my chest, right where my heart was located, running his finger down slightly.

"Right here." He said the feeling of his finger laying there sent a thrill through me. "I noticed when you came into the throne room. You couldn't hide much, there were scars on your back from Drask since I am not able to fully heal. But this one looked different. It's not quite a scar, it's lighter, not exactly white, it's hard to see. You have to be looking to see. But where did you receive it?" His gaze held mine.

My heart was pounding, I kept my face neutral. But I was nervous as memories of that night flooded back. The feeling of that blade plunging in my chest, the blood choking me as it bubbled up...

"Shae?" Faelan pulled me from the memory. "Where is it from?" He asked again.

I cleared my throat. Licking my lips.

I didn't tell him.

"From the many scars Commander Demented left me when we stayed at the inn in Mochan." I lied, not able to look at him. He was silent for a long while, assessing my reply.

"Does it hurt?" He asked, a strange question, I thought.

"No." I said, looking back at him. Everything in me stopped. It was like I was back in that cell, those glowing eyes seeing right through me. I looked away before I was lost in them. "I don't know." I said, "I didn't even know it was there until you mentioned it to me." At least that was honest.

His hand lightly touched beneath my chin, bringing my face back to him. I dragged my gaze up, forcing myself to look.

"Whatever it is, Shae. It is no longer here." His expression was gentle seeing through my lie. We sat still for a moment, neither one of us breaking contact.

He leaned into me, stopping just before my face. His lips a breath away, barely touching mine. "May I?" He asked the brush of contact from his words made my lips ache for more.

"Why do you tease me so?" I asked, frustrated. Then his lips were on mine firm, it took my breath away.

Heat rose within my chest.

His hands were on me, one tangled in my hair, the other on the side of my face, his thumb gently stroking my cheek. His canine brushed over my lip lightly, pressing in just enough pressure to make a rush of pleasure flow. Tilting my head back, I invited him to explore more.

He didn't hesitate

Running his hand from my cheek along my shoulder following it down my lower back. Where his hand fit nicely pressing me closer into him. He pushed me down laying me along the rug, his body on top of mine.

The rug was soft against my skin.

I felt his warm hand slip under the hem of my shirt, gripping my side as his mouth roamed down my neck. A moan released from my lips, my body filled with desire. His mouth was on mine in an instant opening me up, his lips tasted sweet a pleasant aroma filling my senses. My arms lay above my head, I felt his arm reach over his hand clasped onto my wrists easily encasing them both. Holding them firm he pulled away looking me over.

His eyes full of hunger.

My heart hammered in my chest, breathing heavily. I felt his hand roaming up my side, tracing over my skin. His hand reached the center of my chest, fingers lingering just between my breasts. I felt them trace over the slight line from when the Sliske stabbed me.

My body shivered from his touch.

Then his body went ridged, frozen, his hand gripped my wrists even tighter to the point they began to ache. I caught sight of his gaze, his eyes distant some place far away from here. The pressure suddenly left my hands as he sat up, taking the warmth of his body with him. Unmoving, he stared away from me towards the door. Shocked, I sat up from where I laid, I waited as he sat there, arm propped over one knee keeping his back to me. His shoulders started shaking, and he erupted with laughter. When he spoke, his tone was not gentle at all. "Apologies..." He spoke. "I may have taken it too far." He turned to me. Gave me a smile that didn't touch his eyes.

"Taken too far?" I said confused, "I was under the impression we were just getting started." The heat of his touch still lingered on my skin. His laugh was short and rough.

"Yes... well... a female of your age would think so." He got up from the rug.

"What does that mean?" I was even more confused.

He ran a hand through his hair before looking at me. There was no humor in his eyes.

"It means Shae. This was never what you thought. I never truly returned your feelings. You are beautiful and very intriguing, but that is all. We are only here to travel together until I complete my mission. Forgive me if I gave you the wrong idea. It was just a bit of fun to pass the time." He grabbed his bag of supplies.

I sat frozen in place, my head reeling. I looked around the room, confused about what transpired. 'He was having fun?' I thought, 'it was just to pass the time?'

"Was it all really a lie?" My voice broke, "did your words actually mean nothing until now?" My hands shook tears suddenly dripped from my eyes running down my cheeks as I bit my lip. He didn't even look at me when he replied.

"Who wouldn't want to tame a feral cat." Then he left me in the room alone. I rubbed my mouth with the back of my hand ferociously, trying to wipe the feeling he marked me with.

My heart felt wrenched from my chest.

'You fool' I thought, you should have known better. Why did you let him get so close? Just because he showed you kindness. There is no way a man of his renown would truly love you.

You are only cursed.

I laid down on the rug and curled into a ball. My plain and silver tears running down my face mixing together, I allowed my consciousness to disappear into the flames.

31

Morning came.

Laying in the same spot after Faelan left, I got up glancing at my fingers. There was no sign of blood the scrapes and cuts healing well. Scabs formed over the deeper cuts and the smaller ones almost fully closed.

The inside of my stomach twisted at the thought of Faelan. I shook myself and stretched my body stiff from all it had endured during my trial.

I washed my face in the basin and my reflection was horrid, lips swollen, eyes a bit puffy. I splashed another handful of water on my face, rubbing it one more time. I drew my hair up off my shoulders with a leather cord, tying it tight, making certain to partially cover my cursed eye. Drying my face off, I got ready for the day. There was no way I would remain in the room another day. My close-fitting clothes felt comfortable, easy to move in. A pale green top, a dark brown leather vest covered half of my upper torso. Putting on the black pants, I tied the string around my waist. I tapped my boot to the ground, finding my hidden blade still in place.

A knock on the door stopped me short. I looked around, no Faelan in sight, cautiously, I walked to the door pulling it open. Calum stood on the other side.

"Good morning." He said with a smile on his face, which was short lived when he saw how awful I looked. "Shae..." he began, I waved him off.

"I am fine the trials were harder on my body than I would have liked." I lied to him, I allowed my shoulders to relax, unconsciously I scanned the hall behind him in search of Faelan. Inwardly, I reprimanded myself after recognizing what I was doing.

"Come. The King has summoned you." He said turning to leave.

"Oh? That is good to hear." I replied, following him along the hall. Calum was just as dazzling this morning, he wore a bright blue tunic that came to his knees, the sides cut into a U to his hips. His silk pants were a pearl white grasping at his ankles with gold thread running along both. "Does Morfran dress you?" I asked, curious of his elegant attire once again and knowing he had an unusual fascination with beautiful things.

"He used to." Calum said, his expression dark. "I underwent lots of training when I first began serving him. It's.... not a time I find very pleasant to reflect on." He said keeping his pace even.

"For...forgive me." I stammered over my words, chastising myself for bringing up painful memories.

"How was your evening?" Calum asked I kept my face normal, not wanting him to think he touched a sore subject.

"It was... uneventful." I answered, smiling at him. "The rest was good." I added, looking around the garden as we passed by. The boisterous royals returned to their loud gossiping and noisy talk.

"So am I going to be thrown in a dungeon again." I asked playfully. He glanced in my direction. "Let's see if you can behave." He said with a sly smile. I pushed him lightheartedly, which caused him to pause for a moment. I froze thinking I messed something up somehow, my face lined with worry. He began laughing, the sound was musical as it filled the air. "You should see your face." He laughed again.

"Ha ha, very funny." I said, the worry melting away. We continued to walk laughing together, unconcerned of the onlookers as we passed.

We reached the huge doors to the throne room before we entered, Calum returned to his normal demeanor, the fourteen-year-old boy no longer seen. The room was still like a tomb, there were fewer people this time, only the King and his advisors stood in the large room. I noticed Faelan propped up against a wall, his arms crossed over his shoulder. A sharp pain pierced my chest at the sight of him, not revealing any pain or emotions raging inside on my face, I approached the King.

I stopped just short of the large three steps below him and I bowed my head to the king. He stood from his overly large chair.

"Cursed One, you have finished the Trial by Fire as we agreed. You are no longer my prisoner. You are free to leave." He said before he turned, I spoke up.

"If his majesty would allow it. May I stay in the capital a while longer?" I kept my head up.

"You can do what you please cursed one, you are free." He said, turning around. "If his majesty would allow, I would like to stay and get to know the King and his people better." I said unwavering. At that, Morfran shifted in his stance ever so slightly.

"And why would you want to do that Cursed One." Again, with that title I held back from screaming.

"Shae." he paused at my words.

"Pardon?" I could tell he was losing his patience.

"My name is Shae. Majesty, I would like to stay so you can see I am not only known as the Cursed One." I said, then bowed my head lower. I felt the Eleith linger above. As if it agreed with me. I heard him sigh heavily.

"If you wish, I can allow you to remain in the castle for the time being. I assumed General Faelan would keep an eye on you anyway. You may join him for our banquets." He said then waved me away like I was an annoyance he was glad to be rid of. Bowing my head once again, I left the throne room glad to be out of the tomb.

Breathing in the fresh air I set out for the town below, not waiting for anyone or anything. Although the sun was bright in the sky shining over Thornden, the air was chilled. I passed the fountain I first saw when entering the castle with the Commander. The streets were lined with a pale yellowish stone. Reddish bricks made up the homes of the people. Houses lined down one next to another along the street.

The street I walked on continued the pattern of four brick houses lined next to one another that split to allow another yellowish stone street to run through. I walked on that one street for a while until I could hear people in the distance.

I took a right on one street, following the noise of people. There were alleys in between these streets, little dark places easy for a child or criminals to hide. The noise grew louder, I turned left into one of the dark alleyways. Following it through on the other side was a large, stone area, it was not a street but a large open circular area.

Carts and wagons filled the space, masses of people crowded in for shopping. The smell of freshly baked food filled the air. My stomach rumbled remembering I had not yet eaten today. I was even more disappointed when I realized I had no money on me, and I forgot to request the return of my belongings.

I sighed to myself and walked into the crowd of people. The amount of people was more than I had ever seen in one place. I watched as people interacted with one another. Laughing and arguing some bartering others trading and buying. So many people of all shapes and sizes.

"You!" Someone said just behind me. I turned to see a short round man with a round nose, thin lips and his brown hair was balding on the top. I stared down at him, it was rare I stared down at a grown man.

"Yes?" I said, looking at the stout man.

"Are you selling?" His voice was loud and annoying.

"Selling?" I gave him a quizzical look.

"Yes, I can see a few uses with that body of yours." Annoyed, I put my hands in my pockets.

"No. I am not selling. Unless you got an opponent worth fighting, I got nothing for you old man." I said, turning away. He latched his sausage fingers onto my wrist before I moved.

"Whoa, where are you going?" He said clinging, jingling a bag of coin at me. He licked his lips running his eyes over my figure.

"Unless you want to lose those fingers, old man, I suggest you let go." I warned him.

Without giving him a chance to decide I grabbed hold of his thumb and pulled back, the rest of his hand released me with ease.

"Ow ow ow ow." He said over and over.

"I wouldn't touch me so casually." I said, releasing his sweaty hand then walked away. I guess there are nasty people wherever you go.

I pushed past the crowd of people eager to get some space. Just as I broke through the mass of people, I caught sight of an old lady about to topple over from holding a large bag. Rushing over, I caught the woman and bag before she fell backwards.

"Careful there." I said, pushing her back to steady her on her feet.

"Oh. You're too kind." She said in a shaky voice.

The woman was shorter than me you could tell time had pushed down on her spine.

She hunched over slightly.

Her gray hair was braided, reaching to the middle over her back. The wrinkles on her face made her appear as if she had a permanent frown. But her eyes were a beautiful green, you wouldn't think of her old age if you only looked into those eyes.

"Where can I put this?" I asked, standing next to the old lady still holding her large bag with one arm.

The old woman just stared at me.

"My, you have such unusual eyes." She stated, I covered my cursed eye out of habit, not realizing it had become visible. I glanced down.

"Yes, I get that a lot." I replied, giving her a smile. "I will carry your bag for you. Lead the way." I said, insisting for the old woman to stop staring. She turned without warning and made her way through the large amounts of people, not minding them walking back and forth before.

She just maneuvered around them with ease. For an old woman she was sure agile. We turned onto another street this one differed from the other streets I walked on. The buildings here were more run down. The stone on the ground was a dirty gray. Shops were larger and closer together a black current hung over the door of a building a few places down. I saw women and younger boys and girls not quite adults but also not entirely children, scattered throughout the street. Some were going in and out of that building paired up with other people.

That building was a brothel.

The old woman walked up to a small shop made of brown brick it was thin and tall. Her doorway arched, a wooden door with a metal handles the metal looked black, a deep brown for the old wood. She grasped the handle. The door creaked from being swung open.

She beckoned me to follow her.

The room was dark red lights filled each corner. A desk stood along the front of the room to my right it had knick-knacks filled in a glass case. Shelves lined the wall behind it. There were two walls with furniture against them and a table in the center with a large rug underneath. The hair on the back of my neck rose. I swallowed, realizing I foolishly followed this woman into her den. Setting the large bag down, I took a step back.

"I will be leaving now." I took another step back. The old woman twirled around, and the front door slammed behind me.

Dread rose within...

32

"But you just got here." She purred. Her appearance shifted, more sinister as a dark fog hung behind her, those green eyes now all black.

"Witch." I breathed, realizing I had walked straight into her trap. Her laugh that filled the room made my blood run cold.

"My, my, you were rather easy to fool. Has no one told you not to follow witches." Her voice was soothing, like her every word was a spell.

I shook my head.

"As exciting as this is I will be leaving. The King is expecting me." I bluffed. Knowing full well it would make no difference if he never saw my face again. She laughed again, amused by my lie.

"Oh, I know who you are, Blood Bearer." She said, her voice ringing in my ears.

"What do you want?" I tried to sound threatening, but my tone sounded far away.

"It's been a while since I have had such a splendid meal. It would be a pity to let you get away." She crooned. I felt like the walls were closing in on me, my breathing came up short.

"Gen... eral... Fa.. elan... will be... looki..." I dropped to my knees, the room spun, I had no strength in my legs. She hissed.

"That abomination is nowhere near here." Through my blurry vision, I saw her sniff the air. "Yes, nowhere around here indeed." Her voice purred near me, I didn't realize how she got so close.

"Oh dear. Don't worry. I am not like those savage Sliske, taking your soul will be much less... *gruesome*." She paused on that word, letting it hang in the air. I fumbled around looking for anything I could grab hold of to hit her with. I heard her click her tongue against her teeth. "There is no point in fighting my dear." A cold hand caressed the side of my cheek. I heard her breath deep next to my ear.

A wave of nausea hit my stomach as I collapsed to my side, my face felt clammy sweat dripping down my temple. She cackled next to my ear.

"Yessss. Very lovely. You taste sooo sweet." Another deep inhale.

More nausea I had no strength to move, my limbs lay numb on the floor. I laid there, my breaths becoming shallower, it was barely a rasp. Panicked my mind could scarcely form a thought the only thing on my mind was death. I heard her voice off in the distance somewhere more laughter and words I could no longer understand.

A Scream pierced through the haze, strength returned to me in an instant. The nauseous clammy feeling disappeared I sat up to the sight of the old woman crashing all over the room. Something black was attached to her face. Not waiting another second, I pulled the hidden knife from my boot. Lunging forward, I plunged my knife into her thigh. She screeched an ear-piercing scream pulling the black figure from her face flinging it across the room it landed on its paws back arched high ready to attack.

The black cat hissed at the witch, who was once old now looked thirty years younger. She pulled my knife out from her leg, blood dripping from its blade. The wound closed before my very eyes.

I swallowed.

The witch laughed. "Well well, you are full of surprises blood Bearer. You seem to have a guard in the most unlikely places." I glanced at the slim black cat behind me. Its eyes an exquisite deep red.

"I hope you enjoyed your meal." My voice coming out more fierce. "Because it will be your last." A nasty smile sprouted on her face.

"How cute." She mocked, then leapt for me, her hands outstretched the nails on her fingers shifting into long sharp claws. I dove to the side rolling under the table popping up on the other side. The black cat was already on her. Its claws latched on to the side of her face.

My heart raced, licking my lips, I ran my eyes over the room looking for any kind of weapon I could use against her.

I spotted a long staff leaning against the wall, I ran for it. Snatching it up in an instant, I flung the other end straight for the witch's head while she was fighting off the cat. Smacking her on the side of her temple, she toppled to the ground unmoving. Not waiting to see if she was alive, I ran for the door. Wrenching it open, I looked back at the Cat.

"Let's go." I said like it could understand me. As if it did it jumped off the unconscious witch and followed me out.

I ran as far as my legs would take me, I didn't stop to see if she followed. I didn't stop to ask anyone for help or to look for new places to explore. I ran straight for the castle. Never slowing down until I reached the fountain, I passed this morning. Heart hammering in my chest breathing ragged, I collapsed to the ground and leaned back against the cool stone savoring the feeling on my heated skin. I noticed it was dark out by the time I took in my surroundings. I had no idea I was in that house for so long, and I had no idea what she had done to me while I was in that haze.

I jolted when something rubbed against my leg, panicked I looked down and noticed the black cat was still with me. Petting the top of its head, I scratched its ears.

"You really saved my neck back there, Beautiful." I said, while it rubbed against my hands. "Shall we find something to eat?" I said, standing at my feet its eyes glowed in the dark, the beautiful red reflected by the moonlight. "Aren't you fascinating?" I said, picking her up, she purred in my arms.

We walked back to the castle together.

33

The night was calm, bright lights filled the sky high above blues and purples swirled through those stars. My breath came out in little puffs of smoke as the cold air nipped at my nose.

"I think it might be time for me to get a coat, little one." I said, stroking the black cat purring in my arms. Her warmth radiated off her fur as I snuggled my cold nose into her neck. "You have my thanks." I breathed into the cat like she could understand me. "We should head to the kitchen I am sure I already missed the banquet for the night with the King, anyway." I said gloomily. "I bet he was glad I didn't arrive." I was still talking to the cat. I doubt Faelan was even worried of my whereabouts considering what he said last night he would be spending little time with me.

A sharp pain hit my stomach from the thought.

When we reached the castle, I put the cat down and walked straight for the passages the servants used going directly to the kitchen. She remained beside me the entire way, brushing against my leg every now and again reminding me of her presence.

The kitchen was filled with servants they were scurrying around cleaning after the night's feast. There was a table filled with leftover food that wasn't even touched. I snatched hold of one servant running by, "What are you doing with the remaining food?" I asked her. She looked me up and down, a disgusted look on her face.

"It is given to the dogs the rest is thrown out with the garbage."

She said annoyed. Pulling her hand away, "if you'll excuse me, I have better things to do." She said with venom.

I nodded at the girl as she turned away, glaring at me. 'Well,' I thought this was what I was accustomed to. I grabbed two bowls off the shelf filled it with meat and the other with various breads and fruit. Since it's being given to the dogs and tossed out anyway, I'll just help myself. It was a pity, though there was enough food here to feed at least six large families.

What a waste.

Taking a seat at the table Fealan and I once ate, I sat both bowls on the table. The black cat leaped onto the table curling her tail around her legs leaning down she dug right into the bowl of meat. I smiled at her, "not bad for the scraps, eh." Then I dug into my bowl of food. Nobody paid any mind to us while they ran around finishing all the dishes and cleaned up from the normal night's festivities.

The black cat jumped from the table when she was done with her food and roamed around the room. I finished the last of my food, went to an empty tub and washed the bowls we used. Both bowls had no food left in them when we were done. I smiled thinking the cat must have been as hungry as I was. A rub on my leg told me she had returned. "

Shall we head back to my room?" I knelt and rubbed under her neck. "That is, if you'd like to stay a little longer?" Moving my fingers I scratched the top of her head.

"You're welcome to stay as long as you want. Although I may not be the best companion for a feline. I run into a lot of trouble." She stopped rubbing against my finger and sat curling her tail the crimson eyes stared at me. Rubbing my eyes, I left the kitchen and went back to the room I was left in the night before.

My heart thudded against my chest.

I stood outside the door to the room I didn't have the nerve to open it yet. My hands were sweaty, and my heart felt like it would explode at any moment. 'What if he is in there?' I thought closing my eyes tight I breathed out.

"It's fine, we are just two people who are traveling together. No big deal." I took hold of the handle and before I could lose my nerve, I squeezed it pushing the door open with a creak.

The room was dark, quiet, and cold. No one had been here all day.

Another sharp pain in my stomach.

What was I expecting anyway, I only thought we cared for each other? I laughed at myself.

"He's over 400 how could he possibly be in love with you." I walked into the room, went straight for the hearth to get the fire ablaze. After everything, I wasn't fond of staying in the dark alone. A tail brushed over my arm, telling me otherwise. I smiled, "I guess I'm not completely alone."

The fire was warm, I used its flame to light a few candles to light up half the room. I laid on the rug in front of the fire covering with a small blanket, exhausted from the day. The cat curled up into a ball next to my hand.

"Shall I give you a name?" Her eyes snapped open at the sound of my voice. Her stare held mine, those eyes were mesmerizing.

"Crimson." I said, if I didn't know any better, I would have sworn the cat smiled at me. She began to purr, closing her eyes and laying her head back down. "Crimson it is." I was pleased with the sound of it. Laying on the carpet I stared up at the ceiling. This morning felt like ages ago. Tired, I closed my eyes. Tomorrow I will try to meet with the King again. I sighed, not having any idea what I was doing or why I was even still here in the first place. I knew there was more to be done, and I couldn't ignore that warm voice from before.

The throne room was empty this time it really resembled a tomb. The only light was a torch on either side of the throne, the shadows crossing it from the flickering light made it look alive, almost.

It glimmered.

Walking to the chair, I felt compelled to sit inside of it. My footsteps echoed aloud, filling the huge room with each step. Slowly I approached the chair I felt almost possessed, like my limbs had a mind of their own drawing nearer to the seat.

I stopped just before the throne, my shadow cast over its arm. My body moved without a thought sitting in the chair putting my arms on each armrest. Cold air crept down my spine, a breath breathing down my neck.

"What do you want?" I said, knowing exactly what was behind me. A low chuckle broke the silence, proving my suspicions.

"Shae." He purred my name. I felt his cold hand clasp my shoulder as he leaned in next to my ear. "You know what I want, Shae." He said whispering in my ear. "Just you, always just you." His icy hand traced down my arm laying his

hand on top of mine, interlacing his fingers. I didn't dare look, fear kept me petrified. "This could be yours, Shae. This throne, this kingdom. They all abuse their power anyway, the young king is useless, he doesn't care for the well-being of his people. If he did, do you think he would be so easily fooled by that sorcerer whispering in his ear?" His voice was alluring the more he spoke, the more pleasant he sounded. "You could do so much better." He breathed.

"No." Was all I could muster, barely a whisper. Sensing my weak will, I felt his breath on my cheek, a hand stroking the underside of my neck pulling my hair back. They were so cold it felt like it burnt my skin.

"All you have to do, Shae. Is join me. I won't trick you. Not like that, General." My heart was thumping at the mention of him. I licked my lips. "Don't you want to help these people, Shae." Tempting, it was so tempting.

But I knew I could not take his hand. He was dark, and whatever he offered was not what I wanted. As if my very thought revealed truth. Images flashed before me, fire was everywhere, burning homes and people. That dark fog oozed out of the people's mouths as they ridiculed and beat each other. Mother against daughter, father against son, lover against lover, my heart broke from the hatred.

I heard him click his tongue next to me. "What are you doing, Shae?" His voice sounding impatient. His finger on my neck pushed in, pain seared my skin. His nails dug into my hand. "Don't make me your enemy, Shae. I could do far worse than you can ever imagine." Fire shot up my arm, the pain raging under my skin started to boil my inner bone melting.

I screamed.

34

My eyes popped open to find Crimson sitting on my chest staring at me. I sat up breathing heavy, my heart refusing to slow down. I looked around the room the sun was just beginning to break light. Rubbing my neck, it felt slick and wet I looked at my hand and noticed blood dripping from it.

That's when I panicked.

Running to the basin by the mirror I splashed the water over my hand, rubbing the blood away frantically.

Right there on my hand, five claw marks dug into my skin. I searched my arm for boils or missing skin. Nothing.

I dropped to my knees, gripping the side of the desk. My mind raced. What is he? How can he affect me in a dream? I looked everywhere, he knew of Fealan and me, he knew what happened that night. My heart hammered in my chest.

What else did he know? My mind was whirling I must not have heard the knock on the door because it opened. I nearly jumped out of my skin from the sound. Sitting on my hands and knees, Calum and Fealan walked into the room.

A small paw touched my hand I looked down and saw crimson standing next to me. Those intelligent eyes assessing me.

"What are you doing." Faelan's voice so warm... I loved and hated that it soothed me. I got up from the ground, hiding the tremble in my hands. "You're bleeding." He said already next to me lifting my chin. I pulled away from his touch.

"It's nothing." I said, grabbing a cloth and putting pressure on my neck.

"That doesn't look like nothing." He frustration clear in his voice. Crimson hissed next to me, her back arched staring at Faelan. I smiled from her appearance. "Shae, where did that come from?" He said his voice no longer holding concern, only scolding. Crimson passed Faelan and went straight to Calum, rubbing along his legs.

"Oh. I picked her up." I said simply.

"You. Picked. Her. Up." He said disbelieving. "It can't stay." He said his voice fierce, heading straight for Crimson.

"What?" It came out in a panic.

"You don't know where that thing came from. What if it's a trap?" His voice was hard. I ran, placing myself between him and Crimson.

"Crimson is not going anywhere." I said, determined.

"Crimson?" He looked astonished.

"Yes, Crimson. She saved me. When you were nowhere to be found. She saved me. So, she stays." I concluded.

"What do you mean she saved you? And how was I supposed to be near you? You left without a word to anyone." He said annoyed.

"I didn't think it would matter after..." I paused and looked away. "I'm allowed to come and go as I please why would I need to inform you." I said with a harsh tone.

His eyes glowed.

" You cannot just leave on your own I am supposed to make sure you are safe." He fumed.

"YOU! Were the first to leave. I assumed it was no longer implied." I said angrily. Calum cleared his throat behind us.

"I don't mean to interrupt. But could someone help me?" Crimson had knocked him on the bed and was rubbing her head aggressively on his cheek, purring loud enough I could hear. I laughed, forgetting our fight entirely.

"I guess she really likes you." I walked over and plucked her from the bed, tossing her to the side gently.

Calum sat up, brushing his robe down. "May I ask what she saved you from." He looked me over. "Did it have to do with the blood on your neck and hand?" I covered my hand.

"She saved me from a witch." I said, far too casual.

"A witch?" Both Faelan and Calum spoke together intensely.

"Is it that bad?" I asked, Faelan looked down at Crimson his stare was intense not looking at me he replied. "Were you able to kill her?" I watched as Crimson licked her paw.

"I don't think so. I got out of there as soon as I had a chance."

"Where did you meet this witch, Shae?" He asked seriously.

"She was in the market in the lower town where everyone traded and sold goods." I said, still putting pressure on my neck.

"Let's take care of that." Faelan said, reaching a hand out to me. I took a step out of his reach, "That won't be necessary." I said with some bite. He dropped his hand.

"Of course. Calum, I will be gone today please take Shae to see the King." He said his expression was unreadable and left the room without giving me another look.

Pain filled my chest.

Unconsciously rubbing my chest Calum touched my arm lightly. "Why don't you let me look at that." His smile was warm. Hesitantly, I lowered my hand, letting him lead me over to the desk where the basin was. He pulled the chair over for me to sit in with a nod. Obediently I sat down, Crimson leaped on to the desk sitting next to me watching Calum as he looked over my neck.

His hands were gentle, wiping the blood away. "You have a cut along your neck, it's not deep, but I will have to wrap it for the day." I gave him a short nod. "Were you scared?" He asked while gently wrapping my neck.

My heart thumped.

"Yes," I breathed I could feel my eyes glisten tears threatening to appear. I cleared my throat. "I... have. These dreams. Sometimes." I said in a quiet voice. Calum finished his bandaging and placed his hands on his lap, those blue eyes ever patient. "They feel so real." I bit my lower lip, "never once did I truly believe it was real... until... this morning." I said, dabbing my neck.

Running a hand through my hair, I closed my eyes. "Faelan said you are taking me to see the King. Is there anything wrong?" I said opening my eyes finally relaxing from the morning events. Calum's face did not help though.

"King Anwyl was not very pleased you missed the banquet last night after you made the declaration yesterday morning." He paused, "Although you have a good excuse for missing it, I don't think King Anwyl will be very understanding. Considering he is unaware of the coming and goings of most everything good or bad."

Calum sighed, seeming annoyed. "Do you not like the King?" I asked curiously. His eyes searched the room, keeping his voice low.

"It is not that I do not like the King on the contrary, I would like to spend more time with him. He is a kind King who does care for his people. But... he is blinded by his power-hungry advisor's." He stood from the chair and walked over to the door.

"Shall we start our day? It will be a difficult one. Morfran knows Faelan requested you to spend the day with King Anwyl and will be on his tail." I laughed at his statement.

"Yes, I am sure he will be worried." I said but thought of his response in the throne room yesterday and wondered if I was really playing into his hands.

The banquet hall differed greatly from the throne room, many people filled the seats, nobles and royals I assumed with how they were dressed in their fine silks and garments. On the floor a tan marble with creamy lines swirled along it. Smooth pillars also of marble lined along the hall near the walls, white drapes hung along the ceiling between each of them. They sparkled and silver was embedded into them.

Two long tables stood parallel to one another with a huge gap between the two, another long table connecting them at the end. The King sat in the middle of that table; his advisor's on his left an empty seat to his right. My guess that was for me. I whispered to Calum, keeping my head down so no one could see me speak.

"I am guessing you will not be sitting with us." I said already disappointed, knowing the answer. His lack of response confirmed my thoughts.

The room went quiet when they saw me enter, not letting the sudden change in mood bother me I walked straight to the King, Crimson following me at my heels. I bowed my head to King Anwyl.

"Apologies Majesty for my absence last night, I was in the lower town exploring and meeting with the pleasant people of your kingdom." I said, it was mostly true, anyway.

"And how was it?" He asked his tone stiff.

"Very eventful Majesty." I said with a smile. His expression softened.

"Please sit. Although General Faelan was supposed to join, I am not sure where he may be." Calum then bowed to the King.

"Apologies My King he had some business in the lower town and said he will be away for the day he sends his regrets." Calum said, then left the King and stood next to Morfran whose face stayed the same since I entered the room.

After sitting next to King Anwyl, one of his advisor's squealed in my direction. "What. Is. That." He said pointing at Crimson. "Remove it." He demanded. I rolled my eyes.

"She is mine and if she goes I will as well." I said like it would make a difference.

"Good riddance to the both of you." Said the round bald adviser who obviously disliked me from the beginning.

"Counselor if it bothers you so, maybe you should eat at a different table." King Anwyl said without a second thought. Astonished, I looked at the advisor's face who looked just as surprised.

"But.... but... Sire." He began but was silenced with a hand of King Anwyl.

"She is my guest today and I will not tolerate such behavior." Then waved the bald man off who promptly got from his seat grumbling to himself and gave me the death glare. I returned it with a sickly-sweet smile, even threw in a few fluttering lashes.

He left with a huff and waddled off. I looked back, noticing King Anwyl staring at me. I cleared my throat, removing the smile from my face and went to my food placed before me. I caught sight of a slight smile on his face. He really was still a boy I thought.

"How did you come by that creature?" He asked me. Crimson walked around the King's feet rubbing against him, purring aloud. I saw a small smile touch his lips at the action.

"When I was around town... She... helped me find my way." I looked at Crimson.

Leaning over, I asked a servant to bring a bowl of milk out for her. It was the same one from the kitchen last night, she scowled at me before leaving and returning with a bowl shortly after. Before letting Crimson have her milk, I smelled it then had a small taste. I was afraid of poison to be honest. Satisfied there was nothing, I then handed it to Crimson who dug in after setting it in front of her.

"What are your plans for the day?" King Anwyl asked me.

"They told me I will be with you today. So, the question is, what are we doing today?" I said, giving him a soft smile. I could tell he was not accustomed to smiles because his cheeks lightly colored after receiving mine.

"I only have a few matters later in the day. But I spend most of my days in the library." I beamed at the thought.

"Your Majesty that would be wonderful." I said, excited.

King Anwyl returned with a small smile, "then it is decided." Morfran remained silent, observing throughout our conversation, never once interrupting which made me all the more nervous. We spoke with one another briefly in between bites. He mostly asked questions of my village and how I grew up. I told him, leaving out the more abusive parts of my childhood when the villagers set their sights on me. I mostly spoke of my Grams, the stories made me miss her deeply.

I had told no one the many things done to me growing up. I always showed up at Grams with various bruises and cuts. Sometimes it was worse, but I never told Grams how I got them. Something told me she already knew what those villagers were doing.

After we finished, the King stood and left the room, his close guards keeping to his side. The Guard Cynwrig that Faelan spoke with before was among them. I gave him a small nod which he did not return. Crimson and I followed suit Morfran walked beside King Anwyl whispering in his ear. His entire being made my blood boil. I caught up with the small group and walked on the others side of King Anwyl.

Morfran then bowed to him, "Apologize my King, I have urgent business to attend to. I will join you later when you see the council." He said giving me a quick glance. His smile did not reach his eyes. Then glided on his way like the snake he was.

We reached the library in no time we walked in silence the whole way. The room was much brighter this time of day, with the sun out streaming through the windows up high. It showed a beautiful painting on the ceiling that I did not see the last time I was here. It was of the night sky, bright stars filled the painting surrounding a full moon. Colors of gold and shades of blue, pink, and purple swirled around them.

"Beautiful," I whispered aloud, unable to hide my astonishment.

"Yes, it was a gift to my mother from my father when they were young." King Anwyl said, looking up at the ceiling with me. "It was one of the ways he won her favor." He said smiling to himself.

"She must be quite the woman." I said, looking at King Anwyl. His expression darkened.

"Was." He said then walked over to a table with piles of books I am sure he has been reading.

"Forgive me." I said, feeling like a fool.

I watched as the King skimmed through his books and scrolls. His eyes glazed over a moment, I could tell from whatever memory had come to mind.

"What was she like?" I asked, a small smile touched his lips.

"She was similar to you, actually." Slightly taken aback, I let that sink in.

"She must have given you a hard time." He laughed then. It was an innocent sound that filled my heart with hope.

"Cursed One, you have no idea." I dared to put my hand on his, "Majesty please, Shae. Not Cursed One." I asked gently.

He stopped what he was doing, "Apologies. Shae." I smiled at him.

"Now, what have you been reading up on?" He returned my smile and started flipping through all the information that lay before us.

35

We stayed in the library all day, not knowing how quickly the time flew by us. Food was brought to us, telling us how much time we had actually spent there. Crimson roamed around the room ducking in and out of the corners, only coming to sit with us every few minutes, then continued to explore the library. King Anwyl was as kind and innocent as I thought he was.

He cared deeply for the people, but he knew nothing of the crimes, the very people he relied on day in and day out. He spoke to me about how his grandfather was the one who formed the treaty with the Elemental Realm. How every time General Faelan came for a political reason, he would always make time to play with him as a young child. After his father died from a sickness that plagued him for years he ascended to the throne before he could mourn his death. He told me his mother died shortly after his father. As though the heartbreak from the loss was too much for her to bear. He said he remembered her always being very kind.

After we finished the food brought to us King Anwyl told me it was time for him to endure another long-winded counsel meeting with his advisor's. I laughed lightly, accompanied him until we reached a small chamber where they assembled daily. Sadly, I would be leaving the young King in the clutches of these wolves waiting in their den. I left knowing this was not a place I would be welcome, promising to sit beside him at supper.

I walked along the long halls of the castle Crimson dashed in and out of every turn. I found myself led to the training yard for the guards, it was quiet. Deciding I needed to flex my arms, I made my way down to the courtyard, picking through the bows until I found the one I liked.

The targets stood at different meters, I took my time standing in front of the one closest to me. Closing my eyes, I breathed deep, soaking in the cold air and warm sun. Nocking the arrow in place I drew my bow, the feather on the arrow brushed my cheek ever so lightly. I opened my eyes marking the target, I let loose the arrow watching it soar in the air, it landed with a thud in the middle.

I smiled to myself.

Moving to the next target stood further than the first I removed my arrow from its quiver. Steading my arm, I pulled my bow string tight, aiming for the heart, I sent the arrow flying with a breath. It didn't disappoint me, landing directly where I aimed.

The relished feeling I had flew away at the sound of Crimson hissing behind me.

Clap. Clap.

I turned, scowling at the sight of Commander Drask clapping as he made his way down to the courtyard.

He had an expression of mockery, "Well done, well done." He said walking closer. Crimson arched her back next to my feet.

"Feeling better, Commander." I said, glancing at his hand. He flexed his right hand as if I had done no damage.

"The Commander can't go around with a broken hand, can he? Morfran does have his uses." He said, still approaching.

"That's close enough, Commander." I said firmly, drawing an arrow and aiming it directly at him. He stopped. Hands up.

"No need to be on your guard. You are no longer my prisoner, and I have no need to punish you." He said, trying for a truce.

"Is that what you call it? Punishment? I am no fool Commander you stay away from me." He kept his hands up.

"Can we not come to some sort of arrangement," he asked, taking another step in my direction.

I pulled the bow sting tighter.

"The only arrangement I want with you Commander is you

laying on the ground choking in a pool of your own blood." I said with fury. A smile crept onto his face, his eyes excited.

"Never a dull moment when your around cursed wench." That demented look on his face appeared as he took another step. He was within arms-reach now, my pulse thumped, fingers twitch aching to release the arrow directly into his neck.

The Elieth tugged. Giving a warning.

I let out a breath and obeyed, letting the bow and arrow drop to my sides gripping them tightly. "Giving up so soon? Hm... that doesn't seem like you." He said. "There's a rumor the General has been rather.... cold to you as of late. Did he finally bore of you?" He kept pushing, "do you need a bed to keep warm at night? I would be more than willing to share mine." His eyes raked over me, "I don't mind the General's leftovers."

My face neutral, "Commander unlike you I have no interest in torture for pleasure." I said, walking past him. Returning the bow and arrows where they came, I wanted nothing more than to be far away from him.

His hand brushed under my chin pulling me towards him, I slapped it away. "You're too familiar, Commander." I said with a cold stare. Large amounts of footsteps approached in unison. He grabbed the back of my hair while I was distracted, yanking my head back.

"You're here to train aren't you. A few of my men were not pleased with my treatment during the trial." The area was lined with guards covering all exits.

"A few of them requested I let them train with you." He said with amusement.

"I have no desire to train with your men, Commander." I said through gritted teeth. He pulled harder the pain made my eyes water.

"I think you are misunderstanding, whore. You will face three of my men every day until I am satisfied." He sneered, "if you don't agree I will leave you here with all my men and let them do as they please. I can promise you, you will have a hard time picking yourself up from the broken pieces they will leave you in." He leaned in brushing his lips along my jaw, his breath hot on my skin.

"And don't even think about running to the King, that little wretch holds no power here." An anger lit within me from his words.

"You want me to train with your men? Fine. But don't punish

them to harshly when I'm done." I gripped his hand that held my hair. "Now, are you going to let me go or am I going to have to break your hand again?" He laughed, releasing my hair and stepped away.

Entering the circle where Faelan and I once trained, I waited for the first opponent. But Commander Drask had a different idea. Three men stepped into the arena with me each had a wooden weapon, one with a club another with a staff and the third with a sword.

"You fight until you can't get up anymore." He said crossing his arms over his chest, the look of triumph on his face.

I readied as the three men slowly approached, I caught a glimpse of crimson sitting watching her tail flicking back and forth. They moved trying to circle me from all sides, smiles sat on their faces thinking they've already won.

I waited.

Observing their steps and how they shifted in their stance. Which one would attack first?

The one with the club shifted on his foot as he swung it above his head whipping it around, he aimed for my skull. Dodging forward dipping under his arm, my hand pulling on his forearm, launching my other palm directly into his elbow. It snapped under the pressure. He yelled in pain, dropping the club to the ground clutching his arm.

"Cursed Wench! Try not to make them incapacitated they still have to return to their duties." Commander Drask said amused, to make this more difficult for me they weren't planning on pulling their punches. The other two were already on me, taking advantage of his distraction. The one with the staff aimed for my legs, the other with the sword went for my head.

I moved quickly leaping between the two weapons, I spun crossing my arms over my chest, slipping through them as they passed.

I touched the ground lightly.

Catching a glimpse of his sword swinging straight for my neck. Leaning, I arched my back just as the sword swiped over my face. The air rushed past. I leaned forward just to receive a fist on the side of my head. I fell to the side, catching myself just before my face smacked the stone. Sensing another attack, I pushed off the ground just in time for a foot to slam where my head had just been. Standing back on my feet, all three men approached quickly. The man with the broken arm raged as he ran straight at me.

Leaping above I touched my hands lightly on his shoulders pushing off I flipped, landing in between the two men with weapons. I blocked the sword with my forearm, pain slicing into my arm. Grabbing hold of his sword, I yanked it out of his hands. Shoving the end he had back into his nose, blood exploded immediately. He cursed aloud, pressing on his face.

Spinning around, I brought the sword directly down with full force on the staff, snapping it in half. The man staggered back, taking this chance, I swiped my leg to the back foot of him knocking him to the ground. The guard with the broken arm charged stepping to the right I twisted swinging my leg up connecting my foot with his face. He fell to the ground hard.

Before I made another move Commander Drask yelled.

"That's enough. You pathetic excuse for men get up and go home. You are not needed for the rest of the day." He said furiously. I threw the wooden sword on the ground.

"Satisfied?" I glared at the Commander as his men matched out of the quart yard. He shook his head, approaching me.

"Do you really believe I could be content with just this Shae?" My name on his lips made my skin crawl. Stopping just before me, he kicked the man with the broken arm still lying on the ground. "Get up and go find a healer." There was no sympathy in his voice. The man got up and limped himself away, disappearing around a corner. He put his hand under my chin, lifting it towards him again. His touch was so gentle it was disbelieving as he brushed a thumb over my lower lip.

I stood unmoving.

"I could find other uses for you." His dark eyes sparked an idea I am sure included immense pain and more of my flesh being torn off.

I swiped his hand away. "I have no desire to satisfy you, Commander." I felt bad for his next victim. "Why don't you go back to that hell hole Morfran found you in." I said, pushing past him.

Wrong words.

He grabbed hold of my arm, his leg swept under mine tripping me, I fell to the ground. He placed his hand on the side of my head and pushed it into the stone. I felt the dirt press into my skin. He moved his face was close to mine.

"I would think twice before speaking to me like that cursed wench. I am still the Commander, and I only have so much patience." I let out a short laugh.

"Did I hit a soft spot, Commander?" His fingers dug into my skull, pain flashed across my vision. He gripped my shoulder and flipped me onto my back.

"Remember. You are my prey." He said pressing his hand over my throat and squeezed. Crimson hissed, leaping for Commander Drask. He smacked her out of the air. I watched as she slammed against the stone wall, fell to the ground like a sack of rocks. Her body lay there unmoving.

I roared at him gripping his arm I pulled trying to remove his hand. He stared down at me, his eyes sparked with delight and his tongue ran along his upper lip.

"Yes." He whispered putting both his hands on my neck holding tighter. My breath no longer coming out, I felt the pressure build from lack of oxygen. "Where's your General now?" His demented smile spreading across his face. I struggled underneath him fighting in vain to remove his hands I tried slamming my fist on the inside of his elbows he barely moved from the impact.

I could feel my pulse slowing, the pound of my heart weakening. He was going to kill me, I thought. I felt my cursed eye rage in anticipation of my next death. My vision began to blur, my arms weakening against his grip pounding against them slower and slower with each second. I stared up at him unable to do anything as he watched the life escape, holding tighter so tight I thought my neck would break before I suffocated.

Everything dimmed, my arms no longer holding any strength I tried and tried in vain to bring down air until my body went limp, and everything went white.

36

I Breathed deep.

My heart thundered to life as I gasped, my eyes snapped open. Pain pulsed through my veins as I came to. My hands flew to my throat checking for any damage from Commander Drask long gone, as well as the man himself. I sat up rubbing my neck, my breathing calm and heart steady. Crimson still laying on the ground unmoving.

I went to her scooping her up I checked, satisfied she was still alive I went back to the room.

Again.

I came back to life, again.

By the time I reached the room, the sun started setting. I opened the door to the room and noticed a dress was lying on the bed with a note on top of it. Laying Crimson on the bed I rubbed her side, she stirred under my hand sprung up off the bed and began hissing.

I laughed, "it's alright now Crimson, I took care of it." I said knowing my expression didn't match my words.

Satisfied she was just fine, I turned to the dress that lay along the bed. It was velvety a deep green gown, I sighed picking up the note. 'Shae, I had a pleasant time today in the library this is a gift from one of my advisor's. I would very much like you to wear it tonight for the banquet.' I crumpled the note in my hand, annoyed.

I knew King Anwyl meant no harm. This was just another way for Morfran to show he still had a way to get to me, using the King made me even more irritated. I went to the basin which now had clean water, splashing my face I rubbed the water over my neck and shoulders. The cut no longer there after I came back. My body healed all the wounds left and there was no mark on my neck, no bruising, nothing. I brushed my hair draping it over my left shoulder running my fingers through my hair. I braided it from the top of my head pulling a leather cord weaving it in and out of the braid as I went tying it off at the end.

The dress was soft over my skin, the sleeves were long stopping just over my wrists the other half of the sleeve continued passed my knees. The dress touched the floor, covering my feet. A pattern of swirls and tiny butterflies ran down the middle of the dress with golden threading. A golden chain hung around my hips; the long chain stopped at my knees.

The neck was low cut into a square, the hem lay just above my breasts most of my shoulders bare. Even though I was far more covered than when I was first presented to King Anwyl, I still felt extremely exposed. I was debating on leaving my boots on instead of using the thin slippers that laid alongside the dress when the door opened, and Faelan walked into the room.

My heart thumped.

I stood frozen at the sight of him. He was disheveled a few of his weapons were missing. I cleared my throat.

"Did you manage to find her?" I asked, trying to remember how my limbs worked. His eyes ran over my dress, remembering what I wore my face flushed, "um... this is... this is courtesy of the King." I stumbled over my words.

He looked away. "What you wear is your business, I have more important matters to attend to." He said grabbing more of his supplies.

"I recall you once telling me you would pay to see me in a dress." I said, annoyed.

"This is the last time I will come to this room. If I need you, I will have Calum send word." He said, in a cold tone, ignoring my statement. I made fists so tight my fingernails dug into them.

"You still haven't killed the witch?" I said in a mocking tone. "What good is there in even having you around if you can't even take care of a simple matter." I hated the words but couldn't stop them from flowing out.

He smirked at me, "Apologies Blood Bearer I will be sure to not return to this castle until it is taken care of." He looked me over again.

"Try not to let your guard down while I am away. If you die while I am gone, I cannot complete my mission." He slung the bag over his shoulder, no feeling in his words.

"Right. Your mission." Was all I could say. He left me in the room, Crimson resting by the fire curled into a ball. 'Too late' I thought, lucky he doesn't have to worry about me dying I will come back, anyway. I laughed to myself, but the tears started spilling over while I laughed bitterly. My heart felt tight, a lump formed in my throat.

"Blood Bearer." I scoffed. I was beginning to hate that title. I wiped away the tears, opened the door, looked over as Crimson stretched and made her way to follow me out the door.

The banquet hall was just as filled tonight as it was this morning. People whispered as I passed. Ignoring them, I approached the King sitting at the head table. Bowing my head, I greeted him.

"Shae, what a lovely gown you are wearing this evening." Morfran said, his sly smile on his lips, eyes assessing. I only gave him a small nod, not bothering to smile in his direction. He didn't seem surprised to see me. Does that mean Commander Drask didn't mention what happened earlier or did he not realize he killed me.

"It suits you well Shae, you should dress this way more often." The young King said.

"You are kind, Majesty." I said giving him another bow then made my way to the empty chair next to him. Sitting down, I noticed the chair next to me was also empty and I couldn't help but think that chair was for Faelan. Until a familiar figure pulled that chair back and sat next to me.

My anger flared at the site of Commander Drask, for a split second he was unable to hide the shock from seeing me like I was a ghost. Then he smiled wickedly.

"Lovely gown." His tone mocked. He leaned in his head, resting it on his hand propped on the table. I could see the wheels in his head turning, trying to figure out why I was sitting before him when my body should be lying cold on the ground.

"Nice seeing you here." He said, eyes on my neck. Then back to my gaze, I leaned in.

"What's wrong, Commander? Are you seeing ghosts?" A slight smile on my lips. "Maybe you should make sure you finish the job before running off." I whispered. He stared, that wicked smile still plastered on his face.

"No, I finished. I am just wondering why you are sitting here right now." I knew it should worry me about him discovering my secret, but I was too pleased with how he couldn't understand why I was still alive.

I turned my attention to King Anwyl, "How did you fair the rest of your day?" I asked. He smiled, but it did not touch his eyes.

"It was uneventful." He replied, but I could see through his lie. "Will you have time to walk together again tomorrow?" He asked me in between bites.

"Yes, Majesty." I said with a soft smile.

King Anwyl and I spoke to one another, trading simple stories of our own childhoods. His smile kind as he listened to each of my stories. I monitored Morfran in my peripheral, trying to decipher what he could be thinking. He never let his guard down while we chatted, he only ate quietly, speaking to a few people. He kept his eyes on me most of the time but never spoke to me after his first greeting. Something brushed over my arm, and I turned to see Commander Drask's forearm grazing over mine as he reached for his goblet.

"Don't you have duties to see to Commander?" I asked, annoyed.

"That is none of your concern. You are only a guest here." He said then took a long drink. I picked at my food, forcing down bites past the lump that still lingered from my encounter with Faelan.

"Why don't the two of us go for a small walk." Commander Drask said out of nowhere, I glanced around unsure he was speaking with me. When he just stared at me, I realized he really was speaking to me. "I think there are a few things we can discuss." He said. I leaned over whispering near his face.

"Unfortunately Commander, I have nothing to say to you." I leaned away from him, taking another bit of food.

Pain pierced my side, but I kept my composure, "I am not asking." Commander Drask whispered while pressing a knife into my side. I sighed.

"No, of course you're not." He looked amused by my response. Crimson leaped onto his arm, claws latching into his skin, he cursed trying to shake her off dropping the knife to the ground. She let go landing on the ground with a graceful thump then jumped into my lap, curled into a ball and began to purr. I couldn't help but laugh.

"Doesn't look like she agrees with you, Commander." I said while he gripped his arm, marks of blood dripped down. I looked to the king who was astonished with a look of confusion over his face, bowing to him.

"Apologies Majesty, I think I will leave for the night." I said getting up from my seat, Commander Drask latched onto my arm.

"Look forward to training tomorrow, my men hope to learn much from you." He said hidden meanings laced through his words. He dropped his hand from my arm, which ached from his grip. Speaking to a servant, he ordered them to bring him something to clean his arm up with.

"I am sure your men have much to learn Commander, if you'll excuse me." I said and left before anyone could follow.

I changed out of the gown as soon as I closed the door, I was in a bad mood. I laid on the bed, tired from the long day only part of it was enjoyable and I looked forward to seeing King Anwyl again tomorrow. I hoped to see his innocent eyes bright with excitement as he talked of his ideas for the future of his people.

He was a bright boy he knew there were matters he was not good with and matters he was better at. He did not have a problem designating tasks to other authorities, the only problem was there was no one on his side. All of them were dirty, bought with money or bribed with whatever they desired. I clicked my tongue, annoyed at the wolves parading all around him and they had no desire to win his favor because Morfran held all the cards.

I snuggled in the bed Crimson lay at my feet, her purr vibrated the bed. My mind drifted off into darkness and I slept that night dreaming of nothing.

37

I spent the next few mornings with King Anwyl. We would have breakfast then spend time in the library or walk around the gardens in the castle talking to ourselves. We avoided as many nobles as possible to not get drawn into their gossip or complaints.

In the afternoons he would leave and go to the council meetings alone in the den of wolves. I avoided the training yard, but Commander Drask seemed to find me wherever I went. After the second day of being dragged there by him, I just went straight to the courtyard.

I would fight against his soldiers three at a time, they would leave limping and humiliated. It bothered me Commander Drask tried nothing these few days. I would just fight a few and they would leave.

This particular morning chilled me to the bone, there was no clear blue sky, only gray clouds filled it as far as I could see. To top it off, Calum didn't greet me at the door yet again. I hadn't seen him for a few days, and it was becoming worrisome. Dressing for the day I dressed in my normal pants, shirt, and leather vest then went with Crimson to breakfast where King Anwyl would await me.

It was just as boisterous today as every other day and when I came through, they whispered as I passed by the nobles and royals, even the servants glared. King Anwyl beamed at the sight of me. I gave him a warm smile at his welcome. Taking my place next to him.

"Good morning, Majesty." I said, glad to see him as bright as ever, not bothered by the dreary weather.

"Morning Shae, did you sleep well?" He asked, curiously.

"I did." I replied. I noticed Morfran was also missing this morning, so I took the chance before he appeared. "Have you seen Calum? Normally he escorts me in the morning, but I have not seen him in a few days. Do you know where he could be?" King Anwyl looked confused.

"Forgive me, who is this... Calum?" I sighed from his response,

"He is the beautiful blond blue-eyed boy." He still looked confused. "Morfran's servant." I said, a little annoyed. Understanding lit up on his face.

"Is that what his name is?" He said, not realizing how rude he sounded.

"Yes, him. I was hoping the three of us could spend some time today. I thought you two might get along since you are the same age." He looked at me confused again.

"Why would I spend time with a servant?" I leaned back, crossing my arms. I knew this was a response that was ingrained in him, with all the hierarchy.

"Well Majesty, just like how you took the time to get to know me, you could get to know him. Him being a servant doesn't change his good character. I am cursed, but you still like my company after a few days of spending time together." I gave him a warm smile.

His expression was full of confusion trying to wrap the concept around his head. I was glad he was at least considering it. Morfran came out of the shadows. Bowing his head to King Anwyl.

"My King." King Anwyl turned surprised.

"Morfran? You made it this morning." Morfran sat next to the King.

"I only came to give my greetings." He said in his smooth voice the sound left me feeling unpleasant.

"Maybe you can help us Morfran." King Anwyl began. "Where is your servant... Calum?" He said remembering the name. Morfran's eyes sparked ever so slightly as his gaze dragged to me a small smile touched his lips.

"Calum? He was.... in need of training." He said, "he will be indisposed for a few more days. Is there anything I can help you with?" He spoke with a slight amusement in his voice.

"That won't be necessary." King Anwyl said. He looked at me. "Maybe in the next few days we can meet with him. Will that do for you Shae?" I stared at Morfran as he spoke, I knew something was wrong. I nodded, trying to give him a smile.

"Yes. That will do just fine, Majesty." Morfran leaned into the King and whispered in his ear. My heart thumped at the sight of it, I had no idea what to think at this moment. I watched as the young King nodded and smiled warmly, completely fooled by the sorcerer. Morfran gave him a smile and left with a bow to the King.

"Is there anything wrong?" I asked concerned, he smiled.

"Yes, yes, everything is just fine." He said happily. It filled me with mixed emotions by how this kind young boy was being taken advantage of.

"Forgive me, today I won't be able to accompany you, I have... some matters I need to look into." I stood from my seat he took hold of my hand.

"Before you go. Would you be willing to accompany me tonight for a quiet dinner?"

He looked hopeful, I sighed it would be nice to sit away from all the people.

"Yes, I believe so." I said, his face lit up.

"Wonderful, I will send someone to get you tonight."

"I will see you tonight then." I didn't want to leave him but after talking with Morfran I knew something was wrong and Calum was already in danger.

I found a secluded spot and wrote a short message on a small parchment, scribbled on a small parchment. Pulling the leather cord from my hair, I cut it with a knife, making it smaller. I tied the parchment to one of Crimson's legs.

"I need you to get this to Faelan. I know you can find him, a friend of mine is in danger, and I need his help. Please get this to him as fast as you can." It could have been her intense stare or those intelligent eyes, but something in me told me she knew exactly what I was saying.

She rubbed my hand with the top of her head then left,

disappearing into the shadows. I sighed a small weight lifted believing that Faelan will be here. I walked swiftly and silently, moving in the shadows. I had no idea where Morfran would keep him. I only had one place I knew where he stayed, and I doubted that would be where he kept him.

I walked along the wall in one of the servant's passageways. It was dark and quiet, the stone slick under my hand. With the chill in the air today far worse than most days. The warm air from my breath formed small clouds of smoke. There were a few torches along the walls in the servant passages, coming up to the end of the hall where it split, I took the right side.

Checking over my shoulder as I turned the corner, I froze in place. Shocked by the pain exploding in my stomach, blood bloomed, spreading over my shirt. A blade shoved deeper into my abdomen, I grabbed hold of the arm it was attached to. Looking up, I found myself facing Commander Drask. His sinister smile lit by the reflection of the flickering flame from the torch just to the left of us.

My hand warm and slick with blood. I choked out, and felt my eyebrows knit together from the sudden surprise. Feeling the sharp blade slide out sent a shiver in my gut. I pressed my hands over the wound, trying in vain to keep the blood from spilling over. I only succeeded in soaking them.

"Wonderful to see you." Commander Drask said amused. I staggered back, hitting the wall behind me. I felt the cold stone rub against my skin as my legs lost their strength and I slid down the wall. Commander Drask crouched down next to me.

"You're alone today." He said looking around the passage. "I don't see that damned black cat following you wherever you go." He grabbed the front of my hair pulled me up by it. I grunted from the movement, "I think I'll stick around today." He said looking down at me. My breathing became heavy, and everything started to feel cold. I felt his thumb run down the side of my face. I lay there in shock and silent as blood continuously flowed out of my body.

"What a beautiful color." His eyes were fixated, with the flickering light in the passage he looked demented. I felt my cursed eye pulse awaiting another resurrection. "What's wrong you don't have any last words." He said delighted with himself. I only stared at him with loathing, I would not be afraid of him, I told myself.

Excitement filled his face. "That's the look." He said as everything started to fade, I could no longer feel any part of my body. Unable to hold on, my eyes became heavy and slowly closed, then everything went white.

38

I sat alone there was nothing everything was just white.

My body trembled.

I screamed in the silence gripping fists full of hair curled into a ball unable to contain the emotions boiling over. The only sound was the echo of my screams.

"Why?" I yelled to nothing.

I was back in my body, fire flooding through burning everything to its core. I heard a short rough laugh, "So... you can't die." Commander Drask said, his hand over one side of his face, giving off a crazed expression. "Well, isn't that just... delightful." His voice was off like the time when he wrote the message on my back, and for the first time I truly was afraid of him. The horror I felt must have been written on my face because his eyes widened in excitement and his demented smile grew.

"I like that expression." He said licking his lips. I braced myself against the wall, raking my brain for an escape. "Shhh. Shhhshh." He hushed me, petting the top of my head with his rough hand. "Don't worry, this will be our little secret. I can't be sharing such an amazing detail with that greedy sorcerer." I flinched from his movement.

He rubbed his fingertips along the spot he ran me through with his sword. It felt cool on my feverish skin from the recent flame that roared inside. "What a shame... there's barely a mark. Your skin is hot." He removed his hand then touched my face next, slowly running them along my jaw than over my lips, smearing the blood left from his fingers everywhere he touched. He gripped my chin and pulled it up. He examined me as if he tried to figure out a puzzle.

"Your skin is very hot, it almost burns. What about your old scars?" He said repeating his words he acted as though he lost all sanity. Grabbing my arm yanking me to my feet turning me around he shoved me against the wall. I didn't make a move, I just let him lift the back of my shirt and probe for the scars that he once left. I heard him click his tongue. "Well, isn't that a shame, my lovely work has been erased." I felt his cold hands press into my back, fingernails digging into my skin.

"That will be fine... yes, just fine... you are the most wonderful creature I have ever discovered... a permanent prey for me. I can keep you alive while painting this beautiful canvas in red, and when I run out of space, I can just kill you and start over. It's... it's like you were made just for me." As he spoke his voice got more excited and his words came out faster. He laughed overjoyed by his new discovery. "We must leave n..."

I flung my head back, connecting it with his nose. As his body staggered back, I ran.

I didn't look back; I ran as fast as I could. I turned several corners sprinting in the shadows out of site. I couldn't let anyone see me in this state I looked like someone had murdered me, which they did. But when they see no wound, they will think I murdered someone. Or worse, I run into Morfran, and he questions what Commander Drask has already figured out.

I made it to my room far faster than I would have thought possible. My breathing was heavy, darting into the room, slamming it behind I locked the two bolts. My back ran along the door as I allowed myself to slide to the ground. Elbows leaning on my knees, I dropped my head in my hands. I had no idea what to do and to make matters worse, I can't talk to anyone. No one knows about my resurrections, not even Grams, she left before I could even talk with her.

My heart tightened at the thought of her. I felt a pain in my chest, thinking of the memories I once had with her as I grew. The love and care she made me feel almost felt like a dream, too good to be true now. 'It will be fine' I told myself Faelan should return soon with Crimson. We can find Calum and prove what a conniving snake Morfran truly is and how Commander Drask has been working with him the entire time to the King.

It was a long shot, but I had no other idea how I could convince King Anwyl of his true nature. I looked down at myself there was blood caked on my cloths. I sighed, getting off the ground removing all my clothing threw it in the fire. After washing the blood off my skin the best I could. I slipped into some extra clothes made of red silk, I groaned inwardly by the irony.

After slipping the shirt on, there was a light knock on the door. My senses went to high alert. I reached for my weapons and remembered I still haven't gone to retrieve them, I cursed myself for being so foolish.

"Yes." I called out, walking with caution to the door.

"Um... the King sent me." A small voice said behind the door. Was it that time already? It was hard to tell the time of day with the gray clouds coating the skies. Although they spoke quietly, I could hear them clearly. "I was told to help you ready... I came to prepare your bath." She finished. I leaned into the door, trying to hear if there was any other noise around her.

"Are you alone?" I said, it was quiet for a moment.

"Yes." She said, in a small voice. I had no weapon with me and nothing I could use. If all else failed, I could just fight with my hands. If the Commander is out there, I won't be caught by surprise this time.

I unlocked the door, slowly opening it. A girl my height with curly brown hair cut to her shoulders, her green eyes stared at me confused. She had freckles on her small nose and small pink lips. I looked behind her, when I was satisfied there was no one, I opened the door just enough for her to enter and grabbed her arm pulling her in. Closing the door behind us, I locked both locks again.

The girl looked worried, "it has been a long day." I said, apologizing to her. She nodded like the explanation was perfectly understandable and disappeared into the washroom with the bundle she had been carrying. I sat by the fire while I waited for her to ready the bath, grateful for the chance to clean in hot water instead of cold.

"It's ready for you." She said after appearing again, I nodded. "Would you like me to help you wash?" She asked.

"That won't be necessary." I replied.

"I will get your gown ready for the evening..."

"Gown?" I interrupted her. Her head tilted to the side a slight smile touched her lips.

"Yes." She giggled. "Of course, you would wear a gown when you eat with the King." She said it to me like I should have already known.

My head dropped.

"Really?" I said, already giving up. She giggled at me again.

"Don't worry, I will make sure you have a lovely gown tonight." I sighed.

"If I must." She bowed.

"Now wash. You look like it has been a long day." She winked at me. I couldn't help but laugh.

"What is your name?" I asked, she sparked my interest.

"Laise" she said, giving me a curtsy.

"Well Laise, it is nice to meet you. I am grateful for the bath." I went into the room alone. The smell was a pleasant aroma of cinnamon and vanilla. White flower peddles floated scattered in the water. I removed my clothes and dipped in the water. I didn't savor the bath like I would normally do, I just washed the rest of the blood off my body that I missed.

I was in and out before Laise returned from getting the gown. I dried the drops of water off my skin and sat next to the fire stroking a brush through my hair, waiting for her return. I faced the door the entire time she was gone. After a few minutes of sitting by the fire Laise returned to the room a white gown lay across her arms.

It was made of silk, golden thread woven throughout it with flowers and peddles and swirls of delicate design. The sleeves stopped at the elbows, plain white ran down the middle with a thick line of gold thread on either side.

I changed quietly with no complaints it was light on my skin I felt strangely comfortable. The neckline was the same as the green gown I wore the other evening. Leaving my collar bones exposed.

"That looks lovely." Laise said to me beaming at the sight. "Please come sit." She insisted

Obediently, I sat in the chair before the mirror. She gently ran the brush through my hair, running her fingers through she began to braid some of my hair on the left side of my head.

"How long have you been in the castle?" I asked, as she quietly worked her fingers through my hair.

"Around one year." She answered.

I left her to her humming as she worked, pulling the braid back. She swept it across my back, braiding it into a thinker braid and draping it over my right shoulder. The back of my gown left my shoulder blades open. She had little white flowers placing them in various spots throughout the braid. When she seemed content, she stepped away.

"You have beautiful hair it is a shame you only pull it back." She smiled at her handy work with my hair.

"It is nice sometimes, but I prefer something simpler for every day." I looked over all she had done. "I don't believe I have ever looked so well dressed in my life." I said, grateful. Looking over her handy work astonished.

"Have you seen Calum as of late?" She shocked me with her question.

"Calum?" I looked at her, she was staring at the ground holding her hands together. I noticed a tear fall to the ground.

"Are you close with him?" I asked, she lifted her head, and her expression was heart breaking. Grief stricken tears streaked down her face. She shuddered with each breath trying to remain composed in vain. I took her by the hand and lead her to a chair next to the fire and sat her down.

"Do you know something?" I asked, worried. She rubbed her tears away and took a breath.

"He was kind to me, he helped me when no one else would." I waited patiently as she fought to tell her story, probably for the first time.

"It was a year and a half ago I lived in the town below. I worked at a pub, my parents were killed long ago, and it left me to raise my brother and sister they were twins barely seven. I worked hard for them, we had a simple life I could make just enough to keep going. One night a group of guards came into our pub, it was rare, we didn't normally get them in our place, since it is on the outer skirts of town." She paused.

"I did nothing special that night, I only did my job like normal. I guess... I caught the eye of one of the guards because that night he followed me home. I had no idea he was behind me, but he overtook me when I opened the door. Pulling me inside with him…" She stopped talking for a moment, her face twisted at the memory. "He threatened to kill my brother and sister if I didn't do what he asked…" The tears began to spill over while her hands gripped together in her lap. She continued to stare at them while she continued.

"I did everything he asked, and I despised every minute. After a couple of months, he would come once a week to bother me. One night he brought some men with him, they barged into our home and took my brother and sister away, handing a pouch of gold to the guard. I screamed and tried to fight back but he beat me and took advantage of me… he told me… he told me. It was nothing personal he just needed the money… he sold my brother and sister to some noble family." Her hands so tight the knuckles turned white in her lap.

"He said I could get them back if I behaved. But the beatings got worse. The last couple of weeks he started coming to the pub every night. I was losing hope that I would ever see my siblings again. The last night he was particularly persistent and cruel, he took me in the back of an alley. When he was done, he left me on the ground bleeding in the rain. My face was swollen to the point I was barely recognizable I didn't care if I lived or died in that alley. I wasn't even sure if my siblings were still alive. But…. But Calum came out of nowhere I saw him kneel next to me as I lost consciousness." She paused taking a small shaky breath.

"When I woke up, I was in a small home in another area of town. He would visit me once a week and made sure I was healing properly. He spoke kind to me and was far more caring than anyone I have ever met."

She finally looked at me. "He gave me hope again. He showed me there was light even in the darkest places. He helped me get a place in the castle working for the King. He said he would do his very best to help my find my siblings. But he told me I was to tell no one how we met and if I ever saw the person who did that to me to hide. He said he could only protect me so far. I owe Calum everything… I saw him being summoned by Morfran one evening it was strange the look on Calum's face was… strained. I have not seen him since. If there is anything you can do for him, please… please help." She had gotten to her knees at this point gripping my hand in hers.

Just listening to her story filled me with mixed emotions of sorrow and rage. I patted her head gently.

"I am already trying to find him. Don't worry, nothing will stop me from making sure he is safe." Her shoulders slumped in relief at my words she released my hands and wiped her tears away.

"You have all my gratitude," I gave her a sad smile.

"Don't thank me until I bring him back." Hope filled her face as she looked up to me.

She then got up. "It is time to go... you're going to be late." I blinked, "your dinner with the King." She said laughing lightly, I got to my feet. "Of course... I still have to go to dinner." I swallowed down the dread that was building in my throat. The sooner I was done with dinner the better.

39

The gray clouds still covered the sky, making it appear far later than it was. We hurried in the halls of the castle I stayed next to her as she led me one turn after another.

She stopped before a set of stairs angling up. "These will lead you to a red double door, that is where you will meet his Majesty. I will leave you now, I wish you luck." She bowed and gave me an encouraging smile.

"I will send word later." I said before heading up the stairs.

The stairs were lit brightly, I picked my gown up just above my feet, so I didn't trip as I ascended. My footsteps echoed throughout the passage as I kept my pace steady.

I reached the doors undisturbed, to my relief. I knocked twice the doors opened shortly after, King Anwyl stood on the other side smiling. The guard Cynwrig stood next to him. He wore a creamy brown jacket over a white shirt. His jacket had black toggles his pants matched the color of the jacket. He was quite handsome for a young man.

"You made it." He said happily, that will be all Cynwrig. King Anwyl said to him. Cynwrig bowed to the young king.

"Majesty." looked to me gave me and bowed, "Shae." Then walked past me and down the steps. I looked only a moment after him then turned my attention to King Anwyl.

"Majesty," I bowed my head slightly. He turned to the side,

welcoming me to enter. I trailed passed him and waited by the table set up in the middle of the room. A cloth covered it with fine plates set atop and a small pot with white flowers in the middle. It was an empty space with a fire at the far end. Torches lined the wall, lighting up the room. A few couches and chairs lined the walls.

He closed the door behind me.

"Please have a seat." He said pulling a chair out for me.

I sat down, "why the private dinner?" I asked curiously.

"I thought it would be nice to talk over dinner without the watchful eyes of everyone." He smiled to himself.

A servant came out of a doorway I failed to notice when I came in. They carried a tray full of food. Stopping before our table he set the food before us and left just as quietly as he came.

It was a lovely display of food, steam rising from the meats and breads. The smell was mouthwatering, I didn't wait for permission to dig in.

"I haven't seen General Faelan for a few days. Did he leave?" I stopped eating at the mention of his name and looked up to King Anwyl, taking a bite of his own food.

Clearing my throat, "he had some matters to attend to and said he would be gone for a little while." I forced another bite.

"I... see." King Anwyl sounded disappointed.

"Maybe when he returns, we can have another small dinner like this just for him." I said, hoping it would help. His face brightened.

"That would be a wonderful idea. I had hoped I would get to speak with him more before he left again. I am at a loss with the many problems in my kingdom." The brightness he had faded away.

"I am sure he would be more than willing to listen to whatever your Majesty has to say." I tried to be helpful.

"Anwyl." I paused, "please just Anwyl is fine when we are in private company." He said in a small voice.

"Anwyl." I gave him a smile. He was sweet, a little brother I never had. The servant came in again taking our plates giving us some drinks in fine goblets with steaming pies laid before us.

"This looks wonderful." I said, Anwyl took his cup and raised it.

"To new friends." I did the same, tapping my goblet to his we both drank. I set down the cup and went to have a bit of the pleasant-smelling pie. My hand dropped to the table and my body fell back in the chair, going limp.

"Shae?" Anwyl went to stand, reaching over the table. He froze in place, his hand flew to his chest and fell towards the table catching himself just before his body slammed into the table.

My body lay limp in the chair, unable to speak or move. I panicked staring at Anwyl as he gripped the tablecloth and toppled to the floor, all the plates and cups clattering to the ground with him.

"Oh, dear what has happened?" My eyes darted toward Morfran's voice as he walked through the opening the servant had been going in and out of. Anwyl struggled to get to his hands and knees. "Don't bother getting up Sire you only have a few more minutes to live." He said in a pleased voice. My eye flared with rage as I sat motionless, my arms dangling on either side.

Morfran slowly walked around the room with his hands clasped behind his back. "I have to say your highness you made this rather easy for me." He said looking down at Anwyl circling him like a vulture. I heard footsteps and Commander Drask stepped in from the shadows. He knelt to the ground before Morfran.

"The servant is taken care of as you asked master." He said bowing his head.

"Very good Commander, this will all be over soon. I will not have to worry about this naive child for much longer." His face twisted in disgust. Anwyl couldn't hide the heartbreak from the betrayal, he lay there heaving, suffering from the poison given to him. Tears ran down his face as he gripped his shirt tight crumpling it. First, he mouthed it, then he forced the word out. "W... why?"

"For the same reason I poisoned your father, dear boy... power." A smile spread across his too prefect face. "With the Cursed One here who better to take the fall, everyone will blame her. No one will think I had anything to do with it. A private dinner with the King, he forgave her of her sins and look what became of him. The people will demand for her execution. No... They would tear the streets apart for it." He was so delighted with how well his plan worked out.

"That is unless... she is willing to work for me." He said turning his attention to me. "I can't deny you are a very intriguing creature." It felt like my veins were on fire. My lips trembled, aching to scream to jump from this chair and rip those two apart.

"Bastard." The word flew out, his eyes widened.

"My, you are full of surprises… you're not supposed to speak or move for the next few hours." He came to my side with his long fingers, and he traced it over my lip, his stare full of plans and schemes. "It will be such a shame to kill you. The Sliske won't be pleased. I did promise to return you after I used you. But we cannot always get our way, can we Commander." He said glancing in Commander Drask's direction.

Drask stood from his crouching position. "No master we cannot." He said, his eyes flashing.

"We should be off now, don't want to linger when the cute little brown haired servant girl returns to find you've murdered the young king. Or better yet that annoying Captain Cynwrig. If only you had chosen to work with me Shae." He leaned brushing his cold lips over my cheek. "Commander." Morfran glided his way out of the room. Commander Drask knelt to my side instead of following.

"Don't worry, I won't let anyone discover our little secret." He whispered, running his fingers over my hair than leaned his head on my chest and looked up at my face. "I will be sure to take good care of you in my private chambers." He leaned in and pressed his lips against mine I felt the pain as he bit my lower lip, brushing his lips along my cheek he whispered in my ear. "Until we meet again." Then left the room.

I looked to the ground, Anwyl lay on his side now I heard him rasping with each breath short and labored.

"I…. I…. do… don't… w… want to… die." He said through his tears. My heart broke from the sight of him, the burning in my veins continued to rage.

The Eleith hit me with force. I felt the tug far stronger than ever before.

I closed my eyes, and I breathed.

I saw the flames inside, I saw them burning away the poison that kept me motionless. I burned encouraging it to move faster, extinguishing any trace. King Anwyl choked out. My eyes snapped open, and I forced my body to move even with the toxin still inside I rolled my body to the ground. Using my arms to pull my body along with them. 'Just hold on' I thought as I reached him lying on the ground.

The sight was heart wrenching his skin was pale and white substance slid down the side of his mouth. His hand locked in place, gripping his shirt. I sat up beside him moving his upper body I placed his head over my lap. I couldn't stop the tears from falling at the sight of the boy once filled with so much life. No long breathing my gut felt as if someone had ripped a hole in it. My tears fell, sliver sliding down the side of his face.

He laid limp over my lap, no sign of movement.

I shook his shoulders.

"Please, you need to wake." I said more tears falling.

Still no movement.

"Why are you not waking up?" I rasped; I shook his shoulders again. "Isn't this why I am here," I spoke to the Elieth. I waited, staring at the lifeless boy. I closed my eyes and held my forehead to his. I felt lost I didn't know what to do, there was no image this time telling me what to do. The tears still streamed down my face on to his.

I felt a tingle in the back of my neck and a soft brush touched my hair.

"Shae." At the sound of Faelan's voice, I felt something break and gripped Anwyl tighter.

"You will not die tonight." I whispered and breathed gently over his mouth. The pain inside was excruciating I felt like my insides were boiling. I didn't intend to let out a scream, I felt a strong hand on my shoulder squeeze keeping my sanity intact. I lost track of how long I stayed in that state raging in the battle of life for the young King.

When the pain finally subsided, I released King Anwyl and collapsed to the ground. Panting I felt sweat drip off my brow and my pulse race, King Anwyl stirred next to me. Strong arms wrapped around my body lifting me off the ground, I looked to see Faelan carrying me in his arms.

"We need to leave here. Anwyl change into those clothes and keep your head covered. I assume you feel fine." Faelan's voice was quiet.

"Yes," Anwyl said in a surprised voice, "but I..."

"Later." Faelan said cutting him off. "I will explain later, first we need to get somewhere else." He started for the servant's door.

"What about Calum?" I said weakly, remembering Laise's request and my own worries.

"We can't now." Faelan's voice was hard. "The King first then we will help Calum." There was no room for arguing, so I just let him carry me. I didn't have much strength to fight back now, and leaving here was for the best. But I couldn't shake the feeling he needed to be rescued tonight. The Elieth gave an impression of agreement.

Faelan put his cloak over my gown since it would be like a beacon to anyone looking. After feeling satisfied it covered, he left with the King on his heels and Crimson at the end. Faelan moved swiftly and silently he stopped many times hearing footsteps before Anwyl or I.

I had to give Anwyl credit. He moved and obeyed well. We did not delay once because of him. He stayed next to Faelan the entire time quiet and watched for any kind of signal given to him. We came to a dead end in the servant passages, Faelan stopping just before the stone wall.

"I can walk now you don't have to keep carrying me." I said, feeling more energized.

"No." He said placing his hand on one stone. It moved on its own from his touch.

"No?" I said annoyed.

"It will be hard for you to move in that and if anyone is alert to our presence. It will make the night a lot more difficult." His voice was emotionless. Hearing it sent sharp pains in my chest.

A dark passage opened before us Faelan continued forward without another word.

40

We were in the same tunnels I had entered upon my first arrival. There was no light other than the glow of Faelan's eyes. He closed them momentarily when they opened again a small flame sparked to life above us, it floated in the air following him wherever he went. It took us a while to reach the iron gate at the end of the tunnel. The half-moon partially lit the night sky, Faelan extinguished his flame before stepping out into the opening.

He paused, scanning for any guards patrolling this area when he felt all was clear he gave a nod to proceed. We went straight for the trees ahead of us, perfect for cover. He kept his pace the entire way I glanced back to see King Anwyl breathing heavily but kept up with Faelan never complaining once of being tired or demanding answers.

Faelan angled towards the town, I saw lights come into view filling the streets for some festival tonight. Music and laughter traveled to us. Faelan kept to the shadows, never once making a sound. We ducked into one of the dark alleys. There was a door in the middle of the building, Faelan glanced around double checking to see if we were seen then entered.

It was a small one room. A cot along the far end of the wall, a window boarded up. One table with two chairs on either side, white stone walls. Faelan set me on the cot, stepped to the wall and lit a small torch with just a look. King Anwyl went to the table and sat he dropped his head in his hand's tears fell to the ground. I stood testing my strength, "Do you have clothes for me?" I spoke to Faelan, he nodded in my direction, I looked back and noticed small trunk at the end of the cot. Opening it I found all of my weapons and clothes I had with me before being taken into custody.

Relieved, I changed quickly.

"Why am I alive?" King Anwyl finally spoke, his voice quiet. "Why did he do it? How long have you known about him?" He stared in Faelan's direction, his gaze accusing. "Did you know he murdered my father?" His voice rose a little. Faelan remained unmoving; his arms crossed over his chest as he stared at the young king.

"No. Had I known Morfran did so, he would have paid long ago." Anwyl jumped from the table and ran to Faelan slamming his fists on his chest yelling in anger and sorrow. Faelan grabbed hold of him putting one hand over his mouth muffling his screams and held him still with the other arm wrapped around him. "I understand you are suffering Anwyl, but now is not the time to make a scene. Even I will face consequences if we do not do this right." He paused, "I am going to let go now. Can you promise me you will remain calm? After this is settled you can scream and hit me until you are satisfied." Faelan said, slowly letting Anwyl go.

Anwyl dropped to the floor and cried silent tears, "I trusted him, father trusted him." I sat before him on the floor and took his hands in mine. "What Morfran did is unforgivable, and he will pay for his crimes. I stared into the young king's eyes. The puffy redness made his eyes even more radiant. "There will be time for mourning and answers later, for tonight we must be prepared for tomorrow." I spoke to him in a gentle voice, "I can tell you I don't know why you are alive. I only know you are supposed to be here now." I placed my hand on his shoulder and gave him a soft smile. "I am glad you are alive." His expression did not share my words.

"Morfran plans to announce his death by my hand. His plan is for me to take the fall." I looked at Faelan. "We have the advantage he has no idea Anwyl is alive." I went back to the chest and pulled out a few of my knives I only took one of my blades sliding it in between my shoulder. "And what do you think you are doing?" Faelan said, his voice harsh, "I am going back." He finally looked me in the eye "No." His tone unwavering. I placed my knives in a few concealed places. The one by my thigh, two in the sleeve of my inner forearm and another two on the outer of my other forearm. "I am not asking... You know where Calum is we have to get him tonight." I said listening to the Eleith.

"It's out of the question, we stay here tonight and ambush Morfran tomorrow when he plans to announce King Anwyl's death." He pushed off the wall. "I will not risk the King for a half-baked rescue mission." I turned in his direction. "You won't be because you are not coming." His eyebrows shot up. "You think I am going to let you walk back in there?" His laugh mocked me, "And how do you suppose you will rescue Calum when you don't even know the way?" He said like he won the argument. "Crimson will guide me," I said looking in her direction her ears perked at the sound of her name. Something told me she knew the way very well.

I patted King Anwyl's head, "Everything will change for you Anwyl, only this time you will have people on your side." I said as he lifted his head, his eyes full of confusion. I went for the door Crimson dropped to the ground from where she was perched. Faelen latched onto my arm before I reached the door. His grip pressed into my skin.

"You. are. Not. Going. Anywhere." He said between clenched teeth, I yanked my arm away from him.

"I have to do this, Calum is essential to this kingdom. I can't explain it, but he has to be saved tonight we cannot wait." For a second Faelen's eyes shifted, and I saw the gentle expression filled with pain and love. Then it was gone just as quickly. "You should know by now you can't stop me when my mind is made up." He latched on to my hand as I went to leave once again.

"I could stop you." His eyes flashed. "I could stop you." He said again with less conviction.

"But you won't" I said slipping my hand from his. "You have a lot to make up for General." I said bitterly then walked out the door, disappearing into the night.

41

Crimson led the way, we traced our steps back to the tunnels we just left. The moon was still high in the sky we had several hours before daylight would even come near the mountain tops. The people still danced in the streets laughing and singing, drinking their merry ale. None the wiser of the plots within the castle walls.

After entering the tunnels, I realized too late I had no way to make a fire to light the way. But after a minute my eyes adjusted to the dark and I could at least make out Crimson's figure in the dark tunnels. I kept my pace with her, my footsteps light on the ground barely making a sound.

She went in a different direction in the tunnel than when we escaped. I ran my hand along the wall feeling the slick rock beneath my fingers making my insides cringe. It felt almost slimy. My thoughts drifted to Faelan. He had a lot of explaining to do. There was more going on than he has told me, and I will get answers. The look he had was not someone who felt nothing, no. In fact, he felt something, whatever that may be.

As to the reasons why he pulled away from me and became cold, I was not sure, but I was going to find out.

I pushed it all to the back of my mind and told myself later. I will talk with him later, now I must find Calum. We walked in the dark for a while longer. When Crimson came to a dead end stopping just before the stone wall, a hole big enough I could fit my hand in, was at eye level.

"This it?" I asked, like she could respond. She licked her paw then put it back standing up proper waiting for me to open the wall. "All right then," Reaching my hand in, I felt the cool stone and noticed a notch on the inside. Pushing down, the wall to my left moved open. We were in the castle once more. My heartbeat picked up, I took a small breath then followed Crimson, keeping to the shadows.

The further we went the more familiar each turn became. Then we turned down the last hall, and I stopped in place, frozen at the sight of the door that led to the dungeons, proving my suspicions. I could have sworn those lifeless black eyes stared at me past the bars of the door. I shook my head, looking again, finding the eyes were never there.

"Calum is behind there?" I asked Crimson who was already halfway to the door. I sighed, "of course he is." Pulling all the courage I could muster and made my way to the door. I knew once I went down there, I would have to be in and out. I couldn't afford to be caught now. Especially not by Commander Drask.

Sliding one dagger out I quietly picked the lock. It took a few moments, but the door clicked, and the latch flipped open. I eased the door open. "You better stay by my side." I told Crimson, then descended into the dark tunnel. Keeping the door just barely open.

I kept my eyes forward, checking for any kind of movement. The silence made this place even more eerie. My heartbeat quickened with every step. Memories flashed across my mind, the depths of those dark eyes watching, images of the dark creatures scurrying over black marble. The hair on my arms rose. There was little light here, I kept each step silent and my breathing quiet, despite the fear threatening to take over.

We reached the end of the stairs I stopped at the corner just before the straight hall filled with prison cells. Inching I glanced around the wall as the stone rubbed against my skin. There was one guard at the end of the dungeon, he stood in place unmoving. I kicked a couple of rocks at my feet against the stone wall.

He perked up, looking in our direction, he turned and made his way to the sound. As he got closer, I noticed his eyes were pitch black. I swallowed, silently I pulled a knife from my thigh, fingers trembling. I closed my eyes, leaning my head against the stone wall licking my lips I took a small breath. Listening as he approached, one step after another. When I felt he was close enough, I moved like a blur, coming into his view launching the knife. It spun in the air at the man who stopped as the knife landed with a thud in his forehead, collapsing to the ground. His body twitched a moment, then remained unmoving.

I dragged his body into the cell next to me. Pulling the knife out, I cleaned the blood off and slid it back into its sheath.

Closing the door, I left the dead body there.

Crimson was sitting before the door at the end, the one that held the endless ear curdling screams when I was last down here. I swallowed, then placed my fingers over the iron handle. It was cool under my skin. Pressing down, it opened with a small creak.

The room was dark, the only light shined down on Calum who hung off the ground, his hands bound above his head, feet dangling. Shirtless, his well-kept hair lay disheveled covering his face. I moved quickly, pulling a blade out in one fluid motion and cut the ropes binding his hands and sheathing my blade catching Calum as he slumped into my arms.

He groaned.

There were traces of blood that had spilled from his ears and nose. His eyes swollen. "Calum." I whispered, shaking him gently. "Calum." I said once more. He stirred in my arms, his eyes popped open. Tears welled up from the sight of me.

"Are... you real?" he asked, his fingers lightly touching my face.

I smiled "Yes, Calum I am real. Now let's get out of this forsaken place." I said, pulling his arm over my shoulder. He strangely felt lighter than I would have imagined as he put weight on his feet.

"How did you find me?" He said in disbelief.

"Questions later. We must get out of here." I said as we moved forward, making our way out the door. I peeked out satisfied no one had entered we made our way to the stairs one step at a time. We moved slower than I had hoped, but Calum was in bad condition. Although I saw no real external damage, I was sure the torture Morfran did to him took a toll on him internally.

We made it to the stairs slowly, working our way up I kept my eye on the door hoping no one would open it. I got more nervous with every step. Gripping his arm, we were only a few steps away from the door. His breathing was getting heavier.

"A few more steps." I murmured next to his ear. He only nodded in response, focused solely on the goal ahead.

I glanced at the bars, not a soul in sight. I breathed a sigh and pushed the door open. Shutting it behind us, Crimson went ahead. I shifted my weight, pulling Calum's arm further up.

"A... apologies." He managed.

"I don't want your apologies, Calum, you're going to owe me lots of meals after this." He attempted a slight smile, but it vanished quickly.

I followed Crimson down each hall as we kept close to the walls. I could feel the heat radiating off him. I noticed sweat dripping down his face when the sound of footsteps started to echo in the hall ahead of us. I held my breath, looking for a place to hide. There was little light, but we would be caught just standing out in the open. The steps grew louder, and voices trailed in the air. I thought we would have to fight our way out when Crimson appeared from the shadows and disappeared again into a small nook into the wall behind one of the few banners hanging up. Somehow, I wedged us inside, Calum's head slumped on my shoulder.

I put my finger over Calum's lips, warning him to be silent. The echo of the footsteps were getting closer and their words became clear reaching our small hiding place.

"... We will proceed as planned." Morfarn's words made my blood boil. "She will still take the blame for murdering the King, she just escaped before we could catch her, we will put up rewards for her capture dead or alive." Their footsteps stopped before us.

I suppressed the panic, thinking they have discovered us. "But why would she take his body?" Commander Drask's voice spoke in the dark.

"It matters not. What surprised me was her resilience to my poison." His voice sounded excited "She was supposed to be unable to move for another few hours. But somehow, she managed to escape." I heard his hands clasp together. "I am only sad I can no longer observe her..." he paused "I have matters with my servant." Calum's body stiffened by his words. "He shouldn't disobey me again after this." I heard a few more steps than stop. "And Commander. That lovely little brunet servant girl, the one who escorted our cursed one... see to it she is taken care of..." he paused I heard a tap on the ground. "Make

241

sure you don't have too much fun." Then the sound of their retreating steps grew quiet then silence.

My eye raged from his words.

I waited for a while, giving Calum rest and making sure those steps didn't return. When Calum's breathing was more stable, I whispered.

"Do you know what room Laise stays in?" His face shot up at the sound of her name. "Looks like we will have two rescues tonight." I said slipping from behind the banner. "We are going to have to move fast. Do you think you can keep up?" I asked him, worried. He nodded in response.

I still held one of his arms over my shoulder and wrapped my arm around his waist, but he was moving with more urgency, keeping up with my pace. No doubt worried for his friend.

Crimson stayed by my side the entire way. I followed Calum's instruction. We kept to the servant's passages and stayed in the dark. I could feel Calum's pulse, it thumped vigorously under my fingers. I breathed small words of encouragement as we went. One turn after another I wondered if we would ever reach her room in time when I saw a familiar small figure dash past at the end of the hall. It was just a moment, but her image lit in the torch light. My stomach twisted when Commander Drask's figure appeared just behind her a wicked smile lit on his face.

I set Calum against the wall. "Try to catch up." Then I ran, not waiting for a reply. All that practicing with Faelan paid off, my steps silent as the night. A scream came out then was cut off there was a loud thump. I turned the corner, the sight of the Commander crouching down by Laise a fist full of her brown hair in his hand. My speed picked up. I rushed forward and just as my last step made a sound on the ground. Drask's head turned to the sound as my knee came forward slamming him in the nose.

I felt the crunch under the pressure. His body flew back from the force, hitting the wall behind him.

He stirred.

For a moment I thought he would get up then slumped to the ground. Laise lay on the ground, unmoving. I put my hand under her nose when her warm breath brushed over my skin, I looked for any blood. Satisfied there wasn't any I lifted her up and flung her over my shoulder. She felt much lighter than I would have expected. In fact, I was doing a lot of heavy lifting, I felt surprisingly energized for all the movement I had been making tonight.

I shifted from the sound of approaching steps. Calum limped into view; he breathed a noticeable sigh of relief. Then looked to Drask.

"We should kill him." He said with far more edge than I would have thought him capable.

"Yes..." I paused, taking a glance at the unconscious Commander. "But we don't have the time. And we would be no better than him." As if my words summoned them, shouts rose from the other end of the hall. Figuring I would regret this later I didn't give it another thought as we left his limp body on the ground. "Either of you able to find the way out of here?" I spoke to Crimson and Calum.

He looked at me puzzled. Crimson leapt forward, turning down the passage leading the way for us once again. "I don't want to stop until I know we are out of this castle, Morfran will have discovered you missing by now and will be extremely displeased." I gave Calum an apologetic smile. "Do you think you can make it?" He gave me a smile back.

"I feel more alive than I have in a while. There is nothing going to stop me from leaving these walls." With that he picked up his pace, and we made our way outside of the dark passages and into the night sky.

42

We reached the gate at the entrance of the tunnel in no time. It was still dark. I glanced around in both directions, checking for any sign of movement. Satisfied there was no one, I gave Calum a nod, and we made our way into the forest just ahead of us. Crimson walked beside me, I still carried Laise over my shoulder and Calum limped just behind us.

Following the path we had taken earlier; I noticed the festivities had ended for the night.

All was quiet.

Looking back, I checked on Calum. The temperature suddenly changed, and a cold feeling crept up the back of my neck.

I froze.

My breathe puffed smoke in front of my face. Searching the woods, I looked for those dark creatures that have hunted me from the beginning. A small nook in the ground by a large old tree caught my eye. Its roots hid it making it hard to see. Moving quickly, I set Laise down inside tucking her out of sight. I beckoned Calum to come near.

Gripping his shoulder tight, I whispered in his ear. "Stay hidden, stay quiet, and no matter what you see, don't come out. Keep her safe." I saw the many questions flash through his eyes, but he obediently laid next to her, hiding himself with the bush leaves next to the tree.

I walked away quickly; I felt the Eleith tugging in my mind. Two dark forms shimmered out of the shadows to the right of me, one appeared in front of me and two more to the left. Gliding closer, hissing as they spoke, Crimson's back arched as they approached. The Sliske stopped before us.

"We foound her. We did." The one in front of me said to the others. "Yesss, we found her indeed." Another spoke their voices sent shivers down my spine. "What did you find?" I said,

"Hsshss." They snickered. "Silly girl, you know who you are." One moved closer. I slid my good blade out from its sheath. "Oh, you won't be needing those where you're going Blood Bearer." It said closer.

"Forgive me for being the bearer of bad news. But I won't be going with you." I said, with a quick flick I sent a knife straight for the Sliske in front of me.

They shot at me in unison, the one in front dodged my knife with ease. I pulled the next knife out, holding it in my left hand, the blade in my right. Leaning back on one foot, I braced for the attack. The one who dodged reached me first, tearing his claws through the air directed for my chest. I moved back, twisting on my back foot out of its reach. Another had moved behind me, waiting. Pain exploded as His claws raked along my back. I nearly fell to my knees; from the sudden pain. I cursed under my breath for not being quicker.

Another went for my throat. His claws outstretched, swinging my blade up just in time, slicing the end of its fingers off. It hissed in fury at me. I spun my knife holding the blade down swinging around to slice another behind me. My knife only passed through thin air. All five of the black figures disappeared in the dark.

Leaping to the side I turned, readying my weapons, searching for the dark figures lurking around me. Crimson hissed to the right of us. One of them appeared, making its way to us. My back throbbed in pain, 'where was Faelan when you needed him.' I thought.

I caught movement in my peripheral just before the second one darted for us, just as I turned my attention to it, the other launched for me. A large black figure leapt out, knocking it to the ground. Its deep rumble revealed the sound of a black panther. I was so distracted by the sudden appearance another Sliske slammed into me.

Ramming me into a tree force the air right out of my lungs.

I gasped out.

Its claws buried in my shoulder. Dragging them down my arm, tearing through the skin as it went. I screamed, pain exploded in my arm, up my neck and into my chest. It was so agonizing I couldn't move. It leaned its head down the long snake like tongue flickered out. Licking the blood spilling from my wounds. Three of them hovered around us while the fifth was being torn apart by the panther.

The Sliske lifted its face. The red swirls thickened; its mouth widened revealing its long yellowing teeth.

"What a ssssweet tassste." It said whispering next to my face. I pulled my face away in an attempt to get away. A screech reached my ears as the other Sliske cried out, then the sound was cut off.

The other Sliske turned their heads toward their companion, then erupted into blue flames. I watched as its head whipped around, its red swirling eyes wide then dissolved, it didn't even have a chance to scream. I collapsed, no longer any support to keep me up right. Strong arms caught me before I hit the ground. Fealan's deep voice spoke in my ear.

"I got you." My heart skipped by the sound and all the tension left my body. He lifted me in his arms, carrying me once again. The black panther slunk its way to us. I stared as its eyes glowed a deep red.

"Crimson?" I said out loud. Her eyes seemed to smile then she shifted back into the smooth black cat.

I was speechless.

Calum came out of the place he was wedged into.

"What… were those?" He said breathing hard.

"Nothing we want to run into again." Faelan answered. "Let's get moving," he said, then turned,

"Wait!" I said stopping him in place, "can you put me down." He looked at me skeptically. "Truly, I am fine." I insisted, "besides there is another who needs assistance more."

"Another one?" Faelan said, not pleased.

"I'll explain when we return," he finally put me down, and I retrieved Laise. Pulling her off the ground, I lifted her when Faelan stopped me.

"Just let me take her." Grabbing my arm, "you are injured." Unable to argue back, I let him pick her up with ease and carry her over his shoulder.

"Where is the King?" I asked Fealan. He cleared his throat.

"He may be sleeping to some…. convincing." I only sighed at his answer. Calum looked confused and Crimson leaped from branch to branch while we walked.

By the time we made it back to the small room I was dragging my feet, suddenly tired from all the excitement. Fealan opened the door without a sound and allowed us all to file in while he watched the door. Anwyl lay on the small bed, sound asleep. Calum walked over to the table and sat down; he slumped in the chair. The boy looked aged, whatever Morfran did to him I guarantee it was nothing pleasant. I pulled a shirt from my supplies since we were practically the same size and handed it to him. He took it gratefully, pulling it over his head. Then his eyes went to Laise, who still lay unconscious.

"She will be alright." Faelan said, noticing his concern. "She is just knocked out." Calum gave him a small nod. I sat on the ground and leaned my head against the wall Crimson lay next to me. I stroked her fur.

"That's a pretty neat trick you did back there, Crimson." I said aloud. Faelan snorted at my comment. "Something amusing, General?" I said to him, my tone bitter before he made a reply Crimson hissed in his direction.

Putting his hands up, "Do not worry." Was all he said. I tilted my head to the side, confused. Then Crimson leapt onto my lap and curled into a ball, purring. I smiled at her action and decided to let it go.

Everyone was exhausted or knocked out save for Faelan, who remained on the other side of the room from me. He didn't look in my direction for very long, if at all. He remained cold towards me, which even with everything that happened tonight frustrated me the most. I sighed, closing my eyes.

"What do we do now?" I asked aloud. Faelan and Calum both looked over in my direction. "There is no way Morfran won't have something up his sleeve, he is not going to just let us walk up and arrest him." I voiced my concerns. Faelan just leaned himself against the wall in his casual posture.

"There will not be much he can do." Faelan said with confidence. "With Anwyl being alive and Morfran failing to murder him, the King has all he needs to pass judgment over him." He said brushing his hands together.

"I see what you're saying but aren't you underestimating Morfran too much." I said annoyed. "Underestimating?" He said cocking his head to the side he looked a little amused.

"Don't mock me, Faelan." I said, feeling the irritation rise.

"I am not mocking you, I just don't understand how you think this will go." He pushed himself off the wall, then continued. "Morfran is an arrogant sorcerer who thinks he is two steps ahead of everyone. He thinks he will win because he believes the King is dead and no one will believe the word of someone cursed. But he does not know what you can do, and he doesn't know that what he did sealed his own fate." Watching him slowly walk across the room, I hated how I couldn't take my eyes off him.

He was right, and I knew he was right. But there was a part of me that had a nagging feeling we were missing something. He stepped over to me and knelt to my side, placing a hand on my still bleeding shoulder. Their nails always left the blood flowing longer than normal. His touch reminded me of the throbbing pain.

I pushed his hand away. "I don't need your elements." I turned my head. I felt the familiar warm feeling rush up my arm, soothing any pain.

"You may not want it, Shae. But you need it." He said in a cold tone. I clenched my teeth together, fitting any feeling I may have. "Calum needs attention more than I." I said, finally able to look at him. "I don't know what kind of torture Morfran did to him, but he was in bad shape when I found him." Like he was confirming my suspicions, he fell from the chair to the floor.

I moved to get up Faelan only waved for me to stay. "There is nothing you can do so just stay." He spoke with little emotion. It was hard to only get this side of him. I was starting to wonder if there was ever any kindness from him anymore. He picked up Calum who looked worse, his skin pale and clammy. Faelan laid him on the ground and got a coat lying by the wall and propped it under his head. Calum groaned in pain his eyebrows pulled together. I watched as Faelan's eyes blazed to life, his hands touching on either side of Calum's head. "Morfran's type of torture is a mental battle. He attacks them in the mind, sends shock or horrid images directly to the brain. Never giving the person a chance to defend against it. It's amazing he hasn't already gone insane." After he stopped speaking the light in his eyes dead.

"That is all I can do for now healing was never my specialty, although since I have been traveling with you, I have had my practice." He said amused with himself. He brought a blanket over to Calum and laid it over the top of him. "Sleep, Shea. We only have a few hours until we need to leave and tomorrow will be a difficult day." He said going back to his side of the room and leaning against the wall. Closing his eyes he fell asleep or at least appeared to be.

43

Morning came far too fast, I saw the sun stream through the cracks of the boards over the window. I rubbed my eyes, forcing my body to move even though it protested greatly, wishing very much to rest another six or eight hours. Which was very tempting until I noticed movement in the room, I was suddenly wide awake. Faelan sat on one chair cleaning one of his blades. He made no noise. Staring down at his hands, his gaze focused. I watched, mesmerized by his strong fingers stroking the blade and how it gleamed passing under the sunlight. The cloth slowly rubbed over the steel, showing only a few chips and dents from the many uses in battle.

"You should get ready." He said, speaking to me without looking in my direction. "There is no telling if this will go as planned or if Morfran has the guards loyal to him. We might have to fight our way out." He then looked in my direction, his expression which once held compassion and fire now only looked neutral. A sharp pain in my stomach confirmed the feeling in my heart. I ran my fingers through my hair closing my eyes replacing the view of him with sunlight streaming in touching only bits of his face, chest, and arms with darkness. I sighed once then stood up, stretching from the uncomfortable position I had slept in.

The others stirred around me. Crimson curled in a ball on a ledge above the fireplace yawned and stretched out her paws, claws curling past her fur. King Anwyl sat up from his spot on the bed, rubbing his eyes. I looked over to Laise, who remained asleep in the same position we left her. Calum was already awake sitting next to her, his hand placed on her forehead.

"How is she?" I asked him. He looked up to me.

"There is no fever. I suspect she will be just fine. She should wake up at any time." As if Calum had commanded her awake, her eyes fluttered open.

At the sight of Calum her eyes grew big then softened, tears welled until they spilled over running down the side of her face. He pulled her into his arms and gently stroked her hair. "Everything will be fine now." He whispered into her hair. I watched as she gripped his sleeves tight, shoulders shaking as she silently wept in his arms.

I took a leather cord pulling my hair back and tied it up out of my face. I put my knives into place, thinking only of the things I would do to Commander Drask when I got a hold of him. I pushed the memory of his demented look after realizing I was a forever prey, to the back of my mind. The thought brought a cold feeling to my gut. Lastly, I slid my dual blades together on my lower back they clicked assuring me they were secured.

"We have little time." Faelan said, securing his own blade.

"What are we doing now?" Laise asked confused, wiping her tear-streaked face. Calum stood and gave her a hand to do the same. She took it gratefully.

"We will take back the Kingdom." Calum said, with a gentle smile but his eyes were filled with fire.

"Won't they just kill you on the spot?" King Anwyl said unsure.

"That is why you are coming along. Anwyl." Faelan said putting a hand on his shoulder. He then looked in my direction, his eyes caught sight of Crimson rubbing along my legs. He paused for a moment, eying her. I wondered what it was he didn't like about her. Like a spell broken over his eyes, his gaze snapped to me. "It's time." He said and led us to the door.

We all filed out of the tiny room and into an alley, the streets were filled with people all walking in the direction of the castle. Faelan pulled a light brown, almost tan, hood over his head we all followed suit. Everyone in our group was easy to spot save for Calum and Laise, who walked with us uncovered. We mixed into the crowd of people, all shuffling forward. I heard the murmuring among themselves, wondering why they were summoned so suddenly.

We walked together in silence. The crowd slowed, and we started to get shoved together in the mix. I followed Faelan as he made his way through the crowd; slipping through without anyone making a fuss, which was beyond me. Because everyone I touched huffed and spoke their annoyance of my pushing through. We walked single file. King Anwyl behind me and followed by Laise and Calum taking up the rear. Finally making our way past the crowd, we slipped into another alley.

You could see the mass of people all standing together in the open area where the fountain I first saw on arrival stood. With the amount of people gathered, their voice made a low rumble. We walked around the outskirts of the crowd. They placed guards all around the crowd and a line stood in front of Morfran. He stood on the other side of the fountain, the advisor's lined up behind him. Large stairs went up leading further into the castle, it placed him above the crowd. He stood in place with his hands clasped together, a sly smile across his face. We hid ourselves behind a large pillar of stone it stood higher than Faelan and two of us could hide from sight easily. I leaned my head back on the pillar, waiting for his voice to speak out over the crowd.

We had to time it right, if we went out too soon Morfran would never be caught. He could talk his way out of any punishment King Anwyl tries to pass judgment on.

So, we were to wait.

I closed my eyes and breathed slowly in through my nose and out again. I could feel my fingers itch for a chance to attack. Clenching my fists, I willed them to calm. 'Now is not the time' I thought 'this is not a time we want a fight to break out.' My thoughts drifted to Commander Drask.

It's a pity. His judgment will not be by my hand. I glanced around, noticing he did not stand next to Morfran. No, in fact Commander Drask was nowhere to be seen. Then he spoke.

"People of Thorden!" Morfran spoke aloud, silencing the murmurs of the people. "I come to you this day to bring terrible news." He said with a pause, lowering his head appearing saddened. Faelan turned toward Anwyl.

"You will speak loud and bold. Do not give any room to be

interrupted, we will make sure you get there." He looked at Anwyl with a gentle expression and nodded to him encouragingly. Anwyl stepped forward.

"I am ready." He said with a confidence I didn't believe he had in him until now.

"It is with great regret that the Young King has been murdered last night." The crowd responded in kind; the shock obvious in the air. "I know, I know it is an awful incident. But the young King was fooled despite my warnings." The crowd whispered among themselves as he continued to speak. "The Cursed One." He paused, allowing the crowd to gasp in shock. Faelan moved leaning down, he folded his fingers together allowing Anwyl to use them as a step. Pushing him up, the boy reached high grabbing the top of the pillar. Faelan pushed him higher, giving him enough momentum to pull himself up.

Anwyl stood at the top of the pillar. The air round him seemed to slow as he pulled the hood from his head and revealed his identity. He spoke loudly the people turned stunned from the sudden appearance of the King.

"HE LIES!" King Anwyl yelled, pointing his finger towards Morfran's direction. The look on his face was worth every part of our plan. The once conniving two steps ahead, snake stood frozen in place at the sight of the young king whom he truly believed dead. "THIS MAN IS A TRAITOR TO THE CROWN!" He kept his head high and back straight. Anwyl did not make the appearance of a fourteen-year-old boy. No, these people were in the presence of a King.

Then he walked taking a step off the pillar, when he did not fall the crowd gasped. I looked over Fealan's eyes glowed as he used the air to lower the King.

"He pretends to be my aid but behind my back he plotted against me!" King Anwyl continued. "This man gained the trust of my father, and he plotted against him."

In the brief pause Morfran spoke, "But My King, you are being manipulated by the Cursed...."

"SILENCE!" King Anwyl cut off Morfran who was taken back by his authority. "I will no longer listen to your lies traitor!" As King Anwyl made his way through the crowd, the people stepped aside allowing the King through to his destination.

We followed behind him, I kept my hood up for fear my presence would ruin the whole plan if they recognized me. Fealan walked just behind him, a warrior no one dared challenge the guards stood frozen in place at the sight of him.

"Your lies will no long plague these lands Morfran, I have learned the truth, and you will be judged." King Anwyl said, pushing past the line of guards and up the stairs.

"Do you truly believe I worked alone?" Morfran stepped aside, revealing the other advisors who all had panicked looks on their faces. "And do you truly believe I will just stay here and allow you to take me prisoner?" He said taking another step back.

"Guards! Seize them!" Morfran screamed, chaos ensued. Faelan was the first to defend while guards converged on him.

"Get behind me!" He yelled for the young king, who was dazed, I gripped his arm and pulled him out of his confusion. Taking him away from the main battle. I blocked a blow from one of the guards blocking our way. Where he came two more took his place.

"Please," he spoke with urgency, "do not kill them" Anwyl said behind me. I paused for a moment then gave him a curt nod before pulling him further behind me. My blades clashed against the group of them. I deflected and defended with all my effort. Working hard to keep the Anwyl safe. Faelan flashed through the guards with deadly speed.

My moment of distraction cost me as a guard moved past my defenses and went for Anwyl. I ran to take him out before he got to him, but another guard tackled me to the ground. As I yelled for him to run Anwyl stood in fear as the blade went down toward his neck, I screamed believing it was too late. Then Cynwrig came in between him and the sword blocking the blow with his own.

"I will protect you, My King." He said and pressed the guard back. Anwyl stood up on shaky legs. "Men with me!" Cynwrig yelled for his men, "protect your King!" I turned and shoved my foot against the guard at my feet. He grunted but held firm, taking the hilt of my blade, I slammed it against his temple. He crumpled from the blow releasing me. Another guard charged at me I deflected it and rolled to the side coming to my feet.

Before I would have believed we were alone, but guards were fighting against guards while the people fought against the guards trying to protect Morfran. Taking the side of their King. I watched as the battle grew in our favor.

Morfran also learned he was losing this war when he raised his hand to the sky with a quick swish to the ground smoke exploded vanishing his figure. In that instant, the advisors that worked with him began to try to escape.

"Stop them!" King Anwyl yelled. I launched out of another attack and slashed my blade at the guard. He deflected it and went for another until a black figure came from behind and pounced on him. Crimson nocked the man to the ground. I turned and went to stop Morfran and the advisors from escaping when I found the advisors were blocked from their escapes.

Everything happened so fast the dust had not yet settled. I looked over in its direction, annoyed Morfran had got away until I noticed a figure then two figures standing in the smoke. Fealan stood behind Morfran, holding his arms behind his back.

"Did you truly believe I would let you escape?" Faelan said to Morfran. "And don't think you will be able to use your magic sorcerer. These shackles are especially made for your lot."

The murderous look in Morfran's eyes was icy. King Anwyl turned to the rowdy crowd.

"People of Thornden." His voice echoed loud, and silence followed in an instant. The guard that had protected him stood behind him as if to protect him from another threat.

"I have failed you as your ruler. I have wronged all of you and for far too long have sat blind to the abuse you endured. No longer will I ignore the needs of my people no longer will I be blind to the suffering you fight each day. I will work to fight and make this kingdom a far better Kingdom than even my father's father did. Will you help Me? Will you help me be the King that makes this kingdom prosper?" It started low, but it became loud very quickly the cheer from the people shook the very ground we stood.

The king smiled and, in his smile, light glistened off his cheeks as tears streamed down his face. No doubt moved by the reaction from his people, but also pain from the realization of how much he allowed Morfran to manipulate and take over his kingdom.

44

By the time the crowd dispersed into the town below the sun was nearing the mountains making it close to evening. Cynwrig served Anwyl's father years ago when he was young. He became a Captain of his own unit. But was overlooked when Morfran brought in Drask to be commander. It never set well with him, and he felt Morfran never had the king's best interest. King Anwyl, Cynwrig and Faelan already returned to the castle long ago after his speech that moved even within the depths of my soul. I sat on one of the large steps mindlessly twirling one of my knives, crimson curled next to me purring softly. My eyes were fixated on the light ahead.

The sound of footsteps warned me someone approached, to my relief and yet disappointment they did not belong to Faelan. I silently scolded the part of me that was disappointed.

"Shae." Calum said, coming closer. "King Anwyl is asking you to join him for supper." Stopping the knife, I slid it in its sheath on my thigh where it belonged. Looking up at Calum, I noticed his color had returned to normal.

"Will you be joining us?" I asked him, to his surprise.

"Would you like me to join you?" I nodded my head.

"Yes, very much so." Pushing myself off the step I dusted my hands and legs off. "Shall we dine with the King?" I said, giving him a winning smile. He only laughed his wonderful laugh and walked beside me as we made our way to the king.

Crimson followed along beside me. There were more guards stationed than normal. I only assumed it was because Commander Drask was nowhere to be found and Morfran was kept under close watch.

"Will we be having another feast tonight?" I asked Calum as we walked. He folded his hands behind his back.

"No, King Anwyl has stopped the banquets until he deems fit." I smiled to myself.

"Have you had a chance to speak with King Anwyl?" I asked.

"Why would I speak to the King?" He asked confused. I gave him a sympathetic smile.

"Considering you have been under Morfran's control for a while. I thought you might have something to say to the King regarding his inner workings." I noticed Calum's jaw tightened slightly by the mention of his name. "Forgive me, I know it is difficult for you. If you ever need anything from me, you only have to say the word." I said gently touching his shoulder. He halted then turned to look at me.

His eyes glistened, tears threatening to spill over. He bit his lower lip before he spoke, his words came out shaky.

"I... despise... that man." My heart sank at the sight of him. "I still have nightmares from the last time I endured his training." He looked at me and the despair in his eyes made my stomach twist in pain. I lunged forward wrapping my arms around him as he collapsed in my embrace the tears that threatened to spill over soaked my shoulder.

I held this boy and let him cry, the pain and suffering he held in for years that had been kept hidden deep poured out; no longer having to hide what he truly felt. He crumpled to the ground I held him tight as he shook under my touch. I stroked his hair over and over again rocking him back and forth telling him everything would be all right.

"He will no longer torment you Calum. Morfran will never bother you again." I said, as his breathing began to even and his shaking finally stopped. I let the young boy go as he pulled away.

"They will be wondering where we have gone, we should make our way there before they send out a search party." He said, his voice clear. I laughed at his remark,

"That would be the first time anyone has ever sent out a search party for me." I laughed to myself then got up from the ground and held a handout for Calum who took it gratefully. "Everything is going to change Calum, and I believe you will be a big part of that." The Elieth tugged. "You will need to be patient with King Anwyl, the two of you are the same age, you are more mature than him in many ways. But I think there will be things you will learn from him as well." Calum looked at me confused.

"Why would I need to be patient with the King?" He asked me with a quizzical look.

I gave him a kind smile, "You'll just have to wait and see. Shall we?" I said then started walking, "We don't want them to send out a search party." I laughed to myself again. "You know it wasn't that amusing." Calum said following me.

We turned down one of the many halls in the castle Calum led me to the very place King Anwyl and I have been meeting for the past few days. I noticed a figure leaning against the wall in front of the library door. My heart skipped realizing Faelan stood in his casual pose a knife out aimlessly picking at his nail.

"Did you get lost?" His tone impatient.

"I don't see why it makes any difference to you?" I said annoyed. He leaned off the wall placing his knife in the forearm cuff.

"It does when you are keeping everyone waiting." He kept his face neutral. Calum went to speak, I took hold of his arm before he could.

"Apologies General I will be sure to not make you waste your time." I noticed his eyes went to where my hand touch Calum then returned just as fast.

"King Anwyl is inside." He turned then went into the room leading the way. Calum looked at me confused.

"It's nothing you need to worry about." I told him reassuringly, he gave me a kind smile, and we walked into the library. King Anwyl sat at one of the tables. Light still bled into the room from the sunset, giving the room an orange tinge. Upon our approach Cynwrig spoke in a quiet voice to Faelan and King Anwyl. .

"Are we not eating?" Their heads turned to us. My stomach rumbled at the words realizing I had not eaten since, since... well... since Anwyl and I were poisoned. I sighed at the thought.

"It will be here shortly; we need to talk." King Anwyl said, beckoning me to sit.

I obeyed and sat across from him, Cynwrig stood behind him

while Faelan stood to the left of us Calum stood behind me.

"Calum, is it? You won't need to stay." King Anwyl said with a wave of his hand. Calum only nodded and began to leave. I grabbed hold of his arm; I caught Faelan move ever so slightly.

"Actually Majesty, I would rather have him stay." I said pulling a chair out for him. King Anwyl looked stunned but only nodded.

"Yes, of course. But please Anwyl is fine." He said leaning back in his chair.

"Anwyl." I said with a smile. Calum sat next to me; I could feel his body tense from my actions.

The door opened and Laise came in with a tray of steaming food. I smiled as the Eleith's presence brought forth another idea at me once again.

"Anwyl, forgive me to impose on you again, but I would also like to have Laise stay as well." She froze at the mention of her name. King Anwyl looked at me confused.

"I suppose if you must. She may stay." I folded my hands together. He looked up at Cynwrig for reassurance who gave Anwyl a nod of encouragement.

"Yes, I insist." I noticed Faelan shift in his stance again. I could have sworn his half smile appeared on his face. King Anwyl cleared his throat. "Laise? Would you mind joining us?" She stood, still frozen in place. "Please sit." I encouraged her. She only nodded silently and sat down next to King Anwyl. Crimson leapt onto the table and went to paw at the food. I picked her up before she got to it. "Hold on let me get you a plate." I said putting her to the side.

"Yes, we should all get some food." King Anwyl said clasping his hands together. Everyone took some portions for themselves save for Faelan who remained in his usual spot standing against the wall.

After everyone ate their share of food King Anwyl pushed himself back in his chair.

"I wanted to talk with you Shae, because I wanted to know if you would stay at the castle and be one of my advisors." King Anwyl said, getting straight to the point. "When I mentioned this to General Faelan, he informed me you are traveling together. And since he must return to the Elemental Realm, I did not want you to leave without at least considering my offer." I looked over to Faelan, who remained neutral.

I sighed annoyed, I knew I had to stay with Faelan, the Eleith nagged at me that my time here was done. Well, almost. But even though Faelan had pulled away from me. I still knew we were meant to walk this out together through the darkness that plagued the land. It was not something I was meant to do alone.

"You are kind Anwyl. But General Faelan is right, we travel together, and I will go where he goes. But why your realm?" I asked Faelan.

"The queen of the Elemental Realm has requested Morfran be brought to her for judgment." Calum stood up.

"What do you mean brought to her? He is our prisoner." Although his voice was calm, his anger was evident.

"I have already discussed this with King Anwyl, and he has already agreed." Faelan said not bothered.

"Calum, forgive me even though he has betrayed the kingdom. I thought it better to let another ruler who was also wronged by him pass judgment." King Anwyl said. Calum flopped down on the chair, giving up easily. It was the first time I saw him allow his emotion to be seen by others besides me.

I cleared my throat. "King Anwyl before we finish for the night, I wanted you to think about something very carefully and I would like you to decide before I leave with General Faelan. You are vulnerable at the moment, seeing as you have no advisors. Although you have Cynwrig's loyalty there is still a need for those who can give you advice. I asked Calum and Laise to stay because I wanted you to see you are not actually alone." I put my hand on Calum's shoulder and gave a nod in Laise's direction. "Calum has been under Morfran for a few years and in those years, he has seen with his own eyes what went on. He has earned the trust of many people who are willing to stand with you. He has a good head on his shoulders and a good eye for politics and like you he has been wronged by Morfran. I think you should consider making Calum your right-hand man if you are willing. I can tell you Anwyl if you do this your kingdom will flourish." I let go of Calum and looked in Laise's direction.

"Laise has been wronged by the very guards who have sworn to protect her. She is a kind girl with experience in the town below and knows first-hand how hard it is to survive. She can give you a good insight on what to do to help your people thrive and love you as a king if you are willing to make her one of your advisors. I know they are not of noble blood or anyone from the higher families. But these two will not betray you, they will stand next to you and keep you on the right path to being a great king." My words stunned everyone in the room, I looked at the two.

"You will be of great influence, trust Anwyl he will mess up but as long as you two stay true to yourselves and be honest with him there will be nothing that can stop you." I stood from the chair and stretched, "It has been a long day, and I am tired, you guys should sleep on my words." I said, walking towards the door. Crimson leapt down and followed me. I noticed Faelan move as I left the room.

45

It was dark by the time I left the library, I didn't walk far before I heard Faelan's footsteps trail after me.

"Something the matter, General?" I asked, stopping to look behind me. He walked up to me casually with his hands in his pockets.

"That was very interesting how you brought those three together." He said now at my side, I continued walking.

"It wasn't because of me General I was only doing what I felt was right and those three need people on their side." I kept my gaze forward, but could see him in my peripheral.

"You have set a great trio into motion." He rubbed the back of his neck, worry laced in his voice.

It felt strange walking together with him. It had been so long I had forgotten how much I enjoyed walking next to him. I reminded myself that it was never real to begin with.

"Has anyone found Commander Drask?" I asked Faelan, pushing the painful thought away. I heard him click his tongue at the sound of his name.

"That pest got away before anyone was the wiser. Morfran claims he knows nothing although at the sound of his name made his face turn red with furry." He made a short laugh, I swallowed, trying to push down the worry that formed in my throat.

"Why did you tell King Anwyl you are taking Morfran to the Elemental Realm?" I asked.

"Because we are." I stopped, looking at him confused.

"Why would we take him there when he has done so much wrong here?" He sighed whether he was tired or annoyed I did not know, but he answered my question, anyway.

"I sent my regular report to the Queen when she heard of it, she sent word ordering me to bring him there. I do not know why, but I cannot disobey this order. Convincing Anwyl was easy, and it is better he does not have the death of a man on his shoulders, no matter how much of a monster he is." He continued to walk again. There was a part of me that was excited to go to his lands, but another part of me felt it would not be as exciting as I would like.

We reached the room I was staying in. He entered after me. "Are you planning to stay?" I asked.

"Does that bother you?" He stood just behind me; Crimson went straight to the fireplace and lay just before it curling into a ball by the warm fire. I felt his body heat as he towered over me, silent. A shiver ran up my neck from just his presence. He leaned in next to my ear. "Are you worried?" His voice low, and pleasant.

Even though he made no move to touch me my body ached for his fingers to run along my arm and through my hair. I imagined him pressing his smooth lips on the nape of my neck. I swallowed, my heartbeat picked up from the thought.

"Don't worry, I won't lay my hands on you." He said, removing his heat and walked further into the room. I noticed him eying Crimson, who also had one eye open in our direction. Those red eyes assessing to what I had no clue.

Rubbing the back of my neck, I tried to remove any lingering feeling. "Do not toy with me, Faelan." I said annoyed.

"I would not dream of it, Blood Bearer." I froze from the name. I felt as if he had just stabbed me in the chest.

"Don't. Call me that." I said, furious. He paused from removing his weapons and looked in my direction. For a moment I thought his expression looked pained, but then it was gone.

"Apologies Shae, I will try to remember." He said with sarcasm in his words. He walked over to the fire where Crimson lay and sat on a chair, leaning his head back. "I am staying since Drask is nowhere to be found and he had a strange fascination with you. In case he plans something, I will be here." Then closed his eyes.

I went to bed and laid down, only bothering to remove my blades which I placed under the pillow. "When do we leave?" I asked him, knowing it would be soon.

"The day after tomorrow." He said, "It is at least a fourteen-day journey Northwest to the Elemental Realm another three days North after that. We will prepare tomorrow; you can say your farewells before we leave." He said, then turned his head from me telling me he was done with talking. I sighed, lying in bed tired from the last two days. I thought of Calum and Laise and knew it would be hard to leave them so soon after just meeting. I thought of Anwyl, and the Elieth settled on me, giving me a peace for the three of them. I took comfort in it and closed my eyes, falling asleep.

Morning came with it a frost that chilled me to the bone. Faelan was already awake and ready. I sat up groggy from the night's sleep.

"We will need to get you warmer clothes after we eat, we will head into town." He said standing next to the door. "But currently we are late. Again. So, if you would be so kind as to get up and ready so we can leave." He spoke. Impatient and annoyed I got out of bed, I rubbed my hands down my pants in a sad attempt to smooth them out. Not bothering to brush my hair I pulled it up and tied it with a leather string, put my blades in place, quickly splashed my face with water and walked to the door drying it off. "Ready." I said, giving him a smile he only opened the door and walked out.

I huffed to myself. "Time to go, Crimson." Who was already sitting next to me on the floor? We followed the grumpy General and made our way to the banquet hall. Faelan wore his normal leathers, deep brown pants, and pale tan shirt with a black vest over it. His blade lay across his back, barely hiding his shoulder muscles that flexed when he walked. His forearms were a masterpiece of muscle they looked crafted to perfection. Realizing what I was doing, I scolded myself. Honestly, it was hard to look away. I crossed my arms annoyed knowing it.

We reached the banquet hall. I expected there to be many people but there was only King Anwyl, Calum, and Laise. They sat together talking among themselves, smiles on their faces. I watched them, the warm feeling and peace I felt last night hung over the three of them like a cloud. They stopped talking when they noticed us approaching. All three stood in our direction. We reached the table where they were, one by one they each came and embraced me with a warm hug, thanking me for all I had done for them. "We thought about what you said last night, and we decided to do what you suggested. We will work together to make this Kingdom thrive again." King Anwyl said, pulling a chair out for me.

I smiled with warmth at the three of them. "I am glad to hear it." "We know you have to leave soon. So, we got you a few gifts for your journey." Calum said bringing out a bundle of supplies. Laise handed me a well-made dark brown coat, it had light brown fur lining the inside and collar. I stood admiring the handy work, the fur soft to the touch. "Please try it." She insisted, hesitating for a moment she then placed it over me. I slid one arm in after another. The coat warmed my chilled arms, and it was long reaching to the mid of my calves. But it was not constricting at all, it was light despite the fur. I moved with ease. "Thank you, I don't think I can take this." I said taking it off.

She laughed. "Oh, you are taking it. I made it specifically for you. You're not going to make my hard work go to waste, are you?" She said, knowing I could not refuse now. I sighed

"Fine." Giving up. Calum handed me a small thin pouch. My eyes sparked, realizing what he had given me.

"Just in case you end up in a prison again. You do know how to pick locks, don't you?" He said with a sly smile. I opened the velvet black pouch admiring the fine lock picking tools shining on the inside.

"I believe these will come into use." I said laughing to myself. King Anwyl placed a small ring on the table in front of me.

The ring was thin, a red ruby placed in the middle a sign of an eagle etched in the ruby. "This is a sign of my favor. If you find yourself in need, show this and those who stand with me will help you. But be careful if you are in a territory who are my enemies, they will not be so kind." I placed my hand over the small ring.

"I will take this only to show our friendship Anwyl, you are a good man. Your people are lucky to have you as a ruler."

We sat and ate together, talking, sharing stories, Faelan remained silent throughout his mind elsewhere in another world, but his eyes were always watching. It was hard for me not to notice them follow my movements. It left me confused on what he truly felt or thought.

The time came and went far too quickly I spent the evening with the three of them, we talked about where they planned to start first.

They needed to find another Commander so that was their first goal. They planned to make rounds in the town below to see how much his people truly suffered. Since no one knew of Calum and Laise being advisors of Anwyl, it made going unnoticed that much easier. I promised them I would return one day to see them. We said our goodbyes, I walked to my room alone in the dark, Faelan having left ages ago getting the supplies we needed for our journey.

I went straight to bed, not waiting for him to return to the room.

The room was dark, I lay in the bed paralyzed not able to move frozen staring up laying on my back. The bed shook, I felt movement next to me. My heartbeat sped up, my breathing came out in quick short bursts. The voice I knew would come but feared to come whispered next to my ear.

"Shae." He whispered, I felt something brush my cheek, unable to move I could only lay there. "You are doing wonderful Shae." He said, the feeling of fingers traced down my cheek to my chin moving down the middle of my neck. "It won't be long now, soon. You will walk straight into my hands." I felt his lips touch the edge of my mouth, "No one will stop me Shae, your General will die he will not save you. You are mine Blood Bearer." Fire seared everywhere he touched a painful fire that even my resurrections could not compare, a dark fire that threatened to devour me. The pain so severe I screamed despite being paralyzed.

"Shae! Shae! Wake up, Shae!" I heard Faelan calling me from far away. But the fire burned so much, I couldn't break free. "Shae!" I heard him again. His voice trembled. Then the fire vanished, replaced with an icy cool. I opened my eyes, Faelan on top of me his eyes glowed with every breath smoke puffed out of his mouth. Was then I realized his body was frozen.

"What?" I croaked out, my throat parched. I saw the glow in his eyes slowly disappear, he breathed out a sigh of relief letting go of me pushing himself up.

"You were screaming. Your body was so hot I thought you might have burst into flames." He said, in a shaky voice. I rubbed my cheek, trying to rub off where he had touched.

I noticed Faelan breathing heavily. "Would you mind laying here tonight?" I asked, thinking it would be to no avail. He looked at me his eyes distant, only giving me a nod. We laid together side by side, the moonlight streamed in the window. Looking at the ceiling, "Despite everything Faelan, I am glad you are with me. I don't think I would have made it this far without you." He did not make a move to face me.

"I feel the same way, Shae." Was all he said. I let out a small breath. I did not know how far we would travel or who we would face, but this path we were on was only just the beginning.

www.ingramcontent.com/pod-product-compliance
Lightning Source LLC
Chambersburg PA
CBHW020719130726
47899CB00011B/452